**Books by
A. Claire Everward**

The First

Oracle's Hunt
Oracle's Diplomacy

Blackwell: A Tangled Web

A. CLAIRE EVERWARD

THE FIRST

BOOK ONE

Author & sister

First published in 2016 by Author & Sister
www.authorandsister.net
www.annaclaireeverward.com

Print ISBN 978-965-555-934-7
eBook ISBN 978-965-555-935-4

To my sister, whom I'm lucky to have by my side,
and to our mother, for her patience

Chapter One

By the time the airliner touched down in this place she called home, she had put it all behind her. Homecoming and the weekend ahead drowned any thoughts of it that might have remained, and by the beginning of the week a busy horizon was once again the focus of her mind and all memories of what had happened during her vacation had disappeared into the past. It was time to settle back into real life.

Sunday was already well on its way to last week, the sun now closer to its debut into a new day, when the executive jet extended its landing gear and began its descent. Its only passenger turned his head to the window but his dark blue eyes were blind to the distant city below, his mind busily going for the umpteenth time over his next moves.

It was time.

She backed the car out of her parking space and drove through the familiar underground garage toward the gate and out onto the road, unconsciously bracing herself for the day ahead. Mondays were never easy as it was, but a Monday that followed a couple of weeks' vacation, that was even worse. At least she didn't have to work today. Anticipating it would be difficult to return to normal life, she had taken the day off. She always did that when she took long vacations, made sure she returned on Saturday, early Sunday at the latest, so she'd have time to rest, get reoriented in her own time zone, then took the beginning of the week to settle back into her routine.

Errands followed one another mindlessly throughout the day, and she was just turning to drive out of the supermarket parking lot when she braked with a protesting screech of her car tires. There was a man just ahead, standing, watching. Watching her. And something about him . . . He didn't look out of the ordinary, nor did he seem menacing. Young, in his early twenties, she guessed. Well dressed, quite meticulous in his charcoal suit and tieless shirt, yet managing to look casual in them, as if this was his normal attire. Light-haired, a sharp contrast to the clothes he was wearing. Light-skinned. Light, but not pale. Burly, quite clearly. She couldn't see the color of his eyes from this distance, but she could feel their intensity. This man seemed entirely focused on her.

No, he wasn't, not entirely that is. Once in a while he would turn his head and scan the area around her. The parking lot behind her car, the cars around it. The road she was about to drive onto. But his eyes always came back to her, lingering. Watching.

Honking startled her and she realized she'd been sitting there staring at him, blocking the path for other shoppers behind her. But just before she took her foot off the brake and continued on her way, she noticed something odd. Other than this man watching her, which was certainly odd enough. When the car behind her honked, he seemed to stiffen, and his eyes locked on the car whose driver was honking. As if he was ready to take action if needed. To pounce. But the moment passed and he relaxed, and she wondered if she might have imagined it all.

Except she knew she didn't.

As she turned onto the main road she threw a look in the rear-view mirror. The man was gone.

He disembarked inside the private hangar and got into the black sedan that stopped beside the jet. A luxury car with darkened windows and a professional-looking driver, of course, trust Jennison to demand only the best. He settled back into the soft upholstery and sighed. This day had been awaited for so long, it was amazing how only chance brought it to be. Or was it chance? Intervention, maybe?

Either way, it was promising to be interesting.

She felt a little better after the electronic gate of the underground parking garage at her building closed behind her with an audible click. As the elevator reached her floor, she wondered if she had in fact imagined it all. After all, she wasn't anyone special, no one had any reason to take any interest in her. By the time she put the groceries away, she'd convinced herself that it was nothing. Leaning on the kitchen counter with a glass of delicate rosé in her hand, she chided herself on her reaction, and mused that she wouldn't even be thinking about it if not for what had happened on her vacation, its memory now once again vivid in her mind.

Chapter Two

She had just returned from Rome. She traveled alone, invariably so, because she loved the freedom of it, the ability to decide for herself what to do and when. Her everyday life was always so very busy, day chasing day and disappearing into months, so once a year, twice when she could, she would escape it, go abroad, far away, to experience a different culture. She would choose a city, one that had a history, and book a hotel, a small, cozy one. Quaint, when she could find it. Crammed in some small street, surrounded by the local culture, where possible. At a location where she could feel the city, lose herself in it.

And in every city she had ever visited, she would immerse herself in the local life and spend whole days walking through the streets where the locals lived, narrow paths winding through age-old squares. Feeling the city, its people, their ancient ways seeping through to modern times, talking to them about their past and present and searching their eyes to glimpse into their hopes for the future. And at the end of each long day she would return to the hotel through streets that soon became familiar, feeling after a while as if she was returning home.

Young as she was she'd already visited so many places, walked among so many people. Tried, for a short time, to be one of them, even if only to a limited extent. And at the end of every trip she would fly back home with a pang in her heart, not wanting to leave, not ready to return to her reality, but also feeling a bit richer in experience. And after a while, just as the city she had just left would forget her, she too would allow her own life to envelop her again, immerse her in its endless routine, and memories of her last journey would be replaced by the anticipation of the next one she would already begin to plan for.

But Rome was different. Something happened in Rome. It had felt different from the moment she entered the city, and this feeling only grew stronger as the taxi dropped her off at the hotel after driving through old, tiny streets it could barely pass through. The air here felt charged. It was as if the city was watching her. As if unseen ghosts all turned away from gazing at the endless processions of tourists, to her. As if they'd been waiting, for her. The silent bearers of an unspoken secret, eager witnesses of her arrival.

Although she was tired after the long flight, she felt restless. The first time she walked out of the hotel, that same evening she arrived, the city seemed to envelope her, embrace her, as though it had awaited her. Its very air seemed to penetrate through her skin, possessing every cell in her body, whispering ancient stories into them.

She wandered through the narrow streets, ancient

buildings close on both sides, old paving stones under her feet. The falling darkness felt comforting, allowing her to reflect on the ancient city's past, see through all signs of the present into a time long gone. Her path took her among tourists stopping at shops, eager sellers rushing to convince them to buy another memorabilia they simply must have, and among weary workers for whom this was just another end—or beginning—of a workday in this tourist city that had long lost all charm for them. Home, for them, was elsewhere. This place, these people, were just another way to make a living.

She heard the water before she saw it, before she reached the awe-inspiring view of the Fontana di Trevi. There were people around it, sitting on its wide steps, some talking, others silent, perhaps pondering the wish they had made that sunk into the water along with the coin they had thrown in, wondering if there was a miracle here for them. She didn't throw in a coin, it was not her belief, but she enjoyed the beauty, the ambience. The buzz of life.

Except that the statues were looking at her, large stone figures that seemed to be focused on nothing but her. The seagull that had somehow found its way there, standing on a statue high above, was looking at her. The windows of the ancient buildings surrounding her, they too were looking on, and even the gentle gust of wind coming down from the rooftops, caught between the buildings and spiraling down to the Fontana, even it seemed to be there for her, stroking her hair, beckoning, beseeching. She stood up and left. It must be her tiredness, the long day, the flight, she thought. Her imagination was playing games with her. Yes, surely that must be it.

Still, this feeling, that first evening there, did nothing to mar her visit to this magnificent city, and after a good night's sleep she was ready to continue her quest. And her days of travel were most satisfying. The architecture, the history, the people, they seemed to fill something within her, and she felt good here, in this ancient city.

Until she entered that cathedral, with its ancient paintings, its silent statues, its rambling space. And it hit her, the feeling. She halted, perplexed, and looked around her. There were so many people here. Some were tourists walking around, speaking in hushed voices, others were locals, for whom this was their place of worship. Some people just sat, awed, others prayed. Even if they were not religious, this place got to them, it was nothing short of inspiring.

That wasn't what she felt, it wasn't like that, religion had never been a part of her. But then she'd always had the tendency to question what others simply accepted, never feared the uncertainty of the unknown as others did. Did not have the same questions of purpose and fate that they had, their need to believe that someone was watching over them, that they were not alone. She simply accepted that there were things she could never know. Accepted, and decided for herself.

And yet here, now, in this cathedral in the ancient city of Rome . . . no, there was nothing religious about what she was feeling, what she was sensing, really. It was something else. Something she could not define, it eluded her. She stood there, oblivious to the people around her, her gaze searching, trying to understand.

And then she saw him, standing in the shadows, beside a distant wall. The man. Wearing white, all white. A white suit, modern, she noticed fleetingly, a white shirt with a Chinese collar buttoned up. Elderly, white-haired, distinguished. Not one of the clergymen, but not one of the tourists, either. He seemed to belong there. As did the younger man standing beside him, a step back in deference. A big man, burly, light-haired, wearing a well-cut charcoal suit, a white shirt, no tie. Both just standing, looking at her. No, not just looking. The older man was frozen. Staring. As if he was seeing a ghost. She turned, perhaps he was looking at someone behind her. But there was no one there. She turned back and he was gone, they were both gone. She shrugged inwardly and returned to her sightseeing, but it was futile, she knew it was her that man was looking at. She knew.

Just as she knew she was still being watched. She walked around, thinking she might find this man again, but he was gone, they were both gone. There were doorways she couldn't enter, and they must have ducked into one of them. After a while she left. It was difficult for her to tear herself away from this place, but at the same time she felt unsettled at being watched and was unable to resolve that unfamiliar feeling that was tugging at her, mind and soul.

The white-haired man stumbled back through a doorway and, his voice trembling, uttered a single word. In a secure complex far under the cathedral in Rome, all hell broke loose.

The feeling remained. She distanced herself from the cathedral, but that didn't help. It pulled at her relentlessly, the rest of the day, the next, and the ones after that. The feeling just wouldn't go away.

Nor would the conviction that she was still being watched.

Still, it was easy to allow herself to think that perhaps this ancient wonder of a city was getting to her and she could not convince herself to leave, go back to her own life. And when the last day of her vacation arrived, she found she regretted leaving. There was always regret at the end of her vacations, her excursions into different lives, but this time she felt like she was leaving something behind, something important. Like she was leaving part of herself behind. Like she was leaving her self behind.

Back at the hotel, that last day, she walked to the taxi, her bags already inside, and a motorcycle came out of nowhere, whipping by. She would have been hit, but from a corner a man stepped forward, blocking the way to her, and the driver swerved, almost fell, cursed, then continued on his way. She turned to thank her savior but there was no one there. Whoever it was, was already gone. The taxi driver had urged her to hurry, and so she took one last look around her and let him take her from this place she already began to miss. But while she waited for her flight, standing close to the airport's glass walls to see the sky, Rome's sky, for a few more moments before she had to leave, she knew she was not alone, although she could not identify whoever was watching her. And yet she was not afraid. She did not scare easily and, after all, no one had tried to harm her. On the contrary.

She was being protected. She had no idea how she knew this, but she did. She was being protected.

And then she was on the plane, and by the time she landed under that same old sky of the reality of her own life the feeling ebbed, and she could more easily chalk it all up to her imagination, leave it behind.

Except that now that man was there.

The man from the cathedral in Rome, who had accompanied the distinguished old man who had stared at her, looking so stunned.

The light-haired young man, right there in the parking lot of her neighborhood supermarket. In Grand Rapids, Michigan, in the United States.

At the scheduled time a command was activated, and an unattended computer system under the cathedral in Rome sent data that was received on a single laptop in a secure office in southwestern Arizona. The man behind the desk, until that moment busy with the routine tasks entailed in running the organization's main training facility, turned distractedly and opened the message received. When he saw its contents he pushed away from the desk so violently that the back of his chair hit the wide shelf behind him, sending the framed photos carefully placed on it to the floor, glass shattering. He sat still for a long moment, then took a deep breath, moved slowly closer to the desk and read the message again.

He closed the laptop and sat still, his mind churning. He'd known it could happen, of course. He'd spent his entire professional life preparing for this. Still, he'd hoped it wouldn't come to be. Not in his lifetime. Perhaps never.

And yet it did.

And it wouldn't go away just because he wanted it to. It was his responsibility to deal with it, and he would. He knew what to do, and he knew there was no choice. This had to be done.

Howard Jennison straightened up and reached for his phone. "Rhys," he said, and the phone dialed.

In a secluded mansion above Italy's Amalfi Coast, the men and women of the Council stood up in deference as the doors of the Council Hall opened and the old woman entered. Her entire demeanor spoke of elegance and stature, and her eyes had the serenity and wisdom of old-timers. As she moved, her robes flowed around her, all white except for the light-colored band that seemed to encompass all colors, at the edges of the soft fabric.

Usually she would simply approach the large table and sit down, signaling them all to do the same and begin the meeting. They met once a year, traveling from the farthest reaches of the world to meet her in this very room. Once a year, for decades, she would walk in, resigned, and sit in on this meeting that always began the same way.

"We are yet alone."

But tonight hope flickered in her eyes. She approached the table and looked around at her loyal Council, her gaze stopping at the white-haired man immediately on her right. He bowed his head in respect and said the words she and others before her had waited so long, too long, to hear.

"Keeper, She is back."

The old woman sat down. "Tell me."

He spoke and they all listened in eager silence. When he finished, they turned to look at the old woman, who remained silent, her head lowered.

Suddenly she raised her head. "Is She protected?"

"I have put Benjamin Laree, my most trusted man, in charge of Her protection. He has had people following Her since She left the cathedral. We have also managed to collect some information on Her through the hotel, and Benjamin himself has gone ahead of Her. He will be keeping an eye on Her, and will approach Her when the occasion allows. We are being careful not to draw unwarranted attention, of course."

"She must be kept safe. And She must be brought here. Now."

He bowed his head. "Yes, Keeper."

Chapter Three

The black sedan drove through the iron gates. The house was small and not nearly as isolated as what the organization usually used, but then it was rented, and very recently at that—those charged with preparing it would only have been alerted at about the time he himself was called in, which wouldn't have left them much time. The organization didn't keep a permanent complex anywhere near this city, nor the kind of personnel it did in other places, because it couldn't be everywhere. Or at least, that was the official line. The truth was that those who had the say in it didn't want to draw any attention to where the woman was. Ideally she would live—and eventually die—here without anyone outside the organization ever knowing she'd ever been here. Or even that she was still alive. Ideally.

He got out of the car and looked around him. Rented or not, the house was secure. Jennison worked fast. He nodded at a half-hidden camera and went in through the front door that unlocked automatically. He assumed that the man who was coming out of a side room toward him, his hand extended, was the one behind the outside camera.

"Mr. Rhys, I'm Jason Neace. I'll be making sure you have everything you need while you're here." The man chuckled. "Consider me your personal housekeeper, gofer, anything you need."

Kyle Rhys took the man in. Older than him, in his mid-thirties. Short, wiry, with a shock of brown hair. He disregarded the man's extended hand. "Then you received my list."

"Right down to business. Yes, Mr. Jennison said that too. Obey and don't ask questions. Hey, that's me." Neace grinned. "This way."

He led the newcomer to the room he'd come from, where screens stood that showed the perimeter of the house, although evidently this Neace guy wasn't the man behind the camera after all. Another man was watching the screens, and Kyle could see on one of them that yet another was walking the perimeter fence.

"Here." Neace led Kyle to a long table along the wall, laid out with guns, ammunition, military issue binoculars, everything he might need for this mission. And all would be untraceable, it always was. The biometrically secure handheld that lay in the corner would contain the most recent information collected about the target within the short time they had since she'd been marked as active. "And there's a gray four-by-four in the garage. Older model, like you asked for, dead-end registration."

Kyle nodded, satisfied. This would do.

By the time he finished preparing what he would need and finalized his plan, night had fallen, and the only indications of life in the house were a guard walking the perimeter with an alert-looking dog, and the light in the window of his second-floor bedroom. Kyle sat down on the couch near the bed and picked up the handheld again. The data came up. Because the organization was careful not to draw attention to the woman, it left her alone except to follow her location and to periodically check who she was in contact with, so there wasn't much new information about her. Where she lived and worked, neighbors and colleagues. No family, no husband or boy-friend in the picture. Good. That meant no one would get in his way. He read again carefully what little information there was and frowned. Normally he'd have someone follow the target to get more information about her habits, or preferably do so himself, however this time there was no time for that. But then, how hard could it be? Ironically, this was the easiest mission he'd ever had.

An incoming alert appeared on the screen. He let the biometric identifier scan his eye again, unlocking anoth-er security layer, and the last missing item, the photo he was to be given only at the last moment, came up. He stared.

Hours later the first light of the day peeked hesitantly into the room.

He was still staring.

The new day brought with it a calm breeze, without even a hint of autumn yet, not even here, on the balcony of her mid-rise apartment. She held her first cup of coffee of the day absently, her eyes on the city, the people below.

The night before, she finally managed to push the thoughts of her trip to Rome out of her mind and will herself to sleep, but her sleep was plagued by vivid dreams. Just as it had been every night since she visited the cathedral in Rome. Those first nights, in her dreams she was standing in pitch dark, had been for a long time. It felt, she remembered, as if she'd been standing there, in the darkness, forever, waiting. Once in a while she would raise her head and look for a sign of anything— light, life. But the darkness seemed to swallow it all, drown her in its thick embrace, and she felt lost.

She would wake up feeling confused. She'd never remembered her dreams before, and this was an un- settling experience for her. All the more so since the dreams resonated of something long gone, something she'd forgotten, something she knew she must remem- ber. Eventually she would fall asleep again, only to find herself back in the darkness.

But last night the dream changed. In the dark a light flickered. Small, weak, yet she could feel its warmth, beckoning. She walked toward it and it grew, pushing the darkness away until finally it enfolded her, filling her with something new, an energy, a strength deep within her. The light grew stronger and she closed her eyes against its brightness, raised her head to it, breathed it in. And then she heard a harmonious mix of soft voices saying, "Open your eyes," and when she did she found she was part of a circle of women, dozens of women, all dressed with the same flowing white robes that held within them the infinite brilliance of the light, all looking at her with elated smiles. And although they did not utter a word she could hear their voices in her mind, see into theirs, as they welcomed her. As they spoke to her, telling her of times past, of destinies to be. As they showed her.

We are one.

She had awakened at dawn and had been out here since, watching the day brighten slowly with a light that mirrored the one in her dream, growing in strength as it did, full of a new promise as it was. The dream was real. She didn't know how she knew, she just did. She should have felt confusion, disbelief, fear perhaps. Instead, standing here in the light of a new day, she felt only calm.

The sounds of the city now awake below seeped into her reverie. She sighed. It was time to get to work. Her research wouldn't wait. She was on a sabbatical from the Center for Human Behavior, where she was an analyst as well as taught at the center's home university, which was also her alma mater. The sabbatical had been a carefully thought-out decision. For a while now she'd been increasingly restless, and this had been a chance for her to get away for a long enough time to sort herself out. She had no idea what was wrong. Her work at the center was challenging, and she enjoyed the course she was teaching at the university. It was the same course she herself took when she was a graduate student, and had become teaching assistant for when Professor Shell insisted on it after she'd given him hell during the semester she studied it, bombarding him with questions every chance she got.

He'd asked her to take it over as soon as she'd completed her studies, when he'd also recruited her to the center. Professor Shell, now a trusted friend, a rare friend, was also the one to notice how preoccupied she'd become and the one to suggest that some time off might be just what she needed.

She didn't tell him that this restlessness she'd been contending with had always been inside her, gnawing at her, although it was only just recently becoming too strong to disregard. Instead, she took his suggestion, thinking she would do some research she hadn't had time for and hopefully get back on track, perhaps even return to pursue the doctorate he'd been pushing her toward. Except that she'd decided to start her sabbatical with that trip to Rome she now couldn't shake off.

She walked inside, made herself another cup of coffee, took it to her study, and sat down at her desk. Immediately behind her, windows stretched from floor to ceiling along the entire wall, so that when she turned toward it with her chair she could see the park stretch before her. The panorama of green below and the occasional bird flying by on the backdrop of endless skies helped her relax, kept her focused. The entire room, in fact, was designed to make her comfortable in her own little world, and she liked working here by herself, enjoyed the solitude, the peace and quiet.

But more and more lately, she couldn't do much more here than return in her mind to that place inside her she didn't seem to be able to reach, a place she'd been aware of since she was a child but had so far only been able to walk around in her mind, again and again, looking for some way in. She had a sense that whatever was hidden there was important, even crucial for her, but the years had not let her in.

She could never give up, though—every piece of herself was too precious. She had no idea who she was, didn't know where she was born or who her parents were. She had grown up in foster homes that had no interest in her wellbeing, had no pity for this lost child, until she had finally managed to get away, make a life for herself. And these were her only childhood memories. It didn't stop her. She'd learned early on to survive. She was strong and smart and she'd made it through. She'd created her own identity, knew well the kind of person she was, relied on the personality that had taken her through life without losing that which she valued within herself along the way.

She thought that perhaps that's where her fascination with traveling came from, her journeys to cities with an ancient past, people with a history, while she had none of her own. These people did not just exist in the present. They could, at any moment, look back to a past rich with detail, the past of their ancestors, of parents and grandparents and great-grandparents and many others before them. They could turn to memories and photos, share a story, a laugh and a cry, a life, with someone who was as part of their past as they themselves were. They belonged.

She didn't. All she had were questions, and an unrelenting feeling that she was not where she was supposed to be, that she was a stranger in her own life. That and her first name, Aelia. That was hers, the only thing that belonged to her. Her last name, given to her by one of the many for whom she was just another unwanted child along the way, didn't. And so she didn't used it unless she had to, treated it as an unavoidable formality.

She turned her chair to face the park. So many questions and not a single answer. She had tried to research herself but found nothing except what she already knew. That there was nothing out there, no information about her, about who she might be. Nothing.

She leaned back in the chair, her gaze distant. For all she knew, she didn't even exist.

Across the park the sniper checked his aim. He was at the window of an empty apartment in a building not quite opposite the target's. Perhaps not what he would choose if he had more time, but, because of the glass wall of the room she was in, he'd managed to position himself at an angle from which he could clearly see her.

He had her on his sight from the moment she came into the room. He considered shooting her when she sat on the chair with her back to him—the bullet, he knew, would easily go through glass and upholstery. And he wouldn't miss. He never did. He shifted slightly, took careful aim, and began to squeeze the trigger. And then she turned toward the window.

His finger fell off the trigger and he readjusted his aim. He now had full view of her face, which was framed by long black hair that flowed down under her shoulders, slightly pulled back. Even better, a shot to the forehead would be clean and immediate. His eye focused on her face, his finger began to squeeze the trigger again—

And he faltered.

He stared, mesmerized. He couldn't shoot. That is, he could, but . . . he couldn't. Something about her, something that resonated deep within him, stopped him. He couldn't seem to—

Her head turned slightly and she looked straight at him, her gray eyes intense on his through the aim of his rifle. But that was impossible, there was no way she could see him, no way she could know he was there.

The target stood up and walked to the glass wall, her gaze never wavering, seeing what her eyes could not see.

Kyle Rhys raised his head from the rifle and frowned, perplexed.

Someone was watching her.

Aelia could feel it, deep in that unknown place inside her. As deep as her reaction at the cathedral in Rome had been, although it didn't feel the same. This was different, more . . . what? Stronger. No, that's not all it was. She was confused. She couldn't see this person, didn't even know where he was, but he was, he *felt*, familiar. He. She was sure it was a man.

And she was certain that she knew him. Somehow, in

a way she could not begin to understand, she knew him.

She stood there for a long moment, her palm flat against the window, as if trying to reach him, touch him. Her eyes closed, and she tried to search for him in her mind. Then she shook her head and opened her eyes, surprised at herself. What was she doing? She must be going mad, she—

She stopped. He was gone. She couldn't feel him there anymore.

Kyle got into the car, breathless, and threw the rifle case on the passenger seat. He was rattled. And he was never rattled. That was what made him so good at what he did. And he never hesitated when on the tail of a target. He had nerves of steel. He never faltered, and he never ever failed.

And yet now he couldn't seem to get a grip on himself. What the hell happened there? She saw him. Hell, it had felt as if she was looking right into him.

No, it was worse than that.

He *knew* her.

This was harder to push away. She wasn't in Rome, this wasn't some ancient city far removed from her own life, and there was no justifying what just happened. This was the reality she was familiar with, it was what anchored her, and here she was supposed to be as she always was. Herself. And yet right now she felt anything but herself.

She felt as if the ground was shaking under her, and realized it hadn't really stopped shaking since her visit to the cathedral. That what happened just now was simply another highlight in whatever it was that it was now becoming clear was being unleashed deep within her.

In an effort to protect herself, to keep herself anchored in the pragmatism that had helped her survive all these years, she tried to push it away, to convince herself that she was wrong, there was nothing, had been no one there. She tried to get some work done, but couldn't. Tried to control herself, not to think about whatever it was that was happening to her, but it was futile. After a while she went online, and for the thousandth time in her life made another desperate attempt to find some information about herself.

About a child who had appeared from nowhere.

Kyle's instincts finally kicked in, and he drove away. He checked the rear-view mirror automatically. No one was following him, but then no one would. No one knew he was here, and this woman wasn't someone anyone would think would be targeted for killing. She was just an ordinary woman.

Except that she wasn't, was she? Not for him. When he'd seen her photo for the first time only hours before, even then it had hit him. Not just her looks, nor the smile that played on her lips and was so readily reflected in her eyes, making him wonder who she was smiling at, who had taken the photo. No, it was something else, something hidden, something he couldn't define, which pulled at his very core. Something that wasn't supposed to exist in him. He was always ice cold on the job, focused entirely on the target and its elimination. But sitting there, staring at this woman's photo, fragments had surfaced, unbidden. Fragments of memories, of something long lost.

Aware of the importance of this kill he had forced it all away, proceeding as planned. And yet just now, as he watched her from behind the scope of his rifle, saw her in real life, and as she reacted to him, impossibly so, the fragments surfaced again with an unexpected abruptness and fell into place, not nearly enough to form a clear picture but enough for something in him to awaken, and he felt—

He shook his head, angrily brushing off his confusion, and focused on driving. Several miles down he pulled over and took out his phone.

His call was answered after the first ring. "Is it done?"

Kyle remained silent.

"You didn't do it."

"Not yet."

"Kyle, this is the most important mission I've ever given you, the most important mission of your life. It's what you were made for. There's no turning back, you know that!" An uncharacteristically frantic edge slipped into Jennison's voice, and Kyle frowned.

"And I will complete it," he said. "But I need to know more. I need to know who she is."

Jennison's voice hardened. "You have all the information you need. Finish the job." And the line went dead.

Kyle put the phone back in his jacket pocket, got out of the car, and walked to a coffee cart a distance away. He bought a cup of some strong black brew and stood for a while watching the people around him, going about their lives, normal lives the likes of which he never had, never would have. He then returned to the car, started it and drove back to where his target was. He would complete the mission.

In his office, Jennison put down the phone slowly and stared at it. "Go after her." He paused. "And him."

The man standing at attention on the other side of the desk started in surprise. "Sir?"

"You heard me. Get rid of them both." Sharply this time, leaving no room for disobeying.

"Yes, Sir." There was no hesitation this time. "It will be done."

As the door closed, Jennison sank slowly into his chair. No. No!

Chapter Four

It was no use. Aelia couldn't focus, and eventually she decided to go outside, take a walk, maybe it would help. She took an elevator down to the lobby and went out the back entrance of the building and into the park, then strolled up one of the paths winding through it. This time of the day the park was relatively empty, which suited her. The bagel cart was there, its perpetually cheerful vendor chatting with a lone customer. Nearby, several toddlers were playing under the watchful eyes of parents and nannies, and occasionally a jogger would pass her by, intent on the next step. It was all very ordinary, peaceful, and it took only a few short moments for her to relax.

She heard a commotion and walked toward it absently. It was a protest. She wondered for a fleeting moment but then remembered there was a story about it in the local news. The city wanted to tear down a small structure near the edge of the park that was being used as a pub at night, saying it disrupted the peace, but people objected, saying it had been there for decades and was mindful of the residential neighborhoods that had sprouted up in the area over the years, and anyway during the day it served them as a pleasant restaurant. Now the pub was surrounded by police officers and city inspectors, and the protesters were agitated. Aelia was about to turn away when she heard shouts, a brawl erupted and before she could move away she was surrounded by an angry mob. Violence spread quickly around her, and she had no way out.

Kyle moved quickly from within the crowd and half-hid a distance away. It was simple really. The protest was a welcome opportunity to finish the job elegantly. All he'd done was mingle with the protesters, and when they were close enough to one of the inspectors, he punched the guy, all the while shouting obscenities. The inspector, blind with anger, tried to punch back, but Kyle ducked and the inspector hit the protester behind him, who just happened to be a woman. The enraged crowd attacked the inspectors and the police officers and a riot ensued. Kyle was good at that, manipulating situations to suit his purposes. He could easily read people, find their weaknesses. And this particular crowd was easy to stir up. He now stood back, watching as the woman he was here to kill was swallowed by the out-of-control mob. Yes. It worked. It actually looked as though they might do the job for him. And if not, he could always use the confusion to finish it himself.

Aelia stood trapped within the mayhem. She felt the chaos around her, felt the tension build inside her, felt herself react to both—

And then it all stopped. Whatever it was that had been awakening in that place deep inside her now stirred, surged, then flowed through her with growing strength. Instinctively she closed her eyes and let it rise, felt it intensify within her, and within a split second too short to grasp she felt it connect through this moment, this place, to all moments and to infinite existence, on a level she had not known existed. She felt no fear, only a calmness, a certainty, stood oblivious to the rage surrounding her, aware only of what was happening within her, what she had become.

And then she opened her eyes.

Kyle watched in confusion. She just stood there, in the midst of all that rage, did not panic, did not scramble to find a way out. There was none of the fear he had expected. And then before his eyes she seemed to be... to become a light. No, it was as if she *emanated* a light, a flowing, warm light that was becoming bright, so bright, so strong. He could see it, feel it. He looked around him, but no one else seemed to see this, no one but him. He turned his gaze back to her, gripped with the impossibility of what he was seeing, and started in surprise when he saw that she was looking straight at him, quiet strength in her eyes. She held his gaze for a long moment, and then her eyes moved away from his and focused on the people raging around her. And when she spoke, he couldn't so much hear her voice as feel it.

"Enough."

Those closest to her seemed to falter and turned, confused, to look at her, which sent a ripple through the crowd. She walked through them and they fell back, making way for her to pass through. She approached a man who was still grasping the lapel of another's shirt, his other hand raised in a fist, and put a gentle hand on his arm. She was smaller than he was, slighter, and yet he slowly lowered his hand. "Enough," she said again, her voice soft. "You're hurting him." Then she looked around her. "You're hurting each other. Why?"

No one answered but Kyle saw them all looking at one another, confused, men and women alike, as if they were waking up from a trance.

"Yes," she said. "See? You're all the same People. Stand together, help each other."

The two men who'd been fighting only a moment before looked at each other, both visibly ashamed. Incredibly enough, around her people began helping one another get up, pick up their belongings. Subdued voices spoke, inquired, apologized. Offered help.

Kyle looked at them, gaping. She had defused it, the chaos he'd created, just like that. She—

She turned again and looked at him. And where a moment before her eyes were filled with compassion, the compassion and strength that had stopped the fighting, now they were filled with anger. At him. Anger, and a question that he felt resonating through him.

Why?

He took several steps back, her eyes and his still locked. His, he knew, were filled with shock.

He turned and fled.

No more than mere feet away, Benjamin Laree stood, staring. He had followed her as she left her building, almost missed her because she went out the back but caught sight of her in time. He had taken care to stay a safe distance away, all the while making sure no one came near her. He had to be careful she wouldn't see him, it would be hard to explain his presence there if she did. And so far he'd managed to follow her without incident. He thought she'd seen him at the supermarket the day before and had hid quickly, but she'd simply left so he figured he was fine, still undetected. Although he wouldn't be surprised if she did realize he was there, all considering.

He'd seen her approach the protest and had recognized the potential risk, but then all hell broke loose so quickly that he didn't have time to get to her. From his position he saw the man who threw the punch, and then everything happened all at once. The small crowd erupted in anger and enveloped her, and at the same time he saw the man who had instigated it all slip away and stand aside, watching. Watching her, Benjamin realized with apprehension. He began to move toward the crowd to get her out but halted in surprise when she herself stopped the rioters. He stood mesmerized at what had happened next, at her, at the light he could not believe he was seeing, at the force he felt from her, at the perpetrator he saw turn and half run. From her.

He wanted to follow this man, but his first duty was to her. He watched her stagger away from the protesters, who were now helping one another and breaking off into small groups, some already leaving, dazed, not noticing

that she was walking away. He followed her more closely this time, worried, but the man, whoever he was, had
apparently left, and she made it safely home without any
further incident.

As soon as she was safe in her apartment building he
slumped against its wall, allowing the shock to take over.
It was true, it was all true. It was Her. She really was here,
She really existed. He took out his phone and made a call.

The man at the Amalfi Coast answered immediately.
"Benjamin, is She all right?"

"Yes, Sir, but I believe there is someone after Her."

"What? Tell me."

Benjamin told him everything. What he had seen,
what She had become.

"So, it has begun."

The young man heard the awe in his esteemed
mentor's voice, and this only increased his own wonder
at what he had seen. Then something struck him. "Yes,
but, Sir, I don't think She has any idea."

The line was quiet for a long moment. "Yes, that
makes sense. All the more reason why we must protect
Her, Benjamin. We must bring Her here immediately. I
am sending you some help. In the meantime, you must
speak to Her."

"I wouldn't know how to, how do I explain—"

"You must, we cannot wait any longer."

"Yes, Sir. And, Sir?"

"Yes?"

"This man? He's one of *them*, he's got to be. But I
think, I don't know, She seems to know him."

"How so?"

Benjamin told him how she somehow knew that this stranger was responsible for what happened, how she had looked at him, singling him out from the rest of the crowd, how she had, in effect, chased him away. How he'd looked at her, his reaction.

"I think . . . it was almost as if he saw it. The light. But that couldn't be, could it, Sir?"

When the man at the Amalfi Coast finally spoke again his voice shook. "Bring Her here now, immediately." After a pause, he added, his voice low, "And try not to hurt the man following Her. Bringing Her here safely takes precedence over everything, but . . . try."

Benjamin was perplexed. "Sir, if he has the chance he will kill Her."

"No, Benjamin. He won't." The certainty in the quiet voice left no place for argument.

Ending the call, the white-haired man stared at the phone, frozen in place. It couldn't be.

Could it?

Once again Kyle found himself getting into his car in a hurry to leave, and once again he was rattled. But this time it was far worse than before. He couldn't accept what he'd just seen, but he couldn't deny that it happened, either. His mind reeled. This couldn't be real, such things just didn't happen. That light . . . no, people were just people, they didn't radiate that kind of— what was it that he had seen, had felt? He had no idea, couldn't begin to understand. He shook his head. He didn't sound like he was making any sense, not even to himself. He felt frustrated, out of control. He'd never before run away from anything, and here he'd been forced to get away from her, his mark. Again.

He closed his eyes and breathed in deeply. There was a perfectly logical explanation for it, there had to be. She was just an ordinary woman. Otherwise he would have known. Jennison had spent years preparing him for her killing. He'd tell him if there was anything out of the ordinary. Which there wasn't, because such things did not exist. Not in the real world. No. It must be him, there must be something wrong with him. Maybe because of this mission, the importance it had had throughout his life, the expectation that he would be the one to finish this. Yes, that was it. And the best way to end this was to, well, end it. He would distance himself from the situation, regroup.

And then return to finish this once and for all.

Aelia's head was throbbing badly. She was dazed, and made her way home without really seeing where she was going. What happened there, in the park . . . Her mind was jumping from one thing to the next, not knowing what to grasp on to. The brawl, that feeling inside her, the man . . . both men. The one who was out to hurt her —the same man who had watched her in her study, he simply *felt* the same—and the one watching out for her. Nor could she begin to understand how she knew this. It was all foreign, confusing. All except for what she did back there, stopping that chaos. It simply happened, was a part of her, and it felt right, so right. And that raised more questions than anything else. Her mind reeled with the impossibility of it all, and thoughts intermixed with memories her exhausted mind could not keep away, trying to find a reason, an explanation.

She knew she was different. She never belonged. Even as a child she felt she was in the wrong place and wanted to leave, go elsewhere, search for something, though where and what were a mystery to her. And the feeling never went away, not even when she grew up. Nor did she truly blend into society around her. She never went with the mainstream, never gave in to the opinions of others. She did what she felt was just and right and spoke for the truth, no matter the cost to herself.

It took her years before she realized that she was not finding her way. That she was running into walls, that walls were appearing where they weren't a moment before. That she was constantly forcing her way through, as if she was a rogue element that had no place in the very life she lived. But she was strong, and within her there was something that would never bend, an unbreakable will that pushed her on. And so she kept searching, calling out from the depth of her being and longing for an answer. But there was none.

Until Rome.

When she had stood in the ancient cathedral it was as if her mind had linked with someone, something. For the first time in her life, it was as if her mind worked on its natural frequency. It felt right. Belonging—but to whom?

Now back here, in what she deemed her real life, she felt disconnected again, out of place, but it felt worse than ever because of those rare moments in Rome. She had always been so good at pushing this feeling aside, but it was more difficult this time, near impossible. She had adamantly put her mind into it, sure there was nothing else for her but that same life she always returned to, that nothing would change.

She was wrong.

She vaguely realized that her building was looming above her and headed up to her apartment, her privacy. Her hiding place. On the way up she leaned her forehead on the cool elevator wall. Her headache was getting worse.

So was her loneliness.

In the gray four-by-four on the way back to the rented house that served as his headquarters for this mission, Kyle was once again going over what happened. He couldn't let it go no matter how logical he tried to be, how focused, and this only shook him more. He'd never been affected this way. And he certainly never reacted emotionally to a target, he was always detached and cool. Nor had he ever questioned Jennison's orders before. Until now.

He was, he knew, better trained than most. He grew up on a small, well-kept farm, and was raised only by his father—his mother, his father told him, had died giving birth to him. He had no other family. The closest thing he had to an extended family were his father's friends from the military, men from elite units like his father had been in in his younger days. All were already serving in the organization when Kyle was growing up. They'd stayed at the farm many times during his youth and had taken the time to teach him what their training had taught them. They'd even taken him camping in the toughest terrains worldwide, to teach him the art and craft of survival in any conditions. But most of his training was given to him by his father himself, who'd insisted early on that Kyle keep in shape and acquire the type of capabilities a seasoned soldier would envy. And he had the body for it, too. He was tall, well-built, and had stamina that could not be matched by his peers. Already as a teenager he could outfight every adult he knew.

By the time Kyle graduated from high school he was a match for any soldier in any military in the world. But his father wanted more than that. He wanted Kyle to be in a league of his own, and that included training his highly intelligent mind. Intelligence should be constantly honed just like the body should, he'd taught his son, and by the time Kyle graduated, at the top of his class, he already had unparalleled knowledge of military strategy and human nature.

He was raised to be a killing machine, and his father had made no attempt to hide this from him. But while his father was a strict man, he loved Kyle. His entire world revolved around his only son, and while he planned every aspect of the boy's life and did not let him stray from the path set for him, he also made sure that Kyle always knew he was loved and protected. That he had roots, a family to come back to.

By the time the organization called on him to serve it, he was already better than many of its seasoned operatives. Kyle the man, now a formidable force, did just that, answer the organization's call. He did its bidding without question, as his father had told him he would one day be expected to do, and never strayed from the path his father and Jennison, then already the facility's director, had set for him. Nothing and no one could sway him.

Until now.

Until her.

He braked hard and turned the car around, going back.

Aelia wasn't entirely sure how she got back to her apartment. All she knew was that she felt exhausted, had to rest, just for a moment. She stumbled to her bedroom, fell on the bed, and was instantly asleep.

She was back in the circle, and as she looked on all the women merged into one and became a light, the light that had beckoned her before. Gentle, warm, it had a shape now, human almost. It spoke to her again, and as it did it changed, its form becoming increasingly distinct, increasingly familiar, as if she was looking not into the depth of the unknown, but into eyes. Her eyes. Her form. The light advanced and she gasped as it flowed through her, into her, becoming one with her—

She woke up with a start.

And for the first time in her life, she woke up feeling whole.

Chapter Five

This would end now. He would not be stopped, not this time. This time he was ready, nothing could surprise him anymore. He would kill her, complete his mission successfully, and never tell a soul about what he had seen or about her effect on him. Her killing would end whatever it was, whatever she was, whatever games his mind was playing on him. He would then track down that guy who'd been following her in the park and find out what he was all about, and eliminate him, too, to minimize any residual risk.

He never went in without a plan, and, as always, his approach of the situation was measured. He considered breaking into her apartment, but that would only do if she was not there and he was free to wait until she returned and he would surprise her. If she was home it would be out of the question, he wasn't familiar enough with the place to be sure he could break in without alerting her and giving her time to call for help. Either way, killing her at home wasn't ideal. It would be better to do it somewhere public, some place messy enough to make the collection of forensic evidence substantially more difficult than in her apartment, where it would be just the two of them.

And perhaps more important, it would make it easier for him to disguise her kill as random, and random crimes attracted less attention, if at all. In that sense, sniping was the perfect balance between these two factors—a clean kill that indicated the target might have been deliberately chosen, and still would not give a clue as to the reason, or the perpetrator. His sniper's rifle was still in the car, so perhaps that was the best solution. Now that he was ready, he was confident that she would not surprise him like she did last time.

Whichever way he would choose, he knew he had to take the other man following her into account in its implementation. The guy was an unexpected complication that needed to be dealt with. He stopped the car down the street and scouted the area by foot, looking for him. He didn't see him around. Maybe—

The guy came out of the target's building. Kyle could see him clearly now. He was young, couldn't be more than in his mid-twenties, most likely less. Something about him made Kyle frown. He seemed a bit out of place, the way he was dressed, the way he carried himself, and something else, something Kyle couldn't quite put his finger on.

He was clearly agitated, that much Kyle could tell. He kept throwing glances up to where the target's apartment was, even as he walked to his car that was parked in front of the building's main entrance. Eventually he settled inside, facing the entrance.

Waiting. So she must be in her apartment. Which made sense, Kyle thought. What happened in the park, it must have taken some toll—

He pushed the thought away. That never happened, he reminded himself, and focused on the kill.

Aelia felt energized and focused. The dreams never came other than during the night, and yet this time it was still daylight outside, she had slept so little, and still she had dreamt.

She remembered, and felt its impact on her. All the effects of what she had done in the park, and what had happened since that morning, were gone. All except that irritating headache, the result of the strain on her body, she supposed. She got up to get a painkiller but then remembered she had none. So instead she got some ice water in the kitchen, then took a cool shower, which made the pain ebb a bit, and got dressed. Finally, she left to go to a drugstore she knew would be quiet, empty in all probability at this hour. She didn't want to meet people, and she wanted to return here quickly, return and think.

There was no running from it, no evading, no pushing it aside. She had to try and understand what was going on.

The other guy following Kyle's target got out of the car yet again and walked toward the building. Kyle watched him with interest. He seemed indecisive. As if . . . Kyle straightened up as it came to him. The guy was considering going to her, that was the only thing that would explain his behavior. Kyle still had no idea who he was but considering the way he had acted at the park, Kyle's experience told him the guy was guarding her.

Which made him a potential interference that could not be allowed.

Kyle started to follow him but then the guy halted, turned, and returned once again to his car. Kyle raised a brow. This guy was getting to be a nuisance. The problem was that he couldn't kill him before killing the target. That would be too much of a risk. It was broad daylight, and if anyone saw anything, if anyone saw him—

The gate of the underground parking to the left of the building opened and the target's car came out. The guy started his car and followed. Kyle remained in place, a small smile on his face. Perfect.

It was an isolated enough place where it would only be her and him, a place she would feel safe in and would let her guard down, and at the same time a place where her killing could be made to look random, like a mugging gone wrong perhaps. The underground parking of the building she lived in. Whoever her guard—her very unprofessional guard—was seemed to think that waiting outside the building was enough, and Kyle expected him to do just that, wait outside, when the target returned from wherever she had gone, with the guy still following her, no doubt. And what Kyle could only interpret as his indecisiveness as to whether to approach her or not meant Kyle would most likely have time to kill her and leave. The guy would probably think she just went up to her apartment, and keep being indecisive out front instead of following her closely, making sure she was safe and not letting her out of his sight, which was what he himself would do, Kyle thought, then dismissed the thought with irritation. He was her killer, not her protector.

He rounded the building and entered from the back, unobserved by the day doorman who was deeply engrossed in the small television set on his desk, then descended the stairs to the underground parking. Then he simply waited for the target to return.

She finally arrived, and Kyle waited until she parked, made sure they were alone, and then walked toward her with determination. He wasn't worried about security cameras, he'd taken care of those. He wanted to make sure he'd be completely focused on one thing, and one thing only. Killing his target. Now.

She got out of the car and walked to the elevators, a path that would take her through a section of the underground parking lot where he had dismantled the lights to leave it semi-dark, enough for him to approach her through shadows. He walked toward her, the hand holding a gun with a silencer down by his side, then halted. She had stopped in the darkness and was looking around her, as if sensing him. He frowned. She closed her eyes and lowered her head, and he stood still, waiting in the dark silence.

And then she raised her head and turned to look

straight at him. There was no way she could see him where he stood, and yet...

He walked forward quickly, raising the gun and pointing it at her, and when he was close enough that he could not miss, he pulled the trigger.

As he did, something inside him erupted and he moved his hand to the side with a start.

And missed.

Uncontrollable rage rose inside him and he took aim again, his hand on the trigger, ready to finally do it, finally finish this —

He stopped. She never even moved. Just stood there mere feet away, looking straight into his eyes.

She would either run or crumble and beg, he thought, suddenly calm, that part of him that made him so good at what he did kicking in. Fear overtook all of them in the face of imminent death, his experience taught him. Part of him truly hoped she would do either, and that it would break this strange hold she had on him.

Except she didn't. Instead she took a step toward him, her eyes, incredibly, full of anger and irritation. "Will you stop trying to kill me already?"

Both the hand holding the gun and his jaw dropped.

She walked right up to him, stopped close, so close, and looked up at him with eyes that he couldn't help think could look so different, so warm, not as furious as they were now. He was surprised to feel a pang at this fury that was directed at him.

"Fine. There. Here I am. You want so badly to kill me? Then tell me why. You got me, now tell me *why*."

He stared at her, incredulous, and the thing was he couldn't move. At this close interaction, which he was not at all expecting, he felt something within him, that same awakening volcano of unfamiliar thoughts and feelings that had caused him to hesitate twice before and again just now, that same rumbling volcano because of which she was still alive. Except that it had now erupted and was spreading to every corner of his soul, and he couldn't focus, something was wrong, he couldn't.

She winced and her left hand came up to her right arm, and he jerked into focus as he realized that he'd hit her after all. He hadn't missed her when he shot. He hadn't hit her heart like he meant to, but he hadn't completely missed, either. A blood stain was visibly spreading on her shirt where she was hit, and only now he realized she was pale, so pale.

She was irritated and angry and only fleetingly realized that she was not at all scared of this man. At no time since it had all started was she ever afraid of him. Even now, after he'd shot her, it was only fury that she felt, fury toward this man who was after her, she had no idea why, fury at this inexplicable connection she seemed to have to him, of all people, fury at whatever it was that was happening to her, tearing her reality apart. The next thing she knew she was standing right there in his face, prepared to stand her ground, right before she realized her upper arm was warm and burning, and something was flowing down it and it hurt, it hurt so much. Without warning her vision blurred and she felt herself falling, collapsing to the ground, and just before the world disappeared she felt strong arms catch her, circling her body as her killer pulled her to him—

Protectively. But it couldn't be, could it?

She woke in her own bed with this thought and traces of a forgotten dream in her mind. Her head still hurt and her arm throbbed, and when she tried to move, something hindered her ability to move to her right. She breathed in deeply, and opened her eyes. Yes, her bedroom. Her own bed. There was still some light outside, she saw through the gap between the loosely drawn drapes, but most of the light came from the doorway. She sat up with some difficulty, and found she'd been stripped of her shirt to her bra, and her arm had been carefully bandaged. She held the blanket to her neck with her good hand and turned to see that the soft barrier that hindered her from turning was in fact that, a barrier made of her bedspread and decorative bed pillows.

"So you wouldn't turn on your arm and hurt it."

She started at the voice and whipped around. The man who had shot her was standing at the bedroom door, leaning on the doorframe. He had taken his jacket off, and a gun holster was visible against his black shirt. She wondered how long he'd been standing there and found herself feeling oddly self-conscious, exposed. He walked over to the window and opened the drapes a little to peek out, then let them fall back into place.

"I didn't look, if that's what's bothering you," he said dryly. "I was too busy trying to . . . not-kill you." He turned to her and stood quietly for a moment, pondering her. "How do you feel?"

"You patched me up."

"Don't worry, I'm trained to do that. And anyway the bullet just grazed your arm, it's just a nasty flesh wound." He walked back toward the door. "I'll let you get dressed. Try not to get the bandage wet."

"You didn't kill me."

It was a simple statement, spoken factually, with no anger or fear behind it.

He halted, but didn't turn back, didn't answer. A moment later he walked out the door.

She winced as she got up and walked to her bathroom. The face in the mirror was pale, but her bandaged arm held the reason for that. She felt fine otherwise, even the headache seemed to have ebbed. She showered carefully, got dressed and emerged from her bedroom to the smell of fresh coffee and toast in the kitchen. He was at the stove, frying eggs. She walked over to the counter and sat down.

"First you shoot me and now you're feeding me," she remarked. As an answer, he placed a rather appetizing plate of food in front of her and indicated her arm.

"It's fine, I kept it dry. Now talk, and start with your name." This might have come harsher than she'd meant it to, but then she'd had enough.

He put a cup of coffee before her. "Eat first. You need the energy."

She continued to look at him.

He sighed. "Fine." He took some coffee for himself

and sat down opposite her.

"Kyle Rhys." He looked down at the cup in his hands and nodded slightly to himself, reaching a decision. "I was ordered to kill you at any cost."

"Why didn't you?"

"Why didn't you run?"

They looked at each other in silence.

Outside the building, sitting in his car, Benjamin Laree was watching her living room window up above. He'd followed her to the building but didn't go in, just waited outside, not entirely sure how to approach this, and was still there when darkness began to settle and the lights came on in her windows. The man he'd seen at the park hadn't been around all day, and the sensor Benjamin had placed above her apartment door told him no one had gone into the apartment while she was at the drugstore, so he was confident she was alone and safe inside. Still, he had his orders to bring her in. The plane had already landed at a private airfield just outside the city, and the additional escort sent to help him would be here soon, so there was no delaying. This was as good a time as any to talk to her, although he had no idea how he would explain this, convince her to go with him—

The rear door of the car opened and someone slipped inside. Benjamin managed only to glimpse the face in the rear-view mirror before the bullets lodged themselves in him.

Kyle considered his words carefully. He never thought he'd have this conversation, never thought he'd say any of this to anyone outside the organization, certainly not to a target. And certainly not to this woman. Every instinct his father and the organization had instilled in him told him not to do it, but a whole new set of instincts was now taking over within him, and they had an altogether different opinion. One his gut told him to follow. He made a conscious decision to go with the truth.

"I belong to an organization that exists for the sole purpose of eliminating the enemies of humankind."

"Enemies?" Anyone else might have found what he was saying downright insane. But not her, not anymore.

"People who are deemed a danger to the future of humanity, to its existence."

"And by eliminate, you mean kill."

"Yes," he said simply. "They use men and women who are trained specifically for that, and I'm one of them." His smile was mirthless. "No, I'm the best one. I was literally raised to do that."

"What, to kill people?"

"To get to anyone and do whatever it is that the organization wants me to do."

She contemplated this. He expected more questions, but instead she simply stated, "You missed me."

"I never miss." He paused. "I moved the gun at the last moment."

"And the first two times?"

He was no longer surprised that she knew. "The first time I never tried to take a shot. I hesitated. And I never hesitate." Agitated, he stopped, forced himself to calm down. "The second time, I have no idea what happened. Do you?" The question was serious, and his eyes bore into hers but found no answer there. She really had no idea.

She was silent for a long time, and he watched her, curious at how calmly she appeared to be taking what he was saying. He wondered what was going through her mind.

She ate absently, deep in thought, and then raised her eyes to him. "Why me? I'm hardly an enemy of anything. I'm just me."

"I really don't know how to answer that, not anymore." He considered her. "See, I was told—"

Benjamin came to. He was alone in the car and realized that his would-be killer must have left without ensuring that his victim was in fact dead. Lucky for me, he thought, but as he tried to move excruciating pain seared through him, and he almost lost consciousness again. He opened the door weakly and stumbled out. The driver's seat he'd been sitting on was soaked with blood, too much blood, he realized. Willing himself to move, he stumbled to the building. He succeeded in approaching the entrance without anyone seeing him but had to wait until the doorman inside left his station before he managed to slip in and make his way to an elevator. He counted the floors up in an effort to stay alert, stumbled out, and crashed against her door.

Inside, Kyle stopped in mid-sentence and drew his gun. "Go into the bedroom and stay there," he said quietly and waited until Aelia did as he instructed, then walked to the door. He looked through the peephole and opened the door quickly, putting the gun back in its holster and dragging the barely conscious man in. He placed him on the carpet and frisked him, then called out, "Aelia!"

She came out and gasped at the sight of the injured man. She began running to him, but Kyle's voice stopped her.

"I need some towels. We need to get rid of that blood outside your door before anyone sees it."

She changed direction and went to get some water and towels. Kyle took a cushion off the sofa and put it under the injured man's head, then proceeded to look for the wounds. He found three of them in the man's back. A cluster, too close to the heart. He laid him back gently, and the man opened his eyes and met his, starting at the sight of him.

He struggled feebly against Kyle and tried to speak, and Kyle said quietly, "It's all right, you're safe." Then, thinking, he added, "She's safe, too. I promise you that."

The young man stopped struggling and lay back, his eyes on Kyle's, wonder evident in them.

Aelia kneeled beside the injured man and Kyle took the towels from her and ordered, "Stay with him, I'll clean the blood." She looked at him questioningly and he shook his head. This man wasn't going to make it.

Aelia looked down at the still figure and started. Him. "What..."

The man coughed, wincing in pain, and she leaned forward and raised his head a little to help him breathe. In a vain effort to keep him comfortable, she covered him carefully with a throw, but the man was now barely responsive.

Kyle cleaned all signs of blood on the outside of the door, glancing back at Aelia every now and then. The injured man lay still, his eyes closed. After ensuring no bloodstains remained in the corridor or in the elevator, Kyle came back in and closed the door behind him. He washed his hands in the bathroom and returned to the living room. At his approach, the man on the carpet opened his eyes, and, seeing Aelia, raised his hand and found hers. Grasping it with desperation, he struggled to speak.

"It's all right," she said, tried to soothe him. "Don't speak."

But the man struggled frantically. "Keeper, you must find the Keeper—" He began coughing, and bubbles of blood appeared in the corner of his mouth.

"Amalfi Coast"—he struggled to breathe—"the village in the mountains. Find her . . . find . . . Aeterna," he whispered with his last breath, and his grasp on her hand loosened.

Aelia looked at Kyle as he checked the man's pulse. He shook his head and she turned her eyes back to the young man who died on her living room carpet.

Kyle stood up. "We need to get out of here."

She was staring at the body, tears streaking her cheeks.

Kyle kneeled beside her and put his hand on her back. "Aelia, we have to leave. Whoever did this to him will come after you."

She looked at him, not comprehending. He stood up, pulling her up with him. She was in shock, of course she would be. He'd forgotten for a moment that this was all new to her, that only hours before she'd been living an ordinary, unremarkable life. And now there were people chasing her, trying to kill her, and there was a dead man in the middle of her living room, a dead man whose blood was on her hands. She stared from the body on the carpet to her hands, looked around her, grabbed a towel, and began wiping her hands with focused intensity.

He stopped her gently, took the towel from her and sat her down on the sofa, sitting down beside her. He took her hands in his.

"Aelia, listen to me. This man was following you."

"What?"

"In the park, I saw him when I followed you."

To his surprise she said, her voice hollow, "Yes, I know. He was there, and I thought I saw him yesterday at the supermarket, and in the cathedral, he was there too. I'm sure he was there. Why is he dead? He didn't do anything. Why is he dead?"

Kyle frowned. "Cathedral? In Rome? Aelia, you met this man in Rome?"

She didn't understand. How could he know she had

been in Rome? How did he know about the cathedral? She shook her head, her mind reeling, trying to latch on to something, to anything. "No, I just saw him there, he was looking at me, him and someone else, an old man... how can he be here? Why was he following me?"

Kyle continued quickly, worried that she was overwhelmed, knowing he couldn't let the shock paralyze her. They had to leave. Now. "I don't think he came here to hurt you, I think he actually came here to guard you. That's certainly the way he was behaving. My guess is, if you hadn't stopped those people in the park, he would have gone right in there to help you."

She looked at him, confused. Kyle frowned. There was no time for this, and even if there were, he couldn't offer any further explanation. He was, in fact, as confused about what was happening as she was. All he knew was that they had to get out of there now and that they needed to find answers, fast. And the dead man had been their only lead.

He breathed in, then took a leap. "Trust me."

She didn't react.

He knew he needed to convince her, needed her to trust him so that he could save her life, that same life he himself had almost taken just hours earlier. "You knew I was watching you," he said, and as he spoke, realization turned into decision and into acceptance, and he continued, the words flowing now. "You knew I was watching you outside your window this morning, you knew I was the one who started the brawl at the park, and you knew I was there at the parking lot." He paused, then let the words out. "And you *know* me. Just as I *know* you."

Her eyes focused.

"And you know you can trust me. Aelia, you *know*."

She breathed in deeply and nodded, her eyes on his.

"Good," he said, relieved. "Good. Come on then, pack a bag. We're leaving."

She stood up and began walking to the bedroom, then stopped. "Leaving for where?"

"Italy."

She stared at him.

He shrugged. "The Amalfi Coast. That's in northern Italy."

Chapter Six

While Aelia packed a bag, Kyle checked the dead man's pockets and found a wallet and a passport. Italian national, Benjamin Laree. The face in the photo was young, smiling. Alive. He was only twenty-three. Kyle looked at him with regret, then put the passport and wallet in his own pocket, thinking that maintaining the guy's anonymity for a while longer might be a good idea.

He then made a call from his phone and updated Neace at the house, but only partially. He wasn't about to let on what really happened in the past day, and certainly not what he was doing now. Neace was, after all, one of the organization's operatives, and on this mission he was taking his orders directly from Jennison, who was an intimidating figure. And Kyle's gut feeling told him to be careful. There were already too many unknowns in the equation for his taste, and this last one, the question of who killed Laree, disturbed him the most. Still, he had to check in to avoid suspicion.

And he had an assumption he wanted to check.

He told Neace succinctly that the target appeared to have left her apartment, that he'd broken in to learn more about her, and that a man had attacked him while he was there and the body had to disappear. He claimed to have no knowledge of who the man was but was dismissive about it, since—the way he told it—it didn't interfere with his mission, killing the target and disappearing as he'd done countless times before.

The line was silent for too long a moment.

"What are you going to do?" Neace finally asked.

"Follow her," Kyle answered. "There are indications here that she's gone to a friend's place up north. I'll get her there."

"Didn't she just return from a vacation or something?"

Kyle let irritation into his voice. "We know she's taken an extended leave from work, so she can do whatever the hell she wants."

"You think she might be spooked?"

"Why would she be?" Kyle lied. "I haven't actually tried to kill her yet, and this dead guy here made his move after she was already gone."

"Yeah," Neace said after a silence. "Well, you're the boss. You do what you do, I'll take care of her place."

Kyle ended the call, his brow furrowed. He didn't know Neace that well, but he was a good judge of character and his instincts never failed him.

And there was something about the operative's questions. No, not questions.

Interrogation.

He entered a code into his phone. When the designated software deleted everything from the device, rendering it useless, he took out the card and destroyed it. The dead, now untraceable phone he put in his pocket, he would get rid of it somewhere along the way.

He wanted to make sure it couldn't be used by the organization to track him down.

"Rhys just asked for a cleanup at the target's apartment. Says he killed a guy there, that the woman's gone and he's going after her. So, what, you think he's lying?"

On the other end of the line, John Semner looked up at the light in the windows of the target's apartment. He ended the call without answering Neace and contemplated the situation.

He had landed shortly before and had come directly here. He hadn't staked out the place long before he identified the other man who was following the target, as Kyle had updated when he'd checked in earlier in the day. He had to get the guy out of the way. He didn't really care who the man was, but as long as he was there Semner couldn't go in himself and take care of what he was sent here to do. So, once darkness had fallen, and after watching for a while and ascertaining that this guy, quite young and obviously not much of a professional, wasn't really expecting anyone to be watching him, Semner killed him.

He then retreated a distance, intending to watch from afar to make sure no one had seen what he did, but no one even noticed. The car simply remained parked where it was, with the body inside. He finally began relaxing, thinking he'd gotten away with it, and was considering going into the building to get the target—targets, he should perhaps call it as it was—when, to his shock, the car door opened and the dead man—well, not so dead, obviously—stumbled out and proceeded to enter the building. Semner cursed under his breath. Sloppy. This just made everything more complicated. If the man was seen all hell would break loose, and if Kyle was here to see him, that would certainly complicate matters immensely.

Either way he had no choice but to proceed. If he failed because of a mess he himself made, there would be consequences, and Jennison wasn't known for being forgiving. There would be no second chance, especially on this mission. Which meant Semner would have to achieve what he came for, no matter what.

He stayed where he was, watching, waiting to see if there would be any reaction to the man who was stumbling around all bloody before deciding what to do next. He had been contemplating his options when Neace called and had unknowingly provided him with valuable information. That Kyle was in fact there, and that Jennison's suspicion was in all probability well founded and he had turned, and was now helping the target. And of course, that the man Semner had failed to kill had managed to reach the target's apartment and Kyle was aware of him.

The lie about the woman not being there shouldn't have been obvious, but it was, at least to Semner, who was right there outside the building when Kyle made the call. After all, if she weren't there, the man who'd been following her wouldn't have been there either. So Kyle was hiding the truth about the target. And then there was the lie about Kyle killing that man. Or the fact that he had uncharacteristically provided Neace with so much information, or that he had called him in the first place — the target's disappearance, if it had been true, would warrant a call directly to Jennison. So what was Kyle playing at?

Still, none of it meant that Kyle would know who the dead man was or why he was there, especially if the guy died before he could provide any information. Nor would Kyle know who killed him. And he would not be likely to think that the organization was involved. Kyle had always been the organization and especially Jennison's pride, their most prized and protected asset. He would never think they would turn on him. True, there was the problem of exactly how the man was killed . . .

Ah. So that was it. Of course Kyle would check how the man died, he would never overlook such a detail. That's why the call to Neace, the lies. To try to ascertain if someone else from the organization might be there, after all. And Kyle would know who. Damn. Of course. Kyle didn't get where he was by being stupid.

Semner's eyes narrowed. Whatever Kyle did or didn't know didn't matter, nothing mattered, not anymore. Semner would not stop. He would get the job done. He should have been the one chosen to do it from the start, this most critical mission in the history of the organization. Him, not Kyle. That had been a mistake, he had known from the start. No matter. Kyle's failure presented Semner with a unique opportunity. Get both the coveted target and Kyle himself. He shook his head in disbelief at his luck. He wanted this badly. Jennison's precious protégé had finally slipped, and he, Semner, would be the one to pick up the pieces and show Jennison and the organization who its most valuable asset really was.

Yes, he wanted this badly.

Kyle was restless. His instincts warned him to leave, now. As soon as Aelia was ready he steered her to the door, not allowing her more than a last glance at the body in the middle of her living room. He made sure the corridor was empty, and led her to the staircase, directing her to stay behind him and constantly glimpsing up and down, his hand on his gun. But the descent was uneventful, and they reached the underground parking level undisturbed.

They walked through the empty shadows without a word, but then Kyle halted and put a hand on Aelia's arm, signaling her to stop. They stood quietly and listened to a commotion outside. Police sirens were approaching and cut off close, too close, and dogs barked. This had to do with the man in Aelia's apartment, Kyle thought. Laree had been covered with blood. Someone must have seen something.

He frowned. They had to get out. It would be difficult, if not impossible, to explain the dead man in the apartment, and he himself certainly couldn't afford to get caught. Worse, the chaos that would ensue following

Laree's discovery would be the perfect setting for the killer to get to Aelia, no matter how many law enforcement officers were around. He himself would be able to get to her no matter who was around, and he knew that Laree's killer could, too, if his suspicion about who the man was, was correct.

He glanced at Aelia and found that she was looking toward the sounds outside. He realized just then that she might choose to run, go to them to get away from him. I wouldn't blame her, he was thinking when she turned to him and her gaze was calm, trusting. The realization that she was in fact putting her life in his hands, choosing him over them, awakened in him a fierce reaction, adding to the already unfamiliar sensations he felt around her which he couldn't begin to explain.

He had been planning to steal a car in the parking lot, knowing they couldn't use Aelia's car, which would in all likelihood be familiar to her new pursuer. But that was out of the question now, since they could not risk being stopped by the police or whoever was out there when leaving the building by the underground vehicle exit. Instead, he was contemplating the best way they could leave on foot when Aelia spoke.

"There's a service entrance at the side of the building that goes down straight to this parking lot. I don't think it's used much. The one that leads into the main lobby is the one that's normally used."

He nodded, and she led the way to a side door that opened to a narrow, dusty corridor, and up some steps to another door that opened just under ground level, to the far side of the building outside. There were no police out here yet, although they could see red and blue lights reflected on the pavement a distance away, at the front of the building, and it sounded as if police officers were being deployed. Kyle led Aelia hurriedly away in the opposite direction, then into the park and out again in a more isolated area, taking care to remain concealed in the darkness.

He chose a dark blue coupe standing in a small parking lot adjacent to that same pub where the protest took place earlier, now shut down. Aelia waited in a dark corner while he swiftly broke in and started the car, then she ducked in and huddled in the back seat. After a while she sat up and began to ask Kyle if it was all right to move to the front seat, but he cut her question short. "Stay down."

She frowned at the urgency of his voice and settled back down.

"We're being followed—"

She didn't hear the shot, but she felt the car swerve as a tire blew. Kyle muttered a curse and steered the car expertly to the roadside. "Stay inside!" he called out again as he opened the door and jumped out, gun drawn. Aelia sat up and looked through the window. A car passed them and stopped with a screech of its tires, standing halfway across the road, blocking their way. The driver's door opened, and a man came out, poised to shoot again. Without hesitating Kyle took two steps forward and shot him point blank in the forehead. Then he turned around, putting his gun back in its holster, opened the coupe's back door, and pulled Aelia out.

"Let's go." He led the way to the dead man's car, and they got in and drove away.

Someone had seen the open car door and the blood inside and had called for help. Semner was increasingly displeased with every passing moment. An ambulance was now standing close by, its lights flashing, and the police were scurrying all over the place, looking for the person whose blood they had found in the car. Semner clenched his fists. There was no way he would get into the building anytime soon. But then Kyle and the woman wouldn't be able to get out either. A couple of squad cars were blocking the gate to the underground parking, and he could see the police in the lobby, talking to the night doorman and standing at the elevators and at an open door to what he assumed were the stairs. The crime scene people were there too, with luminol lamps. Which would of course help them trace the injured man's bloody path. He looked on in frustration. It was too late for the cleanup, which meant more consequences. All he could do now was wait for them to find the dead man and finish their work. He trusted that Kyle at least would find a way to hide, keep the police away from him, him and her. Otherwise, things would become even more complicated.

Though not impossible. He'd worked with worse. And nothing would stop him getting to his coveted targets.

Nothing.

The dark blue eyes that looked through the windshield at the road as it whipped by were ice cold. Experience had brought him face to face with so much over the years that he was rarely surprised by anything, yet human nature never ceased to amaze him, and greed most of all, the greed for power. Which was why the fact that Jason Neace had decided to take matters into his own hands and go after them himself didn't faze him. Neace must have thought that if he managed to stop them himself, Jennison would see his worth, and he would be accepted into that select club of the organization's elite. And it was no wonder that he thought he had a chance. He knew more than anyone where and when Kyle was on this job, and thought he knew his plans. But he didn't know anywhere near enough about Kyle himself, or else he wouldn't have dared go against him.

Kyle's hands tightened on the steering wheel. He had no compunction about killing Neace. He'd learned long ago that it was best to dispose of problems at the earliest possible convenience and with finality, otherwise they just returned to complicate things. And since complicating things meant in this case further attempts on Aelia and himself, and having to deal with someone in addition to Semner, getting rid of Neace was the best way for him to deal with this.

Semner. He would have liked to be wrong, but he knew he wasn't. He had known Jennison had turned on him from the moment he'd heard just that slightest bit of hesitation in Neace's voice earlier, when he spoke to him on the phone. Neace was there to obey Kyle, not question him as he had. And that feeble attempt Neace had just made on their lives just confirmed it for Kyle beyond a doubt. Neace never would have dared do this unless Jennison had led him to believe Kyle was fair game, even if he didn't exactly know why.

Of course, Jennison himself would never leave such a task—killing Aelia and Kyle—in the hands of someone like Neace. No, he would choose someone close to Kyle's level, another one of his elite operatives. Perhaps his best one, in fact, after Kyle, and the one who knew Kyle most. And that could only be Semner. Semner who, unlike Kyle, who was flexible and decided on how to kill his targets based on the circumstances, always killed the same way. Three tight shots to the heart.

Laree had three tight shots near the heart.

Kyle's eyes narrowed. Semner was his closet friend. He didn't have many friends, in fact Semner was one of a rare few in his life who he ever called a friend. They'd known each other since they were kids. Semner was a couple of years older than he was, the son of one of his father's military buddies, and they'd joined the organization just a few years apart.

The idea that it was Semner who was after them troubled Kyle. For one, the guy was no longer a field operative, having decided instead to climb up the hierarchy ladder by leaving field work and acting as Jennison's right-hand man, a position that Kyle himself had declined. And why would Jennison risk this mission by sending after Kyle the only operative in the organization who was Kyle's friend?

And why would Semner agree to go after him?

Worse, three bullets near the heart, that was a miss. And the fact that Semner didn't make sure his victim was dead, didn't realize Neace was going after them himself, and apparently didn't notice that they had left, that was sloppy. And Semner was good, he didn't do sloppy unless something pushed him off balance. So what the hell was going on?

Which brought Kyle back to the initial question. Why would Jennison turn on him? The decision to actually send someone to kill him, *him*, and without even allowing him time to complete the mission, made no sense.

Kyle realized he was grasping the steering wheel so tightly that the blood flow to his hands stopped, and he forced himself to relax them. There was only one way to find out what was going on, and that was to confront Jennison. He threw a look at the woman sitting beside him, the woman who was the reason for all of this, and his brow furrowed. She was staring out through the passenger side window, her eyes on the night outside. She looked so vulnerable. There was nothing bad, nothing threatening about her. She was nothing like his targets over the years. How the hell did she come to be at the center of this mess?

As if to answer, his mind brought up all he'd been told since he was a child, and what Jennison had confided to him as an adult. But in answer to that, came the memory of all he had witnessed since he had first laid eyes on her. And the as yet unanswered question that had been playing in his mind followed, more insistent than ever. Who was she really?

He focused back on the road with determination. The only thing he was sure of, the only thing he did not doubt, was that he needed, wanted, to keep her safe. So first he would find a way to ensure her safety, and then he would deal with those who were supposed to have his back and instead had turned on him, and get some answers in the process.

She was sitting in the passenger seat beside her would-be killer turned protector, a man she felt safe with even after witnessing him so easily killing another. Aelia leaned her forehead against the cool window and closed her eyes. She couldn't begin to make sense of it, any of it. Why was this happening, what did these people want from her? It wasn't like she mattered.

Unwanted. That's what she always knew she was.

In fact, that was her first clear impression of herself as a child. It was the second time she sat in that small, colorless room at social services, after yet another family had returned her, deciding they didn't want her after all. Two foster homes behind her, a string of homes yet to come, and the feeling of being unwanted with a long, long way to grow.

She learned quickly to hide her feelings, but she never learned not to care. That made her life even harder, but she was a strong-willed girl, with that impenetrable place inside her that never broke, and she survived. No matter what, she survived.

She was smart, and that helped. She spent days on end in libraries. Libraries were warm, had vending machines, and no one shouted at her in them. Sometimes she could even hide and stay there overnight, after the staff was gone. Although she suspected at least some of them knew and turned a blind eye. She was, after all, a good girl, helped them put books back in place or clean up sometimes. And she loved the books. They made her think, and she could lose herself in them. Search for herself in them.

Being smart got her through a lot. It got her work, got her emancipated at sixteen, got her into college that same year. Got her where she was now. But it never helped with the knowledge that no one wanted her. That none of those foster parents chose to keep her. That even her own parents hadn't chosen to keep her. Or at least made sure that she knew something about herself.

Except for the name that had been embroidered on the clothes she had been wearing the day she was found. Her name. Aelia. She'd always wondered about that, that her parents didn't care enough to keep her, but took care to give her a name and make sure whoever found her knew it. That one piece of information, the only thing she knew about herself.

Her name.

Other than that, she was, always had been, unwanted. That was what had been imprinted on her, and it was what had kept her from letting anyone get close to her, what had made her keep a protective wall, an entire fortress really, around her. She was the child no one had wanted, the child nobody had thought worthwhile enough to keep.

And yet now there were people after her. Trying to kill her, protecting her. Two men had already died, and somehow this was because of her. Someone wanted her dead, and someone else wanted her alive.

The unwanted, so very unwanted girl.

This just didn't make any sense.

Nothing makes sense anymore, a small voice sounded in her mind. Nothing, it continued, but she clamped down on it, unable to fully face yet whatever it meant.

Chapter Seven

They got on the next flight to Rome. Kyle would have liked to arrange for different identities, maybe a private plane, but the fact was that they didn't have the time for that. He needed to get Aelia out of there quickly, hopefully without giving Semner or anyone else in the organization a chance to track them down too soon. There had been no apparent indications of interrogation on Laree's body and Kyle had taken all his means of identification, so he figured it would take the organization some time to find out who the guy was and, Kyle had to assume, understand where Aelia and he himself were headed. And they would need to untangle the mess they left behind first, and actually get their hands on the body. Still, the organization had powerful resources and there were other ways to track Aelia and him down, so speed was his only advantage.

He didn't have a safety net to fall back on because he couldn't just do what he always did, call on the organization for whatever resources he required, having essentially switched sides when he turned from his target's killer into her protector. He was alone. And so was Aelia. The way things had gone, the police were certain to find the dead man in her apartment. She couldn't go back now, there would be too many questions she couldn't begin to answer because she obviously had no idea why all this was happening. The upside was that the police would find signs of another man, him, in her apartment, through DNA traces most likely. He wasn't the least bit concerned, since anything they found would be useless. He knew for certain that he was unidentifiable, the fact was that as long as they didn't actually have him in custody, he didn't exist. But the mere fact that he had been there at all did afford a possible explanation that might allow Aelia to return to her home and to her life, if the time ever came. That she was held and then taken by him against her will.

The closest international airport was small and had only one terminal, which limited Kyle's options. He would have preferred the huge, bustling airport of a major city, where they could more easily disappear. He also needed to make sure they would not be seen together, so that they would be more difficult to trace, both by the organization and by the police, although frankly right now he was more worried about the organization. Still, because of its size, this airport was not as carefully secured, which made up somewhat for the limited options it afforded.

In the nearest residential area outside the airport, he abandoned the car they were in and stole another from a used car lot closed this time of night. He instructed Aelia to hide her face to the best of her ability using eyeglasses and a scarf he had taken from the car lot's office, and put on a baseball cap he found. They made it into the airport without incident, the sleepy guards barely throwing a look at them. He let Aelia out not far from the terminal, watching to make sure she entered safely, and then drove to the multi-level parking lot of the airport. He parked in the most isolated place he could find, pulled the cap down low on his eyes and ducked out of the car, making sure he would not be seen by any surveillance cameras.

He then left the parking lot and headed to departures, where he bought a travel bag in a men's chain store—luckily he could rely on there being one in nearly every airport he'd ever been to—and some items to go with it, the bare minimum that would avoid questions when he checked in on an international flight. He expected to have to answer the cashier's curious questions but found her conveniently susceptible to his flirting. He was used to it, had done it so many times before, used his looks and charm to get what he wanted and avoid questions.

He took his newly purchased acquisitions and walked calmly through the terminal, stopping as if to check his flight on the flight board while in fact selecting one, the only flight to Rome available. A flight to Naples, closer to their destination, would have been better, but this airport had none. Still, they were lucky there was a flight available to Rome here, and at such short notice. He then continued on his way, going directly to where he'd told Aelia to wait, in the ladies' room near the airport security. Risky, but he'd rather she fell into the hands of the airport police and not the organization's. He went into the men's room in the same corridor and waited. At the designated time he came out, to walk ahead of Aelia as she walked down the corridor.

They joined the line at the airline desk for the flight Kyle had selected, Kyle first and Aelia a moment later, and bought tickets with the contingency cash Kyle always had on him on missions. Aelia used her own passport, which he had her pack back in the apartment. It made her more vulnerable to discovery if she were flagged at some point as a possible suspect or accomplice in Laree's death or even if she were assumed by them to have been kidnapped, but once again, he had no choice but to work with what he had. For himself he used a fake identification, an alias the organization didn't know he had, one he'd never had to use in the past while he was protected by them but had kept nonetheless. Just as he'd been trained to do—always be prepared to disappear.

Semner cut the ribbon the police had left on the door and picked the lock, then entered the woman's apartment with a last look around him to make sure that no one had seen him break in. He'd had to wait long hours until the police and crime scene techs finally left and he could get into the building.

Using a fake badge to pass as a plain clothes police officer sent to stand at the apartment door so that no one would disrupt the crime scene, he'd chatted up that talkative doorman downstairs. According to him the police had traced the blood to the apartment and had found a dead body inside—covered, and it seemed that someone had tried to help him—but there was no one else there. They found the fingerprints of the woman who lived there and signs that someone else, a man, had been there too, but nothing was known about this man, and no one had seen him. They thought she might have been kidnapped by him and that he might have been the one to shoot the man discovered at her apartment, but weren't sure. They seemed to have no real idea what was going on, which Semner was relieved to hear.

The apartment was in shambles. There was still blood on the living room carpet and bloody towels were strewn everywhere, and the police had conducted a thorough search. Semner proceeded to conduct his own but found nothing to indicate where his targets might have gone. He stood beside the table in the woman's study, staring at it, then abruptly swiped everything off it savagely. How the hell did they get away? He should have interrogated that man before he killed him, it might have given him a clue as to who he was. And a place to start.

Now he had nothing.

He braced himself, stifling an oath, and made the call.

They made the flight just barely. They got two adjacent business class seats on the half-full flight, and Kyle sat Aelia near the window, lingering to check out the other passengers around them before he finally sat down beside her. Still, even long minutes into the flight he was unable to relax. This was the first time since Jennison had called him in that he'd actually stopped, could do nothing but sit here, in this relatively safe place, and his mind was free to fully focus on the precarious situation he was in.

He was on the run, with the woman he was sent to kill. The training and experience he was so accustomed to falling back on were keeping him focused, but the fact was that his entire world had been turned upside-down. He'd lost everything, had nothing to go back to. And he still had no idea why. In fact, with each step he was taking there were more questions, and no answers in sight. He was now going with his gut feeling, against everything he'd ever been taught, and against the people he trusted and had relied on his entire life. And all he knew for sure was that what he was doing felt right, that he could not act differently. He literally could not act differently, as if something was guiding him, closing all doors in this corridor he was walking through and leaving only one path open. He closed his eyes, thought about who he was, his family, the organization that was his home—

A soft hand rested gently on his. He opened his eyes and looked at Aelia. Incredibly, her eyes were filled with worry. For him. She said nothing, but he knew. It amazed him. She amazed him. She had lost everything just as he had, her life had been torn apart, and she had every reason to huddle in a corner, paralyzed with fear. And yet here she was, a quiet strength in her eyes, assuring him. Trusting in him. He nodded and leaned back, forced himself to relax, get some sleep. He had no idea what awaited them in Italy, and he needed to be alert.

For her.

In that place deep inside her she wasn't even aware she turned to, Aelia felt him relax. She rested her head back on her seat and stared through the window at the peaceful dark sky, but all she saw was Benjamin Laree dying on her living room carpet, and that man who'd chased them falling back on the concrete road after Kyle's bullet struck him. Dead. She closed her eyes. How could this be about her? How could all this death be about her?

Jennison threw the phone at the wall in rage. He'd thought the plan was foolproof, that it could not fail. How could it? It was daring and brilliant, and it had been his idea all those years ago, his idea and his doing. It's what brought him to this prominent position in the organization. And it had worked so far. Until now. Until the two of them met. And now, instead of having the best asset the organization had ever had on its side, Kyle had switched sides and all Jennison had was the second best. Except that Semner was nowhere close to being as good as Kyle, no one was. No matter how many the organization had tried to train, no one had ever come close to him. Semner was their best bet because he knew Kyle better than the others did, could perhaps exploit some weakness, maybe even influence him to switch sides again.

Jennison closed his eyes in despair. Yes, well, that was unlikely. After all, that was the whole point of using Kyle and not just anyone else.

He had to admit he had no control over the situation.

He considered his possibilities. One was to wait and try to resolve the situation. Perhaps there was still hope with Semner on it. The other was to inform the organization's governing board of the predicament they were in. But he knew this would in fact be reporting his failure, and that would not be forgiven. Not with the stakes involved and not with the unprecedented preparation that had gone into this. He sighed and let his hand fall from the button that would initiate a conference call. He wasn't ready to give up this mission—or his life—yet.

It was now in Semner's hands.

No one was following them when they disembarked in Rome, and it seemed that Kyle's plan to get away unseen had worked. For now. The organization would never stop, and the power it had would ensure that Aelia and he would eventually be tracked down. And so he wasn't about to stop, or even slow down.

Getting through passport control was not a problem. Kyle had gotten rid of the entry and exit stamps in Aelia's passport to avoid questions about her taking the same trip so soon, and was glad that none of the airports involved had automatic services, which would make the record of her travels too readily available and might have led to a security alert.

Aelia herself was disoriented, finding herself back in the city she had left just days before, the very place where it all started. Wanting to get out of the airport quickly, Kyle put his arm around her, and guided her to a car rental stand where he used his alias to rent a four-by-four, and they set out in the chilly afternoon, a stubborn drizzle hugging the windshield.

Hoping to find some answers.

Chapter Eight

They made no stops except for Kyle to redress Aelia's wound, and quiet roads and the sturdy four-by-four with Kyle behind the wheel brought them to the small village at the Amalfi Coast within a few hours. The village was a short distance up the mountains, out of the way of all but the most curious of tourists and dormant even at the height of the season. It was clearly ancient, yet well maintained, as if a hidden hand cared for it. Kyle parked near a homely looking restaurant not far from a large travertine stone fountain, hoping the location would be central enough to help them find someone who would know what Laree meant, who or what Aeterna was.

The elderly proprietor of the restaurant proudly served them a meal, insisting that they try the local dishes that, he happily bragged, were made by his son, the restaurant's cook. They listened politely as he told them in broken English about the history of the place, which his own grandfather had started and which had served the locals for decades. They steered him gently toward giving them more information about the area —and whatever might be reminiscent of the name Aeterna—several times, but the word only drew silence from him, as it did from other locals they spoke to as they strolled through the quiet streets. Even those who Kyle spoke to in fluent Italian, making them instantly comfortable, were of no help.

They returned to the fountain, and Kyle hurried forward to help a woman whose grocery bag fell apart, sending fresh produce rolling.

"Are you all right?" Aelia asked her.

The woman looked at them both with no understanding in her eyes. Kyle tried to speak to her in Italian, but when he asked her about Aeterna she reacted by hurriedly picking up her belongings and scurrying away.

Shaking his head, Kyle was about to lead Aelia back to the car, thinking they would find nothing here, when they heard behind them, in stammering English, "You, eh, you ask Aeterna."

They turned to find an old man sitting at the edge of the fountain. "You help her, I see. She good woman. You help her," he repeated, nodding.

Aelia walked over to him, Kyle behind her.

"You ask Aeterna," the man said again, still nodding.

"Yes, Aeterna. Do you know this name? Could you tell us who this woman is?" Aelia said.

The man looked at her. "Aeterna."

"Yes."

"No," the man said, and Aelia felt disappointment, but then he added, "No, no woman Aeterna. Aeterna is place."

"A place?" Kyle stepped forward.

"Yes." The man nodded happily and pointed up the

82

mountains. "Big house, Aeterna. We not hear name much here, not many know name, know place but not name. I know. My father told me, I was a child, he told me. Aeterna."

Aelia and Kyle exchanged a look. "How do we get there?" Kyle asked the old man.

"No, no." He nodded vigorously. "No one goes there."

"You've never been there?" Aelia asked.

"No, no one goes. House and mountains around it closed, always closed. No one goes unless they are invited."

They thanked him and walked back to the car, leaving him still happily nodding at the edge of the fountain.

"Right. Aeterna house it is," Kyle said resolutely, and they drove out of the village.

Up the mountains, that's where the man had indicated, and that's where they headed. For a while all they had around them were fields and the scattered houses of the village, increasingly far apart, but before long they found themselves in rocky terrain, huge boulders that seemed impassable except for precarious roads that stubbornly wound around them. They quickly lost track of where they were, only the narrow road they were on guiding them. They pushed on carefully until finally, coming around yet another boulder, they found themselves in a narrow pass with steep rocky walls on both sides.

The pass was blocked by a black SUV. Kyle recognized immediately that this was a reinforced car, but its tinted windows prevented him from seeing who was inside, and the car's low beam lights weren't helping either. Instinct kicked in and he began to back up, but an identical car came up slowly behind them, stopping bumper to bumper against their four-by-four. Two men approached from both sides, appearing as if from nowhere, formidable men with assault rifles, their eyes impenetrable. They approached unhurriedly, yet the intimidation was clear.

"Stay inside." Kyle got out of the car, his hand on his gun, but the audible cocking of a rifle a mere foot to his side added to the realization that these people meant business. His hand tightened on his weapon and he instinctively turned back toward Aelia, prepared to do all it took to protect her, when the passenger side door of the vehicle facing them opened. A man in his late forties, Kyle guessed, got out of the car and walked toward them with the confidence of someone who knew nothing could hurt him here. This was his turf.

"There is no need for that," he said, speaking quietly in Italian. "You are on private property. Go on your way and you will not be harmed."

Kyle was about to respond when Aelia moved. His eyes shifted back to her in surprise as she opened the car door, got out, then calmly shut the door behind her. She walked forward several steps, and the two armed guards raised their weapons. But she didn't seem to care, didn't even look at them. Instead, her eyes were intent on the man she was walking toward. Kyle began to move when the man raised his hand to stop the guards, never taking his eyes off this young woman who was fearlessly walking toward him. As she came closer he suddenly staggered back in surprise, opened his mouth to say something, and then stopped, visibly shaken. Aelia halted a few steps away from him and just stood there, looking at him quietly. Their eyes remained locked for what seemed longer than the mere moments it took before the man collected himself, and to Kyle's astonishment he bowed his head.

"Ma'am, I do apologize. Please, allow us to escort you," he said in fluent English, with a distinct accent that Kyle placed in Australia, maybe New Zealand. He glanced inquisitively at Kyle, then nodded. "Sir, may I join you in your car?"

Kyle hesitated, but Aelia nodded to him and he let it go. Whatever had gone on between her and this man just then, he couldn't argue with that. A couple of days ago it probably would have left him full of questions, but not now. Not with what he'd already seen her do. His eyes followed her as she returned to the car. She met his gaze, and what he saw there convinced him. She knew this was the way to go.

Beyond her, Kyle saw one of the armed men move back and disappear between the boulders, as did the one who'd been behind him. Their boss spoke briefly—and rather urgently, Kyle couldn't help but notice—to his driver, and then got into the back seat of Kyle and Aelia's car. As soon as Kyle himself got behind the wheel the vehicle before them began to move, as did their escort behind them.

The lead car reversed expertly until it reached the end of the narrow road and could turn, then continued ahead. Kyle followed. He wouldn't normally be this compliant, but these men didn't feel like attackers anymore. He didn't question how he knew this. He already knew that this was something he was picking up from Aelia, something she was telling him, their own way. She apparently didn't think they were in any danger. And the way that guy had reacted to her, it wasn't that much different from how he himself had. She seemed to be operating on a whole different level than anyone else he'd ever known, in a way he couldn't begin to understand.

He focused on the road and on the car ahead. I guess we'll see soon enough, he thought.

The road took them deeper between the boulders, then along a cliff, where the magnificent sea stretched far into the horizon on their right, shimmering gold and blue in the setting sun. A short distance farther they swerved off the road into a tunnel built into the mountain, and exited into a landscape of low hills and plains, wild grass and woods, hidden deep beyond the reach of outsiders, breathtaking even in the last light of the day. There were no signs of people anywhere, and, in answer to Kyle's question, their escort, who had introduced himself as Rolly Andrews, said that the entire area for miles around had always been owned by them, but did not elaborate.

They drove deep into the hills, until finally the cars

rounded a low rise and a lake stretched before them, winding out of sight to their left. A sprawling mansion— far from what could be described as simply a house, perhaps what Rolly called it, the great house of Aeterna, was a better fit—loomed on its wider edge. It was awe-inspiring, an ancient, solid structure covered in places with vines that softened it up, as if trying to hide the fact that the place was built like a fortress.

At the sight of the house itself, Kyle suddenly realized what was missing until now. "I haven't seen any gates or guards anywhere," he remarked. "I thought this place was protected."

Rolly chuckled. "Oh, this is one of the most protected places in the world." At Kyle's skeptical look he simply added, "The fact that you don't see it doesn't mean it's not there."

They neared the great house and the escort cars continued down the winding path, while the car Aelia, Kyle and Rolly were in drove up to the main entrance. As they approached it, the doors opened, and a man and a woman, formally dressed, came down the wide stairs. House staff, Kyle guessed at their demeanor. Rolly jumped out before the car came to a full stop and opened the passenger side door for Aelia. As she got out, the two approached her in deference and guided her into the house. With a glance back at Kyle and a reassuring smile, she walked in.

Kyle got out of the car and meant to follow her, but Rolly stopped him. "Let her. She needs to do this herself," he said enigmatically. "My driver called ahead, I assure you She is awaited."

And as the younger man looked worriedly after her, he added, "She is protected here."

Kyle glanced at him, his brow raised, and Rolly nodded. "Yes, I wouldn't believe me either after all you two must have been through. But there's a reason you found your way here. Please, trust me on this. She is safe here. You saw it, She feels it, too." And then he said, strangely, "This is Her place."

He then turned in a different direction and beckoned to Kyle. "Come, I'll explain."

But Kyle was rooted to where he was. He looked around him, at the lake, at the vast grounds beyond. At the massive structure that was the great house of Aeterna. Something nagged at him, something he couldn't quite place. A feeling. No, not a feeling. An elusive, too distant memory.

"What is this place?" The question escaped him involuntary. He wasn't like Aelia. She felt she was wanted here, that she could trust. She sensed, he knew, with whatever it was that he had seen in her. But he couldn't do that, and who he was, who he was trained to be, for him the impossibility of the situation was too much. And he could finally allow it to show, now that Aelia and him were here, in this place that seemed to await them.

To know them.

"Mr. Rhys. Kyle."

He turned to Rolly, who was walking back toward him.

Rolly placed himself squarely before him. "You have

88

questions. I understand that. I assure you there is much we can clarify for you here, just as I suppose there is much you can clarify for us. Now that you are here, both of you, we can finally make sense of it all." His eyes were honest. "I'm asking you to trust me, as I would trust you."

Kyle nodded.

Aelia stepped inside. The feeling that had awakened in her just out of the village and that had grown stronger as she approached Aeterna was now clear and focused, as was the knowledge that they were in the right place, that this was where she should be, although she had no idea why. In that place deep within her, she focused on Kyle. She could feel him always now, knew that he was close, that he was worried because he wasn't with her. But he was safe, as safe as she was.

Returning to where she was, she looked around her with growing curiosity, and the two who had escorted her in fell back and waited patiently. The great house did justice to its name. Where she stood in the huge entry hall, high-ceilinged corridors opened on either side of her, stretching far. Before her, two staircases wound high up, leading to more hidden passageways, and along them hung finely painted pictures of women. Elegant women, older, serene, all with a hint of sadness in their eyes, and all dressed the same. She stepped closer to the painting nearest her, a bit farther up on the staircase to her left, and scrutinized the woman it showed.

"The latest Keeper," a quiet voice behind her said.

Aelia whirled around and saw an old woman not far from her, wearing the same robes each of the women in the paintings did. As she moved, the colored band at the edges of the white garment seemed to catch the light of the many lamps around them, almost giving the illusion of a halo around her.

"Latest before me, that is." The woman tilted her head lightly, scrutinizing Aelia, but not unkindly. Her eyes were smiling, and her face was alight with happiness and, yes, relief, Aelia could see immense relief.

"Who are you?" And it wasn't just this woman she meant.

"I am the Keeper," the old woman answered with unhidden pride. "But *you* can call me Neora."

"Keeper? Keeper of what?" Aelia asked, glancing from Neora to the paintings along the stairs.

"The keeper of your memory. The living symbol of your faith."

Aelia's gaze shot back to her, and Neora was taken aback by the intensity of the young woman's eyes, the paleness of her face. "But, I'm sorry. You have been through so much, you must be so tired."

"No, please. Help me." Aelia took a step toward her. "Please. Tell me what's happening to me. *Tell me who I am.*"

Neora walked up to her, and put a gentle hand on her cheek. "It's all right, child. It's all right. Come, I will explain."

And she linked her arm with Aelia's and led her

away from the stairs to the corridor on their right, and through a set of double doors to a comfortable looking drawing room, where an old-fashioned tea service was already laid out.

Behind them unseen hands closed the doors, leaving the two women alone.

As she poured the tea, Neora began.

"Humans, child, are not the first intelligent inhabitants of this world. There was another species here long before them."

Aelia shook her head in disbelief.

Neora put her hand on the younger woman's, restraining her response. She needed to know this now, had to know the truth before anything else. What they had already learned of her had convinced the old woman of that.

"Ages ago, long before homo sapiens as you have learned of them, before anything that would even resemble human civilization in all its past and present forms, another species lived on this very planet. They looked considerably like the humans you know, although in essence there were marked differences. They lived here alone for a long time, developing, advancing. Evolving." She paused. "We call them the Firsts. And I am one of them, as is everyone else here at Aeterna, and a great many others worldwide."

Aelia's mind reeled and she tried to anchor herself in logic, the only logic she had ever known and that the events of the past days, and this woman here, now, were taking from her. "No, I don't understand. This can't be, we were the only ones, humans are the only ones. There was no one here before us." She kept shaking her head. "And you're telling me there were others, and without us knowing? All those archaeologists and anthropologists and historians, none have identified any trace of another species that lived here before us, and you're saying that they are all wrong?"

"I imagine this goes against everything you've ever learned about the history and origins of humanity, and yet that is exactly how it is. We are, and always have been, an unknown element, because we hid, and still hide even today, all signs of ourselves. And we can and do this rather effectively, because we are still here to do this, to actively protect ourselves, our very existence and origins, from being discovered. Sometimes a sign is found that would otherwise be attributed to us, but so far human scholars have infallibly concluded that human civilization has simply begun earlier than they had thought, and so we remain safe."

Neora continued. "According to the stories of our ancestors, they saw the humans appear, watched them grow. At the beginning, and for tens of thousands of years, in fact, this was very easy to do without their knowing of us. We were so much more advanced than they, you see. And as humans finally progressed to where we might be discovered, we fell back, hid. Lived apart. And continued to watch. Eventually we made ourselves look like them, over a number of carefully engineered generations. This made hiding in plain sight easier."

She halted, biding her words. She wanted to say so much, teach this young woman so much. But considering what Aelia had been through, and how tired she must be, Neora knew it would be best not to overwhelm her. She forced herself to choose what she would say now and what she would leave for later. The most important thing was to let her know that she belonged here, that she must stay. And that what she had been experiencing was meant to be.

"It is impossible for me to tell you our story all at once. There will be plenty of time for that. For now, it is important that you understand who we are, who we always were." Neora spread her hands, her words eager. "We were nothing like humanity. For one, compared to them we were ancient, far more advanced, light years ahead in so many ways even of today's humans. From the beginning, our beginning, we progressed faster, and our perceptions were different. We were highly intelligent, highly efficient. We were also extremely aware of the roads that should be taken and those that must be avoided for us to thrive and prosper. And we were highly attuned to both our own needs and those of the world we have always seen ourselves as guests in—we must, we have always believed, be respectful of our surroundings, of this planet and its welfare." Her smile was sad. "As I said, we were, still are, different from the humans."

She contemplated her next words. "But that is not the only way we were different. You see, over the years, there were among us those who were more attuned to all that is around us. The culture you grew up in would call them spiritual, I believe. With time we became worried that our emphasis on progress and striving to enhance certain, more practical, parts of our intelligence would be our end, lead to the demise of what we held important in our core. And by then the humans were advanced enough for us to realize just how different they were from us, and we worried about what they would do to the world. And to us, if we were discovered. From the beginning they were more aggressive, more territorial in nature than we were.

"With these concerns in mind, with the future of our species in question, we took a leap. We actively decided to cultivate those who would be more in touch with what we worried would be lost, our essence. Keep us from losing our way, and give us something we knew humans would never have. We encouraged those who were more compassionate, empathic. In tune. From the time they were young children, we let them take their own way. They were regular members of our society, Firsts like all others, but we nurtured them as a symbol of what we knew we must keep alive within us, allowed them to be what they wanted, and kept them safe, for they tended toward a sensitivity that made them more susceptible to being harmed by both a word and an act."

She paused, steeling herself for what she was about to say to this woman who had grown all her life among humans, with their history and knowledge in her mind.

"Then, some generations on, something happened that our ancestors did not foresee. A child was born, a girl. At first she seemed like all other children, but as time passed we saw that she was different. She was highly independent, strong-willed. She would intervene without hesitation when she thought injustice was done. She protected the weak. She protected all life. She seemed to know when one of us was hurting, even if we were far away, and would do all she could to help. She had a way of . . . she had foresight. She knew, she simply knew, and she could feel us all, was empathic to the emotions and thoughts of every one of the Firsts in existence. She was kind and emotional, unrelenting and insistent. And strong. She never gave up, in any situation.

"As she grew up her abilities grew. And we let it be, allowed her all the freedom she needed and only watched over her. In all our time in this world, we had never seen anything like her. It was as if she possessed something inside her, a light, a power she was one with. Firsts came to her for help, for counsel, for guidance, and gradually, naturally, she became our leader. First among the Firsts." Neora smiled, her mind on the stories of her ancestors, the past of her people.

"When She died, an old woman, something broke within us. It was as if we lost hope, our Light was gone. It was literally gone. The Firsts were still the same, but all that She had built into us in Her lifetime, all that She had awakened and guided within each of us as individuals and in all of us as a people, was lost." Neora raised her eyes to look at Aelia, her eyes bright. "But then another child was born. A girl with that same Light in her. A new guardian of our people. And after her, another. Always one. Always a girl. And throughout long centuries the Light remained among us and guided us like a beacon that always shines, forever keeping the dark at bay."

Neora paused and sipped her tea, her hand shaking, the memory now becoming an effort for her, a painful one.

"And then She stopped being born. We waited, hoped, but no girl was born with the Light in her since." Neora sighed. "We never lost hope. We don't know why She appeared, why She came to us in the first place, and we don't know why She left us, why the Light had left us. But this is exactly why we could hope, choose to believe, that She will return as She has before. Throughout the centuries we have never lost sight of what She has taught us and never stopped believing that She would come back to us."

Her words were eager again. "That is why the Keeper was eventually created—a woman who is chosen from among volunteers who have come of age, to keep the teachings of the Light alive, maintain the hope among our people. When the Keeper passes, her successor has already been chosen and taught, and immediately takes her place. It must be so, for while the Light guides its bearer, passing her its knowledge, the Keeper is but one of the Firsts and must learn from her predecessor." She smiled proudly. "That is the way it has been throughout the centuries, and it ends with me."

Aelia contemplated incredulously what she was hearing. And then it struck her. "Ends?"

"That is the way it should be. The Firsts have never

stopped hoping, waiting for the return of the Light and its bearer. The child, the girl. She is constantly searched for, and the Keeper awaits news of Her discovery. Once She is here, once the Light is back, the Keeper will make way for Her, and She will take Her rightful place among us."

The old woman smiled and closed her eyes, as if in silent contemplation. "And after all this time, these endless years, the Light is finally back. She is here." She opened her eyes and said, "You are here."

Aelia's mind called for her to protest, to express confusion, disbelief. But her very soul, that place deep within her where that now familiar feeling had been growing, changing her, stopped her. The rationality of who she'd been all her life, which was telling her that what she was hearing could not possibly be real, was faced with the quiet conviction that came from within her that this was all true, whispered by a part of her she could not acknowledge just yet.

She closed her eyes and tried to calm down, organize her thoughts. But the turmoil inside her was too great. She opened her eyes, startled, when she felt Neora's hand on hers. The old woman spoke soothingly.

"I know it is a lot to take in. But the fact is, that although you grew up among the humans of this planet, that is not what you are. You are one of us, one of the Firsts. And not only that, you are our Light."

Chapter Nine

The plush room was silent. Aelia was standing by the large picture windows looking to Aeterna's grounds. Outside, peace reigned on the vast hills, peace that clearly did not reflect in her state of mind. Neora was sitting quietly on the sofa, watching her. No matter how eager she was, how thrilled, she had to be patient. This young woman had a lot to absorb, a lot to accept. There was time. Now that She was here, protected, among Her people, there was all the time in the world. And it would happen. What was destined to be, would be.

The Light would rise again.

Aelia couldn't wrap her mind around what Neora had told her. "It doesn't make sense. Why now?" She couldn't breathe. "You said that in the past they were all identified as children, young girls, the . . . Light. I'm not a little girl, and I'm . . ." —she lowered her eyes and blurted out— "I'm damaged. Those girls, they were protected, you protected them. But I, the world I lived in, I'm not . . . I couldn't possibly be . . ."

"Aelia, look at me." The old woman's voice was gentle.

Aelia kept her eyes lowered.

Neora took the young woman's hands in hers. "Look at me," she insisted and Aelia raised her eyes.

"I was told a little bit about you, you know. Ever since my people"—she stopped and smiled—"our people discovered who you are, they have been trying to collect information about you. And although they have not had much time to do that, I think I have a pretty good idea of who you are. And Benjamin, he told us what he had seen—" At Benjamin's mention her voice broke, and it was Aelia who squeezed her hand gently to comfort her, give her strength.

The gesture made Neora smile through tearful eyes. "Look at you. You are you, do you not see? The life you have lived may have done a lot, but it did not change who you are, who you were born to be."

And as Aelia's eyes reflected doubt, she added, "trust me, child. You will see. The fact that you have become one with the Light in so short a time shows me that it is true, the prophecy—"

The doubt in Aelia's eyes turned into a question, and Neora quickly changed the subject. It was too early, far too early for that. Getting up, she smiled. "But that can wait. Come, child, you must rest. There will be plenty of time for us to speak."

A thousand questions in her mind, Aelia nonetheless complied. She was, she realized, exhausted. The past days, and this place, this woman, the Keeper, her revelations . . . just a bit of rest, she thought. Just a bit of time to absorb it all.

"Where is Kyle?" she asked. "The man I came with. I need to see him. Where is he?"

"I should like to meet him myself, to thank him," Neora said. "But would it be all right if you were to see him a little later?"

"Why?" Even as she asked, Aelia focused on Kyle, found him preoccupied but safe, and she relaxed.

Neora marveled at what she was seeing, and at what she already knew it meant. "He has his own truth to learn," she said.

She bid the young woman good night, and Aelia allowed herself to be escorted back to the main entry hall and its two staircases. She walked up, past Keepers watching her from pictures growing more ancient with each step she took, and was led across the wing and to an expansive set of rooms in which a woman, Sonea, stood ready at her beck and call. But all she wanted was to be alone, and Sonea took leave. Mindless of her surroundings, Aelia went directly into the bedroom, sat at the edge of the bed for a long moment and then lay back, just for a moment, closing her eyes. This must be a dream, she thought. It has to be.

There was no darkness this time, in her sleep. Only the Light, and the kindness in the eyes of her past forms. And the words, deep in her sleeping mind.

Welcome home.

Neora walked toward the stairs, her gait slow. She could finally allow herself to feel the weariness accumulated in her over decades in which she stubbornly maintained the hope she as the Keeper could not lose. After all this time, the girl was here. And while earlier Neora only knew what Benjamin had told Ahir, what he had seen, now she had seen for herself. There were still many questions, and so much more needed to be said, to be done, but that would wait. These past days had clearly taken their toll on Her, and She needed to rest.

The old woman sighed. Tonight, finally, she too could sleep, even though she was still the Keeper and would maintain this role for a while yet, she knew. The girl had to be taught all that She would have known had She grown up among Her own people, among the Firsts. But more than that, because She had been taken to live among the humans and had not been allowed to grow up with the Light, be one with it throughout Her life as would normally be the case, She still needed to transition fully into what She was to be. Worse, from what they had been able to find out about Aelia, She had had a difficult life, and that in itself must have served to hinder all that She might have become long ago. It still could.

And it was not only about Her. Ever since Ahir told Neora and the Council that he believed She was found, there had been voices worrying that because the Light was only awakening now, when Aelia was already in her twenties, She might not fully become one with it and might not achieve Her full potential. Which would mean that She would have to be kept protected at Aeterna, for Her own safety and that of Her people, until Her last day. And then the waiting for the Light would begin again.

But how would the people feel if that were the case? They needed Her now. Would they still hope? They were already rattled by the fact that when the Light finally returned, it happened in this way. They could not understand how She was taken away, subdued for so long, so easily hidden. They would likely wonder what it all said about Her. Would She, *could* She, once again be First among the Firsts?

Neora sighed. She herself was not sure what to think, even now that she had spent some time with the girl—the woman, she should call her. None of the Firsts now living had actually met a Light, nor none for many generations back, and none knew what to expect. All they had were the ways taught to them since birth and maintained by the Keepers, and stories, legends, really, passed on through the ages. None of them had actually *felt* the Light, its presence, that which the stories said that She was able to do, the way in which She connected with Her people. Even the Keeper herself, with what she knew she should be sensing within her, even she did not recognize what it was that she felt from Her. It was too subtle, a trace of an ancient memory long gone. If that was all Aelia could do, could she really awaken in all Her people what the Light had in the past?

Neora straightened up, held her head high. She was the keeper of the faith, and her faith was the strongest. She had made her choice when she herself was younger than Aelia was now, and had not wavered since. She had no doubt—what was to be, would be.

Movement shook her from her reverie. She had now reached the top of the stairs, her lady's maid following close behind her, ensuring the old woman's safety. The head of her Council and her dearest friend, Ahir, was standing there, leaning on the banister and looking down, as if he was having a hard time deciding what to do. He moved hesitantly toward the stairs, then stopped again. Neora motioned her lady's maid to go ahead of her and approached the old man. "You should go to him."

Ahir looked at her, his eyes almost beseeching, and then he looked toward the stairs again. Neora put a gentle hand on her friend's arm. "Go, talk to him, Ahir."

Ahir closed his eyes and breathed in deeply. He opened his eyes, squeezed her hand affectionately, and proceeded slowly down the stairs.

Rolly took Kyle inside through a door that led to a far wing of the great house. On the way he explained that not only was Aeterna constantly monitored technologically, security teams were strategically deployed throughout it at all times, and these worked together with the defense units of the Firsts' defense force, trained to ward off possible attacks. But Kyle found it difficult to believe what the man was saying. So far he had seen no indication of the kind of security layout he was hearing about.

They walked through beautiful, clearly ancient corridors that easily countered Rolly's words, looking more into the past than into the futuristic image he was conveying to Kyle. But then, after Kyle had already lost track of where they were, they stepped through a set of antique doors directly into an elevator concealed behind them. The elevator doors closed, then opened again almost instantly, and Kyle stood in place, gaping. Before him stretched a wide corridor that leaped centuries ahead in time.

Two men stood just outside the elevator, both visibly armed. They stood aside, letting the newcomers through without a word, even Kyle.

"You seem to have some clout here," Kyle noted.

"I'd better. I'm the head of defense and security for Aeterna."

Kyle raised a brow. "Why's the head of defense and security meeting trespassers at the perimeter?"

"Perimeter? You were well inside our territory by the time we intercepted you. Aeterna extends farther than you may think. It even owns miles into the air and sea. If you were unfriendly it would be easier to deal with you on our territory, in our jurisdiction."

"That's commendable. And yet?"

Rolly raised his hands, palms out. "I'm not evading, I will answer. I just think it would be more understandable in the context of things."

Kyle decided to give him the benefit of a doubt, and he focused on where they were, glancing curiously around him. Here, the ceiling was translucent, and Kyle couldn't discern where the lights came from. They seemed to be equally dispersed, yet they also flowed along with them as they walked, as if changing their intensity according to their perceived need.

They passed several intersections with other, smaller corridors, and eventually reached a huge, semicircular room, the entire curved wall of which seemed to Kyle to be a single fluid screen, broken into changing views of the house itself and of the grounds and hills around it. Facing it were individual stations, each comprising a seat in which a person sat, comfortably reclined, intent on a holoscreen showing data and multidimensional images of locations on or above the grounds. All had what looked similar to earpieces, through which they seemed to command the systems and speak to one another. Behind them stood a higher supervisor's station, a half circle coinciding with the screen, which allowed the shift supervisor, a stern woman, to effectively walk behind the individual stations as well as to face any point on the wall views. Kyle was taken aback. The layout was highly advanced, making any command and control center he'd ever seen seem antique.

Beside him Rolly laughed, recognizing his astonishment. "Welcome to Aeterna's control center." He led Kyle inside and showed him around, explaining. Each and every person in the room was intent on his or her work, and despite the size of the place and the activity level in it, it was nearly silent.

"This is where our entire security is controlled from," Rolly said quietly as they walked through the room. "The people you see receive to their individual stations real-time data from the sectors they are assigned. They communicate directly with the technology, as well as with their peers in here or with the security teams outside, through implanted linking devices that they activate through the earpiece, as you called it, which they put on when they are on duty. And if there's any need they're able to deploy either additional security means or the supplemental defense units. All data comes from our equivalents of your cameras and sensors, which cover the entire grounds. We also have satellites positioned—"

Kyle interrupted, thinking he misheard. "I'm sorry, did you say satellites?"

Rolly smiled. "Yes, we've got our own satellites that are invisible to humans'"—he corrected himself quickly—"to the satellites used by the governments or companies you're familiar with. This allows us to have at our disposal constant coverage of Aeterna and numerous other sites worldwide."

He fell silent, took a long look around him. "When it comes to Aeterna, we simply cannot let our guard down. And starting the day She was discovered we've gone to our highest security threat level. It wasn't difficult, really. We didn't know when She would eventually get here, so we've been prepared for, well, quite a long time."

Kyle stopped walking, confused. "Wait, she? You mean Aelia, don't you? You knew she would come here?" His mind went back to Rolly's reaction to her when they had arrived on Aeterna's grounds, to the welcome they received, to the way she was ushered into the great house as if she were . . . someone important. Yes, that was it. Someone awaited.

He frowned. These bits and pieces he was getting weren't enough to do anything but increase his confusion. Nor was Rolly's reference to "humans", which he did not miss.

"No, I don't understand," he said. "This is one hell of a security layout for a private mansion, not to mention the fact that I've never seen anything like this, anywhere. And I've been around. And you can't, what was it, let your guard down? You're on heightened security? What..." He stopped in mid-sentence and stood quietly, thinking, trying to reconcile what he was hearing with what he himself had seen and knew. "Who are you people? And who is she, Aelia?" He raised his eyes to see Rolly watching him, with understanding—and a slight smile.

He let himself be guided out. As they walked back down the corridor, leaving the control center behind them, he noticed that he could see, within what he had thought were only walls, corridors and rooms where people were moving around, or working with technologies he couldn't clearly discern. The walls here were only semi-transparent, the rooms beyond not much more than shadows. Nor could he see any doors that led in. There seemed to be no breaks in the walls on both his sides other than for the intersections that led to the smaller corridors.

Rolly glanced at him. "You really have no idea who She is, do you?"

Kyle only shook his head.

Rolly chuckled in wonder. "In that case I'd love to

have been there, see first-hand what actually made you change sides and get Her here."

Kyle stopped, astonished. "You know?"

"I know some of it. Benjamin had updated us before. . ." Rolly fell silent, clearly thinking about the man's death. "Right. Back to your questions. I was there when the two of you arrived because I'm out there more as part of the heightened security, which, as I've said, we've initiated when we found out about Her, because we knew there was someone after Her, and potentially, then, also after those at Aeterna, especially after we would get Her here. You see, it's complicated to explain why, it is not mine to do, but we have had someone following Aelia for a while."

"Benjamin Laree."

"So you did know about him. How do you know his name?"

Kyle reached into the inner pocket of his jacket and took out Laree's passport and wallet. He handed them to Rolly without a word.

Rolly took the items. "I don't understand. How do you have these?"

Kyle explained briefly.

Rolly nodded. "Thank you," he said, his eyes on the passport he had open on the man's photo. "Thank you for taking these. Benjamin, he was more of an assistant than a bodyguard. I made a mistake allowing him to follow Her alone for so long. I should have sent someone else earlier, someone better trained. But we were taken by surprise, you see, finding Her this way. And we didn't expect the organization to be there, not so soon." He looked up at Kyle. "Benjamin saw something in the park, and he called us." Rolly stopped, not sure how much to say, what this man would think. What he was to know, or already knew.

"I saw it too."

"You saw it?" Rolly frowned. "How is that even possible? Benjamin of course, but you?" It was his turn to be confused. "Yes, he saw you there, and informed us."

"So he told you I tried to kill her," Kyle said evenly.

"He did."

"What he didn't know is that I made three attempts on her life. Not just the one he saw."

"And yet you failed to kill Her. And you brought Her here, to us."

Kyle faced him squarely and held his gaze. "I'm telling you that I was sent to kill Aelia."

"Yes." Rolly didn't waiver.

"And you simply accept that I, what, changed sides?"

"Well, that's a bit more complicated to explain, but yes."

"You don't seem surprised at any of this."

"Of course not. We knew that when She would return, the organization would most likely be after Her. And they are in fact the ones who sent you, didn't they? Yes, well, we now suspect they've always known who and where She is. That's the only explanation."

Kyle was speechless.

Rolly smiled mirthlessly. "They've been after us for so long, we've always known that if they would know about Her they'd go after Her the moment they thought She was a danger to them, maybe even before that. We just didn't know they would find out about Her before us, otherwise they never would have managed to take Her from us in the first place. Which begs the question nobody has been able to answer yet—how did they know who She is and how did they get their hands on Her?" He resumed walking, deep in thought.

"Wait. If you know who sent me after her and why, why did you just show me your entire security? Come to think of it, why didn't you just shoot me when you first saw me?"

Rolly halted and looked back at him. "Because I received explicit orders on how to treat you."

"Who from?"

"The Keeper and the head of the Council, of course. They said to treat you as if you're one of us, and as the man who protected the Light. Do you think I would show our security layout to just anyone?" Rolly returned to Kyle. "Look. Benjamin sent us a photo of you he took on his phone, in the park. We didn't find you in our database of the organization, but we had reasons to be sure they sent you. Head of Council requested to see your photo, and then he requested that you be brought here, alive. The way things turned out, with you switching sides, you made it easy."

Kyle's confusion only deepened. Keeper? Council? Light? He still had no idea what Rolly was talking about and was about to demand a clear answer when something struck him. "Hang on. You say you know about the organization, about Aelia being a target. My target. Why didn't I ever hear anything about you"—he spread his hands to indicate Aeterna around them—"or about this place?" He shook his head, recollecting, "I was taught she was a danger to us, to humanity. Hell, I grew up thinking that she was my greatest enemy. I was told—"

"I guess you were told what they wanted you to know. Who's my counterpart now, still Jennison, is it? Good old Jennison. One of the smarter ones in the organization. Smart and ruthless. Still heads the training facility, does he?"

Kyle's mind was churning. Everything he'd always considered the absolute truth, told to him by those he trusted the most, was shattering into pieces. He no longer knew what to believe, and anger erupted within him. He wanted to stay, knew there would be answers here—Rolly was certainly being straightforward with him—but he needed to go back, find Jennison. Find the truth and do it now, while there was still hope that Jennison wouldn't expect him to double back and wouldn't increase the facility's protection, as well as his own, to the point that it would be impossible for Kyle to get to him. Semner was out there looking for them, but if Kyle could do it fast enough . . .

He focused back on Rolly. "I have to go. But I need to know Aelia is safe here."

"What? Go where? You just arrived, I didn't get a chance to get all the details from you, debrief you properly. And the head of Council, he wanted to speak to you, and we still didn't explain—" He stopped at the look in Kyle's eyes. "Right. Yes, She's safe here. We've always had the Keepers here, so this is our most secure location. And right now, this entire place is focused on Her protection. Everyone here would place themselves between Her and any danger in a heartbeat."

Kyle didn't budge.

Rolly nodded. "I'll show you."

He turned right, straight into a transparent wall, and Kyle had no time to react before a doorway formed out of nowhere.

"Okay, that's new," he said, following Rolly.

"You will learn that not everything is quite what it looks around here," Rolly remarked. "This is not just an ancient mansion."

He walked to a hologram of the great house and its grounds that formed in the middle of the room they had entered, and proceeded to give Kyle the practical specifics of the security layout, answering his questions until Kyle finally nodded.

"It is possible that there is someone else after her," he said, his eyes on the hologram. "Another organization operative, and he's good. I'd tell you to track incoming traffic into the village, which is as I understand the closest access point to this area, but since he knows me he'll do everything to keep hidden, so I doubt he'll come that way."

"We'll keep an eye out. But we haven't had anyone try to come here other than through the village. That's the good thing about it, it's the obvious place people who happen to come around here are attracted to, and they don't usually look beyond it or even suspect that we're here. And Aeterna has supported the village for centuries, so they tend to keep silent about us, and encourage people to stay away."

"An organization killer has already turned up on your grounds," Kyle said, meeting Rolly's eyes. "If I would have wanted, if I hadn't come in openly, with a woman I was protecting, I would have gotten in, and it wouldn't have been through the village."

"Yes," Rolly conceded. "You're right. We didn't expect Her to turn up here this way, certainly not so quickly, and not with you. And had you had other intentions... yes. Understand, we've been safe here for longer than you can imagine. And we had reason to believe that as long as She wasn't back, the organization would stay away." He paused. "And we thought Benjamin would be the one to bring Her here."

"I didn't kill him," Kyle said quietly. "In other circumstances I probably would have. But I didn't."

Rolly said nothing.

Kyle spoke. He began when he first caught a glimpse of Benjamin at the park and recounted everything that would help the man before him understand how his friend died, that he gave his last breath telling Aelia where to go. But he didn't tell Rolly all of it. He left out what he could still not explain to himself.

Rolly was silent for a long minute. "Thank you." He held up Benjamin's passport and wallet, which he was still holding in his hand. "And again, thank you for taking these. As I said, Benjamin was not well versed at knowing how to hide his identity, and had the authorities found these it would have raised unwanted questions. As it is, I can return these to his family together with his body."

"His body?"

Rolly nodded. "We have our methods too, not only the organization. Some of my people were already on their way to help Benjamin secure Aelia and take you in when all this happened. They have managed to, let's say, have his body misplaced. It is being flown home as we speak."

"So that's how you know he died." Kyle looked at the hologram. A thought struck him and his heart beat just that much faster. "Rolly, would the organization know to come here, to Aeterna, even if they weren't tracking us?"

"They are aware of this place. But they also know of us, and I can tell you they would not so easily come here." Rolly's tone reminded Kyle that there was still too much he didn't know. "The question is how quickly they'll make the connection between you and this place. Assuming your actions and ours prevented them from finding out who Benjamin was, and since they obviously think Aelia has no knowledge of who She is or where She belongs, then, if you weren't supposed to know about it either..."

"They might think we're on the run without a clear destination? No. I assure you my people—" Kyle's eyes went ice cold. They weren't his people anymore. "I assure you the organization would ultimately track us here." He turned to leave the room. "I've got to go back there now. I'll give you the description of the operative I believe might be tracking us. I'm hoping it would take him a while, but keep an eye out for him, he's a dangerous guy." He turned back to look at Rolly. "And you know there's a difference between protecting a defined perimeter against an attack and protecting a single person against a designated killer. Put one of your security details on Aelia. I'd put them also on your Keepers or Councils or whoever here you think important."

"I will. But listen, you've made it clear they know you turned against them. They might kill you."

"Oh, they will try if they get the chance." Kyle no longer had a doubt. He just wanted to know why.

There was one more thing he needed to do before he left. "Where is Aelia? I want to see her before I leave."

"I'll take you to Her."

Rolly led him to the entry hall of the great house from the inside, and Kyle found himself facing two long staircases that led up, with portraits of women, he vaguely noticed, some seemingly very old, hanging along them. The question rose in his mind of their significance, but he pushed it aside, keeping his mind on the matter at hand. There was no time.

His attention was drawn to a stout woman who was coming down the stairs. Rolly approached her. "Sonea, Mr. Rhys here needs to see Her."

Sonea halted and looked at Kyle calmly. "The Keeper sent Her up to rest. She will see no one now."

"Mr. Rhys is the one who brought Her here."

Sonea's expression changed, and she looked at Kyle with interest. "You are him then, Sir. Yes, I will show you to Her rooms."

Kyle followed her upstairs, Rolly a step behind. Sonea led them through the plush corridors, but after only a few steps Kyle realized he knew where to go. He stopped at the set of large doors a split second before Sonea did. Glancing at him with unveiled surprise, she turned as if to go in first, then stopped and moved aside, making way for him.

He hesitated.

Abruptly he turned. "Let's go."

Rolly looked at him, began to speak but reconsidered, instead nodding to himself and following Kyle back downstairs.

"Right. Your destination?"

Kyle specified the location of an airport he'd feel safest getting to in southwestern Arizona. "I need to get there fast and quietly."

"And return," Rolly said.

Kyle said nothing.

Rolly frowned. "You sure about this?"

"It's the only way to do this. I need to ascertain who they sent after Aelia and try to stop them from sending anyone else after her." He paused. "And I need to know the truth."

Kyle was taken to a stealth helicopter waiting to take him to the airport, where Rolly had one of Aeterna's private jets ready.

In the great house, Aelia started awake. She sat up, tried to understand what was wrong. She got off the bed and walked to the window, where darkness reigned over Aeterna. She didn't even realize that she was searching inside her, until she realized what it was, what was missing.

Kyle was gone.

Chapter Ten

In the house rented by the organization for this mission that had gone so terribly wrong, Semner stood in the second-floor bedroom that Kyle had used while he was there. Kyle's things were strewn around, and the hand-held with the information about the target lay on the floor at Semner's feet. Semner looked around him in distaste. He'd been through the woman's apartment twice and through this very room countless times, returning to it again and again obsessively as he waited long hours for news. But there was nothing to indicate where they had gone. And that damn Jason Neace was gone too. Semner had the guard downstairs try to track him down, but no luck yet.

He had a theory about this, though. Jennison had of course warned Neace that Kyle had become a target and that he was sending Semner in, and the guard had said that Neace had left the house not long after he had updated Semner about Kyle's actions. So Neace must've gone after the targets himself, for whatever crazy reason. In which case if he actually managed to run into Kyle, he'd be dead by now and probably ended up in a morgue somewhere, unless Kyle bothered to get rid of the body.

Ineptitude, Semner thought. He hated ineptitude, and that stupid Neace who had gone rogue, he was sure, was just the picture of it. He looked down at the handheld, then stamped on it angrily, breaking it. Was there anything else that could go wrong?

His phone rang. High time. The cool voice on the other end of the line informed him that the organization had tracked the targets to a flight to Rome. Which meant that they were most likely heading for one of two places. Semner would shortly have an aircraft waiting for him to take him to Rome, and by the time he'd get there he would be informed which direction to go in, the voice told him. Last chance, it said.

Semner ended the call and looked down at the shattered handheld. Failure was not an option. His life was on the line now, too.

Aeterna's jet waited for Kyle in a private hangar and took off as soon as he was aboard. As he sat alone, away from the security detail Rolly sent along, planning his next moves, he considered the irony of it. It wasn't so long ago that he was on a very similar jet, on his way to kill the same woman he was now trying to protect. He leaned back and closed his eyes, forcing himself under control. He was impatient to get to Jennison.

Rolly's assurance that Aeterna's jet would make far better time than the commercial flight, or any other flight Kyle had ever been on, for that matter, proved correct. Kyle was out as soon as it landed, energized by the urgency of this situation he had found himself in and by his own anger. Every part of him that the organization had cultivated was fully alert, and he was focused on his new mission.

He himself would by now be the organization's target, and he knew Jennison had good people. People Kyle had trained with, others whom he himself had trained. And Jennison himself would be well protected, both in the facility's headquarters and in his home. However, Kyle did have the element of surprise on his side. He also had knowledge, and a lot of it, about how the organization worked, and how Jennison thought. They were both very single-minded when it came to Aelia, which led to a lack of flexibility in their thinking. For them she was a danger like no other, which, when the time came, had to be relentlessly pursued. This was their Achilles' heel. Jennison, Kyle expected, would still blindly focus all thought on her, not on Kyle.

His anger flared. Putting that into the context of what he had seen at Aeterna, the bits and pieces he had time to learn from Rolly, and most of all the time he had spent with Aelia, he understood just how much had been hidden from him, how much he had been lied to. That was the one thing he knew for sure, did not doubt. That he had been lied to by the organization and Jennison. He had time, during the flight, to think about Jennison's recent actions, and about the fact that the first time he had raised a question about the mission and about Aelia's identity, Jennison had written him off and targeted him alongside her. This was unlike Jennison—Kyle had argued with him before about missions and targets, and had even changed missions while they were already in progress, and Jennison had always let him get away with a lot. With anything, really. So why now?

But it was more than that. It was almost as if Jennison had expected Kyle to side with his target, this target. And that was Jennison's weakness right now. Kyle believed, and was about to bet his life on it, that Jennison would never think Kyle would actually leave Aelia and return straight to the organization's midst.

Which was exactly what he was planning to do.

Traveling in a private jet gave him the freedom to choose where to land, and he chose a general aviation airport just outside Glendale, Arizona. The place was small, yet it could easily accept a non-scheduled private jet, and it was designated to serve as a reliever for a nearby international airport, which meant it was a port of entry to the United States. They weren't likely to attract unwanted attention here. And, perhaps most important, it wasn't an airport the organization used.

He left the security detail behind and took off by himself. Wanting to remain untraceable, he stole a car a distance away, where no one would be likely to look for it until morning, and, after making sure he wasn't followed, he drove through Glendale to a place he kept a small storage space in. He had similar storage spaces in several different locations worldwide, all unknown to anyone but him, all kept in cities the organization had no people in.

The building he entered housed hundreds of self-service storage units at a range of sizes. His was paid for ten years in advance, just in case. He wanted to make sure no one would even consider accessing it. Reaching it, he opened the door, revealing that the space behind it had been converted into a vault, with its own emergency ventilation system. An entire wall was fitted with shelves stocked with weapons and cash in a variety of currencies, as well as fake IDs. Against the opposite wall stood a mattress, and beside it everything he would need to spend a few days there in an emergency. A safe house, for all intents and purposes. He took it all in, then entered and chose an outfit that would be most suitable for what he was planning to do, and picked up a small console. Then he armed himself and left, shutting the vault behind him.

He had ditched the car he stole, so he walked in the dark until he came across a motorcycle that fit his purpose. He used the console to disconnect the motorcycle's systems and reconnected them again through it. Soon the motorcycle purred under him, and he quickly left Glendale behind him, due southwest. His destination was about an hour away, maybe less this time of night and on this powerful machine. This one was a small city, much smaller than the one he'd just left behind. Unassuming, mundane. Miles of open spaces around it, some farms on the outskirts, small streets, homes and schools. Shops, not even a mall, nothing that would attract anyone here. A seemingly simple place. A place the organization controlled. Only it's people lived here, their families. And him. This was where he'd grown up.

He knew what to do to avoid detection. He stayed well away from the heart of the place, and headed straight to a building on the outskirts, one he'd known throughout most of his life. From the outside, the simple, concrete one-story building seemed harmless enough. It looked as if it might house a research laboratory of sorts or perhaps serve as an uninteresting storage space. But in reality it was a fortified structure, completely empty on the inside except for a reception desk with two people, a man and a woman, both in fact highly trained organization personnel. Behind them, elevators went down to a number of underground floors, each with its own designation. Offices, an advanced technology intelligence center, a firing range, training areas. Everything, in fact, that was needed to support the army that was the heart of the organization that had been constructed around a single goal—to protect humanity. This, an unimposing concrete structure in an unlikely location, was in reality the organization's main training facility.

Kyle hid the motorcycle some way off and made his way carefully toward the building. Whether they would be on the lookout for him or not, operating procedure dictated that in these circumstances they would be on heightened alert. He knew better than to try to find a way into the building using any type of electronic means, because the facility's systems would automatically flag anything out of the ordinary. These people were far from amateur. And they knew him, his familiarity with the complex. This meant it might be better to go in the old-fashioned way, by simply sneaking in. And the building did have one weakness that would work to his advantage, even given the remote chance that they would think him bold enough to double back and strike at their heart.

Jennison was his father's best friend and Kyle's godfather. As a child, long before he'd begun his formal training in the organization, Kyle spent a lot of time freely roaming the facility. Freely being the key word here. Bored, a child among adults who had no time for him but could not boss him around because of who he was, he spent long days exploring the place in and out. As a result, Kyle the child knew everything about this building that others had long since forgotten. And Kyle the adult was about to use a way in only he knew about.

Back then, the ventilation systems of the underground floors were replaced to accommodate new technology, and a service tunnel was dug to facilitate the work. A very interested young Kyle enjoyed the commotion and spent a lot of his time around the workers. The foreman, who had a child his age, took to him and let him play in a section of the tunnel that led from ground level to the first underground floor.

When the job was finished, Kyle begged the foreman not to seal the tunnel as he was contracted to do. The man did, but he left a narrow way through for the boy, which he even secured to ensure its safety. He said he'd return to seal it after a while, explaining to the boy that he had no choice but to do so because he was contracted to maintain strict security parameters. But he never did come back. As an adult, Kyle could only guess why. Forgot, perhaps, or just decided to leave a lonely young boy this isolated place he enjoyed so much. Whatever the reason, the tunnel remained. When Kyle himself became an active member of the organization, he considered pointing it out and having it sealed but eventually decided against it. Ironically, at the time he thought it would add to the facility's security because it constituted a way in or out, albeit a narrow one, in the event of an attack on the building. So he made sure it could not be found unless someone actually knew where it was, but did not go so far as to tell anyone about it. Not even his godfather.

No one knew it was there except him.

He watched the facility for a while before he proceeded. He had no doubt Jennison was there—he always stayed in at times of crisis—and was eager to get in, but he had to be careful not to be detected by security. The place was covered by multipurpose sensors and cameras, and patrolled by teams dressed as the security employees of a known commercial company, to hide the fact that they were trained at a level that wouldn't shame the best military combat soldiers and were, in fact, organization operatives. He could quickly tell that more teams had been added and that the patrol intervals were reduced to increase coverage. None of them was alone, they walked in twos and were alert. But that was it, which led him to believe that Jennison really didn't expect him to return.

Getting to the tunnel was easy. He knew where each

sensor was and the camera coverage, and anyway the tunnel originally opened far enough from the building so as not to interfere with the current operation of the sensitive electronic security systems. Under the cover of darkness, Kyle went straight to where its entrance was hidden, uncovered the lid that closed it under shallow ground, between thick shrubbery, and slipped in quickly. He had to get in legs first, to be able to secure the entrance behind him, and then had to reverse carefully to a slightly wider cross section in order to turn around. He wasn't child-sized anymore.

The tunnel brought him exactly where he wanted to get to, the first underground floor level. Because no one expected intruders to get through security at the ground level, security here was less than on the outside. Kyle exited the tunnel in the small utility room it led into, took off the black coveralls he was wearing and placed them in the tunnel, then closed it and pushed the panel hiding it back into place. He listened at the door, biding his time, and then walked into the empty corridor, adjusted the cap on his head low over his eyes and walked directly to Jennison's office. He was dressed as the security personnel on this level were, and, as he had expected would be the case, those around him didn't see the obvious. No one expected him to be there, and they noticed the clothes, not the man wearing them.

Lucky for Kyle, Jennison's vanity had led him to take an office on this floor. As the head of the facility he should have had a more secure office on a lower level, but he liked the hum of the offices around him and the knowledge that all the main floors of the facility were under him, that he was in control. His office was at the end of a short corridor, through a heavy door with his name and title on it. Kyle threw a look behind him. The corridor was empty. He wasn't detected yet, then. Hoping the guards behind the closed circuit television would miss looking at the screen of the camera immediately above him just a moment longer, he opened the door and walked in.

Behind the desk, Jennison raised his head up from his laptop and got up so fast that his armchair flew back. "What the..."

"Hello, Uncle Howard."

"How did you—" But then Jennison stopped and let out a hard laugh. "Yes, of course you'd find a way in."

"What? No call to security?"

"No, not you. Not against you. You're family."

"Am I?" Kyle took a step forward. "Then why did you send a killer after me? And while we're at it, who did you send? Semner, I presume? I don't see your guard dog here at your heels, after all."

"I would never send someone to harm you."

Kyle looked at him menacingly.

"I sent someone after your target. You weren't doing the job, so someone else had to."

"No, I know you. And you know me, you've known me all my life. We've had setbacks on jobs before, all of us, and we've never been interfered with unless there was absolutely no choice. And you've never sent someone to replace me on a job, certainly not without telling me. And certainly not on *this* job."

"You weren't functioning as planned."

"You mean I was asking questions."

Jennison didn't answer.

"Well, I've got some more questions, and you're going to answer them."

Jennison walked around the desk and began walking toward Kyle, but the man's forbidding expression made him stop. He sighed. "Right. Ask your questions."

Kyle knew exactly what question to begin with, the same one he'd asked Jennison on the phone only days ago. "Who is she?"

"You know who she is."

"Ah, yes. She who will bring about the destruction of humanity. Danger in its purest form, wasn't that what you and my dad taught me?"

"And that's exactly what she is."

"Is that so? Because it sure didn't look like that to me."

"No, it wouldn't, would it?" Jennison mumbled bitterly.

"What was that?" Kyle walked toward him slowly. "That doesn't seem to surprise you. In fact, it almost seems as if you had expected me to switch sides to hers."

Jennison avoided his eyes.

"So you did. Why?"

Jennison remained silent.

"Why?" Kyle's voice was ice.

Jennison still didn't answer. Kyle thought hard. The events of the past days raced through his mind, contrasting with what this man had taught him his entire life. What he had seen Aelia do. His reaction to her, his would-be target, and her reaction to him. What he sensed, felt, from her and in himself when he was around her, the new instincts she had awakened in him. And memories, shards of memories that simply could not be. These all intertwined with what he'd encountered at Aeterna, the perceived peacefulness of its people, their protectiveness of Aelia, their kind treatment of him, the man they knew had been sent to kill her. Just days ago he would have taken Jennison's words, his description of this woman, the target, as a given, but now he knew it could not be true.

And Jennison's behavior was only proving it.

"Why me?" he suddenly asked.

"What?"

"Why me, why was I chosen for this? I've heard about this 'enemy of humanity' ever since I was a kid, and yet I was never allowed to tell anyone. None of the others knew, only us and dad and his friends, and how many in the organization really know? I was chosen by you, wasn't I? Trained to be the one to stop her because you decided it should be so. Brainwashed almost, isn't that true? Your own family. Why?"

"You were available at the time, it was the most convenient—" Jennison didn't finish his sentence before he was picked off the floor and thrown against the wall like a rag doll. The photograph he hit, which showed him smiling, his hand on the shoulder of a very young, still innocent Kyle, crashed to the floor, the glass shattering loudly into a thousand pieces, although all Jennison was aware of was the screaming pain in his limbs.

The pain was forgotten a mere moment later as he realized the man who caused it was advancing on him, his eyes full of fury. Jennison shied from Kyle as the powerful man bent down and grabbed the lapels of his shirt, repeating, "Why me?"

"Because you're the only one who can!" Jennison screeched as he felt himself being pulled up. "You're the only one who can kill her!"

Kyle let him drop him and stepped back in surprise. His mouth opened to say something, but he found he had no idea what. A fleeting memory flashed, another piece fell into place. His mind reeled.

"Anyone else can only hurt her, believe you me, we tried. We think that you're the only one who can kill her." Jennison continued resignedly, rubbing the back of his head. "You're the one their stories name, you stand as her born champion."

"What the hell are you talking about?"

Jennison got up slowly and sat on his chair with a sigh. "Fine. You want to know, here it is. She belongs to another race that has lived on this planet long before we have. A race far more . . . far more than we are, simply said. Firsts, they dare call themselves. And they're a danger to humanity, they could wipe us out. We've known about them for a long time now. This"—he indicated the facility around him—"all we've done since before my time, has been about them. And the way to get rid of them is to get rid of the force or whatever it is that is their heart, their very being. And that's her. That woman, that . . . that *thing* we sent you after." He said the word with hatred, almost fearfully. He closed his eyes and breathed in deeply. "According to their stories there is a man who is born around the same time as her for one purpose, and one purpose only — to protect her. Always one man." He indicated Kyle with his head. "And that's you. You're one of them."

"One of . . . another race? A force? Are you out of your mind?"

"It's true. Only a handful of people know this, it's the best kept secret of this organization. It's the reason we started this, to stop them. A whole different race coexisting with ours on this planet. And you are one of them. Didn't you ever wonder? Didn't you see what you can do, how no one else here can match you?" He snickered. "Yes, one of *them*. Except they didn't get you, did they? We did."

"What do you mean you got me? And why . . ." Even as he spoke, the picture, as impossible as it seemed, was beginning to form in his mind. "You sent me after her!"

"It was the only way. The only way we could turn the future, our future around was if you were to turn on her. You were born to protect her but you're the one who can kill her. That's their stories, I tell you, that's what they say."

"So by taking me you actually took away her only way to defend herself. And then you sent me to kill her. A defenseless woman."

"Except not really defenseless, is she?" Jennison laughed bitterly. "She has the most advanced species on this goddamn planet on her side. She's got you on her side! We spent years preparing you, and she turned you in what, a day?"

"Which is apparently how it is supposed to be." Kyle murmured to himself in disbelief. In a sudden bout of renewed fury, he lunged at the man before him. "You lied to me my entire life!"

"We couldn't tell you!" Jennison said in panic, half waiting for the iron muscles to crush him. "It didn't—"

"It didn't fit in with your plan." Kyle interrupted savagely, then let go of Jennison with an anguished cry, and turned toward the door. But then he stopped, half-turned back.

Jennison panicked. "I won't tell! I won't tell them you know!"

He cringed under the bigger man's icy gaze. "No, do, do tell them. Tell them if they try to come after her, I will come after them." Kyle closed his eyes. "Answer me one more question. My father."

"He wasn't your father," Jennison blurted out. "He wasn't even your family. We took you from them when you were a child. We had someone on the inside. She saw you, you were a small child, you left your mother's side and ran to a baby, a girl, ran to her and took her hand in yours and you wouldn't leave her. You stayed beside her, refusing to let go. I don't know, the woman who saw you, what she described was absolutely fantastic. She said every one there had turned to you, could not take their eyes off these two young children, and she said people around her said they thought they saw something else, something . . ." He shook his head. "Anyway, we guessed.

We guessed who you must be, who she was. We hoped we were wrong, but couldn't risk it. So we took you away just in case. Both of you."

Kyle let go of the doorknob and faced Jennison, shocked.

Jennison rumbled on, realizing what he'd said. "Yes, I know how it sounds, I know what we did. But we had no choice. You don't know everything, you don't know what we know, what they could do if they wanted, what the two of you together could do if you were who we thought you might be. So yes, we took you. Separately. We placed her as an unwanted baby in a fully human environment, and not a very nice one, on purpose. Yes, okay? On purpose. We watched and made sure, in the hope that whatever she is, whatever the stories say, wouldn't be, that they were really just that, stories. There. That's the truth, there you have it. And you we took, made you one of us. Made you what you were destined to be, but on our side, with her as your enemy."

He sighed. "If it's any consolation, while your father was carefully selected because he was the best man to make you into what you are today, he really did lose his wife, only that was before you were given to him. And he really did come to care for you as his son. That part was not a lie." He rubbed his face with his hands, tired. So tired. All this for a plan that failed. He failed. And he had said too much, he realized. In a sudden burst of frustration, he stood up. "We'll come after you, you know. Both of you. All of you. Until none of you remain."

Kyle turned and left.

He half expected Jennison to raise the alarm and send security after him, but nothing happened. It made sense, in a way. Admitting that Kyle got into the facility unobserved, while he was supposed to be hunted down by another operative sent by Jennison, would only get Jennison into more trouble, it would be perceived as yet another failure. He was after all, Kyle now realized, responsible for Kyle's presence in the organization in the first place. And if what Jennison said was true—although Kyle still couldn't fully comprehend it—Kyle himself was the organization's worst breach of security ever.

He quickly managed to get out the same way he got in, still in the cover of darkness, and was soon walking away from the organization, from the lie that had been his life. As he distanced himself from the facility he walked faster and faster, finally breaking into a run, as if this would take him away from the deceit.

It took a while before he was calm enough to think. Jennison hadn't confirmed that it was Semner he had sent after them, but it didn't matter. Kyle knew the organization's killers and their training, how relentless they were. And if they would keep coming after Aelia and him, as Jennison said they would, it didn't matter in what order. All he could do was return to Aelia as quickly as possible, and make sure she was safe. No matter how good the security at Aeterna was, he needed to be there himself. Jennison's words resonated in his mind. Born to protect her . . . he had more questions now than he did before, but at least now he knew his best chance at getting them answered was at Aeterna.

He found the motorcycle and rode it directly to the airport, ditched it far enough off and continued on foot to the hangar where he'd disembarked from the jet. The security detail was inside, deployed around the aircraft.

"Sir." The head of the detail approached him. "We're fueled and ready to go on your command."

Kyle nodded. "Let's go."

In Rome, Semner stood in the shadows outside the cathedral, looking with unveiled hatred at the people coming and going. He tried to recognize *them*, tell them apart from the tourists or the cathedral staff, the staff that had the right to be there, that is. He switched his weight from one leg to the other restlessly. There was still no lead. The man who was in charge of locating the targets said that the indications were that they were not in the cathedral, but Semner wanted to see for himself. He also wanted to see this place — he'd never before been allowed to come anywhere near here.

He wondered if Jennison would let him come back here. Perhaps after he got Kyle and the woman, perhaps then Jennison's anger at him would be forgotten and he would have the status he'd always wanted. And then perhaps the organization would grant him his wish.

Come back here and destroy them.

Chapter Eleven

The night was yet to give way to dawn, but Aelia was already awake. She was sitting in her bedroom, its lights dimmed, on a window seat that was comfortably cushioned to allow her to lean back and look at Aeterna's vast grounds outside. In the deep of the night, with the sky so clear and the stars so bright and the silence reigning in the great house, it was as if it was only her here, her and the endless questions in her mind. She leaned her chin on her folded arms, her eyes on the world beyond the glass. She would have liked to open the window, or better yet, go outside, but she had been asked not to. Security, she was told. That organization, its killer, was after her, and Aeterna's security was not taking any chances.

This brought her thoughts back to Kyle. He had left while she slept, gone to confront those in his past. To understand why, and to try and stop them from coming after her. She wondered why he hadn't come to her before he left. She wished he had, maybe she would have managed to talk him into staying. She was worried, scared that they would hurt him because of the choice he made, to help her. She kept trying to find him in that place within her but couldn't. Was it because he was so far? Was he blocking her out in his quest for answers?

Would he come back?

She knew she belonged here, with these people. Her people, Neora had called them. But she was feeling his absence. Missed that subtle sense of safety that she felt, with him. Protected, with him, her killer turned protector. Aeterna felt empty without him. And so the peace that she would finally have felt, perhaps, on this quiet night, eluded her.

She wasn't able to sleep again after she had started awake earlier, feeling that he was no longer there. It was only a short time later that Sonea had come, accompanied by Rolly, who had told her that security around the great house had been tightened, that he was putting a security detail outside her door, that it would remain with her, that she must be protected. That Kyle requested that it be so. Rolly was the one who had told her with marked gentleness where Kyle had gone, about the mission he had set for himself.

When they had gone, Rolly and Sonea, she had withdrawn back to her bedroom, to this seat by the window. Looking out into the night.

There, by the window, she must have fallen asleep again, had thought she wouldn't be able to but hadn't realized how tired she was. She slept for a few hours only, but deeply, again without darkness in her dreams. She woke up with the sun on her face, bright and warm, welcoming her to the new day. The great house around her was calm, peaceful, as if a piece essential to its existence, long missing, was now back in its rightful place. She could feel it, the place, its people. She had no words for the feeling, it was just there, a part of her that was beyond her grasp. Perhaps later, as I understand more, the thought passed through her mind.

She stood up and looked around her, really looked, for the first time. The room was spacious, but despite its size it retained a coziness that came from its furnishings, its decoration. Quiet, deep colors, meant to instill peace and a subtle sense of antiquity that would be a reminder of a past, of roots. Of belonging. At the same time, everything in the room, from the lights to the windows, to a semi-hidden control screen beside the door, all responded to her voice, her touch, anticipated her, as if she was in fact not centuries in the past, but miles into the future.

She found she wasn't surprised.

She exited the bedroom and walked through the other rooms. All equally spacious, all equally meticulously furnished and maintained, all equally state of the art where it counted. All so very beautiful, their luxury tastefully understated.

All for her.

It amazed her, the richness and comfort of it all. She seemed to have everything she might need around her in these rooms, this apartment that appeared to have been waiting just for her. She returned to the bedroom, showered, and then walked into her closet for the first time. Even here, there were numerous possibilities of each item, as if these people, who were so attentive to her needs, were trying to ensure she lacked nothing without actually knowing her preferences. It baffled her, this deference she was being treated with. She'd never been treated this way before, never felt cared for in this way. And she didn't feel worthy of this treatment, didn't quite know how to react, act, in the face of all this.

Neora's words came to her mind, the way she spoke, the hope she conveyed, her hope and her people's, for the return of what they had lost. She still couldn't grasp it, couldn't accept that it was even possible, certainly not that it could be her. But just then, standing in this closet, in this smallest of gestures that reflected the extent of the effort these people were making to ensure that she was comfortable, she resolved to do the only thing she knew. To be all that she could, do all that was within her, for them.

The thought, its oddness, struck her. What could *she* do?

She picked out clothes she would feel comfortable with. A pair of blue jeans, a white shirt, a light-color blazer that accentuated the soft gray of her eyes. She turned to walk out of the closet and halted. Along an inner wall, well away from all other items, hung outfits that were difficult to disregard. Robes, white, flowing robes, which she recognized as what Neora wore, as what each and every one of the women in the paintings along the main staircases of the great house wore. Except that the light band of colors wasn't there. These robes were completely white, and the delicate material, one she didn't recognize, looked different, so that the white was just that much lighter, translucent almost. She reached out and touched one of the robes, and it shimmered lightly. A distant image surfaced, too fleeting to catch, and she let the garment go, taking a step back. A frown on her face, she turned and walked out.

A little later she left her rooms, startled for just an instant at the man and woman who stood at opposite sides of the corridor, then realized they must be part of the added security Rolly talked about. She acknowledged them with a nod, not really knowing how to deal with this, with them, then made her way to the main staircases.

Sonea, her lady's maid, met her at the top of the stairs, agitated. "My Lady, why didn't you call for me? I would have come to you."

"It's all right," Aelia said gently. "I just wanted to come downstairs."

"But did you have everything you need? I wanted to see what was suitable for you, so that I can make sure you have what you need."

"It's all perfect, and could you please stop calling me 'My lady'? I'm just Aelia."

"Yes, Ma'am," Sonea said, and Aelia gave up. "Would you like some breakfast? The Keeper was hoping you might dine with her."

"Yes, of course, I'd like that." Aelia was eager to speak to Neora, to hear more, to understand.

They descended the stairs and Aelia stopped beside one of the paintings. She scrutinized it, then looked around her, up and down both staircases, at all of them, all past Keepers. "What all these women are wearing, the . . . Keepers. I've got similar clothes in my closet. And Neora, she wears them."

"Yes Ma'am, the robes. The Keeper's robes. Or"— and Sonea stammered as the realization of who she was speaking to hit her—"yours, I should say, Ma'am." And she hurried down the stairs, flustered, and quickly showed Aelia into the drawing room she had sat in with Neora the day before.

The old woman came toward her with a smile and took Aelia's hands in hers. "Good morning, child. Have you had a good rest? How do you feel?"

"I'm fine, thank you," Aelia answered, her mind still on her unanswered question. "I was just asking Sonea about what the women in the paintings are wearing, what you're wearing. These . . . robes, she called them? I've seen them in my closet."

"Not quite the same ones," Neora said. "For the Keepers it is part of the symbol that we are. From the moment the chosen woman becomes the Keeper, she dresses as the Light did. In Her case, the Light dressed in robes that were made of a special material, which looked white when unworn because of its nature, and when worn captured the Light that She emanated, simultaneously reflecting and containing it. It is a unique material made especially for Her, and for Her only, by us. The robes of the Keepers are of a different material, more like the silk you know, because we do not have the Light within us. Nor are our robes entirely white. A band that encompasses all colors is added at the edge of the fabric used for the Keepers' robes, to signify that the Keeper is not Her."

At Aelia's frown, Neora added, "It is your decision what you wear. The robes were placed in your closet because they are rightfully yours, and it is your choice when you wear them. You are not a symbol, a reminder, after all, you are the real Light." She smiled. "Give yourself time."

The idea of symbolic robes, of the entity they were designed for—Aelia quickly pushed it aside and changed the subject. "You've gone to such an extent to make me comfortable here, there was really no need for this. And I don't understand, when did you have the time?"

Neora laughed. "The rooms you are in, that entire wing of the house in fact, was originally designated for the Light. It has never been used, of course, was kept closed, but it was maintained and renovated periodically. Kept prepared, in case you appeared, as you did. When we received word you were found, it was finally opened for use."

"It's beautiful. This entire house is."

"Yes, I think over the centuries we have managed to keep it in the spirit it was built in."

"But even the clothes in my closet, they. . . well, they fit." Aelia indicated what she was wearing.

"We only had partial footage of you from the security system in the cathedral in Rome, but it was enough to start with. Now that you yourself are here, Aeterna's staff will work quickly to adapt everything to your specific preferences."

"It's too much," Aelia objected, her mind reeling from the way she was being treated, and from the underlying inference of what she meant to these people.

"It is as it should be," Neora said. "You will find that they are all happy to do whatever they can. They had longed to see you return in their lifetime, and they feel privileged that this has been the case. They . . . we have all seen the disappointment of our ancestors, and your being here gives us much needed, much awaited hope."

Aelia didn't know what to say. It all felt surreal. Surreal and undeserved and so very overwhelming. Neora smiled, understanding. "Come, Sonea tells me you refused to eat last night. We'll have some breakfast."

And so Aelia began her first day at Aeterna.

In Rome, Semner answered the call, and a cruel smile appeared on his face. Finally.

Neora was worried about Aelia. The young woman had been torn from the world of the humans she had always thought she belonged in, torn in body and mind, in abilities and knowledge. Neora wanted, on this calm morning, to tell her more about this place she found herself in, to show her that she was home.

And so over breakfast, served to them in the comfortable drawing room by staff who kept sneaking covert looks at Aelia, the Keeper told her about Aeterna. She told her how Firsts have always been in the area, and how they had created a home for themselves deep inside the mountains when humans came here. How, when the humans advanced, building homes and villages, the Firsts built the great house, making a stake for themselves under the guise of rich gentility, which was acceptable back then, and easy to keep through the centuries. Among humans, money and power were still untouchable, and it helped that the Firsts had people in the right places.

The house itself, Aelia heard, had always had a private wing that housed the First's rooms, where Aelia now lived, and an adjoining wing for the Protector. Aelia asked what that was, the Protector, but Neora only smiled, saying she would meet him later. She then took Aelia on a tour of the great house, and they strolled through corridors that displayed a history Aelia had never seen before, while Neora's words took her far into the Firsts' past and back to the present, when they lived hidden in plain sight.

When the Keeper was called away to speak to the Council, provide them with her eagerly awaited impressions of Aelia, Aelia finally exited the house to the grounds outside it. But she did so accompanied by Rolly, who insisted even then that the security detail he had assigned to her remain close by. Nor would he venture too far from the house with her, until the security situation, the fact that there was a killer after her, as he bluntly put it, was resolved.

Wherever Aelia walked she saw people stop, stare at her. Bow their heads in deference when she passed them by. She felt ridiculously watched and even more ridiculously protected, and was glad to return to the drawing room, where Neora already waited for her.

The Keeper answered her questions readily. She spoke of herself, but she was most interested to hear more about Aelia, the life she had. Aelia was hesitant, but she wanted to speak, wanted the Keeper to know. To understand the impossibility of her hope. After all, how could such hope be manifested in her, in Aelia, when the life she had lived was in such a sharp contrast to that which the girls born with the Light invariably had? Theirs was so protected, so carefully made to free and strengthen all that they were. Hers could surely do nothing but destroy it. Still, no matter what Aelia said, nothing changed in the Keeper's eyes. Her faith in Aelia as the Light could not be shaken.

They were deeply engrossed in their conversation when the doors opened and an elderly man stepped into the room. Aelia stood up in surprise.

The white-haired man walked over to her with a smile. "You remember me."

"Yes," Aelia said. "The cathedral, it was you there."

He nodded.

"You were... you looked at me like..." Aelia searched for the right word.

"Like I'd seen the impossible, I suppose." He laughed. "Yes, I apologize for that, I imagine I frightened you. You took me by surprise, I wasn't expecting our encounter."

"You knew."

"Yes. I felt it, as you did."

"Why?" Aelia looked at both Neora and him. "Why there?"

"Ah, that one is easy," Neora said. "That was your first time among your people. And"—she threw a look at Ahir—"a Protector just happened to be there."

The man, who introduced himself as Ahir Kennard, concurred. "We understand now that you had no idea who you are. But also that you must have never come near Firsts, or near enough of us, which has to do with the life you've lived, we believe. If you had, you would have known, you would have sensed it. What must have started your awakening was the fact that you came to Rome, there are many of us there. And when you found your way to the cathedral, I was there, and Benjamin, you know him of course. And quite a few others, we have a center there. So in essence, you walked into a concentration of Firsts. Between that and who I am, that was enough."

Aelia's mind was swamped with questions. "How could I never have met one of you . . . of us?"

Neora smiled at the correction, but the old man's anger was evident. "Those who took you, they kept you where they did for a reason. We have no presence at all anywhere near Michigan."

"But after I returned there, it started again, it . . ."

"Accelerated," Neora completed the thought.

"I saw Benjamin. Was it because of him? But it can't be, when I saw him there was nothing, I just noticed him among everyone else around me, that was it," she answered herself, thinking. "No, nothing marked really happened until . . ." Kyle, she wanted to say, but didn't dare let on what the circumstances had been.

"Until you encountered Kyle Rhys when he tried to kill you," Ahir simply said.

Aelia turned to him, her eyes blazing. "He saved my life, and he lost everything because of it. He would never hurt me."

"It's all right, child. We know." Neora put a calming hand on her arm. "And he didn't quite lose everything. He found everything. He left Aeterna before Ahir had a chance to speak to him, explain as I have explained to you."

"He is one of the Firsts," Aelia said, the sudden revelation leaving her shocked. "He is, isn't he? That would explain so much. But it's different." Her brow furrowed as she tried to sort things out in her mind, to understand. "I can sense him but it's stronger. Much stronger. No, not just that. It's different. None of you *feel* like that. No, you do"—she looked at Ahir—"but it's not nearly as strong, and something there is still markedly different. And what you said, what it took to start this, to awaken . . . Kyle was there alone. How could his presence alone be enough to do this to me?" She replayed in her mind the day Kyle tried to kill her, and their time together since, as they took a new path side by side. Throughout that time, one element stood out. She raised her eyes to look at Neora and Ahir. "Exactly how are Kyle and I connected?"

Ahir chuckled in disbelief. "You're quick. But then I

shouldn't be surprised, should I?" He turned to Neora. "Keeper, perhaps it is time to tell Aelia about the Protector."

"I mentioned it earlier, though only fleetingly. I thought you should be present in that conversation."

Ahir nodded and, motioning them to sit back down on the sofa and sitting himself on a couch nearby, he began to explain. "Well then. In my formal position I am the head of the Council of the Firsts. I am, I suppose you could say, their administrative leader, while Neora is the keeper of the faith. But most important, I am what our ancestors have termed the Protector."

Neora continued. "A long time ago the Light realized that She could not defend herself. That had never been a problem until the humans progressed enough. Certain circumstances, if you allow us to leave that part of it for another time, led to an attack on Her, but one man, one of the Firsts, stood facing Her attackers, stood and won but gave his life in the incident. In thanks and in realization of Her own vulnerability and the impact it could have on Her people, She designated his son to be the start of a line that would stand as Her protector. A man who will be linked with Her through the Light, and who above all others will be able to protect Her."

And together Neora and Ahir told Aelia how the Firsts, an ancient species born for peace, found themselves in the impossible position of having to share their home with the humans, who were so different from them and who quickly overwhelmed the planet in numbers and actions. And the one thing that kept the

Firsts going was the eternal Light they were granted, that signified virtue and hope and gave them strength and endurance. And to keep the Light safe, they were then given a remarkable man to protect Her. She was told how the Protector of the Light was always born only a few years before Her, thus becoming a beacon to Her imminent presence. Told how the Protectors kept being born even after the disappearance of the woman they were created to champion. And so they lived, had families, died. Always had one child, always a boy, and every generation or so the boy would turn out to be the next Protector. Like Ahir, who was the current Protector.

"And as a Protector, I would be able to feel the presence of the First, the Light within Her, at all times. I am not linked to you as your designated Protector is, but still, as soon as you walked into the cathedral I knew who you were."

"Why didn't you say anything?" Aelia asked, and the words came out more painful than she meant, holding in them the uncertainty of the past days, the hurt of a lifetime. "I'm sorry, I didn't mean to—"

"It's perfectly understandable. Considering what you have been through since, I truly am sorry I said nothing. Please understand, it took me by surprise. I am an old man, and I had resigned myself to the possibility that I will be the representative of yet another Protector generation that did not see the Light return. Whenever one of us is born, everyone holds their breath for a number of years, hoping She will appear, and when She doesn't something breaks within us yet again. And then I felt it, I've never felt that before, no Protector had since the last Light passed, and I cannot describe to you what it was like, the hope, and I saw you and—"

The old man was in obvious distress and Aelia could feel it, could literally feel what he was so desperately trying to say, and before she knew compassion washed over her and she reached out and put her hand on his, and that now increasingly familiar feeling flowed through her and he calmed down, breathed in deeply. Only then did she realize that Neora was looking at her, her hand covering her mouth in astonishment. Ahir's face had a similar look.

"I saw it," Neora said. "I saw the..."

"Yes," Ahir said, standing up. And then he bowed his head. "First."

Aelia heard Neora repeat the same title, in the same awed tone. She stood up and looked from one to the other, flabbergasted. "No, please. You two... I'm not..."

Neora stepped forward quickly and guided her back to the sofa. "It's all right, child."

"No, it's not. People here have been treating me like ... No, I'm no one. I'm just me, just Aelia. And you two, you're their elders, their leaders, aren't you? And if you treat me this way too—" She couldn't breathe.

"It's overwhelming, I know. For us too, but it must be putting so much pressure on you." Neora glanced at Ahir and motioned him to sit down. "I promise you, child, we are both here for you. We will teach you all that you need to know and help you in any way we can."

Aelia shook her head, struggling hard to make sense of the words she was hearing even as her very essence, now awake within her, was proving to her that the impossible was true. She tried to grasp on to logic, tried to put everything in place in her mind, tried . . .

"My Protector," she suddenly said. "You keep saying I have a Protector who is not you, Ahir. You called it a line, a family line."

Ahir nodded and spoke. Yes, he had a son. His son, Aelia learned, had not been born a Protector, but he knew that his own son was, and would have raised him as such had the child not been taken and he himself been killed. The child, Ahir's grandson, had not been found, and that meant that he was either killed and gone forever, or was lost, perhaps stolen. They all refused to believe the former, for that would signify that there would never be another Protector and that the Light would never return. And for Ahir that would mean that the last of his family was gone. And so Ahir never stopped believing that the child was alive and would be found, and had searched for him, as he had searched for Her.

The Protectors served faithfully alongside the reigning Keeper, Aelia was told, always on the lookout for the Light, never allowing the search for Her to stop. But for Ahir it had become more personal. And when he had recognized Aelia, felt the Light within her, that day at the cathedral, he knew that not only had the hope of his people finally come true, it was only a matter of time before he would find the Protector, Her Protector. His lost grandson.

Aelia wasn't listening anymore. Instead, she turned her head toward the door. That which had been missing within her since the night before was now back.

Kyle was here.

"Kyle is back," she said absentmindedly, and did not see the look that Neora and Ahir, Keeper and Protector, exchanged. Then suddenly she turned back to Ahir as all the pieces finally fell into place. "Kyle."

Ahir nodded somberly. "Yes."

Chapter Twelve

The shock lurked in the back of Kyle's mind and might otherwise have been allowed more place, but there was no time to deal with it, not now, there was simply too much at stake. Aelia's life was still in danger, and so was his. He had to keep his focus. Any kind of rest was out of the question so he made himself a strong cup of coffee in the jet's galley, some exquisite, aromatic blend he did not recognize, and sat back down.

The possibility that Semner was the one after them, that he was coming after him this way, confounded Kyle. That wasn't the friend he knew. He and Kyle went a long way back, and Semner would have tried to contact him, find out what was going on, instead of marking him as a target without question. Even if that was Jennison's order.

Unless Semner's part in Kyle's past was as much a lie as everything else. Kyle's eyes hardened. That was one more reason to face Semner himself. To hear it straight from him.

He focused on recalibrating his assessment of where they stood. He didn't even consider the possibility that Jennison would call Semner off now, after Kyle's visit, and regroup. It was the smart thing to do, but Kyle knew how Jennison's mind worked, and the hate he had seen in the man's eyes . . . No. Kyle bet he would let Semner follow through, and hope for success, hope that Semner might know of a weakness in Kyle he could exploit, or that Kyle might think Aelia and he were safe now that he'd confronted Jennison, and let his guard down.

Even in his outburst Jennison hadn't given a clue as to how much he knew about their escape, but then Kyle was the enemy now and Jennison wouldn't forget that and let anything operational slip. Nor could Kyle assume that his surprise appearance in Jennison's office would lead him to believe that Aelia was also still in the country. By now the organization would have had enough time to begin tracking them, and all it had to do was find that they had boarded a flight to Italy. And that wasn't impossible. They would go through security footage and flight records in the airports around Grand Rapids. They would find him, and they would certainly find Aelia, since she used her own passport. And yes, Kyle had come back. But he himself had made it clear to Jennison that he would be returning to Aelia's side. And Jennison would have every reason to believe that would be in Italy.

Jennison might first assume that Kyle would choose to stay in Rome because of what Jennison himself had told him, the reason that made the need to kill Aelia immediate—and that was fine with Kyle. If Semner were sent to Rome first that would buy them some time. But Jennison knew about Aeterna. Semner would get there eventually.

He ran scenarios of how Semner, with whom he'd served together for so long, would approach Aeterna, and considered the likelihood that he would not do so alone. The latter he doubted. He knew more than anyone that the organization planned this as a one-man mission in an attempt to contain both the kill itself and any possibility of knowledge about it leaking, even inside the organization itself. Except that this wasn't just a one-man mission after all, was it, he thought ruefully. After all, Jennison had prepared Semner as a backup.

Bottom line was, he had to be there when Semner came for Aelia. The guy was good—damn good—and if he wanted to get to her, he would. And he was not a nice guy. Kyle himself was a trained killer, but he'd always tried to make sure those he killed had no idea what was happening. And he always got them alone, with no one else around to get hurt. Kyle stared out of the jet's window, dark blue eyes seeing past kills. Exactly how far had the organization's lies reached—had he himself killed any innocents? Did he kill friends of those who were now helping Aelia and him?

He pushed the thought away. There was no sense in this, no time now. Semner should be his focus. Semner's targets had no meaning to him. His belief in the necessity of their death was blind, and for him all means were justified. All means.

Kyle thought of Aelia.

Of Semner getting to her.

Defenseless, Jennison had said. But Kyle didn't need him to say it. He already knew that. And Aelia wouldn't have on Semner the effect she had on Kyle. She would be vulnerable to whatever he had in mind for her.

I've got to get to her, Kyle thought, willing the aircraft to go faster. He had talked to Rolly during the flight and knew Aelia was safe, but that didn't mean Semner wouldn't get there at any moment. While he wasn't there to protect her.

Restless, he got up again to make another cup of coffee, aware of the security detail's eyes on him. He was, he knew, a mystery to them. A stranger who turned up out of nowhere, and the next thing they knew they were ordered to obey him.

They were those Firsts Jennison was talking about, the thought popped into his mind. Weren't they? Them, the pilots, Rolly, everyone at Aeterna. Aelia.

Him. That's what Jennison had said.

He pushed that away too. He couldn't even begin to deal with that. Or with the hazy memories that were now more adamantly than ever trying to surface. Or with the fact that his entire life was a lie. That he had nothing.

He sat staring at the steaming coffee. He had no idea who he really was. That was one revelation he hadn't expected. Stolen as a child. But not only him. Aelia, too. Her life was as much a lie as his was. Except that the life she got was nothing like his, was it? He remembered what Jennison said they did to her. Born to protect her, Jennison said that, too. That he belonged with her. That one stuck.

That along with the realization that gnawed at him, that had the organization's plan succeeded, he would have killed her by now. She would be dead, and he would be lost forever. The thought, the truth of it, struck him like a bullet to his heart.

He had to get to her.

When the jet finally landed, the helicopter was already waiting for Kyle beside the hangar. In no time he found himself on Aeterna's helipad, not too far from the great house but a world away as far as he was concerned.

He said nothing to his driver, who obviously knew his way very well, expertly traversing the winding roads in the pitch dark. But the driver noted his restlessness and, throwing him a look, smiled. "We'll be there in no time, Sir. Been traveling these roads since I was a kid, my uncle is Aeterna's head driver. The driver for Mr. Kennard."

Kyle nodded and tried to force himself to settle back. When he finally got out of the car at the great house, Rolly came toward him, scrutinized his face.

"That must have been some talk with Jennison."

"They won't stop until they get to her. And they will get to her," Kyle said evenly. "I would."

"We can protect her."

"Here, perhaps. But for how long? And what happens if and when she goes anywhere? Can you protect her as well in transit? Or anywhere outside this private little world of yours?" Kyle's voice was dangerous. "You don't get it. I could get to her. Even here, I could get to her. Someone like me, who's been trained specifically to kill her, I could get to her anywhere."

"You, yes. You can get to her anytime, anywhere," Rolly retorted. "But you're on her side."

"That's not enough—" Kyle stopped. Aelia was standing at the great house's main entrance, watching him intently. Feeling his worry, he had no doubt. That and everything else. He kept his eyes on her while half-turning his head to Rolly, to excuse himself, but Rolly nodded.

"I'll wait," he said.

Kyle walked to Aelia, and she stepped out to meet him. A member of her security detail appeared of the shadows, another behind her, but Rolly called out, "It's fine, stay at a distance," allowing the two some privacy.

"How're you doing?" Kyle asked Aelia quietly.

"Me? How're you doing? Rolly said you went back there."

"I did. I found out what I needed to know. There's nothing there for me anymore."

Aelia felt a jab of his pain. "I'm sorry," she said somberly, her eyes on his. "It's because of me."

"No, Aelia, I don't think any of it is your fault, or your responsibility. And switching sides, that was my choice." He looked at the great house behind her and shook his head. "I don't know, everything that happened back there, when I was still targeting you, and what I found out now, I think this place might be more of an answer than we both thought."

Aelia nodded. She already knew that was true. "What did you find out?"

"That I was lied to about you." He rubbed his face and sighed. "That I was lied to about everything. About my life, who I am."

"Kyle." She put her hand in his.

He held it, looked at her. "You know, I'm not even sure that's my name. Apparently I was kidnapped when I was a child and raised as someone else. My father wasn't my father, I might not even be"—he shook his head incredulously—"the same species as he. I know how it sounds, but..."

Aelia's response surprised him. "Not as incredible as you think," she said.

He raised a brow. "Looks like you've had some discoveries too. You learned something about yourself, didn't you?"

She nodded. "And about you." The link between them was easier now, stronger, and she could feel his exhaustion beyond the determination that was driving him, the strength in him. She could also feel his loss. "Kyle, you need to come in. There's someone you should talk to."

He squeezed her hand lightly. "I will, I just have to talk to Rolly first. Go back inside, I'll be there in a while." And he added softly, "I won't run off like I did, I promise."

She just looked at him. That wasn't what she was worried about.

"I know," he said. "But I have to make sure security around here is the way I want it."

She nodded, and he walked off in Rolly's direction.

After a moment she walked back inside, her brow slightly furrowed. Neora and Ahir were standing just inside the doors. She walked up to them and addressed Ahir gently. "He needs to know."

Ahir nodded.

Kyle approached Rolly resolutely, and Rolly had to steel himself not to take a step back in the face of the force in the man's walk. He realized he was awed. He knew much about how the organization trained its best, and the man approaching him was a professional of the highest level. But that was nothing compared with who he was. *What* he was would be the best way to put it. And when one added that, the capabilities, the instincts that came with it, it was what ultimately made him a formidable man.

But Rolly wasn't awed just because of the man's true identity, which he had finally been made privy to, as head of Aeterna's defense and security, while Kyle was away, now that this identity had been ascertained. He was also awed by his behavior. The guts it took to help Her, go against the organization, then go back to face them, to face Jennison, of all people. The courage it took to make sure She arrived here, to face those at Aeterna knowing he might be seen as the killer he thought he was. The drive it took to keep him going, keep him focused on his one concern—Her safety, not his own.

Even without him knowing who he really was. Or who She was.

"I ran some scenarios on the way here. You've got some loopholes we're going to close. Aelia's safety—and the safety of anyone else here, for that matter—must be ensured." Kyle's words were spoken quietly but left no place for argument. Rolly wasn't surprised. Without knowing it, this man was already assuming his rightful role.

They turned to go inside, to the control center, and Kyle saw some people not far off to the side of the house, on the well-lit lawns. They were standing around in small groups, talking in hushed voices. His instincts told him they weren't a security risk, but he wasn't one to let his guard down, all the more so since he was in unfamiliar territory, surrounded by people who were taking quite an unusual amount of interest both in Aelia and in him.

He indicated them with his head. "What's this all about?"

Rolly threw a look at them. "They've been flocking here ever since Her arrival. Some of them live around here, others have come from farther away. They are Firsts, all of them, and they've come to see their hope come to life with their own eyes." He opened the door for Kyle. "And more will come. The word is spreading, and Firsts worldwide will soon know She is here, if they don't already know."

"Then I'll have to intercept Semner away from here, I can't risk him hurting anyone or creating a hostage situation," Kyle said thoughtfully, as if speaking more to himself than to Rolly. Throwing a last, wondering look behind him, at these people who were there waiting to catch a glimpse of Aelia, he followed Rolly inside.

They went over Aeterna's security thoroughly again, this time with Kyle simulating a sole perpetrator attacking the security layout from all sides, until each and every one of his questions was answered and he was aware of every manual and technological means employed at every spot on, above or underground, at any given moment of the day. He noted blind spots and was pleased to hear that they were being covered, and raised his own loopholes to which Rolly reacted immediately, making the necessary adjustments with the help of his people, who now surrounded them around Aeterna's hologram under the great house.

Their experience, their loyalty and their perception of the importance of their job were evident, and remarkable. But even so, there was one thing they couldn't do. They couldn't judge their preparedness from his view, the view of a killer trained by the very organization that was targeting them. His view, and Semner's. And it was with that in mind that he made his suggestions, directing Rolly on how to supplement the application of Aeterna's security technologies as well as its people.

Watching Rolly talking to his people and hearing his own safeguards being applied put Kyle's mind at ease. The rest would be up to him. Nodding at Rolly, he turned and left, going back up to the main house to look for Aelia. He wanted, needed to know what she had learned.

He knew where to go, it was that simple. With his connection to his past severed, and now that he had made a conscious decision to return to her, whatever it was that linked them was stronger, and he let it guide him to where she was. He found himself once again in the entry hall of the house with the two staircases that led up, with those portraits that lined them. He passed them without even a glance, his eyes on the woman who was coming toward him. She halted and waited for him to join her, saying nothing. She didn't have to.

They walked together in the direction she had come from, and Kyle soon found himself in a large drawing room looking to the back of the great house. It was comfortably and tastefully furnished with sofas and couches, small tables thoughtfully placed among them. Floor to ceiling picture windows with French doors in two places dominated one wall, and beyond them Kyle saw the grounds closest to the house, lit against the dark night. The room, as did the entire house, in fact, made him feel as if he was in one of the stately homes the likes of which he had seen on visits to the older parts of this continent, houses that spoke of history and heritage, except that this one was lived in and meticulously maintained.

And in fact very advanced where it counted, he knew so very well.

His gaze fell on a distinguished old woman dressed in flowing white robes—like the women in the portraits were wearing, he thought—and on the man who was sitting on the sofa beside her. And even before he looked toward Aelia, he knew exactly where she had come to stand in the room. Even before his eyes stopped on her, standing by the picture windows, looking at him, he knew, he felt her, as he did throughout this great house, as he did just now when he was coming to see her, as if his entire being was a compass that could point to where this woman was. He —

A subtle movement caught his eye, and he realized she had deliberately turned her gaze toward the two other people in the room beside them, guiding him. He turned his attention to them and she introduced them.

"Kyle, these are Neora, the Keeper, and Ahir Kennard, head of the Council of the Firsts, and the Protector."

Where earlier it might have seemed odd to him, the way she introduced them, their titles, so naturally, now Kyle too was ready to accept this despite the questions it still raised. He acknowledged the old woman respectfully and turned to do the same for the man beside her, then stopped. The elderly man had on his face an expression Kyle had never before seen in anyone looking at him. He stood up and walked to Kyle, his face full of emotion. He then reached up to him, fleetingly touched his cheek in what seemed to Kyle to almost be disbelief, then regained control of himself with evident difficulty.

"Kyle," he said. "Is that the name they gave you?"

Kyle's heart accelerated as the realization hit him. This old man knew him. Not just as the man who had tried to kill Aelia, nor as the man who had brought her here. Him, who he was. Before Jennison, before the organization, before he was taken.

"Kyle."

He tore his gaze away from the old man and turned to Neora. Kind eyes reassured him. "Go with him. He is where your answers lie."

Ahir walked toward the door, and Kyle followed him. At the door he looked back at Aelia, perplexed, but his confusion only increased when, after meeting his eyes, she lowered hers, but not before he detected sadness in them. His gaze lingered on her, and then he turned and followed Ahir out the door. If that's where his answers were, it was a good place for him to start.

Chapter Thirteen

Ahir led Kyle up one of the two main staircases to the wing immediately adjacent to Aelia's, and to a set of double doors similar to those he'd stood before when he went to see her. The doors opened to reveal a small man in a tidy suit, who, on seeing them, brightened and moved back in deference to let them in, sneaking a curious peek at Kyle. Kyle followed Ahir in and found himself in a spacious apartment.

"I'm Remi, Sir." The man introduced himself as Kyle took in his surroundings. "I'm in charge of these rooms, and I will be taking care of all your needs here, as I have done for Master Kennard, and as my family has always done for the Kennards."

The words triggered a question in Kyle's mind, but it disappeared into the background when, as he looked around him, a memory surfaced. Something hazy, beyond his grasp. This place, the same sitting room he was in. A woman laughing, sitting on that couch by the huge fireplace in the opposite wall. But he was looking up at her, up from the thick carpet on the floor, and he felt safe, felt as he'd never felt his entire life—

"You remember."

He started. Ahir was standing in the middle of the room, watching him. He walked toward Kyle. "Remi, leave us, please," he said to the valet.

Remi looked from him to Kyle and grinned in elation. "Yes, Sir." He left the room.

Kyle approached the fireplace. He tried to capture the memory, but it eluded him, faded away. "I've been here before."

"You have."

Kyle turned to Ahir, a frown on his face.

"You were born here, at Aeterna."

"I was born in the United States," Kyle said, but he didn't sound convincing even to himself.

"No, you were stolen to the United States."

Kyle's mind reeled, and he sat down on the couch near the fireplace of his memory, now cold and dark. Ahir sat down facing him. He waited until the young man's eyes focused on him again.

"You were born here. Your parents were Firsts, and so are you. Your parents traveled quite a lot between our different regions and centers, as this family's role mandates, but their home was always here." Ahir paused. "When you were four, while on a short stay in Malta, your parents were attacked. They were found shot dead in their car, executed. Your father was at the wheel, and your mother was in the back with your car seat. You were gone. We have been searching for you ever since."

Kyle shook his head in disbelief. This was the second time in less than a day that he heard that the man he thought of as his father wasn't, that he himself wasn't who he thought he was—that he wasn't even human?—and this was just one too many revelations. No, this couldn't be. Even with what Jennison had told him, there must have been some truth to his life.

He tried to hang on to something, the smallest thread of certainty, to what he had never doubted was his. "No, I knew my father. He was a good man. He said that my mom died giving birth to me and that I reminded him of her. I was all he had, and he loved me. He . . ." He fell silent.

"He might very well have loved you," Ahir said gently. "He raised you as his son since you were a small child. That does something to a man."

Kyle thought about the man who had called himself his father. He was a driven man, and Kyle had known from an early age that he was guiding him to walk a very specific path. But he'd thought that he just wanted his son to be like him, and to be able to protect himself in what his father repeatedly said was a tough world. But was there a hidden agenda in his acts? After all, he had to keep this boy he had taken loyal to him as a parent so that he could teach him all that he had, train him to be what the organization had designated him to be.

No, he couldn't believe it. Memories came to his mind, of his father taking him camping, teaching him how to fish and laughing with him when he fell into the water trying to grasp a slippery catch or sitting by his hospital bed day and night when he was shot on a mission that had gone wrong. This was his dad, the only family he ever had. What this man, this stranger was telling him now mixed with Jennison's harsh words, and he shook his head and stood up.

"No," he said and walked away toward the door, ready to leave this man behind, ready to leave it all behind, just as he did hours before when he turned his back on Jennison. These people, their truths, they weren't his either.

"I knew your parents."

He continued walking.

"When your father didn't arrive that day with you and your mother, I knew something was wrong. I just knew. And so did your grandmother."

Kyle halted.

"She never stopped looking for you until the day she passed. And neither did I."

Kyle turned back. The old man walked to him. There was no other way to do this, and there was no waiting anymore. "My son, Kyan . . . you look very much like him. But from what I've seen, you have your mother's strength of purpose, her good heart. She would have liked that. They both would."

Kyle stared. Ahir took his wallet out of his inner jacket pocket and fished out a photo, which he unfolded carefully. An old photo, the creases in it attesting to the many times in so many years it had been unfolded and then refolded again, the losses and regrets of its owner evident in every crease. He handed Kyle the photo with a shaking hand.

Kyle hesitated, then took it. A young couple, smiling happily at the camera, the baby on his mother's lap more interested in her necklace than in posing for this festive family photo.

The resemblance between himself and the man in the photo was uncanny.

"You're my grandfather," Kyle said with astonishment, accepting this one truth he could not deny.

Ahir only nodded, unable to speak through the tears that threatened to flow. His grandson. All these years he'd searched for the Light, never stopped, but not only because this was his duty. He knew that where the Light would be, that's where his grandson would eventually find himself. His grandson, who, like him, was born a Protector. It might take time, he knew, but the Light and Her Protector would find each other, as they were destined to. And he was right. He had found him. And now—

"What's my name?"

Kyle's voice broke the old man's reverie. He looked at his grandson, not comprehending.

"My parents, the name they gave me. What is it?" This one piece of information, this one shred of identity he could begin thinking in terms of, this starting point, was what he would latch onto now.

"Adam. Your name is Adam. Adam Ahir Kennard."

"Ahir."

"Yes, after me, and Adam because your mother loved the name."

Kyle closed his eyes and tried to center himself, to place each piece into its rightful place. His entire life— past, present and future—was rearranging itself in his mind, in his very soul. A touch on his arm pulled him out of the chaos of his thoughts, and he opened his eyes. The man who was his grandfather, his family, was looking at him with what Kyle now realized was a mix of love and relief. It was the expression of a man who'd been given his greatest wish, what he must have searched for, for two and half decades.

"Come," Ahir said. "You have had quite a few days, haven't you? There is much to explain, so much you need to know. So much that I want to tell you. But first, perhaps you would like to change, maybe rest, have you slept at all? Remi made sure your rooms are ready, and I think you will find everything you need there."

"My rooms?"

"Of course. Had you grown up here, eventually you would have been given your own part of this wing. In fact, the day would have come when you yourself would have become the head of the family, head of the Kennards, and this entire wing of the house would have been yours." And this would be, Ahir reminded himself, still unable to believe it himself. "As it is, you were gone, but I still prepared your rooms for the day you would return."

Ahir took Kyle further inside the apartment until they came to a staircase that led up. "This leads to the upper floor of this wing, to your parents' main rooms. I had them renovated over the years, according to your age. The last time was on what would have been your twenty-fifth birthday, I just went up there and thought it would be fitting for the young man you are if I had them changed again, modernized." The old man looked pained, and Kyle felt a pang at what he must have gone through all these years. "Of course, anything you want to change now, it is yours to do with as you please. It's your home."

His only home, Kyle realized. He would never be able to go back to his old apartment. Jennison had probably gotten rid of it already, erased him. He shook his head, not bothering to finish the thought.

Walking up, Kyle was surprised to find himself in a spacious loft apartment, tastefully decorated to suit a man, with a modern feel to it unlike what he'd seen so far in this wing. No, more than that. Worse than that. This loft had anticipation written all over it, hope, while the part of the wing where his grandfather lived had felt as if the life of its inhabitant had come to a standstill. Which was exactly how it was, wasn't it? Ahir's life had come to a standstill the day tragedy hit, taking his family away from him, and since then it was focused on the search for his grandson, for Kyle.

He looked around him. The large space he was standing in had a high ceiling, as was characteristic of the entire house, and the large windows alongside the main wall opened to the back, looking far to the horizon, giving the place an airy feeling. It would, he thought, be full of light during the day, but now it brought starry dark skies in, instilling peace. On one side, the room opened to a half-hidden semicircular alcove, with a new-looking screen much like the one he'd seen in Aeterna's security center. To create a work space, it seemed, and he wondered if it had been installed only now, since he had first gotten here, after he had shown the interest he had in this house, its security. He turned the other way and walked up a few stairs to a bedroom, as tastefully furnished as the rest of the loft. On one side were doorways to a bathroom, fully equipped with anything he might need, and a closet, which he was surprised to find full. He turned to Ahir, not understanding.

"You were here for a short time before you left again, and this was enough. Remi gave surveillance footage that he got from Rolly to our tailors, who spent the past day preparing as good a fit as they could without actually having you present."

Kyle put a jacket on. "That's some fit," he said with appreciation.

"We have good tailors. You should find in there whatever you might need, and it will all be supplemented in the next days. We have our own stores here, managed by our tailors, and they are regularly stocked with the best brands available. And if there's anything else you want, we could get it, or fly you anywhere you want to buy it."

"I can't leave, not now."

"No, of course not. When you can. For now, you'll be surprised what you'll find right here at Aeterna."

Kyle continued to look through the closet, which did seem to have just about anything he could think of. "That's incredible. You keep all these things here?"

Ahir smiled, pleased. "These and so much more. Aeterna is much bigger than you think, there is a whole lot more to it than just this house. There are dozens of people here at any one time, and many have families living on Aeterna's grounds. Firsts come here throughout the year, and the Council convenes in the house itself at least once a year. So we have to be prepared."

Kyle continued to walk through the bedroom, then back to the main space, the lights automatically dimming in the room behind him. He wasn't surprised, he had already noticed the telltale signs of voice- and touch-activated controls, which was as much a part of the great house as its antiquity.

He walked to the marble fireplace, to photos sitting on the mantel that had caught his eyes earlier. He reached out to touch them. His parents, his grandparents, himself as a baby, photos in which he aged until he was a toddler, the age he was taken. Photos he never had, his father had always said photos of him at an early age were lost. The man who had posed as his father, that is.

The words came out before he meant them to. "You really were looking for me."

"Yes." Ahir watched him. He had often wondered what the boy, the man would be like when he was found. Even if the circumstances he grew up in were harsh, he would have the best starting point one could hope for, in his physique, his genetics, the personality he would inherit. And here, the man before him had strength written into his every move, a constant alertness and intelligence in his eyes. But he also had something else about him, a thoughtfulness that pained Ahir. This was a born Protector brought up to be a trained killer. Raised to go against his instincts, the separation from his people, his family, the Light, used against him all too cleverly.

Ahir would have to deal with this, help his grandson come to terms with what had been done to him, what he would have to live with. But not now, not yet. There was time.

He approached Kyle. "There is much you need to know, but it can wait. You should rest, you've had a long day."

Kyle shook his head, instantly becoming what he was. "There will be no rest. Not until I stop whoever is after Aelia."

"Yes, Rolly has been updating me." Ahir wasn't surprised at his grandson's reaction. "You believe Jennison did not call Semner off after you confronted him?"

Kyle raised a brow.

"Before everything, I am what you are. A Protector. And since the beginning I have in fact acted as the Protector for Aelia's stand-in, the Keeper, and for all the Firsts—the heads of defense and security of Aeterna and of all regions answer to me."

For Kyle this only meant more questions.

For the first time, Ahir laughed. "I will have Remi get us dinner, and we will talk. Come down to the main dining room when you are ready."

Kyle watched him as he left. His grandfather. He couldn't wrap his mind around it.

Chapter Fourteen

Kyle took a hot shower that helped relieve some of the tension in his shoulders and chose some clothes out of his new closet, musing at their fit. Someone definitely did their job. He then checked in with Rolly and returned to the main part of the Kennard wing, to Ahir's apartment, eager to get the answers his only living family member had for him.

Coming back to the main room he walked over to where two enlarged framed photos hanging on a wall caught his attention. One showed a younger Ahir, one arm around a woman and the other around a black-haired, blue-eyed teenage boy who looked very much like Kyle. His father, he mused. The other showed the same boy, older. A man. He was standing beside his wife, both smiling widely at the small boy they were holding. The boy, him, was at the age he had first seen himself in the earliest photos he had, photos the man he had thought was his father must have taken immediately after receiving him, or perhaps photos the organization had taken, carefully creating the background they had designated for him from the very beginning. He took the photo off the wall and held it closer, hesitantly touching his parents' faces.

"This is one of the photos I have in . . ." he indicated the direction of his rooms, never taking his eyes off the photo.

"It's the last one I have of all of you together. It was found in the car, wrapped as a present for your grandmother and me." Ahir approached and stood beside him, looking at the photo with him.

"You were looking for me," Kyle repeated his earlier words, his eyes still on the photo.

"Never stopped," Ahir said. "Luckily both your identity and my role alongside the Keeper have afforded me the power to go anywhere and use all the resources we have. Throughout the years I've used our centers worldwide to search for you. But clearly you were not among our people, and finding you among the humans would be near impossible, especially if someone was intentionally hiding you. Assuming they kept you alive, that is." The thought, bringing back old fears, clearly pained him. "I soon realized that the only way I could find you was if now, of all centuries, after being gone for so long, the Light would reappear. Because then you would find each other. This always was and always will be. And when we would find Her, I would find you. So you see, Her being here, Her very return, is an old man's wish come true in more ways than one. And if for no other reason, for that She will forever have my thanks."

Kyle hung the photo back in place and turned to Ahir, his brow furrowed. "There it is again. Aelia, the way people here—the way you—talk about her. And what was it, Protector? Keeper? Light? Everyone here keeps saying these words as if it's natural and expects me to understand and I have no idea what they're all talking about. And come to think of it, what on earth are Firsts?"

Ahir considered this. There was so much he wanted to tell his grandson about himself, about his parents. Memories Ahir had waited to pass on to him for so long. But there were other things he needed to know first. Everything he knew, every context he had, had to do with the humans he had thought he was one of. It was time to change that. And perhaps more than anything, he needed to know why him. Why he was the one who was taken, why his parents were killed.

Why meeting Aelia changed him, changed his life forever.

Ahir led his grandson to the dining room, where, as they sat down at the large table, a cheerful Remi began serving them dinner. Ahir glanced at him. "Remi has been with me for many years now. He has seen me come home tired and discouraged more than once."

"Yes, Sir," Remi said. "It is good to see you smiling, Sir." He walked away with a tray, and Kyle could swear he heard him hum.

"Always loyal and endlessly patient," Ahir noted.

While they ate, Ahir finally began giving Kyle the answers he needed. He explained to him about the Firsts, their beginning, their life, and Kyle listened with growing astonishment. Ahir then told him about the appearance of the Light, how She became the very center of their people, the foundation that kept them strong throughout their existence, gave them hope and purpose. He told him about the Protector and his special connection to Her, how they walked side by side throughout Her existence, how since the last woman with the Light within her passed, the Protectors have never stopped waiting for Her return.

He explained that Protectors were born over the years regardless of the presence of the Light, but never the other way around, for the Light always needed a Protector. Nor was a Protector born every generation— Kyle's father wasn't one. He told him how, after a time that the Light was gone, the Firsts decided to symbolize Her and all that She stood for through the role of the Keeper, and how the Protector had since remained by the Keeper's side. And how they all waited, Protectors, Keepers, Firsts, for the day the Light would return to Her people.

"See, that's what I don't get in all this," Kyle said. "You're talking about a Light within a mortal woman. The fact that she can die—why not let them, the women born with the Light, or actually that first woman, the first Light, live forever? Why have them be born, die, risk the time there is no one like them around, risk them not being born again?"

"It is not our choice, any more than it was our choice for the Light to come to us in the first place. We have no control over who She is who is born with the Light, or when, or how long She is among us." Ahir paused. "I do however have to say that I believe this is how it should be. She who has the Light within Her lives the life span of a mortal. She has the feelings of a mortal, and quite acutely at that, heightened sensitivity you could say. She can love, be sad. Dream. Feel pain. Hence, She is able to empathize with those around Her, their needs, their hardships, their losses. Their pain. She is compassionate and feels the need to help them, save them, *because* She is like them in so many ways."

"I don't know. I would have made her immortal, invulnerable."

"Would you? Think about it. Not the first one hundred years. Two. Five hundred. One thousand years later. Everyone keeps dying around you and you live. Everyone you are close to dies. You make friends, you love, they die and you live on. How long before you stop letting anyone get close to you? How long before you are no longer able to understand the mortal lives, mortal emotions of those around you? How long before you begin to wonder if you are superior to them, before you think you know better than they do because you have lived longer? Before you begin to make decisions for them and try to control their fate simply because you think you have the right to do so—all the more so with the power you have within you? No, it would have to be quite a personality to survive that, I don't mean physical survival but mental, emotional survival. I am not sure any living being would or should be capable of achieving that."

"So she is mortal, and vulnerable. Anyone can hurt her."

"That is why She was given the Protector to stand for Her. We did that."

"I thought you said the Protectors are also simply born and have certain capabilities. How could you do that, make them?"

"And yet unlike Her, the Protector did in fact begin as our creation. You see, when we realized what we had been given, there was awe, as you can imagine. Already with the first Light we felt what She would bring us, what She could make of this world. And we were determined to keep Her safe. So we resolved to create shields, if you will. Men and women who would protect Her."

"So every time She appeared you chose protectors?"

"Yes, based on genetics and capabilities. The best of a selection of would-be warriors. Defensive weapons, if you wish to use a modern day term."

"So how . . . ?"

"There was someone different," Ahir said. "This is what we know. An extraordinary protector. Strong, capable. Loyal. The Light was in trouble, our history tells us. She fell into the hands of humans, and he saved Her where no one could, but he himself was killed. This was after generations of protectors, chosen ones. All brave, all quite remarkable—we got better at their selection. But this one, he was also different in another way. They were close, the Light and he, good friends, inseparable since childhood. And when he died, the Light was inconsolable at his loss.

"That night a child was born, his first-born son. His wife gave birth early because of her grief, and the child had no chance of surviving. And as the mother and child lay there, the Light came to them, and She vowed that as this protector had been loyal, and had selflessly given his life for Her, his sacrifice would not go unrewarded. She decreed that his son would live, and would be the first in a new ancestral line, the line of the Protectors. And that as they would protect the Light, She would protect them."

He fell silent. "That Light died soon after, inexplicably, younger than ever, and just a few years later another girl was born, a new Light. As for the boy, he grew into a formidable man, a Protector, Her Protector, the likes of which had never been seen before. And since then there has only been one Protector, always one, with a unique connection to Her. And no Protector has been killed—in action, you could say—since then, as long as his Light was alive." He paused. "That is what we know about the creation of our line and how the connection between the Protector and the Light came to be, and we understand that that is where our enhanced capabilities came from, that the Light had given us these to protect us."

"So the Protector and the Light are destined to find each other," Kyle said after contemplating what he heard.

"Yes."

"And the Protector has a connection to the Light, they can literally feel each other's presence."

Ahir confirmed again.

"But you are a Protector, aren't you? How come you

didn't find her? How come you didn't find Aelia?"

"For one thing, the Light did not manifest in Her until recently, until She actually made contact with the Firsts, with me, in Rome. We are not sure why, all we can surmise is that it is because of the circumstances She grew up in."

"Jennison said they made sure." Kyle thought back. "'We placed her as an unwanted baby in a fully human environment, and not a very nice one at that', that's what he said."

"Yes. Now that we know Her identity we were able to find out more about Her. I'm afraid Jennison's words were an understatement." Ahir closed his eyes. "What kind of people do that to a child?"

"She's got to be one hell of a woman to become what she has."

"Yes, She is. She certainly is. It seems that while they have done all they could to quench everything that She could be, they have failed. She is here, and so are you." Ahir sipped some water and focused back on what was good and right, on the future that would once again be. "And you are Her Protector. Although I am of the line, I am not *Her* Protector. The Protector of the Light is always born just a few years before Her, so that they can grow up into the life they are destined for together. You are linked with Aelia, not I. I still feel Her presence more strongly than the others, which is how I recognized Her in Rome, but not as strongly as you do. It was not my destiny to find Her."

Ahir hesitated and then decided to say it. "Had you

been raised among us, had you grown up from the start as a Protector and not had your very essence so carefully manipulated, you could have found Her a long time ago. You would have known where to go." He raised his head to meet Kyle's eyes, watched his words sink in, saw a flash of anger, sadness, and finally realization.

"So that's what it was. When I first saw her it felt as if—"

"As if you knew Her, although you two have never met before."

"Yes. And whenever I made an attempt to . . . complete my mission, I just couldn't. Something made it impossible, something I couldn't explain. And even before that, I always felt something was missing. Incomplete." A lot made sense now, and the pieces of the puzzle finally arranged themselves in his mind in the exact places they belonged in from the start, before someone had deliberately taken his life all those years ago and derailed it to serve their own interests.

Kyle—he still thought of himself as Kyle, the only name he'd ever known—was quiet, mindlessly pushing food around on his plate, thinking. "Jennison told me I was taken by them, by the organization," he finally said. "He's my godfather. Or I thought he was. I pushed him to talk, but I don't know how much of what he told me I can trust. He said I was taken by them when I was a small child, to be raised as a human. To be raised as Aelia's enemy, her killer." Kyle found the words difficult.

"That explains a lot. They must have seen something that made them think that She was back, and that identified you as belonging to the Protector line."

"He said someone saw me, I was standing near a baby, a girl, and I refused to leave her side."

Ahir chuckled mirthlessly. "So, they really did infiltrate us back then. We thought as much. We have learned our lesson." He looked at Kyle thoughtfully. "Interesting though. If what he said was true, then that means you and Aelia have met before."

Kyle shook his head in frustration. "I don't remember. All I ever had were fleeting memories, no more than images really. I never told anyone, I don't know why. But there was never enough to make me think. . . I never had any reason to think I wasn't where I belonged, or that they didn't want what was best for me. I was one of them, and I believed them, I believed what they told me. What they taught me." He looked at Ahir and said evenly, "All my life I knew that there was someone out there, that one day I would be called on to kill her, no questions asked."

"You were never told who She was. Or about us."

"Nothing about the Firsts, or about the fact that there was another species living here beside us . . . beside humans," he corrected himself. "They had a whole other set of reasons they used. Ultimately what it all came down to was that there was a woman out there who was uniquely positioned to bring about a combination of circumstances that would lead to the destruction of humanity. And that I had been chosen to deal with her." He shook his head. "Over the years I've seen so much that has taught me there are some cruel, ruthless people out there who would stop at nothing to get their way. For me, she was one of them. I never asked, never doubted."

"Why would you? They raised you as one of their own, as family. Their truth was yours, and they were smart enough to place you in the perfect position to do their bidding at just the right moment, no questions asked. In a way, they did to you what they did to Aelia. Quenched everything that was the Protector in you. It kept you where they wanted you."

Kyle wasn't consoled. Knowing what he now knew, he couldn't help looking back at the life he had led, at the man he was. At the simple fact that he was the perfect killer. He knew he had to push these thoughts away, this wasn't the time for them. But it wasn't an easy thing to do.

Something occurred to him. He raised his head again and looked at Ahir. "Do you know where she came from?"

"Aelia? No, we have no idea who She is."

"How is that possible?"

"You are from the Protector line. We knew as soon as you were taken. But the Light can be born in any family, anywhere among the Firsts. Your parents traveled, you could have met Aelia in any of several places they had been to in the months before you were taken. And She was obviously taken as a baby, before we identified Her as the Light. And since She was removed from among the Firsts and effectively hidden among humans, in an environment specifically designed to subdue Her, Her chances of ever being discovered were near naught."

"But her family, she must have one."

"We are looking into it. We know She was probably taken around the time you were and we know Her given name, which She was found with so we assume it is in fact Hers, and our people will start from there. Other than you two, no children of the Firsts have ever disappeared. So we will be looking at deaths of single adults or couples who we did not know yet had a child, see what we might have missed. We will find out who She is, and if She has a family, we will find them. In the meantime, She has Neora and me." He paused. "And you."

Kyle nodded slightly, his eyes fixed on his plate, his hand playing with the fork, and repeated quietly, "And me." He thought about her trust in him. No matter the threat he posed to her, no matter what he did, she was never afraid. Never of him.

Her born Protector.

He shook his head. "Does she know all this?"

"Yes, Neora and I told Her."

"Neora seems to be good with her, she's made her comfortable here."

"She is a special woman," Ahir said with evident enthusiasm. "Like all other Keepers before her, it was her choice to assume the life she has, to keep the faith, lead the Firsts spiritually, you might say. And she has done so without any regret. She has always been well aware of the importance of what she does for our people, and she has never stopped believing that the Light would return."

"The Keepers stay in their role their entire life?"

"Yes, until their last day, and they live their entire life from the moment they become Keepers here, at Aeterna. And whenever a Keeper passes, she is commemorated with a painting that is placed among those of her predecessors."

"So all those paintings, those women who are dressed the same, along those staircases, were Keepers."

"Yes."

"Exactly how many were there?"

Ahir's sigh was sad. "Too many."

Chapter Fifteen

The phone Rolly gave Kyle beeped and he focused instantly. "We've got a sighting. Just off the cliffs to the south," he said when he ended the call.

Seconds later he was outside, checking his gun as he called out to Rolly, "Until I give you the all clear, keep this place in lockdown. And do not take your eyes off Aelia!"

With a glance at the house, he jumped into the waiting car. As it drove off, he called the man tracking Semner for more information, but the guy barely managed to say a few words before the call was cut off.

Neora looked at the hope of her people standing at the picture windows, her eyes betraying the deepness of her thoughts. Aelia had not left the room since Kyle's return, instead waiting, tuned to him, worry evident in her eyes.

The old woman nodded to herself. She knows him, better than she knows herself. She has accepted him, although she has yet to accept who she herself is.

"I could feel him when he returned, he was all broken

inside," Aelia said, as if to herself. "He'd just lost the only family he's ever known, he's lost everything. He needs Ahir, he needs something real." She turned to find Neora looking at her in wonder.

"I'm not your Light," she blurted out. "What you're talking about, what you're searching for, it's an impossibility. I don't know why I have this thing with Kyle, but what you're saying, it simply cannot be."

Neora was about to answer when Aelia's gray eyes grew intense, her focus shifting. Kyle had suddenly become alert, she could feel the tension in him peak. Before either managed to react movement outside the French doors caught their eye, and Aelia stepped closer to find that security had positioned themselves immediately outside, along the stone terrace. A hushed hiss, and a protective shield appeared on the other side of the glass. At the same time the doors to the room opened and Rolly stepped in.

"Keeper, Ma'am," he said with urgency, "I need you both to stay in here. I've got people outside and at this door. We're in lockdown."

Aelia lowered her head and focused. Kyle had left the house. "The man Kyle was waiting for, he's here, then."

Rolly nodded. "He's been spotted at the edge of the grounds. Kyle went to intercept him."

When he closed the doors behind him, Aelia turned back to the clear glass and the shield beyond it. "All of this because of me." Her voice was barely audible. "Why?" She turned back to Neora. "Why do you need me, I mean the Light? You're the Keeper, and there have been many Keepers before you. You've all kept these people together, led them, guided them. Why not continue this way?"

Neora corrected her. "Not guided. I have led, as others have before me. But the Keepers have led the Firsts based on what the Light has taught us."

"The Light has been gone for a long time, Neora. Things change. Times change. People lose touch with their beliefs and rely on tangible leadership. That's you, the Keepers. You and the Protectors alongside you."

"It is difficult to explain to someone who has not grown up among us, someone who has lived her entire life among humans, with their way of thinking and their perception of belief." Neora contemplated her words. "The Light is not just a belief, and it is not a set of values and rules that were decided in some forgotten past and no longer relevant circumstances, to be followed by people whose lives are completely different from those of its creators." She spoke with passion. "Our Light is real, and She has walked among us, guided through a substantial part of our existence and our development."

She looked toward the sealed windows, her eyes distant. "And yes, She has prepared us for times in which She would not be here, to continue as we have even while She is gone. She did not assign to us rules, She showed us a way of thinking. A way of life. But She has been gone for a very long time, and as the Keeper I can tell you that I feel I am no longer a sufficing substitute. We need our Light back, now more than ever. These are not simple times, Aelia."

"If I am gone, the organization might retreat."

"You have turned an obscure theory of theirs into reality. I doubt they will ever again retreat. And they are not the only threat to us," she added enigmatically. "We need you."

"Me." Aelia shook her head in disbelief. No matter which way she looked at it, she could not bridge the gap between who she thought she was her whole life and what Neora was telling her she was, asking her to be. The pragmatic human she was could not begin to accept that she could be the Light, or that such a force could even exist.

It does, you've felt it, you are *it.* A new voice broke through the logic that was trying hard to keep its place in her mind. *You may not have their knowledge of it, their memories, but you are the only one who has* felt *the reality of it.*

It doesn't matter, she answered herself. Even if it were true, what I am is nowhere near the kind of might the Keeper is speaking of, what her people need. It is better that they remain with what they have come to rely on, to trust, than turn, after all this waiting, all this hope, to what would fail them.

"Still," she said out loud, "they are amazing, the Keepers. To give their lives like this. To lead this way, keep the people's hopes unwavering for so long. You've proven yourselves worthy of this role you've been given."

"Yes. But none of us was born of the Light. We are all just the keepers of the faith, Firsts like all the others.

There is only so much we can do. And we too are guided by the hope, the belief that we ourselves need, that the Light would return someday, when the time is right."

And that's when it dawned on Aelia. "That's why they seem sad. In the paintings, their eyes are sad," she said quietly.

"Yes, they were all sad, especially toward the end." Neora spread her hands to indicate the great house around her. "They have all spent most of their lives here, in this very house, waiting for something, a miracle if you will, that never came. They have seen our people struggle through too many centuries, hanging on to increasingly desperate hope. All Keepers were amazing women who did their best. But ultimately the Firsts have known all that time that the Light was no longer among them, that the Keepers cannot guide and protect like She did, that we are only . . . stand-ins." She sighed. "We have all had to live with the question of why the Light has stayed away for so long and whether She would ever return. We have never had such a long time go by without Her returning, never more than a generation or so. And it is taking a toll on us. We need Her."

Neora stood up and began walking to the windows, stopped when she remembered the shield was still there. Outside, beyond it, she knew, it all looked the same, as if the world of the people she had been called on to lead all those decades ago had not changed, as if the Light herself, the awaited First of the Firsts, was not right there in the room with her. She had to succeed in this, had to make Her understand. Had to help her people, could not let their struggle continue.

Aelia approached her, wanting, needing to help. She felt the old woman's despair, felt it flow from her in waves that hit Aelia with all their strength. "Don't, please, you're in pain and it's so deep, it runs through you all the way far into the past." She closed her eyes and shook her head, bewildered, but could not shake it off, could not stop it. "I can feel it, I can't—" The words flowed out of her, unchecked, and she saw it, saw it all, *felt* it all. "This whole place is in pain, the people, they are all aware that I'm here, every single person here has me on their mind this very moment, and they are all so scared, so afraid to feel hope, afraid to *lose* their hope." Tears flowed down her cheeks and she opened her eyes, out of breath. "What's happening to me?"

To her surprise, her tears were mirrored in the old woman's face, except that Neora was laughing and crying at once. She took the younger woman's hands in hers. "You are waking up, child, what normally happens in years you are going through in days." She tried to find the words to explain what it was now time to tell her. "Your connection is not only with your Protector. That is only the connection designed to keep you safe. At Her height, the First can connect to *all* Her people, *all* the Firsts. Connect, feel and be felt. And"—she nodded slightly, remembering the stories the Keepers were privy to—"defend, when She needs to. That is the true power of the Light, Her ability to do what no one else can. That is why She has remained our hope for so long, She is what no one else can be."

"But I'm . . ."

"This *is* you," Neora interrupted gently but insistently. "The real you. What those who took you did only delayed the Light that you are from growing as should have been from the start. But they did not kill the Light, they do not have the power to do that. You are still you and no one can take that away from you."

Aelia closed her eyes. "I don't know what to do."

"Yes, you do. You are already doing it. You are the only one who can. It is that simple." The Keeper's hands tightened around Aelia's. "And I'm sorry, child, but you have no choice. We need you."

The driver, a member of one of Aeterna's security teams, drove toward the cliffs above the sea, to the coordinates the scout who had followed the intruder had given immediately before his call to Kyle was cut off. Some distance from their destination, Kyle got out of the car and instructed the driver to leave. Rolly had already deployed more people to the area, which was also being watched by satellite, but Kyle had told him to keep everyone away. He would deal with Semner himself.

The car drove off and Kyle walked up to the edge of the cliff before him, where he could see the dark water far below. He watched the light of the moon reflect in the water as a stray cloud moved away, then turned to walk along the dark rock.

Almost immediately he stopped. He closed his eyes, listened in the darkness surrounding him, let his training guide him. Finally he opened his eyes and nodded slightly to himself. He turned back toward the water and waited.

"Hello, Kyle."

He turned slowly.

Semner and Kyle faced off.

"Well, well," Semner sneered. "If it isn't the . . . what are you? The superior race or whatever you call yourselves? What, you're with them now? Come to defend your people? Or just that woman?" He huffed. "What'd she do to turn you?"

Kyle was astonished by the extent of his old friend's knowledge, and even more by the hatred in his voice. "What happened, John? We've known each other how many years now? We were friends, good friends. We've worked missions together, been in some tough situations."

"We were never friends. I've known who you are for years." Semner's laugh was cruel. "You thought you were Jennison's star. But it was me he trusted with his most precious secret."

"You knew?"

"No reason not to tell you now, seeing as I'm going to kill you. They came to me, Jennison and the others, back when they recruited me, long before you think they did. Swore me to secrecy, said I was about to learn the most well-kept secret of the organization, that if I did as they said I'll get far." Semner moved back, keeping a careful eye on Kyle, and sat on a low boulder. "They told me about *them*, the first race or whatever. About how they're a danger to us, how they're biding their time and eventually will take us over, go back to being the controlling race, the only race. And how you are one of them, how they took you when you were a kid, plan to use you against your own people."

"So you knew all this time."

"Knew, reported to them on your every move, every thought. How'd you think they controlled you so well? Their own personal puppet."

Kyle felt the blood in his veins turn to fire.

"But I told them," Semner went on with unhidden glee, "I told them it wouldn't work. I saw things they didn't, told them you'd never truly be one of us. Told them eventually you'd turn on them. And when Jennison told me about that woman, how the only way to stop *them* was to kill her before they took her back and she helped them go against us, and that he was sending you after her, I knew you wouldn't do it. I knew you'd finally fail. And I was right."

He got up, and suddenly there was a gun in his hand. "I've waited for this day too long. This is as good a place as any to kill you. And when I finish with you, I'll get her. You won't be able to protect her this time."

Kyle was more focused than he'd been for days, his training taking over—with a twist. His newfound knowledge of who he was. He went for Semner's weakness, his ego.

"A gun? Really?" He sounded amused.

"You're right," Semner said viciously, taking the bait. "Let's play this out for real." And he threw his gun aside.

He drew a knife from the sheath strapped to his hip and lunged at Kyle, opening an ugly cut in his chest. Reacting to the searing pain, Kyle stepped aside and punched Semner in the side, and Semner roared in anger, turned, and lunged at him again. They wrestled, each using tactics that, inevitably, the other knew. It was more a question of stamina than anything else, the stamina of each man and the one's hatred against the other's preservation instinct.

Moments later found them locked in a deadly embrace, both putting all their strength into it, with Kyle trying to maintain his footing, his muscles straining against his shirt, Semner's knife at his stomach. He had the past days against him, with barely any rest and the constant tension of having his life turned upside-down and facing a new reality he could not begin to grasp. He'd been going on adrenalin, but against this man, who was not only trained as well as he but also knew both his strengths and weaknesses, he finally felt the exhaustion win, and his strength drain. He felt the point of the knife penetrate his shirt, then his skin, right at his spleen. Which would kill him fast, would—

Aelia.

The thought popped into his mind without warning. And with it the realization what his death would mean. The burst of energy came from nowhere and he moved fast, faster than ever before. The surprised Semner lost his footing and stumbled, and Kyle used this to get behind him and place his arm around his neck. He had Semner in a tight grip now, barely allowing the man to breathe, but Semner still struggled and uttered in hate, "There'll be others after me. One day you'll leave her and we'll be there."

His mouth at his former friend's ear, Kyle whispered, "I'll never leave her." And he broke the man's neck with the easiness of newfound strength.

He let Semner's body fall and straightened up. He was still looking down at the man he had killed when the cars came from behind him, their headlights on him. Rolly jumped out of the lead car and ran to him. It was only then that he turned his back to Semner, finally feeling that he was leaving it all—the organization, his past, the only identity he'd ever known—behind him.

The Protector's eyes met Rolly's. Rolly took a step back and nodded once in deference. "We'll take care of it, Sir."

"The man who had followed him?"

"We found the body half a mile from here. Three bullets to the heart from behind."

The Protector nodded. "Stand down but keep watch," was the order he uttered in reply. "No one was sent but Semner, but as of now the organization's plans are an unknown." He began to walk away but then stopped and turned back. "And send the body to Jennison."

The man who was no longer Kyle Rhys got into Rolly's car, which took him back to the great house. He got out and walked through the front door, heading for one of the staircases.

"Kyle?" Ahir came toward him, and began running when he saw the signs of his struggle with Semner.

The young man turned to him, and Ahir halted in mid-stride. Protectors past and present, grandfather and grandson, stood a distance apart in the grand entry hall of the ancient abode of the Firsts.

"Adam." Ahir's voice was no more than a whisper.

Adam nodded once. "I need to see Aelia."

"Yes, of course, Son." Ahir indicated the staircase. "She went up to her rooms just a short while ago. She asked to be alone."

Behind Ahir, the Keeper came toward them. She gasped at the Adam's appearance. "Are you all right? You need a doctor, I will call for her immediately."

Adam raised his hand to stop her, and bowed his head slightly in thanks. "I'm fine." He turned and ran up, taking the stairs two at a time.

The security detail he'd ordered to stay with Aelia until his return began walking toward the rugged man striding toward them, but then moved aside without a word as they recognized him. Adam walked through them without slowing down and touched the screen beside the double doors to Aelia's rooms without giving it a second thought. The security system recognized him and gave him access, unlocking the doors. He opened them and stepped inside, closing them behind him.

The spacious sitting room he found himself in was silent and empty. He crossed it to another set of doors at its opposite end, and stepped into the inner apartment. He walked on without hesitation. Finally he halted, letting the fresh night air, a hint of the sea in it, wash over him, bringing with it memories, still too fresh, of what had taken place earlier at the edge of the seaside cliff.

The silent figure standing on the balcony in the dark turned to him, and they faced each other. Not a word had to be said. She took it all in, the blood, the torn shirt. It was she who moved first, indicating for him to sit on the balcony sofa and he did, wincing. He'd had worse injuries in the past, far worse, but this was more than just his recent struggle with Semner he was finally feeling.

Aelia came back with a soft towel that she had wet with warm water, and, sitting beside him, helped him take off his shirt and tended to the cuts Semner's knife had made in his chest and abdomen. He wanted to tell her that not all the blood was his but found that he couldn't, nor could he meet her eyes.

A soft hand rested on his and he held it, squeezing tight, then raised his eyes to meet a somber look.

"You had no choice. You didn't ask for this," she said.

"Does it matter? I was a part of the organization for a long time. I trained with Semner, and I helped train some of the people Jennison will send after you now. And they'll keep coming, they won't stop. Semner and I, we were just the first."

She kept her eyes on his. "Then let them come."

"They've got some of the best trained killers in the world. The best, Aelia. And you need to understand, you're the organization's most wanted target. Killing you, or at least disabling you if they can't kill you, is the one thing they will not give up on, no matter how long it takes or what they have to do." He shook his head. "Look at the lengths they went to with me."

"Yes, but now I've got you," she said, and then realized what she said. "I mean, no, you don't have to stay, not now. I know what they say about us, who we're supposed to be, but you really don't have to do this. I just thought, because these last few days, this started to look like it's our fight, like we're in this together, I guess." She faltered, unsure of herself. With everything they had been through, with everything she had discovered about both of them, the shock of it, she never had a chance to stop and think about it. About choices. Their choices. And she realized he probably didn't, either.

When she spoke again, her voice was stronger, determined. "They'll settle for me, won't they?"

He frowned. "Yes, I suppose they might."

"Then go. This doesn't have to be your fight, you didn't choose any of this. Decide for yourself, choose what you want. Not what you were told you must do or were born to do." She met his eyes again. "You did enough. I'm among the Firsts now, and this is a secure place. If you want to go, I promise you I'll stay here, I'll never leave Aeterna, so if that's what you're worried about you can rest assured that I'll be safe. Please. You can always come back, you now have a home to come back to."

"You didn't choose this either," he said, not taking his eyes off hers.

"No. But I can't leave them. And you won't leave unless I stay, will you?"

In her eyes he saw the same sadness he saw in them earlier, when she knew what he didn't yet, the role he was destined for as the Protector and what it would mean for him. Choice. She wanted him to have a choice.

"They took so much from you, Adam."

He started at her use of his name. His real name.

"Please. Go, live a life that's yours, find what's true for you. Something you can believe in, after all those lies. Something real."

"I did."

She shook her head and turned her gaze to the darkness beyond the balcony, leaned back. "What they need me to be . . . I don't see how I can be that."

He didn't answer immediately. She thought, he realized, that he had meant the Light. Of course she would. That's what everyone around her must have talked about since she got here, her as the Light. And it was what had started it all, and the only reason, or so she would think, that he, her would-be killer, ended up sitting here beside her as her Protector. He decided this was not the time to correct her, instead choosing to focus on what she still couldn't believe about herself, knowing now that this belief would be central to her safety. All considering, nothing was more important right now.

When he spoke there was real conviction in his voice. "I've seen you be what they want, what they need. It's not a choice, it's who you are."

"What they want is impossible, such things aren't real. It's just a belief, a myth, a story they heard from their ancestors."

He mused at her attempt to convince herself. Wondered what she would think if she saw herself through his eyes.

She didn't notice, she was too agitated. "And how many have already died because of it? Two?" She raised her eyes to his. "Three? How many more will die because of this belief? Because of me, what they think I am? And what about you, how much more will you be hurt?" She let out a breath. "Maybe if I turn my back on what they want me to be, the organization will leave us alone, the Firsts and me. And you'll be free."

Adam sighed and leaned back, wincing again. "No. They'll still come after you. And I'm still your Protector. Apparently that's true no matter what you do."

"Look at what it's doing to you."

"Being the Protector isn't doing this. Neither is being with you. Those after you, after us, heck, after the Firsts, they're doing this. And if anything, look at what I found, what I've got, since I met you." His eyes were intense on hers. "You want a choice? This is mine."

He meant it. She didn't need the link between them to know that. Or to see that he was exhausted, for that matter. Everything that happened from the moment he first laid eyes on her, to this night when he killed a man who he had thought was his friend, was finally catching up with him.

She indicated his wounds. "Someone should have a look at these," she said, "and you need some sleep."

"They look worse than they are, and you cleaned them nicely." He smiled tiredly. "And I think the bruises

I'll feel by morning will be worse. But the sleep, I'll take that." He got up. "I actually have an apartment here, you know? The closest to this one."

"Ahir told me." She finally smiled. "Walk you there?"

"I don't think so. With Aeterna's security following us? That'll be a sight." He chuckled softly. "I'll have them removed tomorrow, by the way. Once I'm sure I'm completely back to form."

At which time he would be taking over her protection, she knew he was saying. So his decision to stay was final.

She nodded.

Chapter Sixteen

The first underground floor of the facility was silent. Everyone who did not have to be here had left, and anyone who had no choice but to be here was tiptoeing around, staying well away from the office at the end of the short corridor. No one wanted to feel the wrath of the facility's director, who had been raging mad for hours. At this very moment Jennison was walking around his office like a cooped-up tiger, his anger out of control.

Semner hadn't checked in, and Jennison had no idea what was going on. The last he heard from him was when the killer had been told to go to Amalfi, and nothing since. Neace had finally been located in a morgue, which was a loose end since the authorities would now try to determine his identity and initiate a homicide investigation. The body of the Firsts' man had vanished along with all forensic evidence collected and Jennison had no idea how that came to be. The police had no clue who Kyle was, and they never would, if the organization could help it, but they were treating it as if he'd kidnapped the woman and killed the man they had found in her apartment, which meant they would continue to actively look for him. The only bright side was that the organization's techs were smart enough to remove all records of the fugitives' presence in the airport or on the flight to Rome. At least someone did their job around here, Jennison thought with renewed rage. He hit the table with his fist. How the hell did it all go so wrong, so fast? He no longer had control over anything—the target's whereabouts, Kyle, Semner.

Kyle. Now that was a mistake, an unprecedented investment gone so wrong it would cost him his life if the board found out just how bad things had gotten. He'd managed to keep the lid on the visit Kyle had paid him, but the longer this failure persisted, the less safe he himself was. This had been his idea, his doing. Taking the child, keeping him alive when he was told it would be best to kill him, raising him as one of their own, training him to become what turned out to be their best operative ever. Just in case there was more to the Firsts' stories than just that, stories, he had thought all those years ago. And why not see what would be if one of them was raised as a human, unaware of what he really was?

Yes. His idea and it had backfired so easily.

The worst thing was, it even made him doubt. Could it all somehow be true? He himself had controlled everything Kyle was taught since the day he was taken, every single ideal and belief instilled in him, had even handpicked who would be in his life, down to who his friends were. The man that child had become had obeyed the organization, and Jennison himself, without question, completing missions and eliminating his targets without fail. And yet this woman, he'd only come into contact with her once—once!—and it was all over. The man who'd spent two and half decades in the controlling hands of the organization had so easily switched sides to hers, and years of careful planning were lost.

But it was more than that. Although Jennison had originally made the decision to keep the child Kyle alive just in case baby Aelia somehow survived what the organization had in store for her, he had never truly believed she would survive. None of the selected few in the organization who knew about her had thought she would. After their initial attempt to kill her had inexplicably failed, they had placed her in an environment no child should ever live in, hoping that this would kill her, or at least turn her into something that would be useless to the Firsts if they ever did succeed in finding her. And yet, not only did she survive, she had turned into quite an individual. And then she'd managed to turn Kyle, the same man who the Firsts' stories said had that connection to her. So could it be... could it be?

He shook the thought off. No. He prided himself on being a rational man and none of it could be true. Humans had their beliefs too, and they were nothing more than baseless convictions rooted in myths, folktales. And her survival in that hell, that was a mix of coincidence and character, had to be. And Kyle... Kyle was harder to explain. Jennison knew him too well, and he had no explanation for what happened to him, none at all. All he knew was that whatever it was, the Kyle who had paid him that unwanted visit was a different man. Worse, he was obviously already well on his way to the truth. Which meant he had to die. As far as the organization was concerned, Kyle, who knew too much, who simply was too much, had to die.

Which brought Jennison back to Semner. Where the hell was he? Did he find them? Was he still on the mission? Was he dead—did Kyle kill him? The worst case scenario, Jennison knew, was just that. Kyle killed Semner, and he and the woman were now at that place, Aeterna, among the Firsts.

Jennison breathed in deeply and forced himself to think. He needed to do something. If the worst case did in fact happen, he needed to let *them* know they'd better not dare retaliate. Had to show them that the organization was ready, strong, and could and would get to them if it wanted to. Under other circumstances that would be a huge risk, what with the status quo that was reached all those years ago, but if the Firsts already knew that the organization had breached that, which was just what Jennison's actions had done . . .

It would all fall on me, he thought. No sense delaying, he had no choice.

Time for drastic action, and he had just the action that would rattle them.

Adam slept. Despite the events of the night before, he actually slept quite well. But then he wasn't really surprised. Whatever had gone on inside him when he had gone to see Aelia, by the time he left to go to his own rooms he was able to breathe easy again. Her knowing, understanding, her being there was all it took.

He got up feeling better than he had in days. His body didn't feel as bruised as he had thought it would, either, and his energy no longer came from adrenaline running in a body that had been through the equivalent of a meat grinder over too many days.

He walked to the mirror in his bathroom and had a look. The wounds still throbbed, but they looked as if they had been inflicted days, not mere hours ago. His injuries had never healed this quickly. He frowned. Aelia had tended to them, that was the only difference this time. He stared at the worst cut on his chest, now just an angry red line. The Light had her own way of protecting the Protector, he remembered Ahir saying. Had Aelia unknowingly made him heal faster, body and soul, just by touching him?

Ahir. His grandfather. His family. He had to get used to that. He wasn't a human, he belonged to the Firsts. And he was standing in his rooms in the Kennard wing. He was a Kennard. Adam Kennard. The Protector. Damn. This would all take time to get used to. Except that last one. That one was easy.

He would have pushed his way to be beside her, protect her, even if he wasn't born to do it. It wasn't because of what he had seen that day in the park or what he since learned her true identity was. It was because of who she was. Her choice to intervene and stop the brawl in the park, despite the danger to herself. The way she tended to Benjamin as he lay dying and cried for this man she didn't know. Her standing up to him, despite knowing he was there to kill her. Her choice to side with him, trust him, even when the alternative arose. Her acceptance of him despite where he'd come from, what he'd been.

He met his own eyes in the mirror. That was the one thing that for him was a given. Even if he wasn't one of the Firsts, even if he wasn't the one who was her Protector, he would have found a way to stay. She was right, of course. He hadn't asked for this. And it was the Light who had created the link to the Protector, he had no doubt she could block it if she wanted to. This Light, Aelia, who wanted to give him his freedom.

He wasn't going anywhere.

He showered and dressed, and then descended the stairs to meet Ahir, who was still worried about him. After returning to the Kennard wing the night before Adam had once again refused to have a doctor look at his injuries, showing Ahir that Aelia had tended to them and saying he just needed some sleep. So Ahir tried once again to convince him to do so now.

Adam unbuttoned his shirt. The old man's jaw dropped, and he looked at his grandson in question.

Adam nodded.

He then checked in with Rolly to ensure that the heightened alert level at Aeterna was still being maintained despite Semner's death, and pulled the security detail from Aelia, to allow her the freedom she wanted. With Semner gone and no imminent threat, at least not a known one, Adam had initially been concerned that

Aeterna's security would become too lax, but Rolly reminded him that with the Light there that would not be the case. Aeterna would not go below the highest security level from now on. Having already seen what that meant and knowing that now he himself was with her, this put Adam's mind at ease.

To an extent. This was only the beginning, he knew. The organization would not stop until they got Aelia, and he would now be a target, too. And the question begged itself—what did it all mean for the Firsts? For the Keeper, for his grandfather? What would Jennison's next step be, especially when he would get Semner's body and understand that he had failed once again and that now both Aelia and Adam himself—Kyle, for him—were out of reach?

But Adam could do little more than speculate on what would happen now. Obviously from the start he'd been given only a small part of the picture by the organization, and even that had been a lie. And so all he could do was rely on what he knew about the organization and the people who were behind it, and on what they had made him, and use it all to do all it took to protect those around him.

A little less than two hours later Adam was having breakfast with Ahir, Neora and Aelia in the main dining room of what was now his and his grandfather's wing of the great house. Neora and Ahir were at the table with him, tea cups before them—his was coffee—and Remi and Sonea were clearing the dishes. Aelia stood up yet again and walked to the window, as she had done several times already, to look outside. There were many more people out there now. She watched them, subconsciously tuning herself to them.

"All those people out there . . ."

"They need you."

Aelia started, realizing that she had spoken her thoughts out loud, that the three at the table were listening.

Neora's eyes clouded, and once again Aelia felt sadness, a bottomless, timeless sadness from her. She glanced at Adam and saw him looking at Neora too, frowning. Ahir put his hand on his old friend's.

"We lost so much." Neora shook her head. "We used to be so alive, so hopeful, always looking to the future. We created, we nurtured, we believed. And when the Light left us, we lost our life force. It was still there at the beginning, the first, second, tenth century after you left us, and later, too. We continued proud, confident. We had a rich past, strong foundations to stand on. We stood for so much, were certain of who we were. We had what the Light had taught us and kept it alive with flourish, because we were certain, so certain that you would return to stand among us, guide us. Protect us. But you did not return. This time, you did not return to us."

Aelia's eyes filled with tears at the pain in the old woman's voice, the pain of the Firsts.

"I and the Keepers before me, we tried to help, to be there for them, keep their hope alive, but it has gotten more and more difficult with each century. And we ourselves, the Keepers—and the Protectors—we ourselves needed you, and needed to continue believing, for ourselves as well as for our people, that you would return. But you did not and by then there was no one who had lived at the same time as the Light, who remembered how it felt when the Light walked among us. There hasn't been someone like that for so long now, and every year, every single year since I became Keeper, the Council would convene and I would be given the same news, always the same news as too many before me have. The silence of your absence. I thought I too would eventually pass without you coming back, but I simply could not stop believing. I haven't even allowed them to choose the one who will replace me yet, do you know? I knew you had to come back, you simply had to. Our people are tired, Aelia, they are at their wits' end. And this world, so much is happening, so much bad, and we are so few, and underneath it all our people, your people, are crumbling in their struggle to keep it all alive, to keep themselves alive. We need you, you see. We need you so much—"

Her voice broke, and Aelia watched her, wanting, needing to take the old Keeper's pain away, and she tried to find within her the way to help, she just had to do something—

Then so be it, she thought, *let it be. Please, show me how to help them, how to let it be.*

She turned back to the window. Outside, people stood in the distance, speaking to one another, throwing looks at the great house. She closed her eyes. The Light. First of the Firsts. Neora was talking as if she was nothing short of amazing, and what those people out there were calling for, awaiting, what they were thinking that she was, that was so much beyond her. What she felt within her, what she was, it wasn't that, it wasn't anywhere close. She was just Aelia. Aelia with that subtle, prodding feeling inside her that was there, but it was a shadow, just a shadow. It wasn't enough. They needed her, and she wanted, needed so much to help them and she wasn't enough.

She noticed the silence behind her and turned. They were all looking at her. Adam stood up, concerned.

"I . . ." She faltered, unsure of herself, felt she was letting them down. "I'm sorry, I can't . . ." She ran out.

Adam moved to go after her, and Neora touched his arm to restrain him. "Adam, let her go."

Adam stopped but continued to look toward the door.

"Let her go. She needs to do this herself."

"Do what?" Adam looked at Neora, not understanding.

"Know who she is. Become what she is," the old woman said, a force to her voice. "You know. You've seen it, you've felt it. But she doesn't believe it yet, she doesn't believe it could possibly be her."

Adam's mind went back to the conversation he had with Aelia the night before. He was about to answer Neora when a commotion sounded outside, the door crashed open and Rolly burst into the room, his face ashen.

"There's been an attack." He shook his head incredulously. "Rome . . . there was an explosion in the cathedral."

Ahir stood up, the chair he was sitting on nearly falling over. "Our people?"

"We're still checking. Our systems in the underground complex registered the blast data, but it just happened, so we don't have anything else yet. I've already had contact with Denole, he says the explosion was outside our perimeter."

"Do they need anything?" Ahir asked.

"Our people in the relevant places are already on the move. We're also waiting for media coverage, it should tell us if we're compromised." Rolly frowned. "Denole reports possible casualties." He turned and walked back to the door, where Adam was already waiting and security details were standing ready to take position and protect their leaders once again, Aeterna having re-initiated a lockdown.

Rolly updated Adam and Ahir on the way to Aeterna's control center. A short while before, what seemed to be a deliberately placed charge exploded immediately outside the rear of the cathedral's left wall. Luckily there were very few tourists around, because the place hadn't opened yet for visits. At that hour only the cathedral personnel and its clergy were there, and any Firsts that were among them were all inside. The Firsts' hidden complex under the cathedral was already fully active at that hour.

The three came to a stop before the curved screen. Its entire main section showed the inside of the Firsts' underground center, which seemed unaffected, the area immediately outside the wall where the explosion hit, the inside of the cathedral, and the entire cathedral from all sides and above, at a growing distance to allow for more coverage of the surrounding streets. The devastation, in and out, was clear, and rescue and law enforcement forces were still arriving. Both inside the cathedral and outside it, paramedics were already treating injured and dazed people.

On Adam's right, a section of the wall he had thought was just that, a wall, shimmered and then broke into a matrix comprising news screens as media worldwide began breaking into newscasts, reporting the explosion at the prominent religious and tourist site. He couldn't hear what they were saying, but work stations facing the screens had people listening to every word being said, as well as to the chatter of police and rescue forces in the area. On his left, others were intent solely on data coming in from Aeterna's extensive security layout. Some subscreens were focused only on the great house, and several of the watchers' individual screens, he saw, were dedicated to the part of the house Aelia and the Keeper were in. Yet others focused on the people outside on Aeterna's grounds. Rolly and his people were leaving nothing to chance and had obviously implemented all the safeguards Adam himself had suggested. And he was impressed with the professional calm at the control center. There were many more people here now than before, and the activity was substantially heightened, yet the noise level was hushed and there was no sense of panic.

"Our complex under the cathedral, our Rome center,

is of course in lockdown," Rolly said for Adam's benefit. "It is safely located far under the multiple basement floors of the main structure. The moment the blast was registered, access to and from the complex was automatically sealed on all sides, and our people were cut off from the outside. The only remaining access is through an underground tunnel to the secondary site. We have designated personnel among the humans, in the cathedral and among the authorities and the rescue forces, so we have a significant presence there. We are safe."

Adam turned to him, frowning. He didn't know anything yet about the Firsts' global security—he didn't know anything about the Firsts themselves yet, come to think of it—but in his experience there was no such thing as safe. Certainly not at a bombing site.

Rolly nodded and spoke quietly to the supervisor overseeing the room. She acknowledged and gave a quiet order, and the satellite view looking down at the cathedral from above distanced itself quickly, until the cathedral was invisible within the city around it. "You're looking at continuous satellite coverage," Rolly said. "That's in addition to technological and other measures applied in and around the cathedral in general and in our underground complex in particular, which are unaffected by any system installed by humans around them, nor are they detectable by any means currently in existence. Our sensors weren't even close to incurring damage throughout the entire event, they just recorded it. And, most important, each and every one of our people in Rome is already accounted for and is monitored. We are," he added somberly, "used to living alongside humans without being discovered, regardless of what happens."

"Still, the attack wasn't identified in progress."

"True. But who thought they would attack their own to get to us? This is a prominent cathedral. A holy place for the humans, with humans inside and around it at all times."

"We'll have to reassess our security." Ahir's frown was deep with worry. This was a new escalation.

Adam forced himself to take a mental step back. Not because he felt better about the safety of the Firsts, but because he realized he didn't know enough for his experience to lock on to what should and shouldn't be done when it came to them. He knew all about the reality of the humans he'd lived among all his life, and nothing about the reality of this hidden species he'd just met.

"So nothing like this ever happened before?" he asked.

Rolly shook his head. "There has never been an intentional attack aimed specifically at the Firsts, assuming that's what it was."

"It was."

Ahir and Rolly turned to him. Adam's eyes remained focused on the screen, his eyes cold. He was sure of it. This had all the markings of panic, specifically Jennison's. And the timing only confirmed it. He knew the man. Although Jennison was the very vision of professionalism, of careful planning—and Adam's own carefully planned life was the best evidence of that—he was, nonetheless, prone to the occasional rash decision. Adam recalled times when he had had to pull Jennison back from a decision that would have led to premature action that would have impeded a mission, and then put a lid on it to hide the fact that it was ever even considered. He doubted more than a handful in the organization knew of this side of Jennison. But Jennison was his godfather, and he had let his guard down around Adam. Adam knew him better than most.

And yes, this had the markings of Jennison's rash decisions, an action taken too quickly, with too little planning, in a rage. To make a point.

Rolly was still watching him. "Jennison? What's he doing? Starting a war?"

"No. It's still only just the organization reacting, and I don't think it's even that, I think it's just him." Adam was thinking out loud. "It's a message for the Firsts, and for me. A warning to refrain from reacting to his recent actions. Which will allow him to regroup, deal with the internal implications of the failure of his plan, maybe cover up. Or more likely create the story he wants, maybe use it to mobilize the organization. Then come after us again."

"You think we should expect something here?" Rolly asked.

It was Ahir who answered. "No, not now. Certainly not after this. They would know that an attack on Aeterna would not pass quietly, especially now that we know what they did to our Light and the Protector in an attempt to destroy us. And if by chance they did succeed in such an attack, they wouldn't be able to stop there. They would have to attack Firsts everywhere, and you don't do that lightly. Not even Jennison. That's the organization risking exposing itself and us, and starting a war."

Adam concurred. He indicated the bombing site on the screen, awash with police and red ambulance lights. "And if Jennison would have thought to attack Aeterna, he wouldn't have bombed another site first. Now he no longer has the element of surprise going for him, and he doesn't need people to start asking why someone is bombing sites all over Italy." He turned to Rolly. "Just the same, I assume you increased security on Firsts everywhere, not just here?"

Rolly confirmed.

"Good. I'm not entirely sure how much in control of himself Jennison is right now, and even if he can't send an army, he could still try another Semner on lower-ranking targets elsewhere. To create fear."

The media screen was now packed, the entire world was reporting. None were showing footage from the site itself yet. Adam imagined it would take time to get news vans through the emergency vehicles blocking the ancient city's streets.

Denole, the head of defense and security of the Rome center, was available after some time to report to them. He sent them footage from the Firsts' systems that showed the entire sequence of events, beginning some time before the explosion. They watched it on the holoscreen of the supervisor's station, while Denole watched it along with them in his own office under the cathedral.

"There," he said when the section of the footage he

was looking for appeared. The couple on the screen approached the cathedral from the piazza behind it, seemingly like the many other tourists who normally frequented the place. The hour might have been somewhat early, but it wasn't entirely out of the ordinary, certainly not so that they would stand out. They spoke to each other and laughed, looking up at the cathedral, walking around it, as if they were just a couple of sightseers.

Here the view changed. "They knew there were no security cameras at this angle, cathedral security didn't think it was needed," Denole said. "But they didn't know about our security."

On the screen, the two, apparently assuming they were not being observed, approached a semi-hidden door in the cathedral's side wall, to the rear. As they did so their demeanor changed. While the woman was keeping an eye out, the man crouched, lay his bag beside the wall and adjusted something inside. He then turned his attention to the door and was trying to open it with a set of tools he had taken from his pocket when the charge exploded. As the dust settled the devastation was clear. The view switched to the inside of the cathedral, showed it shake, heavy stones fall from above along with a part of an arch. People on the ground were running to all sides, trying to avoid them and the broken panels showering them, the blast having blown precious mosaics apart.

"The door he was trying for leads to the cathedral's first basement level, but an inner door at that level opens to an elevator to us. We wouldn't normally think there was any connection to us, since we do not exist as far as anyone is concerned, but with the Light back and the recent attempts on Her life, and the message we intercepted that was sent by our systems here soon after Mr. Kennard identified Her, we have to take this possibility into account. I don't know what made them think they would manage to get to us, but then they don't seem to have been very well prepared. And that explosive, the way it just went off..."

"Could you go back before the explosion, zoom in on their faces?" Adam asked Rolly, who did as he asked. Adam frowned at the realization that he'd been right.

"You know them, Sir?" Denole asked.

"Never seen her, but the guy, he's one of the soldiers at the organization's Italy office. I've met him. He's not even one of their high-level operatives, just a soldier for local missions." This strengthened Adam's assumption that this was a hasty job ordered by Jennison. He was authorized to mobilize people everywhere, but using an operative at Adam's level, and from outside the facility, would require him to report to the heads of the organization, so he would have had no choice but to use lower-level operatives. Who could, on the upside, be more easily intimidated to obey without question.

Rolly nodded appreciatively. Having a former operative of the organization here was proving useful. He called over one of his people and issued some orders to be passed to all other centers, then directed him to set up briefing calls for Ahir and him with all heads of defense and security as soon as possible.

Adam's eyes were on the bombing site views on the control center screen. These are my people out there, my people who are being attacked, the realization dawned on him. "What do we do to help our people in Rome?" he asked.

Rolly glanced at him quizzically. "We watch and wait. Those under the cathedral will lie low, and those around it will do their job and take care of what's needed. If need be, the complex can be evacuated to the secondary site through a secure passage."

Adam nodded, his frustration mounting. He needed to know more.

He didn't see Rolly exchange a look with Ahir, nor the smile that passed on Ahir's face. The latter nodded his confirmation and Rolly spoke. "You're welcome to join the conference calls with the defense and security heads of our worldwide communities, it would be a good time to make the introductions," he said to Adam as they turned to leave the control center. "And anything you've got to say, we'll listen."

"I just got here, I don't know enough. My interference with security outside Aeterna could risk people." Adam stopped and turned to Rolly. "And you don't answer to me. You answer to my grandfather."

"I answer to you both, and so do all heads of defense and security. Mr. Kennard here is the head of the Council and we all answer to him. But you are the Protector now. You are the only authority on the protection of the First and the final authority on the protection of all the Firsts."

"When I know more."

"Knowledge will come quickly. We'll all make sure of that. But the man behind the job, you're already him. I've seen enough to know that." Rolly was dead serious.

Adam turned to Ahir, dumbstruck.

"I agree with Rolly," Ahir said. "Sit in on the calls with us, start getting an idea of what's involved with this side of the Protector's role, the defense and security of the Firsts."

"Aren't you worried Aelia's protection will suffer?"

"That's why you've got us," Rolly said. "Wherever Firsts live, there is someone local who oversees their safety. And we've been doing this for a long time, we're good. We'll be out there for you, your people on site."

"Adam," Ahir said, putting his hand on his grandson's arm. "Trust me, be patient. I've been doing this for decades, I know what you're facing. But you, you've got something else going for you. You're the Protector of a living Light, and that takes you to a whole different level. You'll be able to do so much more than I did." He smiled. "You're not just a legend either."

The Keeper had gone back to the main drawing room of the great house, and Aelia had joined her there. The three men walked through the open doors to see the two of them standing before media coverage from the bombing site, showing on a previously concealed screen. The old woman's hand was on her mouth, a horrified expression on her face. Ahir walked over and put a supporting hand around the longtime leader of the Firsts, and Rolly filled her in about the cruel attempt to harm her people. Adam came to stand silently beside Aelia. Around them in the room, a distance away, stood others of the house's staff, Remi and Sonea among them. They were all looking at the coverage of the explosion, some spoke in hushed voices, tried to make sense of it.

Beside Adam, Aelia listened to Rolly. But within her, she was listening to what remained unsaid in the room. She turned and looked at them, at the shocked faces all around her. A slight furrow in her brow, she walked to the French doors and looked at the people outside, standing in small groups. Waiting. News of the attack had made it to them, too, and they were being kept informed. Not far from her stood several members of the security details Rolly had reassigned to her and to Neora, looking out. She heard one of them comment that there were now so many people out there, he'd never seen anything like this before.

She didn't look at them, but knew their gazes moved to her.

In her mind she heard what Neora had said earlier that morning, and what she had replied before when Aelia had asked her why all these people were flocking here. "They have waited so long, dared to hope for so long. They had to come," the Keeper had said then. "And for each, there are so many others who have not come, who are out there, waiting."

They had done nothing wrong, these people, nothing but live their lives. In peace. In hope. And yet now they were under attack. Aelia closed her eyes and listened to them, to them all. Gradually the voices in the room faded, replaced with their voices within, then others'—outside the room, in Aeterna, beyond it. She opened her eyes and placed her hands on the door handles, her gaze far away. Then she opened the doors and stepped out onto the terrace. The security detail stationed outside turned in surprise and began to walk toward her protectively, but her look stopped them. She walked forward and they stepped aside in reverence, their heads bowed.

"What the—" Adam sprinted after her, Rolly at his heels and Ahir and Neora following, everyone else behind them. Outside, Aelia walked down a few of the terrace steps and stopped. She stood there, looking at the people waiting in silence, in expectation, with hope, as far as the eye could see.

Adam was about to move closer to her when a hand restrained him, gentle but firm.

"Wait," Neora said.

"Look at her, something is wrong—"

"Wait," the Keeper insisted, her voice hushed.

Oblivious to them, Aelia looked at the crowd. All and each, one by one. She saw them, saw within them, saw all the way through to what they held on to so preciously, with stubborn conviction. Saw pain and hope intertwine, reaching out to her in a look, in a thousand looks, in countless beseeching looks now within her. Saw them, and saw herself through their eyes. And she felt them, could feel all that they were, their lives and thoughts and hopes, as if she was them. All of them, those standing before her, around her, and so many others, others all over the world, stopping now wherever they were, closing their eyes in bewilderment, feeling, knowing. Asking. Engulfed by a world of emotions, by her people's desperate cry, her own powerful need to help them finally reached the force needed for the walls of that hidden place deep inside her to break apart, break into a million pieces, and they finally crumbled. And inside her she felt the Light rise, felt it grow and strengthen, felt it reach for her, become one with her. And standing on the terrace steps in Aeterna, before the eyes of Firsts present and in the hearts of Firsts worldwide, she accepted its force, her duty, and instinctively reached out to her people with all she had.

"Can you feel it?" Neora whispered, her voice filled with awe.

But Adam was no longer listening. He involuntarily stepped forward. Yes, he felt it, felt her—and he saw the Light. He could see it emanating from her, enfolding her, one with her. As she stood looking over them all, he felt it inside him, the power flowing from her, boundless might intertwined with endless compassion.

As the First answered her people's call without a word being said, a ripple seemed to go through all those around her. In Aeterna and worldwide, the people, her people, knew their hope had been answered. She was here. After all this time, the legacy their ancestors had left them had come to life.

I am here.

Chapter Seventeen

A day had gone by since the bombing at the cathedral in Rome, and only the devastation in and around it remained, that and the endless speculations of the humans and the somber realization of the Firsts. Because of the early morning hour of the bombing and the haste and, luckily, incompetence in which it was done, no one had been killed except for the two perpetrators. Nor were there serious casualties. Two were moderately injured, an elderly priest inside the cathedral and a groundskeeper, a few people incurred minor lacerations, and several others were treated for shock. No Firsts were harmed, and since they were the only ones who were not plagued by questions and by the uncertainty that accompanied the shocking attack, they were doing all they could to help their human peers.

The authorities had no leads. The perpetrators could not be identified, and the only images available to the police and to the global enforcement agencies that offered their assistance were vague stills taken at intervals by a camera on a building close by, at the wrong angle to be of much help. Because of the religious nature of the site, extremists were suspected, but no group had come

forward, in fact all adamantly stepped up to deny involvement in this attack they knew would bring the
wrath of the world on their heads. Intelligence agencies
were already inclined to believe that the perpetrators were
working alone—a fact to which their unprofessional act
seemed to attest—and no one had a clue who they were
or why they attacked. For now, at least, it seemed that
no questions would be answered anytime soon, although
everyone would no doubt continue to investigate.

As the daylight grew brighter, crews began arriving
at the site to assess the damage, plan the repairs, start
clearing. The cathedral would soon be rebuilt. But while
stone and artifacts could be restored, the trust that was
now replaced with heavy suspicion would not be so easily
fixed.

It was also a day since the Light had erupted in full
force, finally returning to Her people, and this morning
the bombing was nowhere near the minds of the Firsts.
Those who had flocked to Aeterna were gone now, gone
back to their homes, to their families, to friends, but not
quite to their lives yet. Firsts worldwide were still coming
to grips with the unbelievable—the Light had returned.
Those who had been there told of what they had seen,
but everyone, each and every one of the Firsts, had felt
the Light reach out and touch them, uniting them all in
an instant as She had at the beginning of time, when She
had first come to them. In a fraction of a second, a place
that had been left empty and hollow deep within them,

within all the Firsts back to a past too long to remember, had filled, connecting them to one another as they hadn't been since the Light had last left them, and to Aelia in a way that would allow her to reach out to them at will, even after she finally lowered her head and closed her eyes that day, allowing the Light that she was to recede, leaving the air charged with its presence.

The feeling among the Firsts was a mix of awe and elation. For them, the belief in the Light had been their very essence. For this peaceful species that could no longer find its place in an overwhelming world, and that was increasingly fearing discovery, the fear that came with the thought no one dared utter, that the Light might never again return to guide and protect Her people, was unbearable, bringing with it despair that threatened their very survival. Grasping with all their strength on to memories that lay dormant in their very souls, the Light's people had been crying out for help, for Her return, for too long.

And now She was here, right there at Aeterna.

The time had finally come.

Neora and Aelia strolled along the lake. Aelia liked it here. It was peaceful. There were no people around them now, in fact the only person she could see was Ahir, who was sitting on the stone terrace of the great house.

Loud quacking caught her attention and she turned to the lake, where a flock of geese was landing. The area was rich with wildlife that was obviously enjoying the protection of Aeterna and seemed to easily coexist with it.

She watched the geese, gazed at the gentle flap of wings of a colorful butterfly that flew past, felt the gentle play of sun, clouds, and wind surround her. It was all clearly felt, heard, and seen, but ever since the day before it was more than that. She sensed it all on a new, subtle level. Elemental, was the word that came to her mind. As if she was now somehow a part of the very fabric of existence.

Beside her, Neora was silent, keeping a respectful distance. Like Firsts everywhere, the keeper of the faith too had felt the Light. But unlike them, she, like her predecessors, had been taught Her full essence and force. And not only that, what she had seen, Aelia's impossibly fast transition to what She was born to be, that which had erupted within Her at Her own bidding as She sought to help Her people, led Neora to believe that more than just the Light and its bearer, what she was witnessing was what no other knew. No one but the Keepers.

That which had been foreseen by the first bearer of the Light *would* be. In fact, Neora believed it was already happening. But she would not tell, would not say a word of this prophecy of ancient times, not even to Aelia, the First of the Firsts. She would stand by Her, teach Her, but, as was foretold, would say nothing and let it be as it should.

Ahir sighed at the sight he never ceased to hope he would see in his lifetime—the Keeper and the First standing together beside the lake. He felt more at peace than he had in decades. The Light was here and his grandson had been found and had already stepped into his rightful place as the Protector. True, there were many more challenges to come, but now the Firsts had what they needed to contend with them.

Movement brought him out of his reverie, and he smiled as Adam walked over. Adam placed his hand on the old man's shoulder as a greeting and sat down beside him. He settled back and rubbed his neck, stifling a yawn. The day before had been long, as was the night. He had spent a large part of both at the control center with Rolly and Ahir as they spoke with each head of defense and security, briefing them and revising each community's respective security protocol. The organization was not expected to act again immediately, not after the frequency of its recent actions and the publicity of the most recent one, the bombing, but eventually it would act, and the Firsts had to be ready. And then, after he'd returned to his rooms, he had gone directly to his own screen, and connected to the control center that never stopped humming throughout the night, to follow the incoming information both from the bombing site and Aeterna itself.

It was dawn when Adam finally got into bed, and still he could not sleep. His mind was on Aelia. Just like all the Firsts, he too had felt her reach out, touch him, awaken that which was dormant in him as she did in all the others. What he saw, standing not far from her, was so much stronger than what he had already seen before. What he felt was powerful beyond reason. But unlike the others this also affected his connection with her, the part of him that was her Protector. He had felt it intensify within him, respond to the Light, the synergy between them strengthening it. And him. When the Light around her receded, what he now was did not. He was, quite simply, the Protector in full force. And with this finally came the sobering realization—he was responsible for the safety of she who held the fate of the Firsts in her hands.

And so lying in bed, his mind would not relent, constantly going over everything, trying to think if there was anything about her security he might have missed, realizing he still had so much to learn about the Firsts, about their capabilities, before he could hope to keep her as safe as he wanted her to be. And before he could truly know what would be needed to keep the Firsts themselves safe as they went about their daily lives worldwide.

It was on his way back to the control center that he'd seen Ahir outside and had decided to join him. He already felt comfortable with the old man, but this didn't really surprise him. Ahir had been behaving toward him as if Adam had never been gone, as if he was a grandfather just spending time with his grandson as he always had. And Adam was reacting to this, it was making him feel at home.

They watched Neora and Aelia as the current and hoped for leaders of the Firsts sat down on a bench by the lake, under a huge tree whose branches arched above the two women, providing a gentle shadow in the day's clear sun.

"You've lived with a lot of uncertainty. About me. About her. It must have been hard," Adam said.

Ahir nodded. "When your parents were killed and you were gone, I searched for you, I traveled everywhere possible. And when I didn't find you, I could not go on. And I could not come back here, where everything reminded me of all of you. By then I thought you must be dead. Otherwise, why could I not find you? I wasn't thinking clearly anymore."

He indicated Neora. "It was about a year after you were taken. Neora flew to see me, against security's opinion, mind you. Leaving Aeterna is something the Keepers never do. But she did, she knew she was the only one I might listen to. I was a mess, I will be the first to admit it. And she sat facing me, and she said it straight. 'If the boy is dead, we all are.' Which was obviously true because you are the last of the Protector line, and there has never been a Light without a Protector. And without the two of you, it would be the end of the Firsts. And then she says, 'So tell me where Adam is.'

"And I started thinking clearly again because she was right. And I told her, 'My son and his wife, that was a professional kill. Whoever took the boy had to have targeted him specifically, must know who he is. Must have something they want him for.' 'The Light,' was all Neora said, and I realized what must have happened. The organization had to have taken you. I kept an open mind over the years, you should know, looked everywhere and at everyone, just in case. But the organization was always the most likely bet. If for some reason they thought the Light was back, they would want to get rid of Her. And they would need you for that. They could always kill you later and stop the Protector line, and that would be the end of it. And in the meantime, they would have to keep you away from us, hide you until you grew up, until the time came when they would decide to kill Her." He smiled. "I remember it as clear as day, Neora stood up and said, 'Let's go then, we have work to do. This will not end with us.'" He chuckled softly. "I got on the plane back with her. And she was right, wasn't she? It will not end with us. It starts again, with you two. I tell you, I owe her my life."

He paused and turned to his grandson, his eyes somber again. "I'm sorry. I am so sorry I did not find you earlier."

Adam shook his head. "I can tell you one thing. Looking back, you never had a chance of finding me."

"They changed your identity and masked your existence. You were too young to remember who you were, and they would know how to make you forget what you did remember. Knew we would be searching. Knew exactly what to do to keep you away. I know. I have told it to myself a thousand times. It does not make it any better."

"I'm here now."

Ahir smiled. "Yes, yes you are."

Something Ahir had said triggered something in Adam's mind. "You said the organization needed me to get rid of Aelia, that that's why they took the risk of taking me."

Ahir didn't answer immediately. "You are the only one who can kill Her," he finally said.

Adam started. "That's what Jennison said when I went back to confront him. I thought he was just trying to play me. What does that mean?"

"I can only tell you what we know. Once She who has the Light within Her is born, the Light remains one with Her until She dies, and protects Her. To an extent. She is mortal and can get hurt, and She can be harmed, but She cannot be killed. And yet for some reason, the Protector can kill Her. Why is a mystery to us. The Light Herself had created the line of Protectors, which is linked with Her like none other is, and had gone to the extent of giving any Protector who is in fact protecting a living Light enhanced abilities—instincts, strength, durability. And yet the Light has also given Her Protector, and only him, the ability to kill Her." Ahir shook his head.

"So she needs the Protector to keep her safe, and yet she had chosen to give him the ability to kill her, essentially making herself most vulnerable to him." Adam looked at the woman sitting beside the lake, a frown on his face. A memory rose unbidden to his mind, the split second he had shot her. He forced it away.

"I know, Son, but we do not have answers to everything. I remind you that we do not even know the origin of the Light, why She first came to be and how. All we know is that She is."

"She trusts me."

"Yes, She does."

"No, I mean, back there, she had her chances, she could have gotten away from me. Told someone around us what was happening."

"I know what you meant," Ahir said quietly.

Adam was still watching Aelia. His way. She was calm, comfortable. Good.

His eyes narrowed suddenly, and he turned to Ahir. "How did they know?"

"I'm sorry?"

"How does the organization know? About me, about our family, about the Protectors, the Firsts and the Light? How does the organization know so much?"

Ahir was silent, but Adam wasn't about to relent.

"Grandfather."

Now it was Ahir who started and turned toward his grandson. Adam's eyes, bluer, darker than the old man's, were intense on his.

Ahir braced himself. More than anything, this was hard to admit. "We told them."

Adam thought he heard wrong. "Sorry, what?"

Ahir stood up. "Come, Son. I imagine Aelia has the right to hear this too."

Adam followed him down the terrace steps. "You and Neora, you go back a long time." In fact, it seemed that they barely needed a spoken word to understand each other.

Ahir looked at him questioningly.

"You're very familiar with each other."

"We were both young when we assumed our responsibilities. Neora was in her early-twenties when her predecessor died and I was just a bit older when I officially became her Protector that day. I've served alongside her for, oh, almost sixty years now." Ahir stopped and turned toward Adam, "But it is more than that, Son. She is and will until our last day be my dearest friend." The old man nodded slightly to himself and resumed walking, and Adam followed him with a smile. Then something occurred to him.

"Wait, what happened to the previous Protector? He didn't die too, did he, before you became Protector?"

Ahir laughed. "My father? No, not at all. He passed when he was a hundred and nine."

"So he simply retired?"

"Yes. He decided it would be best if Neora and I started our way together, and I had him to guide me for years after, so it worked out well." He chuckled. "And don't you worry, Adam, now that you are back, and the Light is finally here, I plan to be around for a long time. I wouldn't miss it. My guess is Neora would not, either."

They approached the bench and Neora took her old friend's hand in greeting. Ahir saw in her face a happiness he had never seen before, as if a weight had been lifted off her shoulders. Where her predecessors' death was the only release of their burden and unrealized hope, she had lived to see the Light return to take Her rightful place. His eyes moved to the other end of the bench, where Aelia sat, his grandson, Her Protector, now standing beside Her, his eyes unconsciously sweeping the terrain around Her even in this most secure place of all, watching out for Her without realizing he was doing so. Adam's gaze came to rest on Aelia, and Ahir smiled. The connection between them was already unmistakable.

Chapter Eighteen

Ahir sat down beside Neora. "Adam just asked me how the organization knows about the Firsts and about the two of them."

"Ah, yes." She sighed. "Well, no question can be left unanswered, Ahir. They have a right to know it all. In fact, they would need to know it all."

Ahir nodded and turned to Aelia. "As I've already told Adam, the organization knows so much because the Firsts themselves told them."

Aelia looked from him to Neora and back at him in disbelief.

"It's true. You see, decades ago, after another one of the terrible wars of this world, the Council made a decision to break the vow the Firsts made when humans first developed enough to be seriously considered. Back then, the Firsts vowed not to interfere with the development of this young species, but rather to live hidden on this planet. This vow had not changed even as humanity grew, and even as the Firsts knew they would have to live among them. But by then it was meant to protect us."

He tried to find the words. "You need to understand, we have seen war after war, and that last great one, the last world war, what we saw in it was simply too much, and we thought it was time to try to show humanity there was a different way. A better way. And our people themselves needed this. They felt lost, the Light—" He paused and looked at Aelia, as if the realization that She was actually there hit him all over again. "*You* were gone for so long, and the Council worried that our people might be losing hope, starting to think that we would remain alone, and life here had become so difficult for us, we had to try to find a way, to do something. Think about it, a small species having to coexist alongside a huge one that keeps growing and spreading and fighting, so much violence, so much hate and destruction, and they simply did not learn.

"But still there were many of them who were different, who tried to do some good in this world. It was because of them, the kind ones, that we wanted to reach out to humankind. We hoped that if we managed to teach them, show them how we had chosen to live, maybe one day we would be able to truly live alongside them, and not hidden, exiled in our own home. So the Council made the decision to expose us, and the previous Keeper agreed, though the Protector, my father, did not.

"It was done so carefully, and yet it went so terribly wrong. A delegation of the Council contacted a tiny organization that had taken upon itself to bring peace to the world. We watched them for a while, and they seemed to be an honest group striving to transcend the differences between countries, religions and cultures, to bring humanity together. Unfortunately, once their governing board heard us, understood who we were, they became split in their opinions. Some welcomed us and what we brought. But others became convinced that we were a danger to humanity, that we were a threat to them for the mere reason that we are a different species. They were convinced that we were simply trying to learn all we could about them, infiltrate them. That we, the advanced ones, were bound to want the entire world for ourselves, despite the fact that we had not done anything to warrant this opinion and have never harmed humankind, never even interfered with them." His tone turned bitter. "We were so wrong. We thought they were ready to move beyond the old thought patterns of destruction, of selfishness and greed. Patterns that defy coexistence even within the human species, let alone with a species outside it.

"So you understand, ironically it seems that it was their meeting with us that changed the organization. Before they knew about us, they were all about 'peace for the world', meaning peace for humanity of course, although we did not know this then. Their people were diplomats, negotiators. The only ones who were armed among them were bodyguards that they kept for their interventions in the more dangerous regions of the world. But after they met us, the newly-formed hawkish faction removed, if I may be so delicate, the more peaceful core of the group, and effectively took over. It then embarked on turning the organization into a militaristic operation, aimed at forcefully removing any threat to humankind.

"Unfortunately, the potential of this new organization

they created seems to have made them greedy. Within a very short time their objectives evolved, no longer having anything to do with peace or with what was best for humanity, and everything to do with ultimate control. Their aim was, and still is, to become the power that runs the world, to bring the organization to the position where one day it would lead humanity. Control its fate."

Adam's brow furrowed. He more than anyone knew the extent of the organization's capabilities, the way it was run. But these goals . . . run the world?

"Yes," Ahir said. "They may have become smarter in hiding their true purpose, but I remind you that we were there at the beginning, when they were still forming, deciding. When it was still easier than it is today to follow their actions. Luckily, they want to achieve their goals without encountering resistance, so they are careful to avoid outsiders knowing about their existence, and this has slowed their progress. However, our existence also stands in their way. We are the rogue element in their equation. Even without the fact that we know who those behind the organization really are and that we would never bow to their will, imagine what would happen if we decided once again it is time for humanity to know about us—now there is a world changer." He sighed. "And so we became the enemy."

"So it was during the talks with the original organization that they were told what they shouldn't have?" Adam asked. There really was no other way to put it, from where he stood.

"It was a little more complicated than that," Ahir

answered. "At the beginning they really were not told much. We knew that the fact of our existence was in itself significant enough information for them to have. And we would never intentionally let them know how technologically advanced we really were, because at the time the information would have been too overwhelming. Which is lucky, imagine where they would be today with our technology and our knowledge. They were not told about our origins and history either, only enough to make them understand that our way is peace and that there is so much we can teach them." He stopped.

It was Neora who continued. "In an attempt to explain more about who we are, our delegates tried to explain our . . . beliefs, you could say, in terms familiar to humans', in the terms of their own faiths. And so they told them a story, about a light that appeared and guided us, and its protector. And about its symbols. The two children born among the Firsts."

"Symbols?" Aelia asked.

"Well, knowing humanity's way of thinking and its beliefs, the Council at the time did not believe they could handle that much of the truth. All the more so if it came together with the news about an ancient species coexisting alongside them, which was already a lot to take in. So the delegates made it seem as if the Light and its Protector are just an ancient story, much like the stories underlying humanity's religious beliefs, and that every generation two people are selected to serve as symbols of them."

"All in all," Ahir said, "nothing they were told should

have been enough to do harm. If not for the next mistake we made. We thought that trust should begin with trust, and so we did not watch them at first, and had no idea that they had already changed, already made up their mind about us. So, in an effort to give them a better understanding of who we are, our delegates took them one step farther. While they were careful not to tell the organization anything about where the Firsts were in the world, they did tell them about the Rome center, under the cathedral, and about Aeterna." He paused. "The delegation wanted, and the Council agreed, to show them something of ours, let them meet some Firsts. They only spoke about Aeterna, but the cathedral center they took them to. Not only that, in the spirit of cooperation our people there talked freely with them, since we, and we thought they, too, came in the hope for a long-lasting friendship."

"How naive we were." Neora's sigh was deep, regretful.

Ahir put his hand on hers and continued. "They came out realizing just how much more technologically advanced we are than them, even though we thought we were careful with what we exposed them to. And this seems to have made them think, or at least enforced their already existing belief, that we are a threat. But not only that, in retrospect we understand that they must have learned from our people there just how much we await the light that we had told them was just a story, its return in the form of a woman who is identified by the man who is her protector, is protected by him, and can only be killed by him. So that even if they still did not think that our belief was based on facts, they now knew its importance to us. For humanity, their beliefs, their religions turn the world. And that is what they perceived our belief was for us. They came to understand that this was our Achilles' heel. Take this belief and the Firsts will lose what drives them. Have the organization destroy this belief, and the Firsts will fear it and bow to the humans." He paused, let what he was saying sink in.

"It was after that visit that everything happened, and very quickly. One moment the two sides were talking, and the next half the people we had been negotiating with were dead, and the remaining half turned their backs on us, but not before they made a deal with us, a cold truce, in a manner of speaking. We would stay quiet, hidden as we were in the past, and they would leave us alone. It was more complicated than that, of course, but that is the essence of it. We decided to take a step back and reassess our failed attempt, reassess humanity and its danger to our people, some even said. There was talk of leaving Aeterna and the cathedral, but eventually we kept both. As far as Aeterna is concerned, they were told about its existence but nothing else. They have never been here, and Aeterna has always been the abode of the Keepers. A well protected, conveniently placed abode. As for the cathedral, it was part of the truce agreement and a testing point for us, for their intentions then and at any time thereafter. And they haven't approached either until now."

Ahir took a breath. "Following that fiasco the majority of the Council was replaced, and the decision to remain apart from the humans was reinforced, with all Firsts being briefed about the attempt and cautioned to be careful about trusting the humans. Sometime later I replaced my father, and Neora replaced the Keeper. We have honored the truce, but we have also kept a careful eye on the organization over the years, saw it grow and strengthen, become so much more dangerous. But for decades they did nothing. Excluding, of course, what we are finally certain of now. Taking the two of you, and the murder of my son and his wife." He addressed Aelia. "And we have to assume that your family was somehow their victim, too. We are looking into that," he assured her.

Adam mulled what he'd just heard, then addressed Ahir. "Denole said something about a message that was intercepted the day you first saw Aelia."

"Yes." Ahir shook his head in distaste. "Wanting to show the visitors that we are willing to share our knowledge, the delegates showed them a sample of our technology, to demonstrate how we can help advance humanity. Specifically, they showed them data transmission technology. Keep in mind that this was long before humanity had the computer technology it has today, so what the visitors were shown was hugely impressive. Not only that, they were given that sample of the technology, as a gift. And that was another bad mistake, because giving away such a gift to a friend is one thing, but when that friend turns on you and targets you as its worst enemy, well . . ." He spread his hands in unhidden frustration.

"Then several years ago we discovered that the organization has kept the data transmission component we gave them, had integrated it with the humans' now advanced-enough computer technology and were using it to try to get information from our systems. However, immediately after our talks with them had failed, all those decades ago, we prudently discontinued our own use of this technology and have only kept it in a stand-alone system in the cathedral center, to alert us if the organization would ever attempt to misuse our gift. So all they managed to do was hack into and reconfigure the equivalent component at our end to periodically send them data, specifically messages sent to and from the cathedral center." He shrugged. "We, of course, were alerted as soon as they made the first attempt. Considering the nature of this act and the fact that it violates the truce, we decided to learn more about what they were up to. There was obviously no danger to us, since the component cannot connect to our main systems, and we now reconfigured it to allow it to intercept some low-security messages to and from Aeterna, so that they would think their ruse was working."

He coughed, embarrassed, and looked at Aelia. "The day you came to the cathedral and I understood who you were I sent a message to Aeterna. A short message. 'I found Her, She is here.' Except that I sent it through the low-security system. The wrong system. With my authorization, it did not try to stop me." He shook his head. "I'm sorry, both of you. It was my mistake. The cathedral center has always been so careful, so strict, and I was not even supposed to go anywhere near their systems myself, but I confess that I was in shock and I did and the most important message of all our lives was intercepted by those who had hurt you both." He bowed his head. "I truly am sorry."

"Why?" The question came in unison, surprising both Ahir and Neora.

"Because of that message, the organization sent me after Aelia," Adam said, and Aelia continued, "And us meeting is what triggered it all and is how we ended up here. I doubt anything you could have done otherwise would have been this effective."

"Benjamin died," Ahir said.

"True," Adam said. "But, no disrespect, only Benjamin died. And that's because everything that happened took place where Aelia was then, and not here. There, it was only me and her, and Benjamin and Semner. Without that message, even if you had somehow been successful convincing Aelia to come here, it would most likely have also brought me here when I was still on their side— the organization was watching her, they would still know that she was gone, would figure out that she came here. I still would have been sent after her. And here, I would have had to go through I don't know how many Firsts to get that first contact with Aelia, the contact that would have made me realize something was wrong. Who knows how that would have turned out."

"So everything is as it should be." Aelia concluded the matter.

Chapter Nineteen

Adam and Aelia remained sitting on the bench, alone. Aelia was deep in thought, and Adam could feel her worry. He remained silent. Where normally he might just go ahead and ask, with her he waited, knowing she would sense the question, that she would speak when she was ready.

The woman who was the Light was torn. The day before had changed it all, as what she had been destined to become finally came to be. She now felt her people, their connection with the Light alive within her, and she knew what she meant to them. But the harshness of the recent events was still fresh, and what she had just learned about the organization, about how these events came to be, left her deeply worried.

"In the balance of things, am I more a danger to the Firsts than help?"

Adam turned to look at her. Her uttering the thought only served to intensify what he felt from her.

"They have lived for so long without the Light," Aelia said, "led by the Keepers and the Protectors, and I know what I mean to them, but at least they were safe. Even the organization stayed away for so long and might have left them alone. You yourself would never have been taken, Adam, never raised by strangers, never targeted like you are now, your parents, my family, they might still have been here. Ahir, the loss of his son, the life he's had looking for you, how can that be worth it? And these past days, just a few days, and look what has already happened. Without me Benjamin would still be alive, that bombing wouldn't have happened, the Firsts would still be safe." She counted them off, one by one. "And that's only the past," she continued, her voice barely audible. "What about the future? You, all of you, your future?"

She turned and her eyes met his. "Am I a danger to you?"

Adam turned his gaze back to the lake. He thought about the life he might have had, the man he might have been. Always a Protector, never a killer. Adam, always Adam, and not Kyle, never Kyle.

And no Aelia.

His next thoughts he spoke out loud, his voice quiet, but clear. "Yes, you were the trigger. But I assure you, Aelia, that even if you hadn't been born, at some point the organization would have decided that the Firsts are in their way, or, in the least, have an immediate potential of being a disruptive factor in their plans. And then it would be either getting rid of them or finding a way— and not a pleasant one—to control them. And then what?" His eyes were intent on hers. "Believe me, you have no idea what they're capable of doing, if—no, when—they decide it's time they take over, and come after the Firsts in the process. Look at what they already did. They had no qualms about kidnapping two young children of the Firsts, sending one into their version of hell in an attempt to destroy her and turning the other into a killer, then sending killers after both and trying to bomb a center of the Firsts—even though there was a place of worship for humans right on top of it."

"But you would have grown up here, among the Firsts. You would be here to help them."

"True. But there's another way to see this. With what I know about the organization, what we all know now, we have a better chance of protecting the Firsts. And the way I see it, having lived among humans, having been raised by the organization, and with what they've made me into, I'm guessing I'm exactly what I need to be in order to be the Protector of *this* Light, *this* First of the Firsts. Which I'm thinking will be just the right person to deal with everything that's happening as soon as she realizes she's the only one who can."

She shook her head, stood up, and walked to the edge of the water. "People got hurt. People died."

He followed her, turned her back toward him and held her eyes with his, his voice harsh. "I know you feel responsible, but you're not. You don't need to decide to take your place among the Firsts for people to die, Aelia. The organization will continue coming after you and after them, after us, no matter what you do. And you know what, you're forgetting that the organization isn't the only one out there. As it is these are different times. How much longer do you think the Firsts will succeed in remaining hidden? What happens when humans do discover them? At least as the Light among them you can help them fight back. With you they have a chance. You're giving them a real chance."

First of the Firsts. That's what Neora had said too. Aelia remembered Neora's description of the first Light, how she had guided her people, led them, how her next forms did the same. She thought about the challenges of the Firsts in this era, so different than the past. Thought about the need to be more than just the Light within them, about being the one who guided them, protected them, in the reality of this world she knew only too well. "There's a huge leap between what I did yesterday and what they would need."

"There's a huge leap between the woman I had at my rifle's scope just days ago and the woman standing before me now," he said evenly. "And you're forgetting, you've only just begun. What will the Light show you in the coming months, years? What will you become?"

She was listening to him. Good. "Look, whichever way you look at it, you weren't born into a peaceful reality in the first place. Maybe things are in fact getting worse for the Firsts faster than they would have otherwise, and yes, the organization is now in danger of actively coming after them. But frankly, with what I've seen these past days"—He chuckled incredulously—"and what I saw yesterday, I'm getting that what you are is actually impossible to even imagine. And that's probably the only variable that can tilt the equation in favor of the Firsts and against the organization. They'll have no idea how to even begin dealing with you. And who knows, on the way you might even be able to help humans. You've lived among them, Aelia, you know that there are a lot of good people out there."

She gazed at the water, her eyes far away. The wind played gently with her hair, trying to get her attention, but she didn't heed it. Eventually she smiled a little. "Apparently there is more than one way to protect me, Protector." She turned to him. "Thank you, Adam."

He smiled.

She took in a deep breath. "If I want to help the Firsts, there's a lot I need to learn."

"You will."

"And then there's dealing with the organization."

"I'll deal with them. It's my job to keep them away from you."

"No," she said thoughtfully. "We do this together. I know you want to protect me, but ultimately it's up to the two of us to protect the Firsts, and we'll both have to deal with those who are a threat to them." She looked at him with resolve. "You didn't ask for it, and I didn't ask for it. But we are it. And we do this together."

His wanting to protect her made him want to argue, but she was right. Whatever happens, it would hit her too, hurt her, either directly or through her people, to whom she was now connected. She would be a part of it, there would be no way around that.

He let it go at that, knowing also that it would be easier to protect her if she didn't feel she had to hide what she was doing from him thinking he might try to stop her, be overprotective. He'd been a bodyguard before, for the organization. He knew what to do. And this wasn't a temporary mission like in the past, either. He was with her for life, and the First and the Protector, Aelia and Adam, would have to figure out how to do this together.

Somehow, he wasn't worried about that.

Jennison got out of the car and walked to the entrance of the facility, leaving his driver to park. He had finally gone home after watching the media coverage of the bombing for hours, and the first thing he'd done when he got there was to turn on the television. Restless, he came back to the facility just a few hours later. At least here he could think more clearly.

They had no clue, he was relieved to see. No clue at all. The media was his only way of getting information, because he didn't dare employ the organization's resources for that, not now. He'd already called some people at the Italy office, people who were loyal to him, or at least afraid enough of him to obey him and not the organization, and had them remove any sign of his involvement in the bombing, or of the fact that the bombers were part of the organization at all, so that the board would not discover that this botched act was a result of his decision. Once he had done that, he dared not contact the Italy office again, lest his interest arouse suspicion. He smiled bitterly. In the past, it was Kyle he would send to cover his tracks. Of course, most likely if Kyle had been here he would have talked him out of doing it. How ironic.

He disregarded the greetings of the guards at the front desk and rode the elevator down to the first underground level. Mercifully, at this hour this level was nearly empty. He walked directly to his office, and, sitting behind his desk, turned on the television screen on the opposite wall. He switched channels. The bombing was already being replaced by other, newer stories. Soon enough the entire event would be forgotten.

He muted the volume of the television and threw the remote on the desk. First Kyle turns, then the woman gets away—with Kyle, then Semner's body turns up as a delivery to Jennison himself at the airport—that's two of the organization's best men, and now the failed bombing, which, frankly, was lucky for him that it failed. If it had succeeded, if the cathedral had been destroyed, if clergy or tourists had been killed, if the Firsts had been exposed to the world, or perhaps worse, if his actions would have brought them to retaliate against the organization... Which they still might, he realized. He had no idea how the Firsts would react but had little doubt they would trace the bombing back to him, considering his—and the organization's—past actions. And worse, they now had Kyle and his knowledge. Yes, too many ifs, too many mistakes. He knew he had no more leeway with the board, not at all if they found out that he was responsible for the bombing, that he had involved the organization in such a reckless act, endangering it on so many levels.

Right. Okay, what was done was done. It was up to him to fix this, up to him to succeed in such a way that would convince the board to keep him around despite his recent failures. He just needed to do something that would impress them. Yes, something . . . No, not against *them*, not against those blasted Firsts. It wouldn't solve anything, and would only antagonize them more. No, he needed something more effective, he needed to take away the very foundation of their strength, hit the one thing that would make any plans they might have to retaliate against the organization crumble before they even took form. Well, two things, really.

He sat back and thought, an idea forming in his mind. After a while, he got up and walked briskly through the corridors to the elevator, and rode it down to the indoors training range.

He couldn't get to Kyle and the woman. But he could make them come to him.

Chapter Twenty

The elderly man closed his office door, ready to end the day. He thought about the next day's lecture. He loved days when he lectured, loved seeing the eager faces of his students, loved their questions. His work at the Center for Human Behavior was his main activity, and he appreciated its importance. But he loved teaching. He put the key in his pocket and turned away from the door, taking his briefcase in one hand and his coat in the other. At sixty-five, nights like this were already too cold for his taste.

He walked through the corridor, his normally light gait heavy today, his head hanging. It would all be perfect except for Aelia. He was terribly worried, terrified for her since that news broadcast that talked about the murder in her building, the body they had found, the woman who was missing and who was thought to have been kidnapped by the unknown murderer. The police hadn't released her name at first, saying this was for her safety and necessary to avoid impeding the investigation, but he had tried again and again to call her and her cellphone was turned off. He even tried to go to her apartment but found it was cordoned off, and no one would tell him anything.

Finally her neighbors and the building's doorman spoke to the media, and soon the terrible news had been confirmed for him, that it was his Aelia. He had immediately contacted the police, told them about her, about his protégée, and this seemed to convince them that she was indeed innocent in all this. But it did not help find her. He answered all their questions, told them all he could, but could not offer any more information. They had kindly tried to reassure him that they were doing all they could to find her, that her kidnapper was probably keeping her alive, otherwise he would have killed her right there, in her apartment. But he was not to be consoled. He was worried, and this was taking a toll on him. His wife, Sarah, was equally distressed, both about Aelia, who had a long ago become a part of their family, and about him, and had asked him to remain at home, wait for news there, but he refused. He needed to keep busy.

He walked down the wide, circular staircase of the center down to the lobby, greeted the night watchmen and exited the building through the doors that automatically opened before him. He stood for a long moment in the chilly night air, breathed in deeply, and turned his face up to the cloudy sky. He uttered a prayer, "Please, please let her be safe." Then he sighed and walked slowly to his car, which was parked a short distance from the entrance. He opened the car door and was about to get in but froze when he felt the gun at the back of his head.

In the Firsts' Rome center under the cathedral, Denole frowned. For the first time ever, a message was coming in to the standalone system that held the data transmission component the organization had established a link to. The organization would be well aware that this act would betray their attempts to spy on the Firsts, and yet they had chosen to do it.

It was a message that startled Denole into urgently calling Rolly.

"Aelia?"

"It's Stan. Professor Stanley Shell."

They were in one of the rooms along the corridor immediately outside Aeterna's control center. The message Rolly had played for Aelia, Adam and Ahir had ended, and only the photo of the organization's prisoner remained on the screen. The elderly man was sitting at a table, looking dazed. He had a glass of water before him, and no one seemed to be in the room with him. He didn't seem to be hurt, except for the obvious fear this trauma must have been causing him, but the message was clear. The man would be disposed of unless Aelia and Kyle came alone and gave themselves up to Jennison at an address that, Aelia recognized, was in one of the new neighborhoods at the edge of the city she and Adam had recently escaped.

"Yes, I know," Adam said.

She threw him a questioning look, and he explained, "The information I got from the organization about you, my target, listed him as your mentor at the university and your boss at the center."

"The Center for Human Behavior," Aelia said absent-mindedly. It seemed so far away now, a part of the different life of a different person. She shook her head in disbelief. Now that was an understatement.

She turned her attention back to the image before her. Jennison had Stan. The anger came out of nowhere, and she made a conscious effort to control it. She knew that she would not radiate this feeling to those around her, or to any of the Firsts, other than the Protector. The part of her that held her personal feelings was isolated, kept safely away. Her predecessors, knowing they sometimes had to mask their own emotions and concerns as they led their people, had, over the centuries, learned to do so, and the warning that she should do the same, together with the ability to do it, had already been passed to her through their memories within her. Still, she couldn't afford to have anger mar her judgment right now, and so she forced herself to suppress it.

"He matters," Adam stated, intending this to be a question but at the same time wanting her to know that he knew he did.

"I thought you received information . . . ?"

"Not that much. There was no time, no need."

She nodded and said nothing, her eyes on the man on the screen. When she finally spoke, her voice was quiet. "We go back a long way. I couldn't get into college, the competition was high, and I only had a GED, I didn't finish high school because I worked. So I went there and found a way into the Dean of Students' office, and that was Stan. His secretary tried to kick me out, but he listened. Next thing I knew I was in with a full scholarship." She was quiet for a moment. "And it wasn't easy, I was an outsider and there were times when..." She trailed off, remembering. "He kept an eye on me all the way. The first person who ever helped me. Talked me into continuing to graduate school, gave me a job, he and his wife are the closest thing I had to a..."

"Family." Ahir completed her thought, understanding.

Aelia didn't answer. Then she turned to Adam. "Maybe Jennison didn't tell you, but he obviously knows Stan is a friend. Otherwise he wouldn't have taken him." Her gaze now included all of them, Adam, Ahir and Rolly. "He helped me in more ways than I can ever convey. And he's innocent. I want him safe." Her voice, though low, made clear the finality of the request.

Rolly shook his head. "Ma'am, we cannot put you in danger—"

Adam interjected in a tone that did not allow argument. "The First and I will go to meet Jennison," he said, intentionally using, for the first time, Aelia's formal title, and placing a hierarchy on the conversation.

"Rolly, we'll take one of Aeterna's defense units." He brought up on a holoscreen a map of the city and zoomed in on the meeting place. Satellite images followed immediately. "That's the place. Jennison claims he'll be alone, let's assume he's not. If he's once again acting on his own, and I'm betting he is, he'll only use people from the facility. Their actions he can hide more easily."

His eyes were sharp and focused. "In this type of place, he'll be taking a sniper, but that sniper will be trained on the main targets only, that's Aelia and me." To Rolly's question how he could be sure, he answered, "Because I prepared quite a few such missions for him."

He continued. "He'll have people ready to attack us and will be expecting us not to come alone, which means he'll want to bring more operatives than he needs. But he can't pull people from missions without questions being asked, and there are only a few, if any, operatives of my level there at any given time. So most of those he'll take are the organization's trainee operatives currently on site at the facility. No more than a dozen or so. Even that is enough to raise questions but he can find a way to get away with that. Still, don't be mistaken, these aren't rookies. Trainee operatives start at military level." He contemplated the image before him. "Place our people here, here and here," he indicated on the screen.

Aelia nodded slightly to herself and left the room, leaving them to lay out a plan. She walked along the corridor and back up to the main house, aware of her people stopping to watch her as she walked by.

The plane ride was strained. Aelia stared out of the window, but saw nothing except the clouds they were flying through, clouds that reflected the haze of worry over her heart.

Adam, Rolly and Aeterna's elite defense unit, fully

armed, were up front going over their plan. Basically it came down to her and Adam being the bait. They were what Jennison was aiming for, and everyone on that flight knew that. And their plan was ultimately designed to achieve one goal, and one goal only—get her in and out of there and back to Aeterna safely.

Hers was somewhat different. She was going to get Stan Shell away from Jennison, and she wasn't going to return to Aeterna without Adam, Rolly, and each and every one of her people, people she was responsible for, returning safely with her. No life was expendable. That was not what she was about, and the sooner her people understood that, the better.

She closed her eyes and listened to them, in more ways than one, then opened her eyes again when Adam came and sat opposite her. She met his gaze. This was a far stretch from their flight in the opposite direction just days before. They now had their answers. But they also had more responsibility than they had ever imagined they would, and right now that responsibility just happened to involve a human who had done nothing but look out for a girl who had no one and who needed his help. He was an innocent victim.

And Aelia was not about to accept that either, an innocent victim.

Jennison was antsy. The time of the exchange was almost here, and soon he would finally have them. The men he had chosen were already in place—six in this building,

eight around it, ready to move if the targets brought
any of *them* as reinforcements or to join their peers in
the building if the meet turned messy, and a damn good
sniper. None of them knew the truth, all thought they
were after a rogue operative who had betrayed the
organization. He would have liked to use more people,
employ a more elaborate plan that would leave nothing
to chance, but time was short and, in any case, that was
all he could risk. As it was, other than the sniper and two
of these men, the others weren't the caliber he would
have preferred to take for such a mission.

Still, these were a lot of people for one man—even
if it was Kyle—and a woman who had no training at
all, all the more so since they wanted his prisoner alive,
while he himself couldn't care less. He had no intention
of keeping the terms of the exchange. He was holding
the guy alive only for leverage and was planning to
silence him when this was all over anyway. He figured
Kyle would guess that by now, but what the hell, he had
still agreed to the exchange. That had always been the
problem with Kyle, his stupid weakness. Best killer ever
but he never touched anyone except his target, taking
too much care to plan his missions so that no innocents
would be around.

Jennison checked his gun for the hundredth time. If
all went well, by the end of this thing the woman would
be in the organization's hands again and Kyle would be
dead. Or better yet, maybe they would both be dead. He
felt no remorse about Kyle. He was one of *them*, after all,
and Jennison had never forgotten that, not even when

Kyle was just a child, and even after all the years Kyle had been with him, virtually a part of his family. Kyle had to go. He was no longer useful for the purpose Jennison had taken him for, and the organization couldn't risk having him on *their* side.

And Jennison was tired of him getting in the way.

Jennison had chosen a neighborhood that had never quite become that, a live-in neighborhood. Under different circumstances it might have become another proud cluster of family-friendly apartment buildings interspersed with playgrounds and parks on the outskirts of Grand Rapids, but after yet another in a line of too frequent recessions hit, it ended up as nothing more than ghost buildings at different stages of their finishing.

Aelia looked through the passenger-side window of the reinforced SUV she was in, flown in from Aeterna. The buildings looked forlorn, shadowy giants against the dark sky, but then perhaps that was what made them such a fitting meeting place for this. Beside her, Adam maneuvered the vehicle to the rear of the outermost building and parked close to its wall, using it for cover. There were no other structures anywhere around them on this side of the building, only barren land that was originally supposed to be a park, the city's optimistic master plan had shown. It would allow a quick getaway if need be, Adam had explained to Aelia, and was better than parking on the other side, in the midst of the neighborhood, between buildings that could be used for hiding by Jennison's men. Not ideal, he said, but then that's precisely why Jennison would pick this place.

As they were instructed to do by Jennison, they were alone in the SUV. Nor did they see anyone around them, although Adam had warned Aelia that Jennison's people would not hesitate to try to get to her, and asked her to stay close to him, and certainly not to assume they were safe at any point. She didn't need the warning, not with everything that had happened around her, and not with the knowledge that her people could be hurt by her actions, that they would jump in to protect her without heeding their own safety. But she had acknowledged Adam's worry. She knew he needed to know she was safe to be able to operate freely.

"We're here," Adam said quietly, and Aelia heard Rolly confirm in her earpiece. It was time. Adam got out of the vehicle and walked around it, looking around as he did, his gun in his hand down by his side. He opened the passenger door, and Aelia got out. He motioned her to walk between him and the wall, and they walked into the building through what might have been the back entrance to its lobby. The concrete under their feet was bare, sadly covered in mud and littered.

They moved carefully, Adam guiding Aelia through the safest path, and ducked through a broken doorway into the staircase. Adam was vigilant, but no one approached them. The building was dark and deceptively quiet. They walked silently up to the first floor, where Adam stopped and listened, then exchanged a look with Aelia. They turned left, as Jennison had instructed, and followed a wide corridor until they came through the doorway of what would have been an apartment, to a living room that was lighted with mobile lamps. All lights were directed at Stan Shell, who was sitting on a chair in the middle of the room, his arms and legs bound. The elderly man looked tired and scared. Behind him, Jennison was leaning against the wall, his arms crossed on his chest. His eyes were on them as they approached, and there was unveiled hatred on his face.

Adam and Aelia stopped several steps from the professor. Aelia disregarded Jennison, her eyes on the prisoner.

Her old friend looked horrified at the sight of her. "No, Aelia, go, run, he'll kill you!" he called out in a hoarse voice and Aelia's heart broke. Even now he was looking out for her.

"Enough!" Jennison's voice boomed and Stan winced visibly.

Not heeding Jennison, Aelia walked over and kneeled before her friend. "Stan, it's okay, we'll get you back home—"

Jennison's voice rang with anger. "I said—"

He fell quiet as Aelia stood up slowly and met his eyes. He had expected her to be afraid. He'd monitored her over the years, saw with astonishment how she came through the cruel life he had placed her in, wondered about her. But still, who he was, he had always been sure that when it came down to it, she would be intimidated by him. Except that the woman who was standing before him, her eyes gray ice, wasn't the least bit afraid of him. No, he realized, it was more than that, more than him. She had no fear in her at all. And there was something about her, something different. Something that hadn't been in the woman he had sent Kyle after, the woman who had always seemed withdrawn, hesitant in a way.

His eyes moved to Kyle. He'd changed too, but then Jennison had already realized that when Kyle broke into his office. Jennison had been scared that day, the first time ever he'd actually had to face the killer he himself had created. There had been a moment back there when he had thought he would not get out of his office alive, and had been relieved when Kyle simply left without killing him. Still, this, now, this was worse. Kyle was clearly with her, and one of *them*. Jennison went chilly with the realization of what he had done, bringing Kyle into the heart of the organization and making him its best trained operative, and then sending him straight into *their* hands, inadvertently creating the perfect weapon against himself and the organization.

This thought made him focus. He took a step toward Aelia. "It's you, all this is over you. Walk away from this, from the Firsts, from who they believe you to be, and we'll leave them alone, them and him." He indicated Adam. "You don't even have to come with me now, and I won't come after you or go anywhere near anyone you know. Just walk away."

Aelia's eyes never wavered from his, and she remained silent.

Jennison was stunned to feel a pang of fear. He took

a step back, then forced himself to stop, to calm down. There was no choice, then. These two had to die. With a renewed sense of urgency, he called out, "Now!"

Four of his men charged the room with their guns drawn. Adam, who'd easily known where they were hiding, shot two, disabling both, before either of them even got a shot out, and the third got a shot out that nearly grazed Adam's arm before Adam shot him, injuring but not killing him either. The fourth found himself being tackled and thrown at two more who were coming through the door, and they tumbled back, getting up dazed to find themselves looking at the barrel of Adam's gun as he motioned them to stay down. Not a word was uttered.

All that time Aelia did not move. She remained standing in the same spot, her eyes on Jennison, throughout the entire commotion around her. She felt it all through Adam without having to look—the position of every person in the room, their moves, their reactions. He stopped them. He stopped them and he wasn't hurt. Rolly and the defense unit were not hurt, either. Eight more, yes, there were eight more of the organization's men who they intercepted outside the building. Her people she could read easily and knew they had acted efficiently and safely.

And there was the last one.

The guy in the opposite building. The sniper.

She closed her eyes and focused on him, and Adam turned to look at her as several members of the defense unit ran in and took over the captives he had kneeling at gunpoint. He felt it. He asked and without turning to him, without a word, she let him know. He ran to her and placed himself between her and the unglazed window through which the sniper was aiming, keeping an eye on Jennison, who looked dazed.

In the opposite building the sniper had the woman on his sight. He saw what happened in the room, and knew he was up. He began pulling the trigger, and then Kyle Rhys, the operative tagged by Jennison as rogue, moved in, hiding the primary target, but almost immediately she moved half a step to the side, raised her head, and *looked at him.*

Which was impossible because there was no way she could have seen him, no way at all, it was not humanly possible, it was—

The blinding light came out of nowhere, filling his eyes, flooding his mind. Pain shot through him and he gasped, confused, disoriented.

He passed out.

"Shoot, dammit, do it, take the shot, take it!" Jennison shouted, realizing he was losing his chance to get what he wanted. At least she would die, he thought, waiting, but his earpiece remained silent. In a final, desperate act of rage, he drew his gun and was about to aim it at Aelia when the weapon was wrenched out of his hand and he was thrown against the wall. He crumpled against it in defeat, Adam standing above him.

Aelia untied her friend and helped him to his feet.

She supported him out of the room, while Adam took one last look at the man he had grown up believing was his family, and left him with three unconscious operatives, motioning the defense unit to follow him with the remaining captives.

Rolly met them on the way and accompanied them to the front of the building, where the vehicles were now standing, including the one Aelia and Adam had arrived in. Her people had positioned themselves, some beside the SUVs, others with the captives. They were still alert, but no one else was coming. Jennison was past trying to go after them.

When they drove away, a line of dark SUVs with solemn Firsts in it, they left behind them the organization's operatives unhurt and tied at the front of the building. When Jennison would come out he would stand looking at some of the organization's best potentials tied in a row on the ground before him, unable to move until he cut their ropes. Which would be after his cry of rage chilled their blood. His only consolation was that these were his men, from the facility he controlled, and who would not want anyone to know of their easy defeat, so in theory he could control this failure.

Yes. Perhaps he could. Or so he thought until he did the final head count.

The sniper was gone.

Chapter Twenty-One

In the SUV that held Adam and a driver in the front, and Aelia and Stan Shell in the back, Aelia turned to her old mentor. Stan looked exhausted, but otherwise he seemed physically unharmed.

"We're taking you to a hospital," Aelia said with concern.

The older man put his hand on hers and shook his head. "No need, I'm perfectly fine. Those people, they didn't hurt me."

"I'm sorry, Stan. They were trying to get to me through you. This is because of me."

"No," he said, squeezing her hand in admonishment. "This is because of them. Whatever their reasons, they chose to take me, it was their choice, not yours."

She looked at him incredulously. "Same old Stan. Ever the wise mentor."

"Well, someone has to be." He laughed and winced a little.

"Stan," she began, but he shook his head.

"I'm fine, really. A bit tired maybe. I would much rather go home, Sarah must be so worried."

"We'll take you there," she said.

"Ma'am," the driver intervened, using the form of address he knew to use with humans around. "I'm afraid we can't go anywhere near the professor's house. He is considered a missing person, and the police are there."

Adam turned to look at Aelia. "And you're a missing person too," he reminded her.

She frowned, but Stan was the next one to speak. "Of course, I didn't think about it. They're right, you'd better drop me somewhere and leave." He gazed at her for a moment. "Although I must say, Aelia, I would very much like to know what's going on. Where have you been, what happened to you? Who were those men—and who are they?" He indicated Adam and the driver. "This, all these cars, these people, it looks like . . . like a motorcade. The police think you were kidnapped, but you weren't, were you?" He shook his head. "Why can't you go to the police? Why can't you tell them?"

"I can't, Stan," Aelia said quietly. "Not while those people are after me. When it's over, when I can, I'll straighten this mess out." Her eyes were somber on his. "And you can't say anything either, Stan, or tell anyone what happened tonight, no matter what they tell you, what they say about me. You can't even say you saw me."

Stan was quiet, and when he spoke again Adam understood why Aelia trusted him so much. "Why didn't you call me? I would have helped."

"I know you would have. But this is simply too complicated, my friend. It's too big. I didn't want to put you or Sarah in danger or make you accomplices in all this.

As it is look how it turned out, they still got to you, you could have been killed."

"That's what family is for, Aelia. Didn't I teach you that?" And indicating Adam and the driver, he asked her, "Any of them the man who was in your apartment? The man who they say took you?"

"That would be me," Adam said, catching the professor's eyes in the rear-view mirror.

"Did you kill that man?"

"No," Adam said evenly. "The people who took you did."

"He saved my life, Stan," Aelia said, "and he has been watching over me ever since."

Stan contemplated this quietly and then asked, his voice calm, "Will they come after me again? After Sarah? My kids?"

"No," Adam answered, and the eyes that held Stan's left no place for doubt.

Stan surprised Aelia by saying simply, "I believe you." And then he shook his finger at Adam. "You take care of her, you hear?"

"Yes, Sir," Adam answered, equally serious.

"Good," Stan said, leaning back and closing his eyes. "But I want to hear all about it when it's over."

Aelia looked at him quizzically. He was far too calm about this.

"Well," Stan surprised her again by speaking, still not opening his eyes, "you never were an ordinary kid, were you? I knew long ago I was getting into something there, whatever that would prove to be."

She smiled, and kissed the old man's cheek affectionately. He responded by hugging her hard. "You keep safe, you hear?" he whispered in her ear with a choked voice.

The convoy split in two, the vehicle with the captive, Jennison's sniper, moving off with one escort car while the vehicle Aelia and Adam were in, accompanied by the rest of the convoy, drove to let Stan off near a private clinic a friend of his worked in whom he trusted to keep quiet. They then made their way to the small airport they'd used, not far outside the city. The convoy continued directly to the hangar they originally disembarked in, while the SUV Aelia and Adam were in entered the adjacent hangar. Aeterna's official jet stood in its middle, ready to take off, with an Aeterna security detail positioned around it. As the SUV approached the jet, another security detail filed from inside it and surrounded the SUV. Adam and Aelia got out of the car, and Adam walked around it toward her.

"This jet will take you back to Aeterna." He indicated the stern men and women around them. "These people are the Keeper's security detail, they'll fly back with you, and Rolly will join you."

Rolly appeared through a side door and approached them. "The guys are securing the captive. You'll be good to go in a bit."

She tilted her head slightly in question.

"The jet we came in is still in the next hangar. That's where the rest of our people went. I'm taking it and them with Jennison's man."

The question in her eyes did not change.

"Time they knew."

He didn't have to say more. "Be safe," was all she said.

Adam smiled and winked. "This is the easy part."

He waited while Aelia walked up the stairs, closely guarded, and as the second security detail filed in, with Rolly in the rear, giving him one last wave before closing the door. As the hangar doors opened, a satellite above changed focus and Aeterna's control center issued a go, and the jet with the First on it rolled out. Adam watched it pick up speed and take off, and then walked into the adjacent hangar. Fifteen minutes later the second jet took off, carrying him and the captive, and the defense unit that had helped free Stan Shell.

On the top floor of a skyscraper in New York, no one was standing at any of the windows enjoying the magnificent view of the city outside. All those present in the large conference room were intent on the matter at hand. For them, at that specific moment, nothing else was more important.

Nothing at all.

Jennison sat alone at the front of the plane. He moved uncomfortably in his seat. These weren't the luxurious accommodations of one of the organization's executive jets. He had chartered this simpler one to avoid the records that went with the organization's formal flights, as part of his attempt to keep what he was doing from the board.

The three wounded men were flown separately to the facility. They would be treated on the medical floor there, under the guise of having been injured on a legitimate mission. The others were sitting well away from him, obediently quiet. He had already debriefed them and heard how other than the six who had been in the building with him and had actually made it to the attack on the targets, the rest were all intercepted either on their way into the building or while still positioned around it, virtually all at the same moment, which did not allow them to alert one another or him. None had seen their captors before they were captured or would be able to identify the masked men, and none had been hurt by them.

Jennison rubbed his eyes. He'd taken good men, none of whom had trained with Kyle, and yet Kyle seemed to have been one step ahead of them. If only more men had made it into the room he had that professor in, maybe they would have managed to at least hurt Kyle, or the woman, and if that damn sniper had done his job, it might all have turned out differently. He thought he had it all planned. He and the professor in that first floor room, the sniper ready to fire if need be, four of his men rushing the targets in the room and killing Kyle and hopefully the woman, with two following immediately, as a redundant addition, he'd hoped, and the rest stationed immediately outside and ready to act if anyone else tried to interfere. He'd even taken the risk of remaining in the room, where he himself might get hurt in the mayhem. Just to see it end.

He seethed with anger. Not only were Kyle and the woman not even hurt, they just walked out of there with the professor. And one of his men. This was supposed to be easy—fifteen trained men against one of their own, albeit the organization's best, an untrained woman and a chubby old professor. And yes, *them*. Kyle obviously brought help, better people than Jennison had expected, but whoever they were, they weren't in that room. At least that part of his plan should have worked.

He breathed in deeply. He had to get himself under control, there was no room for mistakes now. He needed to concentrate. He was already thinking of a cover story, a training mission gone wrong. And the men would not talk, not if they wanted to advance. And, well, live. Yes, there was still a way to salvage this. There always was.

Adam stopped in an isolated corner of the lowest level of the underground parking lot, and got his captive out of the car. The guy, the sniper Jennison had brought with him, was already tied up, but now Adam connected the knots he'd prepared for this purpose in a way that restricted the captive's movements, and stood still behind him. He could feel the guy's fear. He was trying to turn his head within the restraints, desperate to get a look at his captor. And this guy knew who Adam—whom he knew as Kyle—was. He was looked up to in the organization, respected and feared. Everyone knew who he was.

Adam waited, motionless, letting the guy's panic rise. Then, at just the right moment, he stepped forward until he nearly touched him, and, as the captive involuntarily jumped, pulled at the restraints just enough for the guy to know what would happen if he made a wrong move. Then he warned, his voice low, "Try something and you're dead. Play it right and you'll live to tell all about it."

The captive chuckled bitterly. "Yeah, right, you mean live for Jennison to kill me."

"I'm not taking you to Jennison," Adam said, and felt the guy relax a bit.

The captive did not resist when he led him toward an elevator. Adam knew the building well. He'd been here before countless times, most of them as part of a protection detail. Which was how he knew just which systems Rolly's expert who'd accompanied them throughout this mission had to remotely disable in a cascading sequence, and which entrance to drive in through at just the right moment. The camera and the security alerts in the elevator Adam chose were disabled too, at just the right time for him to enter it with his captive and to allow him to pull out the control panel and rig the override control so that the elevator did not stop on the way up to the building's top floor.

As the elevator doors opened again he pulled out his gun and, using his captive as cover, led him out before him, stopping so that he himself stood between the doors, which he rigged to remain open. The operatives stationed on this floor drew their guns and aimed, but Adam only said quietly, "Tell them I'm here."

He stayed where he was, the armed operatives surrounding him at a safe distance, confused at the situation before them. They knew him, each and every one of them. And while he'd recently been flagged as a security risk, a rogue operative to watch out for, these were all veterans who'd known him for a long time, trained with him and relied on him in missions, and all respected him for the man he was. None of them, he knew, would shoot him unless he made a move against them first.

The door to a room on Adam's left—the security control room for this floor—opened and a man came out. Adam knew him. Jon Melake, the organization's officer responsible for the protection of its more sensitive ranks, and these operatives' direct commanding officer. He would be here for the meeting of the organization's governing board, of course. Melake was the first officer Adam had served under in the organization, back when Melake was in charge of breaking in new recruits. He was a fair, no-nonsense man, and Adam had worked closely with him over the years in protective missions.

Melake walked over and stood facing Adam and his captive, but looked directly at Adam, disregarding the guy he had at gunpoint. The two men assessed each other. And then Adam did what none of the operatives around him expected him to do—he put his gun away.

The operatives around him moved, but Melake ordered, "Stand down." The surprised operatives stopped advancing and looked from him to Adam and back, unsure what to do. Gesturing for them to fall back, Melake turned, walked to the conference room door and entered, closing the door behind him. A short moment later the door opened again, and the board members came out, gaping at the sight before them.

Adam stood still, letting them have a good look at him. He said nothing. He'd made his point. Then, abruptly, he allowed his captive to fall on the floor—which caught everyone's eye—even as he himself stepped back into the elevator. He hit the button down to the underground parking floor and before anyone had a chance to stop them the doors closed and the elevator began descending. As soon as it did Adam opened the ceiling hatch and pulled himself through. Standing on top of the elevator car he counted the floors down, and on the first floor he jumped onto the edge of the outer elevator doors, holding on to a cable. He pushed up the latch beside the outer doors to release them, and came out, allowing the doors to close behind him again.

He moved quickly toward the staircase. They'll follow the elevator to the underground parking level he'd set it to go to, he knew, where the car he had come in was. But he had no intention of returning to it. He exited the staircase on the lobby floor, nonchalantly buttoning the jacket of the meticulous suit he'd changed into on the jet, knowing he would not look out of place with it here. Then he simply walked out through the front doors of the building, where none of its security guards were alerted about him. Not an oversight, he knew, just the organization not wanting to attract too much attention to itself and maybe too sure that he would be where they expected him to be. Although Melake, he was good at his job, the best, Adam thought as he walked down the street, then through an alley to where one of the SUVs waited for him. Melake wouldn't have missed him walking out of the building like that. Unless he wanted to.

Richards looked with distaste at the man at his feet, and from him to the closed elevator doors. He then turned around and looked from each board member to the next, reading on each an expression identical to his.

"What the hell is going on?" he hissed, then turned to Melake. "Get that thing up and bring him inside."

Melake gestured and two of his men rushed forward, untied the captive and helped him into the conference room and into a chair, where he sat cowering under the stern eyes of the board. Standing at the head of the conference table, Richards nodded at Melake, who sent his men out, closed the door and approached the seated man.

"Who are you?" he asked, his voice low.

The youngish man cringed.

Melake's eyes narrowed. This man was wearing an outfit of the kind issued to the organization's field operatives on black missions. He was obviously one of them, as Melake already suspected because of the identity of the man who had brought him here, and the fact that Kyle had in fact brought him *here*.

Melake stepped closer and commanded in a harsh, clipped voice. "Stand up!"

The man stood up automatically, coming to attention and confirming Melake's assertion. "State your name!"

"Sam A. Jones, Sir!"

"Your role?"

"Sniper, Sir!"

Melake frowned. "Where are you stationed?"

Jones didn't respond.

"Answer me!"

"Sir, I was given orders, Sir!"

"By whom?"

He didn't respond.

"Who is your commanding officer?"

No answer. Melake's frown deepened. Hierarchy at the organization was strict, especially in its field ranks. Melake had on the civilian suit he was wearing the organization's insignia indicating his position in it. This man should have answered him without hesitation.

"Do you know who that man is who brought you here?"

Jones hesitated. "That is the target, Sir."

Melake paused. This was odd. "Who gave you this target?"

The man was silent.

Melake frowned again. He took another step forward.

"Do you know who I am?"

Jones's eyes flickered to the insignia on Melake's jacket. "Yes, Sir!" Came the obedient answer.

"And these"—Melake indicated the men and women behind him—"are the organization's governing board. Your commanding officer's bosses. My bosses. Everyone's bosses. Do you understand me?"

Jones nodded, the fear clear on his face.

"There is no question that you will not answer in this room," Melake said menacingly.

"S-Sir," the man stammered, "he'll kill me, Sir."

Everyone in the room leaned forward expectantly.

"Who?" Richards asked.

The man's eyes moved from him to Melake, as if he didn't know who to fear more, and he finally answered, "Mr. Jennison, Sir. This was his mission."

The room was silent except for the man's frantic breathing.

"Talk!" Richards ordered.

And Sam A. Jones did.

Chapter Twenty-Two

A second SUV picked up the men who had flocked from their strategic positions around the building immediately after Adam exited it. The two vehicles rendezvoused with a third one that held the systems expert who had cleared the way for Adam inside the building, and now had eyes on all municipal and non-municipal systems. He was ensuring they were not being followed, and blocking recognition and tracking of the SUVs. They made it back to the airstrip without incident and were soon on their way back to Italy.

The men caught up on much needed sleep, but Adam couldn't rest. This had to work, he thought. But then, with Melake there the chances of this move of his achieving its purpose were far greater than he could have hoped. Melake would know there had to be a reason for what he did. And the board, Adam had met them, some he'd spent prolonged time with. These people weren't stupid, and they took their jobs very seriously. What Jennison was doing, they would never allow it if they knew the extent of his actions and the risks he took.

At least Adam hoped they wouldn't. He knew enough now to understand that they had motives he hadn't been aware of, and he expected that he, Aelia, and the Firsts would have to continue dealing with them, and with the organization they controlled. But he didn't want to deal with Jennison anymore. The board might have sent him after Aelia, but he was pretty sure they never would have bombed the cathedral, and they certainly never would have taken Stan Shell the way Jennison did. They were dangerous, infinitely so, and yet this wasn't the way they, and the organization under them, did things. Jennison was out of control, bordering on irrationality, and the idea was to stop him before he came up with another disruptive idea that might hurt someone.

And Adam really wanted him out of the way.

In Aeterna, the cars approached the great house. Those in the front and in the rear, the augmented security due to the First having been outside Aeterna, and without the Protector beside her, continued to the belowground parking of the security vehicles, while the car holding the First stopped at the main entrance. Rolly, in the front passenger seat, quickly got out to open the door for Aelia but she already did so herself.

Glancing up at the great house, Aelia marveled at the difference between her return now and the first time she arrived here. If then she was a stranger to this place and had come here lost, seeking answers to the sudden twist her life had taken, now she returned here as the Light and future leader of these people, and this was her designated home. Where then bits and pieces were only beginning to awaken within her, now she was whole. And she could feel her people constantly, all of them, as if her very soul was connected to them by countless invisible threads, as if their existence formed the backdrop of her awareness. And right now she felt their worry.

In going back to the United States, she had made a choice. She could have let Adam go alone with Rolly and with Aeterna's defense unit. The latter were, she knew, the elite of the Firsts' defense force, and Jennison's operatives would be no match for those trained to protect the leaders of the Firsts. But she chose to face Jennison, the man who had done this to Adam, to the Firsts, to her. And she chose to be there herself for the man who had helped her all those years ago, who had stood by her like no one had. She couldn't just send others, because she would not allow even the possibility that Jennison might, seeing that Adam came alone, hurt Stan.

But that meant that she had left Aeterna. And that had sent a ripple among the Firsts there, a ripple that had already begun reverberating among Firsts worldwide as word got out. A ripple of worry, of the fear that comes with uncertainty, and she felt it clearly. The Light had only been back for a short time, and they needed to know that she was here to stay, here for them, as was in the past. Instead she had left, exposed herself to danger, had run the risk of being gone again. That she could not die, this her people knew. But they had also thought that the Light would not leave them, and yet she had disappeared for so very long. They had thought she would be among them, protected, when she was eventually born again, and yet now they knew that the girl had been taken from them so easily, and years later it was a woman who returned, one who had not lived among them as should be, as always was. And so their hope was interlaced with old fears, along with new fears she herself had added to by leaving Aeterna.

But while her people were uncertain, she was not. The Light saw past and present, and understood their impact on the future as no one else could. With every day that passed she was growing stronger, and was seeing more of that which was and that which was to be, the path to walk. Not all, no one could foresee that much of the future, free will was too much of a factor to allow that. But she knew enough to understand that the Light that she was would need to play a different role than her predecessors did. No, not different, more encompassing, with active boundaries, she thought. A Light like never before. And she knew she would need to reassert her people's confidence in her presence, so that she could give them the guidance they would need.

Standing there now, beside the car, looking at the great house before her, Aelia knew that it was time to move forward, to leave behind who she had thought she was and be who she was born to become. And this also meant shifting her focus away from what had happened these past days, and placing Jennison and the organization, and their attacks on her, those that were and those she knew would come, at the fringe of her attention. Her life would now be in the hands of the Protector, and the Firsts' in hers.

The First acknowledged those around her with a nod, and they quickly stepped forward. A door closed behind her and the car drove away, doors opened before her and she entered the great house. She walked upstairs to her rooms, showered and dressed in the clothes she asked Sonea to lay out for her. Once again she stopped before the white robes that hung along a wall in her closet, but this time she looked at them at length before opting to wear her regular clothes again. Shortly later she was walking down the main staircase, surrounded by Keepers past, on her way to meet Neora and Ahir.

Jones was taken away by Melake's men. He had followed orders, and the mission he had been on was sanctioned by a senior member of the organization, which was what Jennison still was, and so he would not be punished. There was the matter of his capture, and the failure of his peers alongside him. They would all have to be removed from the facility, debriefed and reassessed, at which time their fate would be decided. However, if their loyalty to the organization—and not to Jennison—could be ascertained, an effort would be made to retrain and reinstate them. These men were of significant value to the organization. Like virtually all its other operatives, they had grown up in its community, in families that were themselves a part of the organization, and had its causes and vision instilled in them since childhood. Perhaps they could still be used.

Especially since it seemed they had no inkling of the truth.

The board was reseated after a long break, which ended once Melake informed them that the search had been futile, that Kyle was not caught. But then no one was surprised. Or worried, for that matter. Kyle had obviously come for one reason, and one reason only— to bring Jones to them. Sometime during that botched mission he had chosen not to leave this man behind as he did the others who had been captured, according to Jones himself, and he had also elected not to kill him. Most important, he chose not to give the captive back to Jennison, but instead took a great risk and brought him all the way to New York, to this meeting place of the board in a secure office building right in the middle of the city. He would obviously know where and when the board was convening—this was the senior field operative of the organization, he'd been everywhere and had seen everything over the years, and had been privy to a staggering amount of information. He was the best, and they had used him as such, it was as simple as that. And frankly, they had never expected him to turn against them, and so they had no real contingency plan to stop him, or even restrict his access to them.

He came alone, and he did not try to harm anyone. He just gave them his unhurt captive and left. That was what caught Richards's attention. Kyle wanted them to hear the man out. He wanted them to know what Jennison was doing. Richards had no doubt about it.

Of course, Kyle had no way of knowing that the board already knew quite a lot. It watched its directors carefully, and Jennison was more than that, he headed the organization's primary training and dispatch facility. Still, they had no idea what happened since Jennison tagged Kyle as rogue and sent Semner after him, which was the last thing he reported to the board. Now they knew it had all gotten out of hand.

They needed to know more.

Less than an hour later the meeting was adjourned. It would reconvene when the information they called for would be available.

Rolly walked to Adam as he was getting out of the car. Adam took an assessing look around him, then walked with Rolly toward the great house. Aeterna's head of defense and security seemed to be keeping a respectful distance. Throughout their recent mission to rescue Aelia's friend, in fact even before, as Adam decisively assumed his rightful role as the Protector, he had already felt this change, as if Rolly was seeing him as his superior. Adam didn't like that. He appreciated Rolly's experience and his professional attitude, and considering that Rolly had been Aeterna's head of defense and security and Ahir's right hand for years, while Adam just came out of nowhere, this sudden respect bothered him. He hoped it was brought on by his actions, rather than by his identity.

As if to confirm this, Rolly commented, "I'd like to have been a fly on the wall."

Adam glanced at him.

"When you brought them the guy." Rolly shook his

head incredulously. "My people say you just left them outside and went in alone with him, in and out in no time, as calm as a . . ." He searched for a word, then gave up.

"Let's hope it does the trick."

"If they'll make him talk."

"Oh, they will," Adam said somberly. "No one disobeys the organization's governing board."

Chapter Twenty-Three

Richards stood by the conference room windows, the sprawling city far below him. His forehead was deeply furrowed, and he was listening to the board members behind him. They were still reacting to the information that had awaited them when they reconvened.

It was easy to get it, now that they knew what to look for. They had all served in operational positions in the organization at one time or another, and knew how get what they needed in a way that did not alert Jennison. And they were the governing board and were not to be trifled with, and no one in the organization dared disobey them when they requested anything, information included.

The secrecy was crucial, and had been for a while as the board had come to understand that Jennison was becoming increasingly unpredictable, and more recently that he had begun hiding his actions from them. They had originally approved using Kyle for the mission he was abducted for, after the message sent from the Firsts' cathedral center to Aeterna had been intercepted. It was a move so carefully planned and so sure to succeed, and yet its failure was so immediate and absolute that the board had been left deeply concerned.

They had then given Jennison the benefit of the doubt and had approved him sending after Kyle and the woman the organization's second best field operative, because Semner knew Kyle so well. However, they now knew that, in reality, Jennison had sent Semner after Kyle before asking the board's permission to do so, which he did when Semner was already dead. And apparently, so was another organization operative and also one of the Firsts, which meant that the board still did not have all the information about what happened. All they had was a messy involvement of the local authorities, and, worse, they had to be extra careful because the original target, the woman, was now considered taken against her will, and there was too much attention on her.

To make matters even hazier, Jennison was no longer updating the board about anything, and did not bother asking permission for two missions that he knew had to be sanctioned first—a bombing and a kidnapping involving humans, of all things. But then Jennison knew they would never be approved, Richards thought angrily. Both were reckless missions that were not thoroughly thought through, and both were botched. Stupid, stupid actions that were designed to cover Jennison's own failures, and that were now endangering the organization and its plans.

Although it was an oversight of the board that Jennison had been allowed to do so much damage for so long, Richards had to admit. They had, perhaps, placed too much trust in him, but then when Kyle was still around, he had been a valuable stabilizing influence on Jennison. Richards chuckled bitterly to himself at the irony and turned his mind back to the matter at hand. It had been quite easy to complete the information Jones had given them about Jennison's most recent venture, to uncover the mission that wasn't really a training mission, as Jennison had logged it in the facility for the sake of the commanding officers of the people he had taken with him, and to speak to more of the operatives involved. Now the board knew for certain that Jennison had kidnapped a human, a university professor, of all things, risking exposure, risking a police investigation, risking what had in fact happened—the police connecting his kidnapping with the disappearance of the woman. All to flush his targets out, make them come to him.

The board also knew the professor was back at home, alive and well. They couldn't even consider killing him to keep him from talking, because Melake, who knew Kyle well, had made it clear to them that by bringing them Jones Kyle had conveyed that it was now their responsibility to act, and act differently than Jennison. And since it was Kyle who had released the professor, if the board would try to hurt him, Kyle was certain to turn on them. And that's without even considering the police investigation that would follow if the professor died now.

Richards did order the professor's home and work surveilled, but so far there was nothing. If he knew anything, he wasn't talking about it. He seemed intent on simply going back to his life and had even gone to the university to lecture today. He certainly didn't say anything to the police, instead claiming he had no idea who had taken him and why. Most likely Kyle didn't tell him anything so as not to involve him more than he already was, and either way, the professor, Richards was willing to wager, would choose to protect himself and his family by keeping silent.

Richards cursed under his breath. What a mess. All that effort to create the perfect operative—and now they had to worry about him coming after them. So much for Jennison's genius plan. And that wasn't even the worst thing. In effect, Jennison had initiated a direct armed interaction between the Firsts and the organization. He had actually placed the Firsts in a situation where they had to send armed people against it. And by now they were certain to know what the organization had done all those years ago, taking the children. Damn it, Jennison should have known better. He did know better—what the hell was he doing? The organization had managed to avoid a confrontation for so many years, and now... And that was without even taking into account the bombing. A direct attempt on the only center of the Firsts that the organization had ever been given access too, so of course it would be traced back to it. So much for the truce.

Richards was hoping to God this would not end in a war.

The stillness behind him drew his attention. His peers were now silent, waiting for his decision, his resolution to this unfortunate situation. He walked briskly to the head of the table and stood looking at them, saw their anger and concern mirror his. He nodded. The future of the organization, its plans, humanity, was in their hands. They would resolve this.

"Jennison has been allowed to accumulate too much power, for too long. It is time to remove him. We will move simultaneously on the facility and on the Italy office, and clean them up. We will then comb through every one of our other offices and facilities, and clean them from those who should be loyal to the organization but instead are loyal to him. This cannot be allowed." He paused for effect. "We must reassert our leadership, our principles and our vision. We must unite the organization and remind our people why we're here. We must now be stronger than ever before."

"And Kyle Rhys? The woman?" the man on his left asked.

"The Firsts?" the woman beside him added.

Richards's eyes narrowed.

There was nothing more Adam could do now. It remained to be seen whether the board would act against Jennison, and only time would tell that. It also remained to be seen what the board would do next about him, about Aelia, the Firsts, but that, that definitely only time could tell. And time wasn't going anywhere today.

He rubbed his neck, working the kinks out. Once again he'd been running on adrenaline, and his body was finally feeling the exhaustion. He tried to remember when he last slept but couldn't. That should be his next order of business, he thought. Except right now he wanted very much to see Aelia.

He found her standing on her balcony. The way it was built made it solitary, and it was fast becoming her favorite place when she wanted to be alone. It was secure, which was his criterion for where she should be, but then if it weren't safe he would have found a way for it to be. The way things were, she needed a place she could escape to, even if for a breather. Like now.

She didn't turn when he approached her, and he leaned on the stone railing with his back to it, facing her. She knew of course he had arrived back at Aeterna, and had then gone to see the recent events from the view of its control center, to wrap them up, make sure there were no loose ends. Knew when he finally walked into her rooms, before he'd even been to his own. Was waiting here for him.

He watched her. Like him she hadn't slept, but then he didn't think she would, not until he returned safely, he and Aeterna's defense unit. Knew she would follow him, not as Aeterna's control center had but as only she could, distance no longer a hindrance to the connection between them. For him she had been in the backdrop of his mind but had stayed back, only subtly felt, just to let him know she was safe, know that he was too.

Too subtly, still. He was here and she was pulling back. Trying to, at least.

"When it's possible, I'd like to see Stan again. Talk to him, explain as much as I can. I owe it to him."

She still wasn't looking at him. He frowned. Something was wrong here. He thought for a beat, then did something he hadn't done before.

He used the link between them to get to her.

And then he could see it. *Feel* it. She was hurting. He turned to face the vast grounds of Aeterna beside her, standing just that much closer. And waited.

She glanced at him. "It can wait, you know. You've only just returned."

He smiled slightly. Since when was it like that between them?

Her expression mirrored his for just a moment, before it became somber again. She breathed in. "The sniper, I did that."

He nodded. The satellite told them where the sniper was, but when they got to him he was unconscious. When he finally did come around, it took quite some time for him to return to himself. The guy had no idea what had happened to him.

"I hurt him. I didn't mean to." She thought back, played it in her mind yet again, that which she would tell no one but him. "He was about to shoot me, and then you moved in between us and I just reacted. I stopped him."

Adam had guessed it was something like that. He looked at her. Her eyes were still on the horizon, but her mind was back in that abandoned neighborhood in the dark of night.

"If I hadn't pulled back at the last moment, I would have . . ." She couldn't complete the thought.

"What if you hadn't stopped him?"

"I know. I also know I'd do it again in a heartbeat. But that doesn't make it any easier."

She was quiet for a long time. "I'm not even supposed to be able to do that, you know. Have this effect on a human. Or know he was there in the first place."

He contemplated this. "I think that all considering, we need to keep an open mind about what you can and can't do."

She said nothing.

"In a way, I think that's our advantage."

She glanced at him.

He shrugged. "Considering the surprises we seem to be in store for, we and all the Firsts, could be good if we had some surprises of our own. Maybe that's another reason the two of us, *this* Light and *this* Protector, fit here specifically now."

She turned her gaze to the night, and he watched her. Had she turned to look, she would have seen the concern on his face. He thought about the park, her need to stop the fighting, help them. Her need to help her people, strong enough to unleash the full force of the Light in her. Her need to be there herself to help Stan Shell, even at a risk to herself.

Her need to help, it was that simple. Hate and violence were painful to her. What she did to that sniper was painful to her. She would do it again, would do anything to protect him, he knew. And she would do anything to protect her people, he knew that too. And this situation she was in, who she was in these complex times, with too many who would want to hurt her and hers, would in all likelihood mandate her doing just that. But it would take a toll.

A bad one. And he wouldn't always be able to shield her from it.

But he could stand with her through it.

Richards was still at his desk. There was no sound in his well-isolated office, none at all. A bomb could go off outside his office door, and he wouldn't hear it. Which suited him just fine. He liked the quiet, it was most conducive to thinking, and that's what he needed to do now.

Think.

The meeting had adjourned without the big question being answered. Yes, the organization would be cleaned, thoroughly so, and nothing would remain of Jennison and his loyals. This would cost it time and good people, both valuable resources, but it had to be done. The organization itself and the community it was part of would rally, and eventually things would continue as they should have in the first place, before Jennison went off on a bender and embarked on his line of failures. Richards would make sure of that.

But the question remained, and in light of recent events it had become more acute than ever, which was why he was sitting here alone now, racking his brain.

What to do about this species that had approached them all those decades ago, a species that had preceded humanity, the humanity he had sworn to protect. A species that could, at any moment it chose to, upturn world order. And if the humans ever found that the alien race they were constantly looking to the skies to find was right there beside them, that's exactly what would happen. So yes, that was one question that was now on his mind. That and the other one.

What to do with the two who were the very foundation of that species' existence.

Chapter Twenty-Four

Sleep cannot be overestimated. Good sleep, that is, not the kind plagued by uneasy dreams, distant memories, or the constant expectation that someone will shoot you. That was Adam's first thought when he woke up, more rested than he'd been for days, as if the hectic events of recent had finally given him some reprieve. Him, and he was hoping Aelia, too. He'd left her walking into her bedroom, promising she would go to bed.

He uttered a voice command and the blinds opened, letting light into the room. A new day. He wondered how it would be, if it would finally be a normal day, as normal as could be under the circumstances. Which got him to wonder if Jennison was at that very moment sitting in his office, planning another surprise for them, or if he was already gone. He sat up, rubbing his face, feeling the stubble. When was the last time he shaved? He wasn't sure. Now would probably be a good time. He got up and walked into the bathroom, thinking that maybe, just maybe, today Jennison would be someone else's problem.

He found Ahir streaming global media coverage on a small holoscreen on the dinner table before him, while drinking a cup of tea. The table was set for Adam, too, and he realized how famished he was. As if on cue, a smiling Remi brought a steaming coffee pot.

"I try to keep up with what goes on in the world. Well, what the media tells the humans, that is, and how they react. I find it quite informative." Ahir sipped his tea as the small images changed yet again. "It will be different for you, I suppose. You know their nuances from a different angle than I do."

Adam tilted his head slightly, savoring the strong taste of black coffee. "And then some. It's a must in my line of work." He raised a brow. "My previous line of work, that is."

Ahir shut off the screen and looked at him. "How are you doing with that?"

"How do you mean?"

"Your past."

Adam contemplated this quietly. "What I don't get is how you all seem to accept it."

"We know something you don't."

"And what's that?"

"We know you."

Adam was surprised at the bitterness that erupted in him. "Really? Who am I?"

"You are the man who left the only family he had ever known, knowing that his actions would mean he could never go back, and in fact that the organization would go after him with all it had, just to save a woman he didn't know, despite what he had been told about her. There was no future in siding with her, and yet you protected her and brought her here, to a different country, a different continent, no less. You left your life until that point and chose to follow the man you are." Ahir stopped for a breath and then sighed. "How many times in the past have you helped someone, Adam, when the organization didn't know? When you knew it could get you killed? How many lives have you saved?" Adam's expression confirmed to Ahir that he had hit the mark. He nodded. "While they were building the Kyle they wanted, Adam was there inside him. The child was growing into the man he is, the Protector, and no one could stop that." His voice softened. "We are peaceful people, Adam, that is our nature. And the Protector, while he is first a warrior, he is also a good man. You are a good man." He tapped his grandson's arm affectionately and commanded, "Now eat!"

Adam smiled despite himself and did as he was told.

"Speaking of the organization, Rolly updated me. What do you think we can expect from them?" Ahir asked.

"Not much for a while. They'll either choose to watch Jennison for a time, in which case they will not allow him the freedom to act again if he even tries, or they'll remove him from office immediately, in which case the new director of the facility will take the time to clean it up. In fact, once Jennison is removed there is bound to be an organization-wide cleanup, that's what I would do." Adam's eyes narrowed. "Either way, Richards is smart and highly calculated—there's a reason he heads the board. I'm betting he'll take the time to assess the impact of Jennison's actions and my and Aelia's escape on the organization. And he'll also want to consider the possible repercussions for the relations between the Firsts and the organization and our possible reaction to the attacks on us." He nodded thoughtfully. "He'll stay away for the duration. What happens after that, that's a different story."

Ahir's face betrayed his worry. Adam noted how drawn the old man's face was, and felt a pang of concern. "Grandfather?" he said quietly, hoping the familiar tone would draw him out.

"This mistake, the contact we established with the humans all these years ago, had cost us so much." He sighed. "I'm sorry, Son. It looks like you and Aelia, you who have already paid so dearly for our mistake, will continue bearing the consequences. You, and our people."

"We can handle it."

Ahir was surprised at his confidence. But Adam only repeated, "Aelia and I, we can handle them. And we'll protect our people. We'll protect the Firsts."

"Adam, if they haven't already figured out the truth after all that has happened, they will eventually. Look what they did when they thought you two were just symbols. What will they do if they realize the crucial role you actually play in our existence?" He shook his head. "They will come after you with all they have."

"Let them."

Aeterna was awake and already bustling with activity, and Adam found himself acknowledging its staff with every step he took. He realized this was the first time he'd walked among them this way, without the air of a man on a mission about him. He'd already made a name for himself, and he was after all the first Protector of a living Light in a long time, which accounted for their awe. But at the same time he was encountering the enthusiastic interest that came from the fact that he was, quite simply, the grandson of a man they all knew and cared for. Some had known his parents, some had even known him as a toddler, and for all of them he was a lost son returning home.

He found Aelia walking beside the lake. A security detail was following her at a distance, and Adam indicated for them to leave, taking over. He fell in beside her and contemplated her. The night before he'd learned that he could use the connection between them to see what was going on inside her. It seemed that the Protector had more insight than he had thought into the Light's feelings, which would, he knew, only add to his ability to protect her. It made her even more vulnerable to him, he realized all too well, but he wasn't about to pull back from it, from her.

That's how he knew that the weight of what had happened with the sniper had lifted somewhat, and that he'd done that. But something else was there, something that had already been there the night before but hadn't been the focus it was now.

"I thought that was done with."

He heard, not just felt, the irritation. She didn't like having a security detail following her. "All considering, I'd like to keep a detail around you for now. As an added precaution," he said.

"I'm constantly watched. Unless I'm in my rooms or with you."

"Yet you're out here." It was a question, not a statement.

"I like it here. I've never been in a place with so many trees and a lake and no endless buildings. It's almost peaceful."

Almost, but not quite, he thought, and an idea began forming in the back of his mind. He put it aside for now, waited to hear what was on her mind.

"I've been reading a bit of what we have about the organization, beginning when the Council initiated first contact with it. It seems to be inclined toward thoroughly planned actions that are carried out with military precision. And yet Jennison..."

Adam wondered where she was going with this, but he went along. "He always seemed to be a thorough man. In his actions, and in his words. He's the one who taught me that every action must be planned from start to end. Always plan contingencies, always be several steps ahead, always be prepared. Even when I was still a kid." He chuckled mirthlessly. "I never thought... looking back, he was always teaching me. Training me. Planning ahead, wasn't he?" He shook his head. "Anyway, it wasn't until I began working closely with him that I saw the cracks. Not many of them, mind you. Just a tendency to panic, take rash action, when something went unexpectedly wrong, when he no longer had complete control over the situation."

He looked at her. "Thing is, Jennison is good. He didn't become the director of the organization's main facility, in charge of its top-tier operatives, by being mediocre. That place is crucial to the organization's survival, and it has been very well run for many years now—by Jennison. Even when he wasn't completely in control, he's always managed to come out of it somehow, and no one ever really noticed. That's why he was never removed." He paused. "More recently things had gotten worse but I'd managed to curb most of his panics, or at least mitigate the consequences, depending on whether I was away on a mission or not when he lost control. Still, between that and his recent actions"—he shook his head—"it is as if the Firsts finding you and my changing sides caused him to go off the deep end. And there's no one there to stop him."

"If Richards removes him, the organization might revert back to its efficient self." It fit what she'd read about it and what Adam had told her about Richards.

"That's a fair assumption. Jennison will be replaced by someone more stable and the organization will clean up after him and attempt to resume its previous course."

"Come after us."

"I think by now you and I are major part of it, yes. The organization no longer has us, the Firsts do. So Jennison being gone won't mean that we're safer. It just means the organization is more likely to come after us more efficiently."

"What do you think they'll do?"

Adam shook his head.

They walked in silence. Finally, Aelia spoke. "Adam, we can't just sit and wait for what the organization will do. We need to act, prepare, do what we are here for. You were right last night, we are different and we'll be doing things our way."

He came to face her, forcing her to stop walking. She turned her eyes away, struggled how to put it, still working it out herself.

"Not with me," he said.

She looked up at him, not understanding.

"You don't have to search for the right words with me," he said, and saw the wonder in her eyes, her wonder at him.

She nodded. "I'm out here now because I wanted to let our people here see me. I wasn't entirely right to leave Aeterna as I did. I left, and it had an impact on them. I could feel the news traveling, felt the uncertainty, the fear." She let out a breath. "They need me, Adam. They need us, Light and Protector. And we have to let them know that no matter what, we won't leave them. But we also have to make them understand that they need to trust us to do what's right. They've lived with the stories, now they must understand that the stories do not make the Light and the Protector. It is we who make the stories. And they must know that whatever we do, we do it with them, and for them."

Her brow furrowed, and she looked at the great house. "I spoke with Neora and Ahir while you were gone, to understand more about what they do, what they have been for the Firsts, not in faith but in their everyday lives, in practical terms. And I understand now that by returning as we have, the two of us, we have destabilized the Keeper and Protector foundation our people have relied on for centuries, the foundation that has given them consistency and order in their daily lives, yet we are not able to give them an alternative one that is based on us, not yet. There is much we still have to contend with before we can. So we need to create something new, for them."

Adam marveled. Most people, with what she'd been through and the danger she was still in, would be paralyzed with fear and indecisiveness. But not her. She was resilient, and he could feel the determination in her, could feel her growing stronger, taking a direction. He thought of the irony. What might have taken so much longer was happening lightning fast because of the same actions that the organization took that had been meant to stop her. Instead of slowing down, she had hit the ground running.

And she had obviously thought this through. "How do you want to do this?" he asked her.

"We start with the Council. It's time they met us."

Rolly came to them, to the drawing room that was already becoming the meeting place of the two generations of the Firsts' leaders. They were all there, Neora and Ahir sitting, Aelia and Adam standing together nearby. Rolly stopped at the door, taking them all in. Now that's something you don't see every day, he marveled. A unique seam in the history of the Firsts.

He wasn't sure who to acknowledge first, and Adam helped him by beginning, and getting straight to the point. "Rolly, how can we bring the Council here?"

Rolly focused. "We can't. With the organization's recent actions and the truce void de facto, we can't vouch for their security." He stopped. "But then you would know that, of course."

Adam confirmed with a brief nod. "So, how can we bring them here?" he repeated.

Rolly sat down on the couch Ahir motioned him to. "Okay, what do you need them for? Practically speaking, that is."

"A meeting," Adam said.

"One meeting?"

"Yes," Neora said. "But we need them here, and all at the same time. Not simply a conference call, but a real meeting."

"We could use holograms. We'll do this in the Council Hall, use mobile devices to construct holograms of them. You'll all be here, and the Council members will be holograms placed in their exact places around the table."

"That's here," Adam said. "But what will they see? How do we get the same effect for them?"

"Well, usually if the Keeper wants to speak to all of them we use the wall screens at every center, so that each Council member can see all the others, as well as the Keeper and the Protector." Here he faltered. "I mean Mr. Kennard." He stopped again, quite comically confused now. "You, Sir." He turned to Ahir.

"It's quite all right." Ahir encouraged him on, and Rolly nodded gratefully and continued.

"The thing is, if you want everyone in the meeting to feel as if they're actually here, we can just use a simulated environment. You might know it as virtual reality," he said to Adam and Aelia, "and we've had an advanced version of it for a while. We use varied applications of it for training, consequence assessment, technology trials and medicine, to name a few. All our centers have it, and it can easily be applied—all we have to do is have Aeterna take control of all the simulations in all the participating centers at once. We already have a Council Hall simulation, for security training purposes." He was clearly enamored with the idea. "We'll still run it in the real Council Hall, with some adjustments the simulation will play perfectly in it and it obviously already has the privacy Council meetings normally require. Yes, we'll take out the conference table, take out everything in fact, leave the Council Hall empty and run the simulation. And we'll need to have the respective centers make some adjustments too. Nothing major, if Aeterna controls the whole thing. If we do this the way I'm thinking, for the Council members it'll be as if they're actually here, in the Council Hall, with everyone else. It'll work."

Adam looked at Neora and Ahir, and it was Neora who smiled. "These are your decisions now," she said.

He bowed his head in acknowledgment and turned to Aelia. She nodded once, and he turned to Rolly. "Let's do this."

Chapter Twenty-Five

Aelia and Adam spent the next hours learning about the Council, with Ahir as their teacher.

"The Firsts are scattered all over the world," he explained. "We are all the same, not divided like humans are, by borders or origins, or belief, obviously. But Firsts in different regions do live in different circumstances —different regional characteristics, different types of human neighbors and accordingly different degrees of involvement with them and security concerns, different community occupations, different needs. We have long ago learned that a good way to ensure everyone's well-being is to maintain local councils that would know best how to cater to the needs of their own communities. Their members are regular members of the community, and their role is simply to make addressing issues that arise more efficient. There are no heads of local councils, no hierarchies, but every council does have a representative who participates in cross-community conferences and who, periodically, comes here, to Aeterna. These representatives form a central council, the Council of the Firsts, and I am its head."

"And you yourself don't represent a specific region?"

Adam asked.

"No. Aeterna does not constitute one of the regions, it is simply known as the seat of the Keeper and the Protector. I oversee the Council, and through it all locations the Firsts are in. And the security of all the Firsts, of course, this has always been the responsibility of the Protectors." He paused and added, "And, first and foremost, I am the Keeper's right-hand."

"And her friend." Aelia smiled.

"Yes."

"Is that a prerequisite of the Protector?" she asked, her smile widening.

"No." Ahir laughed. "I suppose not. But when two people spend so many years together, they get to know and trust each other. Understand each other. And it is more than that. When you are in positions such as ours, you find yourself necessarily isolated. No one can really understand what you are going through, and you cannot speak freely or voice concerns to the same people who look to you for answers. So this friendship in which nothing needs to be hidden becomes precious to you."

His smile had decades of memories behind it. "Neora and I, we got along from the very beginning. She was there when my son"—he turned to Adam—"your father, was born, when you were born, and when your parents were killed and you were taken. She was there beside me in my search for you, and was my only remaining comfort when your grandmother, my wife and companion of many years, passed away and I remained alone. She is my friend, and I am hers," he said simply. For a long moment he remained deep in thought, then looked up at both of them as if suddenly remembering they were there.

"Why is she alone?" Aelia's brow was furrowed.

"I'm sorry?"

"You were married, you had a son. Your grandson is sitting here. Why is Neora alone?" She looked at him, perturbed. "Ahir, were all the Keepers alone?"

"Yes, that is how it has always been."

"Why?" The pain was evident in her voice.

"She is a symbol of something huge, her role is . . ." His voice tapered off at the look in Aelia's eyes. She wanted the truth. He nodded. "Because the Light was."

"She was alone? Why?" It was Adam's turn to be baffled.

"We have no idea. Unlike the Protector she was not always an only child, often she had brothers and sisters. But she grew up to be alone, never with a family of her own."

Aelia turned inward, looked back. Not all answers were there yet, not all realities were clear.

"So in choosing to be the Keeper, these women elected to live alone for the rest of their lives?" Adam asked.

"That is how it has always been," Ahir said again.

"Always is now over," the Light said. "I don't want her to be alone."

Ahir looked at her, and something flickered in his eyes.

"She doesn't have to be alone," Aelia repeated gently.

"That was nice," Adam said when they left Ahir, having learned quite a bit about the Council, including about its current members whom they were about to meet.

"What was?"

He threw her a look, and she smiled. "So you don't mind?"

"Of course not. They're obviously very close."

"I can't believe the Keepers were alone. Symbolizing the Light is one thing, but giving up. . ."

Love, was the word she wasn't saying, he noticed. "Any idea why your predecessors did?" he asked gently.

She shook her head.

They walked to the Council Hall, curious to see the preparations. The huge place was buzzing with activity. It had already been emptied of all furniture, and only the supplementary technology was there, placed so as to simulate an actual Council meeting where the participants would stand exactly where they would normally be sitting. There would be no conference table in the simulation, either, there would be no need for it.

Aelia and Adam walked over to Rolly, who was energetically giving last minute instructions.

"So, basically, we're here and they're not, but we see them as if they are, and wherever they are they see all of us, including the other Council members, as if we're there. So that it's as if we're all in the same room," Aelia mused.

"That's correct." Rolly's eyes never stopped following the work around them.

"Right," Aelia said. "That'll take some getting used to."

Rolly frowned at something he didn't like and walked off, preoccupied.

"You nervous?" Adam asked. "You don't feel nervous."

Aelia smiled at his choice of words. "I'm ready for this." She threw a look at him. "And so are you."

He nodded. "We really should get out of here, though. We're disruptive." He indicated the workers, who were more interested in them than in the tasks they were assigned. The two left the hall, just as Ahir and Neora entered it and joined Rolly in the final preparations for the awaited meeting.

It was time. The Council Hall was silent, even the technology was quiet. The simulation was being supervised from a room off the control center, and the only people physically present in the Council Hall were the two generations of the Firsts' leaders, present and future. Aelia, Adam, and Ahir stood beside one of the walls, outside the simulation perimeter, and Neora, Keeper of the Firsts, stood where the Council table normally was, in the middle of what would now be the open circle of its members within the Council meeting simulation. And as in every meeting, in fact as she had done since the day she became the Keeper, Neora was clad in her white robes, the band of all colors rippling at its edge, majestically reflecting the lights in the spacious room.

On either side of Aelia, Ahir and Adam glanced at her. She was leaning against the wall, her eyes on Neora, focused in concentration. Both could feel the intensity in her, but neither could discern its origin. She wasn't worried or tense, and she was clearly not nervous about the pending encounter. Yet there was something on her mind, the same thing that Adam had felt earlier when they were walking beside the lake and that had been behind her words, the same thing that had been evolving in her since she returned to Aeterna after her friend's release. And it was strong now, finally focused.

In a sudden bout of clarity, Adam thought he might have an idea what it was. She was making decisions. Since the day she was first identified in the cathedral in Rome, every move she made was decided for her, by the organization and Jennison's actions, by him, even by her own destiny. But for the first time, the Aelia who had stopped the brawl in the park, who had stood up to him even as he was pointing a loaded gun at her, and who had stood unwavering before Jennison, the Aelia who he knew was so right to be the Light, First among the Firsts, was taking a stand.

Movement caught his attention. Neora confirmed she was ready, and all members of the Council of the Firsts appeared in the Council Hall, surrounding her. As the simulation in each center worldwide activated, the Council members acknowledged the Keeper with respect, bowing their heads in turn. Neora returned their greeting, welcoming them all. She then walked to where her place would normally be among them, nearly completing the circle. The only empty position in the formation was that of Ahir, who remained standing with Aelia and Adam, who were now looking at the newcomers curiously.

Neora opened the meeting. And that's when the onslaught came, question feeding on question—where was the First, they wanted to know. Was it true that She left Aeterna? What was She like, what kind of a person was this woman who was the Light yet was raised by humans and not by the Firsts? What did that, and the manifestation of the Light at such a late stage of Her life, imply for Her, Her force, Her ability to protect Her people? Would She be what they needed Her to be? *Could* She?

The questions came to the Keeper from all sides, the rush of feelings behind them overwhelming her in their force. Adam watched the Council thoughtfully. These people were worried, on the verge of afraid. They were obviously torn between their own exhilaration at the return of the Light and their need, as the representatives of their respective communities, to answer to the people who looked to them for answers, people who were hearing a constant flow of news and rumors. They were perceived as being privy to decisions made at Aeterna, where the Firsts' leaders reigned, and had no choice but to remain pragmatic.

Adam could understand why, while the return of the Light was received with great relief, it would also raise among the Firsts questions about what would happen now, about the future. These Firsts had never lived with the real Light in their lives. For such a long time, she was for them a belief, a guide to live by, a hope to await the return of. And now, after so many generations, and with no one who had actually lived in the Light's presence around to guide them, she was here, a real person, an adult woman ready to take her place among them. That, and the fact that for the first time ever for them they were actually *feeling* her presence, the presence of the Light, must be unsettling them, Adam thought. They—

His train of thoughts was interrupted as beside him Aelia moved, and stepped into the circle. She walked right in, passing Neora, and stood in their midst, letting them all see her. She had chosen not to dress in the customary clothes of the First, the flowing, unblemished white that signified the Light and that would catch the brilliance of the force within her, reflecting it to those around her. Instead, and in a sharp contrast to the Keeper, she had chosen to dress in black—black slacks, black boots, a black blouse, which accentuated how trim she was, how delicate, and along with her long dark hair countered the striking gray eyes that were now gazing at the Council surrounding her. Everything about the way she looked contrasted the effect the robes of the Light were meant to give her. Everything, but her.

Because it was the Light they saw step into that circle. Even as She walked into their midst it erupted from Her, visible in the Council Hall and in each of the simulations worldwide, seen with the same brightness even though they were all far away, as if She herself was there, right there with each and every one of them. And then they felt it, felt Her force, felt it surround them, flow through them, felt its intensity, its strength, nothing like the gentleness with which She had connected with them thus far, leaving no place for doubt, no place for question as to Her power. In the Council Hall under the great house of Aeterna, all Council members stepped back in awe, as did the Keeper, and near the wall the old Protector stood mesmerized, while the new Protector took an instinctive step forward, not even realizing that while the Light blinded them all, so that they could now barely see Her, he could.

One by one the Council members bowed their heads in reverence. And when they all did, when all in the Council Hall did, all except Her own Protector, the Light changed, deepened, acquired a new dimension, enveloping, protecting, uniting. In a fraction of a second too small to grasp, She connected powerfully to the point of Her origin, ages into the past of this ancient species She had chosen, and surged back into the present, expanding to all sides, in all dimensions, fast, faster, bringing to the Council and to all Firsts beyond them that which She now finally was.

In their very midst, they knew, was the everlasting Light of the Firsts.

Gradually, the Light withdrew most—but not all— of the power in Her back into Herself. She left Her people with just enough sense of how powerful She who had returned to watch over them was, but the representatives of their councils, them She left feeling just that much more of the power of this implied promise.

And then She broke Her silence.

"The Keeper will continue to reign, with Ahir Kennard

by her side. They will lead the Firsts as they always have."
Her voice was quiet, yet the unchecked strength in it
reverberated in every word.

Everybody in the Council Hall looked at Her in
surprise.

"Our people need continuity. They need their leaders, at Aeterna and in the local councils, to continue
addressing the needs of their day-to-day lives. Their lives
must not be disrupted more than they already have been.
And that is how it will be." She paused, including Neora,
Ahir and Adam in her gaze. "More than ever before, the
Firsts are now facing new challenges that endanger their
very existence. It is precisely in these times that their
sense of stability must be assured, and this lies in their
ability to carry on their lives as they have done until now,
for as long as possible. That is what you will ensure, to
the best of your abilities, under the experienced, reliable
reign you have always known."

She fell silent again. "Yes, the Firsts have been alone
for too long, and the Light is needed. But I should walk
among you, not hide here, in the safety of this fortress
you have built for me, not while you need me out
there, with you." She continued, Her voice picking up
force. "You do not need an administrator or day-to-
day leadership, you're doing well yourselves, under the
Keeper and Ahir Kennard. You do not need a symbol
for your belief, you have had that for too long. What you
need is the Light as was given to you all those generations ago. Not as a symbol, but as a reality. You need the
Light to guide and defend you in the challenging times

ahead, and that is what I will do, I and my Protector beside me, until our people, our future, are safe once again." She paused, letting the meaning of Her words sink in. "Be patient. I *will* walk among you. And with time, what should be, will be."

She turned to Neora, who nodded and stepped forward. As Aelia stepped out of the circle, Neora addressed the Council. "So it shall be, then. What we have done we will continue to do. I will retain my duties, with one marked difference. We no longer need to keep the faith alive. We have the Light among us." She turned slowly, looking at them all. "Approach Her, speak to Her, call to Her. You and the people of your communities. She has returned for *you*."

The members of the Council nodded, and the excited murmur grew louder as they spoke to one another, to the Keeper, and to Ahir, who bowed his head to the Light and stepped forward to stand at the Keeper's side. The Light had spoken, and Her people were ready to proceed. Already they were speaking of matters at hand, and the Light felt in them, and in all the Firsts, the certainty that the protective being which their ancestors had turned to in times past for matters beyond them, was here to stay.

Again Aelia leaned against the wall, outside the view of the Council. Beside her the Protector stood straight, his hands folded on his chest, his eyes on her. If before Aelia allowed the Light to be felt by the Firsts just to let them know of her return, now she had in effect positioned herself in an active, tangible role, among them.

And none of them would forget soon the powerful force that they had felt in their midst.

He more than everyone in that room understood why she had done this. It would allow her to deal more effectively with the challenges her people didn't yet know they would be facing. And it would allow her to leave Aeterna without worrying that that in itself would cause uncertainty, giving her the freedom to do what she needed, what they both needed. Protect the Firsts, without their every move causing speculation and fear.

And it would also, he knew only too well, allow her to try to draw the unwanted attention of their enemies to herself, without putting her people in harm's way. That was one way of increasing their sense of security, he thought, and impeding her own safety even more, which was why the Protector was ready to take his place beside her as she had decreed. Aelia had, quite simply, just told him she was putting her life in his hands.

And they would be coming after her. Those who already knew about her and those who would learn of her. She would always be their primary target, all the more so once they realize that the Light was real and that she was key to the survival of the Firsts.

Neither moved until the impromptu Council meeting was over and the Council Hall was silent again, silent and empty except for the two generations that the Light had now designated to work together for the sake of her people. Neora, Ahir and Adam turned to look at Aelia.

She addressed Neora. "You've been a leader to the Firsts for many decades now, and I can't begin to imagine how weary you must be. And yet I need you to remain with them. They trust you, your leadership, your judgment. Only you can provide for them the continuity they will need now."

"But it is you who will need to guide them. You are their living faith."

"And that is why we, you and I, will do this together."

"Eventually, you will have to become their only leader."

"And I will. But I can't tell you how long it will be before I am able to do that." Aelia paused. "This is not about me learning aspects I have yet to know about leading the Firsts. It's not about rules and administration. It is about ensuring their survival."

Neora looked worried. "You cannot put yourself in danger."

"My first duty is to ensure my people are safe. Whatever it takes."

Neora shook her head in sudden fear, and the Light took a step forward. "*I will not leave you again.*"

Neora started at these words, as they brought to her mind that which her shock at Aelia's decision had led her to forget. That which only she knew, the prophecy foretold and passed only from one Keeper to the next. She nodded slowly. "Yes, I do believe you will not," she said quietly, with a sudden confidence that made both Ahir and Adam look at her curiously, and even Aelia tilted her head lightly in question. But once again

Neora was not about to explain. Not even to the Light, especially not to Her. The fact that She was not aware of it said it all. It was not yet time for Her to know.

"It will be my privilege to remain the Keeper as long as you need me too," was all she said.

Aelia nodded her gratitude and turned to Ahir, who nodded too. "I will remain with Neora. Although"— he turned to Adam—"the title of Protector I have, I believe, already relinquished to its rightful holder." He frowned. "This would be a grandfather's dream, if it were not for the challenges that await you. I fear for your safety, Son." He looked at Aelia. "Both your safeties. This is an era never before seen in the history of our people."

Adam's eyes were still on Neora, his brow furrowed. This was the second time the Keeper had been enigmatic in her words. But this time was different. For him. "Perhaps," he said. "But then, nor have the Firsts ever seen such a Light before, have they?" He addressed Neora, testing an assumption.

"A Light, and a Light and Protector," was the only thing Neora would say, although she was confounded at the insight of this new Protector.

Adam nodded slightly. "Right. We need a place to move to, somewhere not in the Firsts' very midst. A place I can secure," he said to Ahir.

"We have quite a few such sites," Ahir said. "You can choose, and it will be prepared for you in no time."

As they approached the entrance to the Council Hall the doors opened, and Aeterna's staff on the other side jumped into action, rushing in to remove the simulation technology and restore the room. Adam instructed that Rolly meet him in his rooms and headed that way with Ahir, while Aelia walked with Neora to the drawing room in the main house, where the Firsts' leaders would begin to discuss the new form of leadership of their people.

Chapter Twenty-Six

Perfect.

They were in Adam's work niche, and the screen was showing an image of mountains stretching as far as the eye could see under the clearest blue sky. The mountains surrounded a lake that wound lazily between them, its end unseen, its shores lined by thick trees that extended up to the mountains in places and tapered into green meadows in others. Whoever took the image was standing on a small pier that extended onto the lake, the only apparent artificial feature in the wild terrain, and the image now changed to one that was taken from the same mooring but in a different direction. It showed the other artificial feature of the place—a beautiful stone cottage, set back from the lake and against a huge boulder that merged into a rocky hill beyond, and half-hidden between trees.

It was breathtaking. Breathtaking and isolated and peaceful. And that's what made it so perfect. They had been going through possibilities for hours, but this was the one that made Adam get up from his chair and walk right up to the screen, as if by doing this he could step through it into the real world out there, to this place that, even as an image, seemed to have the power to instill peace in him.

The search for ideas, after he had explained to Ahir and Rolly what he wanted, was done here, in his rooms, to ensure that the Light's new residence would remain confidential until it was ready and secure. The Firsts had whole regions that were theirs, some were places humans had not set a foot in. And that was what Adam was looking for, not a place in which Firsts lived among the humans, but somewhere where they lived completely apart. He wanted a property in a region that was strictly the Firsts', in which no humans resided. Nor would all such properties fit—he needed a place that would effectively be a safe house, yet one from which Aelia could travel to be among her people, as she promised she would, and one to which she could always return safely and find some peace in, a sanctuary. And the same went for him. They would both find themselves traveling, dealing with the needs of the Firsts. And with whatever unexpected might occur, he thought somberly.

Perhaps more complicated, it had to be a place with unique protection parameters in that they had to be highly flexible and yet hermetic—without the need for added manpower. A place where the Firsts' technologies and his experience, his mere presence there beside Aelia, would be enough. The whole idea was not to have an army there around her. Ideally, it would house only the two of them. Almost peaceful, she had said about Aeterna. Almost peaceful because of its vast grounds, the feeling of nature, yet in it she was always surrounded by people watching her.

His brow furrowed. He would have liked to keep her here, at Aeterna. The place was a fortress, a beauty designed for comfort above the ground with a secure underground complex that had existed long before the Firsts had decided to build the great house. And as far as he was concerned, security was damn near perfect here for this woman he was set on protecting. But if he couldn't convince her to stay here, he would find a place just as good.

A couple of properties seemed close. They had good security parameters but were either too small or surrounded by too many people, and he was sure she would be restless there. And that, he knew from his experience both with people he had guarded and people he had targeted, was no less of a security issue. No, he wanted some place that she would feel comfortable in, that she would actually want to retreat to when she needed, and she would, increasingly so, as the pressure on her would increase. Some place big enough for her to be isolated and not feel she was cooped up in like a prisoner, and with some sort of a Firsts civilization close by, for a whole set of reasons. Yes, he knew what he was looking for, and he knew that he'd know when he saw it.

And he did. That place, right there on the screen. That was going to be their new home. Aelia's sanctuary.

Seeing his reaction, Rolly was already pulling up data about the property and the area around it, something he assured Adam only the head of Aeterna's defense and security and a Protector could do for all Firsts locations.

Other heads of defense and security could only access data about sites they were responsible for.

"I know this property very well," Ahir jumped in with unhidden enthusiasm. "This is where I escaped to when I couldn't find you, after your parents were killed." He took over replacing the images on the screen. "The entire area for hundreds of miles around it was purchased under human laws and classified as being under private ownership more than two centuries ago, and has since been maintained by us in its original state. It has a single village, the original settlement the Firsts built there. It is small, but make no mistake, it is highly advanced. Its residents are the ones who maintain the entire area. They chose to live a simple life, and the village is effectively self-sustainable, although it does not have to be, since Aeterna takes care to provide such areas with all the support they need. It is," he said, flipping through the images, "one of the gems of the planet, and we assign great importance to its preservation. And, better yet, this is an area the humans have not taken take an interest in, and it is surrounded by an even larger region yet unexploited."

Ahir zoomed in on the cottage. It was a cozy structure, built as two main wings joined by a spacious common living area. It also had a small single-level detached wing to house guests or perhaps household staff. Both main wings were slightly drawn back toward the trees and the boulder, while the common area protruded toward the lake. The detached wing blended well into the trees, away from the lake and beyond the main cottage.

"The cottage is actually quite far from the village, and the entire property it is on extends for miles around it. No one lives anywhere near there. The whole idea was to keep the cottage private and isolated," Ahir explained.

Adam turned from the screen and looked at him, his brow raised.

"I should know, I was the one who had it built," Ahir said with a wide smile.

Adam didn't budge. That wasn't what he meant. It was all just a bit too simple. Too apparently simple. One thing he'd already learned was that this was not how the ancient species that had to hide in plain sight among the humans, all the while protecting itself, did things.

Ahir chuckled and nodded to Rolly, and a smile passed Adam's lips. That was more like it.

The multilayered images that now appeared on the screen showed a complex deep under the village, and another, far smaller complex immediately under the cottage, with a long, narrow extension connecting the two below ground. While the Firsts had their main complex, with the control center in it, under Aeterna, and smaller-scale ones in its main communities worldwide, it also had dormant ones scattered across the globe. This was one of them, Ahir explained.

"Originally, only the underground structure had been there," he said, "until the Firsts decided to build the village to signify to human settlers that the area was already taken and lived in, to keep them away. The choice had been to build the village above the larger section of the complex, away from the lake, because the location was the least disruptive to nature around it, since the village would include both homes and fields. At the time nothing had been built above the smaller, control center section, where the cottage now stands."

He sighed, remembering. "That's where I lived when I first went there, in that smaller, isolated complex. I spent I don't know how many days beside that lake. No one dared come near me until Neora finally came to take me back to Aeterna. I returned there about a year later and had the cottage built, and it became a sanctuary I could return to once in a while, to regain my strength by remembering the hope Neora instilled in me that you were out there, alive. I would take your grandmother there." Sadness seeped into his voice. "The cottage was built with your return in mind. I thought we might need to take you away for a while when you returned, for you to recuperate." He indicated the screen. "One wing would be where your grandmother and I would stay, the other was supposed to be yours. The detached wing I thought Remi would be in, he had just started with us back then." It was easier to talk about it now, with Adam safely there, even with the lost years that would never return.

"Some years ago I thought the Keeper needed to get away, and that's where I took her, then and a few times after that, although not for a while now. I used the part of the wing my late wife and I always had, and Neora used the other. That is how I can tell you it would fit Aelia and you. Obviously with the Keeper there we needed increased security, so I activated the control center below, and that's where the security detail stayed, too, along with Rolly. It is highly comfortable since it was originally designed for long-term stay."

Rolly brought up the blueprints. The cottage had an access way down to the underground complex through an elevator that opened outside the control center, which the images that came up beside the blueprints showed was indeed a smaller version of the one at Aeterna. That part of the complex also housed an infirmary, a large space that was prepared for use as a residence for security teams or for a defense unit, if needed, and a separate space that was designed especially for the Keeper and for the Protector and his family. That, Ahir explained, could be found in every underground complex of the Firsts.

There was no direct access by vehicle to the cottage above ground, no roads. But that was because the underground complex had its own parking area, which was where the elevator from the cottage above descended directly to. The parking area opened to an underground passage that led to the only road to the cottage that could comfortably accommodate vehicles above ground, a couple of miles away.

"Is this the only access to the cottage?" Adam asked.

"It was the original road to and from that part of the underground complex. I never added others for security reasons," Ahir answered. "But the village has its own private airfield, and there is an underground passage from under the cottage directly to it."

"The larger complex, under the village, was designed to comfortably house its residents for a prolonged duration," Rolly remarked. "It's still maintained by the villagers, although it hasn't been used since the village was built, there has never been a need for that. The smaller complex, under the cottage, is the operational one. The passage between the two was technologically sealed when the cottage was built and the security classification of the area for several miles around it had to be upgraded because of its use by the Protector, and later by the Keeper. So, in fact, the road out and the road to the airfield are the only ways a vehicle can travel to and from the cottage."

He was now showing on the screen blueprints of the cottage itself, and Adam was astonished at how perfect it was. He could work with this. The cottage was certainly enough. Aelia and he could each occupy a wing—each wing had, according to the blueprints, a spacious bedroom, a large bathroom and an equally large walk-in closet, and a convenient niche outside the bedroom that could perhaps serve as a private sitting area or a work area. The Keeper preferred the former in her stays there and Ahir the latter, he said. The use of the detached wing remained to be seen, simply because Adam wasn't sure. It could remain empty for guests, if they had any, he supposed. Both Aelia and he were used to taking care of themselves, and despite the fact that at Aeterna their every need was taken care of, and he understood that this was bound to be the case from now on, he wasn't sure either of them would want or need anyone to actually live with them.

Of course, that wasn't the only issue they'd have to deal with, he realized. This cottage had a great potential for being the peaceful, private sanctuary that Aelia needed, and he wouldn't mind that either. But the fact was that if he chose it they would be facing a new situation for both of them. Aelia was used to living alone, and so was he. And now they, virtual strangers in that sense, were about to live together in the same house. And this wasn't the great house of Aeterna. Adam looked thoughtfully at the cottage on the screen in front of him and found he had no idea how he felt about this.

His thoughts were interrupted by Ahir. "When the Keeper and I stopped going to the cottage, the underground complex was shut down and cleared again, except for the control center technology, which hasn't been replaced since. The cottage was simply left as it was."

Rolly nodded. "And if you're serious about taking the First there, the entire security layout of the place will have to be reconstructed."

"And enhanced," Adam said. "We'll replace the control center systems and reactivate it, it'll be the power behind the cottage's security. I want the technological layout to be good enough not to require the constant presence of a security detail."

"She's got you there, Protector, that's a bunch of my people put together," Rolly said with appreciation.

"Don't take me into account either," Adam replied to that sternly. "The starting point has to be enough to keep the First safe without the need for anyone who could actually get hurt, which would reduce her protection."

Rolly understood what Adam was going for. "Right. I'll arrange for us to go there with the necessary techs."

"Good. I also want a satellite on the place from this moment on, but not on shared time with anyone else. Nobody sees this feed unless they're authorized."

"That I can do," Rolly said. "You'll get full-time separate coverage that only you can access and that the unmanned systems at Aeterna and the cottage will watch. If there's an alert it will cascade, first allowing Mr. Kennard and myself access, and we can pass it on to field teams if needed. Only you and Mr. Kennard will be able to override anything at any given time."

"You'll also need to refurnish and restock the underground complex, to be ready for the two of you if you need it for any reason, as well as for any security or defense teams you might have to call in if anything happens. And no less important"—Ahir brought up images of the inside of the cottage—"the cottage needs to be completely refurbished. It used to be maintained by a caretaker who lived in the village. His son has taken this responsibility some years ago, I believe, and he can continue to help you take care of the place, but everything inside needs to be replaced according to your preferences, yours and Aelia's."

Adam nodded. Ahir was right. Before they would even begin to deal with the reality of actually living together, they needed to make the cottage their own. "I'd like to have a holographic projection of the cottage to show Aelia, in addition to the area's images. She's not going anywhere near the place until I secure it and it's ready for her to move to." He contemplated the images he'd seen so far. "We'll put in place an initial security layout before work starts so that every single change being made there and every person who goes near the place can be monitored, and once it's ready—as in ready to live in—we'll complete the layout and run it. I'll try to get in several ways, see how the security measures react."

Rolly and Ahir concurred.

Adam and Ahir continued to go over the information about the area, the village and the cottage, with Ahir filling Adam in from his personal experience. Rolly left them, his mind busy with what he needed to do. He should be worried at the prospect of the First leaving Aeterna to live so far away, he thought, in the middle of nowhere, but having Adam as Her Protector made him confident it would be fine. The man was something the likes of which he'd never encountered before. He'd never seen anyone adjust so fast, or learn so fast, for that matter. And he certainly wouldn't want to engage in combat with this guy—he'd seen the security footage of him and Semner.

But perhaps most of all, he remembered the day he first met Adam, when he had been prepared to attack Rolly's armed men for this woman whose real identity he did not even know.

Yes, he had no doubt. Adam Kennard would keep her safe.

It wasn't the night, it was the peace. It just happened to be available to her only at night, when Aeterna wound down around her, and she could withdraw to her balcony, be surrounded by the privacy of the hushed dark. While parts of the great house were still humming with activity even in the small hours of the night, those, the parts that dealt with security, she was oblivious to. The constantly alert control center was deep underground, isolated and unheard, and the security teams on call were in positions they could immediately be deployed from if the technological measures indicated a need. For all intents and purposes, despite the Firsts' advanced measures constantly trained on her, or perhaps because such means were available to them, she was alone up here.

A cricket chirped not far from her and she turned toward it, savoring the sound of this innocent life form in the peace around her. Sounds like these, like a chirping cricket or the rustle of leaves in the gentle breeze, or the sight of fireflies dancing in the rays of the moon on this unusually warm night, were precisely what helped her just . . . be. And being now meant an entire world, an age-old existence.

Tonight was so different, she mused. Different from the nights, the moments, that had been her life these days past. There were no questions tonight, no uncertainties or concerns. Just wholeness, and knowing that whatever was not yet there, whatever was not yet known, would come.

The cricket chirped again and she smiled at the peace

it was reminding her of. All tension left her shoulders, and she leaned back and closed her eyes, letting herself go beyond.

In his rooms, Adam was alone. Ahir had gone to rest. It had been a long, eventful day, and the old Protector no longer had the energy that the young Protector of the Light did. He was enthusiastic, as if finally finding Adam and seeing the coveted Protector and Light duality come to life in his lifetime was giving him new strength, but still, Adam worried about him. Both Ahir and Neora were up to the task Aelia had asked them to undertake, continue in the role they had served in until now, Adam was certain, but he was glad that Aelia and he would be shouldering the major worries.

His brow furrowed as he thought of his grandfather's role, the role the Kennards had always had in the lives of the Firsts. There was so much he needed to learn. He needed to know everything about the Firsts, everything past and present, everything that would have implications on their safety—everything he would have known had he grown up here, among them. And he didn't have a lifetime to do that.

The Protector, he thought incredulously. Only weeks ago he was . . . He shook his head. He didn't know what was more incredible. That or the fact that it was coming to him so easily, that he was absorbing it all so quickly. It was as if every piece of knowledge he was given had a predesignated place in his mind, as if it all belonged there.

No time to think about any of that now, he thought, focusing. He had work to do. Rolly had sent him detailed information about the cottage, the village, and just about everything around, above and under them, including the holographic images he'd asked for. He resumed going through it all, his mind already integrating security weaknesses and the capabilities that would be needed to close them. And that was before he himself would run scenarios.

Scenarios of how *they* could get to her.

Hours later found him leaning back in his chair, his feet on the desk and his fingers interlaced on the back of his neck, his eyes staring intently at the now dark screen. Abruptly he stood up, grabbed the small holoscreen off the desk, and strode out of the apartment and to Aelia's rooms. He went straight to the balcony. It was late, or early, one could say, and the sun wasn't even considering waking up anytime soon, yet she was here, sitting outside, her eyes closed. Exploring, he thought. What she was doing now, he knew, she didn't need a database for, or the stories of those around her, the Keeper, the old Protector. She was learning about herself and her people, spanning this world they were living in, their past and present, her way.

He approached her and sat down on the sofa beside her, put his feet up on the low table before them, and leaned back comfortably, as she had. She opened her eyes, turned her head to him and smiled. Saying nothing, he put the holoscreen on the sofa between them, and the images came up, one after the other, slowly, lazily. She turned her eyes to them and sat up, her expression gradually showing what he wanted it to.

"What's that?" she asked.

"Serena Cottage. Home," he answered.

Chapter Twenty-Seven

Adam stood at the very point from which the first image he had seen of this place was taken. Here winter was promising an early arrival, but he wasn't worried, they would have the place ready by then. And anyway, indications that winter would soon arrive here were not what he was looking at. It was the sheer beauty of the place. The endlessness of it. The images he had seen did not do this place justice.

He tuned in to the sound of Rolly speaking in his earpiece. Good, the techs they had brought had communications up and ready. He didn't want to use the existing infrastructure, since Rolly said it was too outdated and might be susceptible to eavesdropping. And Adam was not about to take the chance of anyone—anyone— knowing the reason they were looking around. Not until this place was as secure as he wanted it to be.

He turned and walked toward the cottage. It was indeed perfectly suitable for what Aelia and he needed, but it needed work. It wasn't that it was in bad shape, it was well maintained and was originally built very well by these people who had also built the fortress that was Aeterna. It looked like a stone cottage, but Adam knew that if a bomb exploded outside it, it would barely be scathed. In fact, that was one of the parameters he had checked for it. Inside, though, it had been designed to suit the tastes of Ahir and his wife, and later the Keeper's, and had last been used some years back. So it needed to be refurbished. The kitchen and bathrooms needed to be replaced, and all rooms needed to be redone, all according to Aelia's and his tastes. And that was after the new security measures were installed. But once it was ready... He nodded appreciatively.

The only thing he didn't like and had immediately instructed be changed was the absence of direct access between the two wings Aelia and him would be occupying. To get from his rooms to Aelia's he would need to go from the niche outside his bedroom half a level down to the common space, cross it, and then go up the stairs half a level to her rooms, which would take time and leave too much chance for outside interference. What he asked the architect he had brought with him to do was to add to the cottage a secure access corridor that would connect the two wings at the level their rooms were on. He trusted the Firsts' peripheral security, it would ensure they would be safe in this property. But he was the Protector, and most of all he trusted his connection to the Light and his own role in her safety. And he wanted to be able to get to Aelia quickly in an emergency.

Rolly was waiting for him just outside the living room that opened to the lake. The techs had been given their instructions, and would remain here to carry them out, as would the architect, while Rolly and he would go back to Aeterna. The sun would be setting soon and they had arrived well before dawn, to canvass the property. Adam planned to return here after the security measures were installed and the house was renovated, before it was furnished, and again once it was ready for Aelia and him to move in, to ensure it was as secure as he was determined for it to be. In the meantime, he would oversee the progress of the work from Aeterna, while Rolly and Ahir would be the ones traveling here. He wanted to minimize the time he spent away from Aeterna, from the woman he was there to protect.

He took one last look around and nodded to Rolly, and they proceeded without a word into the cottage. They crossed it to a section of the far wall behind the kitchen that shimmered and then faded away as they approached it, revealing an elevator. They entered it and it slid down silently, taking them to the underground complex. Moments later the four-by-four they were in was on its way to the airfield, not far from the village, where Aeterna's jet was awaiting them.

They skirted the village and drove directly to the airfield. The jet stood ready on the runway, a security detail from Aeterna beside it, although the satellite watching the area indicated that all was safe. For security reasons, this jet could not be identified as being Aeterna's, nor would the organization be able to track it, thanks to the technologies that the jet, which only looked like other human-made private aircraft, actually held. As for the Firsts in the village, they knew it was one of theirs because of how it registered at the airfield's control systems, and they knew it originated in Italy. Which might have led to speculation except that Ahir himself had cleared the visit with the head of the village, so they knew it most likely had to do with Aeterna.

This would still not disclose who was on this jet. But Ahir knew, as did Adam, that because in the past Ahir had used the cottage for the Keeper, the Firsts in the village would assume that it was the Keeper it was now being renovated for. It made sense. With the Light back, and not yet knowing Aelia's plan, only recently shared with the Council, they would assume that the Keeper might be retiring to her chosen sanctuary, perhaps with the old Protector. Good, Adam thought. That's what he wanted. He didn't mind anyone thinking the Keeper was the one who was going to live there. She wasn't a target, and she was someone the villagers were more used to having around. By the time they figured out who the new residents really were, the cottage and the area immediately around it would be secure to his satisfaction.

The SUV approached the aircraft, and Adam embarked, alone. The vehicle with Rolly in it turned around and headed for the village. At Adam's request, he was going to speak to the head of the village, to clear the next steps with her and thank her for her help. While there, Rolly encountered enough Firsts to realize that they were in fact quite sure that the cottage's resident would indeed once again be the Keeper, and were happy about being chosen as her place of retirement. Rolly left them pleased. Ahir was right, these were good people, the right people to have around the First. She might not like it, She who was as protective of those around Her as they were of Her, but, Rolly thought, these were the type of people who would rush to protect Her without hesitation.

Adam was busy at work when Rolly embarked and closed the door behind him, signaling the crew that they were ready to take off. He didn't indicate that he noticed they were in the air, instead continuing to analyze all he'd seen this past day. They spent the flight discussing possibilities, and by the time they got out of the car at Aeterna's great house they were ready to send back the right people with whatever equipment would be needed. Serena, the lakeside cottage, was officially chosen.

Adam stopped listening to Rolly as soon as they walked into the control center and he saw Aelia up at the supervisor's station, intent on a holoscreen. He watched her. She was focused, listening to the supervisor, asking the occasional question. She didn't look at him, but he knew that she was aware he was there.

"Adam?"

He turned his attention back to Rolly. "Yes. You were saying?"

They resumed their conversation, setting the final details of what was now their major focus, Serena. Rolly then left, but Adam remained where he was and continued to watch Aelia. She straightened up and looked at him, a question in her eyes. He nodded, and she came toward him.

"We're moving forward with it," he told her as they walked up to the main house.

"What's it like?" she asked.

"Perfect," he answered, finding himself smiling, now that he knew the place was indeed all he'd hoped it would be.

"So what now? Can I see it?"

"Not until it's secure. You'll leave Aeterna for an equally secure place, no less." His tone was quiet but left no place for an argument. He would not compromise on her safety. He continued, knowing that she understood. "In the meantime, our transport is also being prepared, so travel will be both secure and flexible."

"Our transport?"

"Our jet."

"Our what?"

"Our jet. We can't keep using Aeterna's official jet or even its secondaries, they need them and we need one that will be at our disposal at all times. A secure aircraft," he explained. "It'll stand at the airfield not far from Serena, in its own hangar, and the aircrew will live in the village."

"When did all that happen?"

"About five minutes after you declared that you were leaving Aeterna."

She shook her head in disbelief. It just might take longer than she thought to get used to this.

"Anyway, initial security at Serena should be up in no

time, and then the builders will be able to start on the cottage. The architect should have the plans ready in the next day or so, and we'll need to approve them immediately, and then we can decide on the furnishings." He indicated the great house around them. "Here we had everything prepared for us, there it would be best if we decided ourselves."

She looked at him skeptically, and he laughed. "Neora said she'll have Aeterna's decorators, the ones who did our rooms here, sit with us. That should make it easier. So, all in all, we should be able to move to Serena in a matter of weeks."

She said nothing for a long while, and he glanced at her.

"It has to be done. We need to be both safe and comfortable there."

"No, yes, I know," she said, and he looked at her, concerned. She was that Aelia again, the Aelia he was sent after what now seemed like ages ago.

"Hey." He touched her arm gently.

"My apartment, it's still . . ." she began and stopped.

"I know," he said softly, realizing where her mind was.

"And I want to talk to Stan, too. I need to explain. Before we leave."

And obtain closure for that part of her life, he thought. "Come on," he said, leading her. "Let's talk."

He chose the privacy of her balcony under gently clouded skies to tell her. He recounted everything he knew about what happened since they left her apartment

—with Benjamin's body in it—that night. "You should know that Aeterna has never stopped following the situation there," he said. "From the moment you and I arrived here, Ahir has had people monitor for anything that might be mentioned about either of us by the police, in the media, and anywhere or by anyone else for that matter. We know that your disappearance was handed to the FBI, and it has no clue where you had disappeared to, or who the man who took you was. The Firsts have people in the right places there and they've ensured that the case's priority would be reduced, which really isn't difficult considering the FBI's workload and the fact that no one has been pushing them to work any faster. The only one who had shown that kind of concern about you was Stan, but he had now obviously let the matter go, since he knows you're all right and doesn't want to inadvertently lead them to you."

Adam paused. "The media was even simpler. They lost interest in the story because there was nothing new to report. Even Stan's connection to it, because of his abduction, died down almost immediately after he returned because he refused to cooperate, and there was nothing new to build a real story on."

"What about Stan?"

"He did exactly what I instructed him to do. He denied knowing who took him and why he was released, and claimed he didn't see the faces of his abductors— and he did so publicly, as I told him to do, so that the organization would not believe him a danger to them. And he never told anyone that he was in fact rescued, or that he saw you." Aelia frowned and he added, "Yes, we're watching him. But it's only a precaution. Once they're sure he won't say anything, I've no doubt the organization would leave him alone, keeping in mind my warning to them to do just that. And the FBI knows something is fishy, between your disappearance and his abduction, but the fact is that he has committed no crime, and they're willing to consider him a victim in whatever is going on. Someone who's involved in this only because of his connection to you."

"Aelia of that life needs to disappear for good," Aelia said after some time, her voice so quiet it was barely more than a whisper.

Adam turned to face her. He waited, saying nothing, until finally she met his eyes. The words he now spoke were factual, but his tone was sensitive to what they would mean to her. "After you showed yourself to the Firsts as the Light I prepared a file for you that imitates what is done in the witness protection program, along with clear instructions as to how to implement it. Including how to deal with the media and with local police, your colleagues, neighbors, the doorman in your building, the guy who does your dry cleaning, everyone. I gave this information to our people at the federal level, to be applied at my order, which would be if the situation there got out of control or if you decided to take your place as the First and not go back to your previous life." He paused. "The day you spoke to the Council I instructed our people to implement it. As of some hours ago, implementation was complete. Aelia of that life no longer exists."

"Witness protection program," she repeated, the shock clear in her voice.

"Yes. That way you never need to go back, talk to the police, the media, anyone. With the media, there was the concern that the story of the woman who had disappeared under rather extreme circumstances and who, after quite some time, still has not been found, would be picked up again at some point unless its resolved. But this way, if they think you're an innocent party who got entangled in something she wasn't supposed to and had to leave her life and the people she cared about behind for her own protection, they would talk a bit, maybe run a marginal story, and let it go. No questions asked. And since you've been living pretty much under the radar as it is, if you ever turn up somewhere they're not likely to recognize you and put two and two together. They ran a photo of you the first couple of days after the incident in your apartment, and that's it. It will not be shown again, our people took care of that." Something dark passed across his expression. "I've made quite a few people disappear this way, hid them from the organization. And nobody is as relentless as them."

Aelia said nothing and turned back toward the peaceful horizon she had learned to find solace in, her eyes far away. Adam took a step closer. Close enough for her to know he was there. Close enough for her to know she was not alone.

The physical meeting with Stan Shell could not be, for obvious reasons, but there was another way to do it. The next afternoon, morning in the United States, Aelia stood in Adam's work niche off his living room, leaning on his desk, her head lowered, arms crossed on her chest. Only Adam was in the room with her, casually leaning against the wall where he would not be seen by the man with whom a secure remote connection was now being established by the supervisor in Aeterna's control center. He was watching Aelia with concern he already knew there was no need to bother trying to hide from her. He wanted to be here with her for this, the virtual meeting with her old friend, a good man who had brought her into his family and had stood by her no matter what. What she would tell him could lead to her losing him. Or maybe not. But either way it would put a final wall between who she used to be and who she was now.

The screen came to life, and the man on the other end of the connection squinted. "Hello? Aelia? You there? I could never get the hang of these things. Do you hear me?" Stan Shell fell silent as Aelia's image appeared on his computer screen. She was standing by herself in a comfortable-looking room, and when she raised her head to look at him he smiled, his heart so much lighter. She was fine, she looked so very well, he thought. But there was something different about her. He'd already seen that when she came to help him with that man after he was captured, but it was only now that he could look at her at leisure and try to figure it out.

In her eyes he saw what he had always seen, a soberness, the kind that came from having been through too much, seen too much. But there was also an air of strength about her. A confidence. A certainty, that too. He frowned. That was new. The first time he'd seen her, when she'd come to convince him to let her enroll as an undergraduate in the college where he was dean of students, she'd been determined, and that determination had never left her. But there was also an uncertainty there, uncertainty and the sadness that tends to accompany it. As if something in her was missing, as if she didn't quite belong. Whatever it was, it was gone now. Wherever she was, she was safe. She was . . .

Home. She was home. In that place she was in now — and in her own skin. Yes, that was it. He frowned. She looked at him, saying nothing yet saying it all. And all of a sudden he became aware of something inside him, a gentle feeling that washed through him, filled him. It had a subtle force to it, a quality he could not quite put a finger on, and it was telling him —

She was telling him. His Aelia. And he understood.

Beside the wall Adam frowned and straightened up. He was wrong. She wasn't speaking, she'd chosen a different way to explain. Her way. And the man on the other end of this encounter somehow understood.

When she spoke, it was simple. "Thank you, my only friend."

Stan Shell smiled. With blurry eyes, he pointed at the screen in admonishment. "You keep safe, you hear? And you come to me if you need me."

Aelia answered his smile with her own. "And you. You can reach me through this connection whenever you need to."

And with that, Aelia left her past behind. She lowered her head, the screen before her now dark. The only people she would keep in her heart from its other side were Stan and his wife, who had taught her that there were people she could trust. Maybe someday she could sit with them someplace, and really explain. One day when it was safe. Safer.

She hoped that day would come.

That same afternoon a moving van stopped at the service dock of an apartment building in a neighborhood that was quite calm, despite the murder that had occurred here only recently. The impassive movers who got out of the van rode the elevator up to a floor high enough to see the park at the back of the building stretch down below, entered the apartment that still had a torn crime scene ribbon on its door, and proceeded to pack all but the furniture.

On its way out of the city, the van stopped at the home of one Stanley Shell, distinguished professor. The movers unloaded some of the boxes, carefully stacking them where the professor asked them to in his study. The books, documents and electronic media inside would be sorted, some he would return to the center he worked in and some he would keep. Other boxes they stacked in the garage, under his wife's watchful eye. These would be donated to charity, along with the furniture that still remained back in the apartment. As for the few items remaining in the van, they were flown to Italy, to the great house of Aeterna, where they would wait, packed, to join the items that would be moved to Serena. These were the only items the First would keep from her life as a human.

Chapter Twenty-Eight

The next days were mercifully undisturbed, and the Light and her Protector pushed on with their plans. Once the techs activated the preliminary security layout, the designated security surveyors, comprising the heads of Aeterna's defense and security response teams and its operational planners, mapped Serena toward the installation and application of more advanced measures. As work began and progressed, a designated team observed at Aeterna and ran failure scenarios. The architect finished checking the cottage and the complex under it and planned the necessary changes, both changes mandated by the fact that neither had been used for some years and by their new designation, and changes that Aelia and Adam asked for after going over the original blueprints and sitting with Aeterna's decorators, and the builders began their work, the decorators working alongside them.

At the airfield, the hangar Adam had ordered built was completed without delay to facilitate the transit of the teams working at Serena, although it would not be fully fitted to house the First's official jet until it was no longer needed for its other interim purposes. Only then would the final security measures be installed and activated and the lockdown procedures applied. The hangar would be attached to a security building that was being built above the previously sealed entrance to the underground passageway that connected the airfield directly to Serena. While this building's upper level was designed for the convenience of the security detail that would occupy it, a car going through the passageway from Serena would come out inside its lower level, instead of outside. The Protector was leaving nothing to chance.

For Adam the days were busy. He watched from afar as Serena's preparations progressed steadily, flying in once from Aeterna to check the preliminary security layout before allowing the actual renovation of the cottage to go ahead. The rest of his time he spent with Ahir, both as his grandfather, his link to the family he never knew, and as the previous Protector, his link to the Protectors of the past. There was much that he wanted—and needed—to know.

But he did not only learn. He also took time to teach what he knew to these people, his people, whom he was entrusted with protecting. He went so far as to train many of Rolly's people, teaching dozens of men and women what the organization's former killer knew and what the transition from its killer to their protector had already taught him. He watched them train, corrected, added, advised. Their Protector, in everything he said and did. Finally, he had them go up against him, aiming to feel their capabilities on himself. None of them could match him in any way, neither alone or in groups. He was faster and stronger than they were, and his mind constantly calculated, predicting their moves and strategizing with uncanny efficiency. But it wasn't until he turned from them to see Rolly and Ahir watching in astonishment that he realized that it wasn't that those he was testing weren't good enough. He was simply better. They then put him through a training simulation and tested his abilities, but no matter what scenario they tried, he came out on top. At the end it was he who stopped, and as he walked away it was with the realization of what being the Light's Protector had made him.

As for Aelia, she spent much of this time alongside the Keeper, observing, asking. Learning. She was present in virtual meetings, with the Council but also ones that the Keeper and Ahir held with individual council representatives. Except that other than those present at Aeterna, the participants had no idea she was there— she had tried participating, but her presence was too disruptive. The presence of the Light was too new, and the way she was perceived by her people made it impossible for them to focus on the matters at hand—which was what they needed to do—and not on her. So she took a step back, observing from afar, being there for them only through the presence of the Light within.

Their last days at Aeterna were the busiest, but there was a calmness to them, a confidence that was felt also by the people around them. Those who lived at Aeterna had seen Aelia and Adam arrive as strangers who were clueless as to who they really were and gradually turn into willing protectors of their race, choosing to assume the destinies they were born for. They had immersed themselves in the lives of the Firsts and were an active presence among the people at Aeterna. And so while the Light took care to always be felt by her people worldwide, it was the Firsts at Aeterna who felt her presence most, and they were the ones who knew beyond a doubt —and passed on that conviction—that even when she would no longer reside at the great house, the Light would never leave.

On a gray day that left nothing to be hoped for, the organization's Italy office was raided by Jon Melake and his people. Hours later anyone who had been loyal to Jennison and not to the organization, and the director who had not seen what was happening and who had allowed the bombing of the cathedral in Rome to come out of his office, had been removed and replaced.

In the first underground level of the organization's main training facility, in southwestern Arizona in the United States, a disheveled Jennison sat behind his desk, his head in his hands, the realization that the consequences of his catastrophic failures had actually caught up with him mercilessly dawning on him. Failure, total and absolute failure, was the only thought that kept repeating in his mind this day when he knew it was finally all over. He didn't even react when the door to his office opened savagely and the men strode in. He knew who it would be. Rozner. Rozner had been waiting for this day, for the moment he could take over and do things his way. For the day Jennison's star would come crashing into a thousand pieces, so that not even he, the master manipulator, could put it back together.

In the silence that ensued, a silence that reverberated through all corridors, all floors, every person in the facility who was witnessing his fate, Jennison slowly raised his head and stood up. He fixed his tie, took his jacket off the back of his chair and put it on carefully, closing every button, and straightened his cufflinks with slow deliberateness. He then faced the newcomers.

Rozner didn't even try to hide his glee. He signaled to the two men he brought with him, and they positioned themselves on both sides of Jennison and escorted him out, into the short corridor, across the floor and to the waiting elevator. Outside in the parking lot, just before they placed him in the waiting car, Jennison stopped and turned around, taking one last look at his life's work. He closed his eyes tightly, one thought in his mind.

How could this have happened?

In what used to be Howard Jennison's office, Charles Rozner looked around him in distaste. Everything that signified Jennison's presence in this room, in this facility, had to go.

Everything.

Time to start over. And he, he would not fail.

Adam, Ahir, and Rolly were sitting in a room off Aeterna's control center, engaged in a conference call with the head of defense and security of yet another community of the Firsts, when the call came in. Rolly tilted his head, listening on his ear comm. He indicated to Adam and uttered a command in a low voice, switching between the calls, then explained that Denole was calling from the cathedral center. The face of the center's head of defense and security appeared before them. He came straight to the point.

"A message came in just now, same as last time. Except it didn't come from Jennison, it came from Richards."

Adam's eyes narrowed.

"What does it say?" Rolly asked.

"I've forwarded it to you. But in a nutshell, the organization claims that it is standing down. It says that the recent actions against the Firsts were the acts of a rogue director, and here Richards actually names Jennison. He claims that the organization stands behind the truce it has with us and that Jennison has been removed and detained."

As Denole spoke, Adam operated a screen embedded in the table and viewed the message. Yes, that sounded like Richards. Short, factual, unapologetic. By a man who expected to be believed. And obeyed.

Rolly instructed Denole to maintain the lockdown at the center, and ended the call. He turned to Adam. "What do you think?"

Adam's only answer was raised eyebrows.

364

"Yeah," Rolly said somberly.

Ahir looked from one to the other. "I'm sorry, what?"

Rolly turned to him. "Right, yes. Sir, when Adam left here the first time, to go see Jennison, he took a listening device."

Now it was Ahir who raised a brow and looked at Adam.

Adam nodded. "I initiated a bit of an altercation with him. Put the recorder in a safe place." He shrugged. They won't find it easily. They sweep for bugs electronically, what I took was organic." He indicated Rolly. "His idea."

Ahir nodded appreciatively. "That's impressive, Rolly."

Rolly chuckled. "You think that's impressive? The man breaks into their most secure facility, faces its director, and plants a bug in his office in the process and gets out again unseen, then just days later he walks right into the midst of their board with one of their own operatives captive, hands him over to them and walks out again like he's got all the time in the world. Now that one I'd like to have seen. Takes nerves of steel to do that, and—"

"Point is, we've been listening in on Jennison's office," Adam interjected. "Not much, but with the sensitivity on that thing it's not a little either. We already knew they removed Jennison and who his replacement is. Charles Rozner."

"You know him?" Ahir asked.

Adam's eyes narrowed again, and when he answered, his tone was troubled. "Yes. He's a big gun. Calculated, ruthless. He'd opposed Jennison's moves every chance he got, they're sworn enemies. And he's the same rank as Jennison in the organization. It's no surprise he got the facility, he's been after it for a long time. Good thing is, he's going to need some time to clean it up of Jennison's loyals, and he's the type to err on the side that would be in his favor, so he's likely to get rid of more people than he needs to. Which means he'll need to move in his own loyals from other offices, assimilate them, and train new operatives. That'll take time." He paused. "Bad thing is, when he's done, we're going to have quite a bit to contend with, and he doesn't have Jennison's weaknesses."

"You think he'll come after us like Jennison?"

"Oh, he's far worse than Jennison," Adam said.

Ahir was about to ask, but Rolly spoke. "The day he took over he told his second-in-command that there's only one way to the top, and one way to get what he wants. And it starts with eliminating the Firsts from the equation."

Ahir looked at Adam, appalled.

"His words," Adam said quietly.

Twenty-four hours later the center under the cathedral in Rome was deserted and sealed, as were the secondary site and the tunnel between the two. The space had been stripped clean and then filled using Firsts technology, to ensure that the center could not be accessed and to avoid it even accidentally registering as empty space under the cathedral, although human technology was unable to do that yet, not with the way the center was built. The system that Richards used to transmit his message to the Firsts was moved to the center's new site, a dormant property that was now quietly activated.

This was the Protector's order. He wanted to get the Firsts in this place the organization had become too daring in approaching out of its reach and moved to a more secure location, one the organization knew nothing about. One, in fact, that had been set up long after the organization had made the Firsts its enemies decades before. Whether the organization would know that the cathedral center was abandoned—or rather when they would discover this—that Adam didn't care about. For now, he was all about protecting.

Chapter Twenty-Nine

Finally, Serena was ready. Adam flew in, taking the opportunity to test the First's aircraft and to get to know its aircrew better. He had chosen to use one of the Keeper's two aircrews, the one that had been on the jet that had taken Aelia back to Aeterna after Stan Shell's release. He'd been impressed by how professional they had been. That and their experience, their training that was specifically designated for their service of the Keeper, had led him to agree when they asked to be assigned to this new addition to the Firsts' fleet. They proved him right already on the jet's first flight to Serena, and as it touched down lightly and taxied to its new hangar, Adam contacted Ahir to ensure that their accommodations in the village, and that of the family of the pilot, the only one among them who was married, would be finalized to their satisfaction.

He was also pleased with the ground crew that met the aircraft as it rolled into its secure hangar. It was local, carefully selected from among this airfield's staff. There was no sense in keeping a permanent ground crew here for this one aircraft in an airfield that otherwise had sparse air traffic, and the local ground crew needed very little training to deal with this jet. The security detail, however, had been moved here from Aeterna. All its members had expressed enthusiasm about moving to this beautiful place in the First's service, and had been carefully retrained by Adam for this prolonged mission. They would live a good life of their choosing here, but at the same time were expected to be at the First's disposal, if so ordered by Adam, either at Serena or in her travels.

This time Adam would spend several days at Serena, alone, to thoroughly test the security layout. He wanted Aelia and him to move here and settle in as soon as possible. The sooner they did, the sooner they would be ready to react to whatever might happen. The changes made in the organization worried him. The fact that Richards had taken the trouble to contact the cathedral center meant that he was playing a game here, wanting them to believe his peaceful intentions while in reality his giving Rozner the facility — and too much power for Adam's taste — spoke to a stark contrary. This was not looking good.

The cottage, where he would be staying for the first time, was now live in ready except for their personal items that had yet to have been brought here from Aeterna. It was perfect, its exterior strengthened and cleaned, its interior entirely renewed and refurnished, a state of the art affair masked by the coziness of a home. As he walked around it, before going in for the first time, he stopped at the one feature he had asked be built that Aelia knew nothing about — a roofed porch that was added in the back of the house where it opened to the lake, with a sofa on it, couches and a low table. Small and cozy, much like her balcony at Aeterna. Her sanctuary within a sanctuary.

Yes, this is it, he thought.

He continued around the cottage and stood looking up at the second feature he'd requested be added. Their separate wings were now connected by a corridor, an external addition on the side of the cottage away from the lake, where the two wings pulled back toward the trees. The corridor was elevated a distance up from the ground and extended all the way up to the roof, and the architect cleverly added above it and around the rooftop a stone balustrade. Inside, Adam knew, the corridor stretched between what would be their bedrooms, its two ends fitted with doors that would open automatically only for Aelia and him.

Adam walked inside the cottage, and through rooms he had so far only seen in images. Both wings were done as Aelia and he had chosen, while also showing the luxurious touch of Aeterna's decorators and their deference to whom it was they were meant for. Each bedroom opened to a comfortable niche that led to a flight of stairs that went half a level down, to the common area of the cottage. The niche in his wing was a workspace from which he would be able to follow Serena's security and connect to Aeterna and through it to the other Firsts sites, and the wall screen dominating it was already running images and data for Serena. The niche in Aelia's wing was designed as a natural extension of her bedroom, a place she could sit comfortably in, although he suspected she would prefer the cottage's porch for that.

As for the common area, the decorators had blended in it the needs and tastes of both the woman and the man who would live here, and quite remarkably so. He was impressed. Both Aelia and he preferred warmer colors, the feel of a cozy room, both were used to this being the only way to quiet the turmoil in their hearts and minds in the days when they had lived lives that were not theirs. And the decorators had managed to attain just that, he thought as he leaned on the living room fireplace, looking around him.

He spent the rest of his time in Serena testing its security. Four times he managed to get from outside the property's vast grounds all the way into the cottage and to Aelia's bedroom, and four times he sat in conference with Ahir, Rolly, and the techs as they adjusted the settings of the security layout, they from Aeterna and him at Serena. The fifth time he couldn't get anywhere near the property, no matter what he tried. Still, although he then approved Serena's preparedness, he would not rest confident. He trusted his experience and instincts to lead him to think and rethink his moves until he would find a way to get to her. And if he could, he had to assume others could, too. And he would not allow that to happen.

Still, there was nothing to stop him from bringing Aelia here, to her new home away from Aeterna. Which would finally allow her to do what she wanted, take the next steps into her destined role in her people's life.

Adam stood looking at the cottage, then turned around slowly, looking around him as the sun rose high over the peaceful horizon. Finally he nodded to himself, satisfied, and returned inside. He walked through the living room, skirted the kitchen and got into the elevator. As it descended, the cottage locked down above him, sending data to the designated handheld he had with him.

In the underground parking, he got into one of the secure SUVs that were now parked there and drove out and up to the road that would take him to the village. Several miles later he passed the newly installed gate that was only there to be seen, his eyes flickering to where the real security measures were installed that would make sure no one would go back the other way, into Serena, unless his command permitted it. As he drove away, the chirp from his handheld confirmed that Serena was in full security lockdown. Despite appearances, meant to preserve the tranquility of the place, nobody would be able to get in.

He drove through tranquil, solitary landscape, heading for the airfield. As he drove through it to the hangar, he noticed there were more people than usual around. This didn't surprise him—the new private jet he'd arrived in a few days earlier and that was now closed in the hangar had been noticed. That, and its official registration. It was registered to Serena. And then of course there was him. If on his earlier visits he had taken some care to disguise his identity and they had thought him to be one of the workers who were there to prepare the Keeper's new home, this last time that he landed, in this official jet, ready to take full charge of everything Serena, he disembarked as himself, in full daylight, and he knew that the secret would begin to unravel. By now they would all know he was the Protector. Which meant the speculations were probably at their height—they also knew whose Protector he was.

His phone registered an incoming call, and as the voice on the other end of the line spoke he thought, well, they're about to have a bit more to speculate about. He parked beside the closed hangar and got out of the SUV. A flash in the sunny sky drew his attention, and he looked up as one of Aeterna's jets descended. It taxied toward him and stopped, the ground crew already moving toward it. The door opened and Sonea peeked out curiously. Adam smiled. Sonea had been adamant that she would be the one to come to Serena with Aelia and him. She would have it no other way. She had looked after Aelia since she had come to Aeterna, had taken it upon herself to make her comfortable, behaving much like a doting aunt. She quickly came to care about her, so much so that she no longer took notice of the fact that the younger woman was the awaited Light. And Adam knew that Aelia liked Sonea, and trusted her care.

An unexpected incentive for her moving here appeared in the form of Nolan, the caretaker of the cottage and its grounds, and the son of the previous caretaker. Adam found that he liked the shy, kind-hearted man, who took his responsibility very seriously. His obvious familiarity with the property appealed to Adam, as did the fact that despite knowing early on who Adam was, and guessing that the cottage was being prepared for two young people, one of them Adam himself, and not the Keeper, Nolan never breathed a word of this to anyone. So when Nolan expressed his wish to continue maintaining Serena, Adam had readily granted the man's request. And then, when Adam brought Sonea to see the place, so that she could prepare better, and introduced her to Nolan, whom she would be working hand in hand with, the two were obviously taken with each other, as was quite apparent in the calls the two had held since, after Sonea had returned to the Aeterna. A few days earlier Nolan finally dared offer that she move in with him into his house at the edge of the village, and Sonea took the offer enthusiastically. Things, Adam thought then, sometimes worked out so well, so unexpectedly.

Sonea saw Adam, and her face broke into a wide smile. She waved at him and came down the stairs energetically, and before Adam could move Nolan came running from across the runway and met her, extending a helping hand. Yes, Adam thought, unable to stop his own smile. These two would be just fine. And he trusted them for what he needed. Sonea would take care of Aelia and him, and would be responsible for all housekeeping duties. Not a difficult job considering the size of the cottage. And Nolan, he would help her and carry on his job as caretaker. They would not even have to commute to Serena every day, there was no need for that. And Adam already had a new SUV waiting for them at their home this very moment, a surprise present for them both.

The jet didn't take long to unload. Sonea's belongings had arrived earlier, and Nolan already had them in the house she would be sharing with him. This load contained mainly Aelia's and Adam's things, mostly clothes, from Aeterna. Neither Adam nor Aelia had been at Aeterna long enough to have accumulated much. Adam himself had nothing left from his life before, it was all in the organization's hands, and Aelia did have the couple of boxes brought to her from her old apartment, but she chose to leave them at Aeterna for now. And so there really wasn't that much for them to bring from Aeterna, and a short while later Adam was driving back to Serena, Sonea beside him and Nolan lounging in the back seat. A loaded SUV driven by a member of the security detail, Milen, was following them, and Aeterna's jet was already back in the air far behind.

Adam left Sonea to orient herself while he helped Nolan and Milen bring everything into the cottage. She began on the ground floor and then went up to each of their wings, inspecting what was done since she was here last. When she came back downstairs she was already ordering Nolan and Milen around. By the time Adam sent her and Nolan to their new home with Milen, intending to give them time to get settled, his closet was organized and his bathroom set out—which surprised him. She must have taken the time to learn all she needed to about him from Remi. A glance showed him that Aelia's rooms were ready for her, too, organized the way she was comfortable with at Aeterna.

Once again he spent the night alone in Serena, and the sun rising over the horizon found him leaving it locked down and fully active, its systems and those of the control center below it seeing every particle for dozens of miles around, the eye of the Firsts' satellites constantly on it. Serena was monitoring itself, and as an added precaution for this newly activated site, it was also being watched from Aeterna. It was ready.

The car Adam was driving this time moved silently and swiftly, and was a far cry from the SUV he'd driven around here until now. It was brought to Serena on a flight just four days before—a secure car, built especially for the Protector. It was also preferably the only car the First would be in while she was here, and preferably only when the Protector was also in it.

All but one of the other newly sent vehicles parked under Serena, one of them the SUV he'd been driving, were vehicles nearly identical to those used by security at Aeterna, and would remain in the underground complex until they were needed. But the one he was driving now was a status car meant to be recognized as holding at least one of Serena's two residents. This was on purpose, in consultation with Ahir. In the village they would be among friends, Ahir had said when he placed before Adam the make and models he would choose from. Friends who should know who was among them. They would, he had said, learn to recognize this car, know who was in it, and would always keep an eye out for it. And protect it if needed. The Protector had relented, thinking that yes, this car would be recognized. So that if the day came that the First was targeted, it would be easy to draw attention to it while getting her out of there another way.

As he approached Serena's hangar, the huge doors opened slowly and he drove through. He parked in a secure space inside, then embarked on the ready jet as the hangar doors continued to open. Inside he sat back, ready for the flight to Aeterna.

It was time to bring Aelia home.

Chapter Thirty

Richards sat on the couch, legs crossed, staring at the drink in his hand as if mesmerized by the ice cube that floated in it, growing smaller as the seconds passed by. Like his hope for a peaceful resolution to this, he thought. Or that it would go away altogether, as if none of it ever happened. In the garden outside, beyond glass sprayed with stubborn rain, strong winds bent his wife's favorite rose bushes and he wondered fleetingly if the delicate plants would survive this winter, forecast to be another in a long line of violent seasons. Perhaps he should build her a greenhouse, it was a good idea for an anniversary present. God knows she deserved it. He'd been preoccupied these past weeks, barely home, and when he was here, he was hardly an attentive husband. Maggie didn't deserve this, the patient, loving woman that she was. He sighed. She was in Miami now, visiting their grandchildren, their son's kids. A reprieve for her from his worry-plagued, nowadays far too introverted company, no doubt.

A greenhouse. The melting ice cube in his glass let out a burst of tiny bubbles of air, as if mimicking an ironic laughter. If only he could build a greenhouse to protect humanity, if only it were that simple. This legacy he had gotten, or rather the legacy his predecessor got from his—that being of course the man who had headed the board when the truce was agreed with the Firsts—was inconceivable. And Jennison . . . the name alone was enough to send a ripple of rage through Richards, and his hand tightened around the cool glass he was holding. What a mess he had made of it all. And what made it infinitely worse was that Richards had no idea if this very minute the Firsts were planning a retaliation of some sort to Jennison's stupid actions, or to what they now knew—that the organization had stolen from them two children, *the* two children. If he were them, he'd be certain by now that the decades of quiet truce were a sham, that the organization had been ill-meaning from the start and had waited for an opportunity to destroy the Firsts. He'd be suspicious, angry. Vengeful—yes, that, too.

What Kyle Rhys had done, though, bringing his captive to the board the way he had, gave Richards a glimmer of hope. He had understood immediately that the man was putting the ball in their court. Warning them about Jennison, because he wanted them—trusted them?—to act. Did that mean he was giving them a chance to uphold the truce, to make things right? But even if so, did he have any influence among the Firsts, could he stop a retaliation, if that was what the Firsts wanted?

Richards sighed, exasperated. It was useless, he had no idea how these . . . whatever they were, thought. He didn't know nearly enough about them, information was so scant. He knew they had been the ones to approach the organization all those decades ago, that it was co-existence they had claimed to want, and that, despite the organization having turned their backs on them, they had remained peaceful all these years. Peaceful and unseen. But would that still be the case now?

Richards's predecessor had been stupid enough to actually honor the truce to the letter. True, the man had focused on strengthening the organization and had poured huge resources into it—it was thanks to him that the organization had a global presence and was so powerful. His aim had been to be prepared to protect humanity from the Firsts, if ever needed, and it was he who had approved Jennison's plan, it was under him that the two children of the Firsts were taken. But that was all he had done. After years in which the Firsts had retreated, never again making contact with the organization and virtually disappearing, he had felt confident that the truce would hold and hadn't done enough to observe or find out more about them. As a result, the organization had no idea just what the Firsts could do.

Richards's grim thoughts were interrupted by a knock. The door opened, and the facility's new director was shown into the den. He walked in with the arrogance of a man who knows he's got the upper hand, and Richards moved uneasily in his seat. He didn't like Rozner. The man was dangerous. Richards was well aware of his insatiable drive for power, and of his rather problematic views—this world belonged to humanity, that other species was too much of an unknown, it should have been brought under the organization's control long ago or, if that was not possible, eliminated in its entirety, and humans were not capable of deciding for themselves and would eventually have to be controlled too. That was it in a nutshell, and he made no effort to hide these views from the board, all except that last one. That, he had voiced earlier in his years but had more recently stopped, knowing that the board was split in their opinions as to the when and how, and to what extent. But he had let it be heard enough for those who remembered to know what he would advocate when the time came.

These views, and in such a man, made Richards wonder if the day would come when Rozner might decide that the organization's board was not acting decisively enough, and would seek to bring them down. Which made Rozner's recent commission, which placed too much power than Richards was comfortable with in the man's hands, rather ironic. The facility, of all places. Yet there was simply no other choice. They needed Rozner. If it ever came to it, he would be the right person to have at the organization's combatant front. And he was not reckless. He understood the need, considering recent events, to regroup, and position the organization where it could act against the Firsts at will in a way that would not allow them to respond. He wasn't the type to charge his prey—be it either the Firsts or humanity. He preferred to find a way to exploit its weaknesses and subdue it without a fight.

"Well?" Richards finally asked, still staring at his wife's poor rose bushes.

"We're clean, Sir."

"What have we lost?"

"Department heads, some deputies. I kept all training personnel, I don't want any delays in training new people. They have a good commanding officer now. I brought in a guy I've worked with for years to replace Larson, who chose to retire. It was a long time coming anyway."

"Field operatives?"

"All trainees remain. We've got time to watch them before they become operational, see where their loyalties lie, but their involvement in the facility's politics has been limited so it's looking good. All level operatives remain except those who participated in the kidnapping. I don't want them there." Rozner's tone was final. "There are still questions as to the loyalty of some of the remaining level operatives, we'll have to see if they're Jennison's or ours. Most of them won't go beyond level operatives anyway." He paused. "Our problem is the tier operatives. We can't afford to lose any. We lost Rhys and Semner, and Leaner and Joyce were injured in that botched kidnapping and are out. That's two tier-one and two tier-three operatives gone. I exchanged some tier operatives with other offices, brought instead some I trust not to have been loyal to Jennison. Plus I have some trustworthy level operatives ready to advance to tier, I've already put them into the necessary training."

"So what's the problem?" Richards asked, a tad impatient.

"These tier operatives, tiers all over the organization in fact, they've all trained with Rhys. Worked with him.

He's gotten quite a few of them out of a jam one time or another. They know him. Respect him." Rozner regarded Richards. "Thanks to Jennison, we've got a whole Rhys-tainted facility. Hell, we've got a Rhys-tainted organization."

Richards closed his eyes. He was well aware of that. His mind went back to Melake and his security team, who had stood looking at Kyle Rhys and his captive at a respectful distance, right there outside his boardroom. If it had been anyone else, they would have shot him right through his captive, shot first to protect their board and asked questions later, as they had been trained and ordered to do. Yes, the organization had a problem.

"What do you suggest?" he finally asked.

"Reposition him."

Richards raised a brow.

"Other than a selected few, everyone else, everyone who knows Rhys, they all think he's one of us."

"So?" Richards didn't need to be told the obvious. "We took him as a young boy. Even those who grew up with him wouldn't remember that far back, most people don't. And we ourselves protected him, reinvented his past. No one has a reason to think he's not one of us."

"Right. And he'd served the organization alongside them, so they think him completely loyal, to be trusted blindly."

"And?" Richards felt a headache coming on.

Rozner thought it was rather obvious. "So what if we change how they see him?"

"We've already told them he's gone rogue. Didn't do

much good, did it?"

"Because we didn't give them a reason, we just gave them an order. This time, why not actually turn him from loyal to traitor? Think about it, our field people are out there protecting humankind, which includes also their own families, their friends. Their peers. Going against enemies that threaten their own. Human enemies, but still, it's the enemy concept we've put in their minds. What will make them feel more betrayed than one of their own turning out to be one of those enemies? We can make them think he sold out to someone. And this time we'll spin it through their commanding officers. Those who like them have served in the field, but now, in their current positions, are perceived as being more knowledgeable about the upper ranks' decisions, about what we know, why we make these decisions in the first place. Like why we made Rhys rogue. They can pass his 'treason' down to the people they're training and commanding, make it seem like they're leaking info they got from above. It can stick. All we need is an enemy Rhys has joined."

Rozner saw the wheels in his boss's mind turning. He had his attention. He ventured forward. "And I'm thinking maybe we should go a step further. Make them think he sold out to the Firsts. Obviously we can't say we were the ones who took him from them, how would that look? So, say, yes, he's a human, one of us, who'd chosen to betray us. That'll looks a lot worse to them, one of their own betraying them to a species that's out to destroy the humanity they're risking their lives protecting."

Richards began to speak and Rozner continued quickly, knowing where the objection lay. "I know it's been important to conceal the existence of the Firsts from them, but under the circumstances, maybe it's time to rethink that. I'm not saying we should tell everyone at once. But Sir, as it is, if this thing with the Firsts doesn't die down, we'd be better off if at least some of our field people knew about them, would not be surprised and be ready to pass on what they know and to control the reaction of the levels under them. I mean, what if they attack us? We can't have our best people freeze in shock because they didn't know about this other species. Look, we can start by letting just a few in on their existence. A couple of department heads at the facility, maybe, to begin with, and the head of training I brought in, definitely—I want new training routines, new capabilities anyway, it'd be better if we could tell him why, make him more creative in his thinking. I'd tell certain tier operatives, too. People who can . . . reeducate those around them without telling them too much, or telling them gradually, break them in."

Reeducate. As in manipulate. Poison the mind of, Richards thought with distaste.

"What I'm saying is, let's see if we can replace their attitude toward Rhys, reposition him as an enemy who's dangerous to them, to their families, to the humanity they are sworn to protect. Use that to de-Rhys the organization, and at the same time begin to build a designated force that is aware of the existence of the Firsts." And that would not think twice before they go against them when the time came, shoot first and ask later, or not ask at all, Rozner thought, although this he did not say out loud. If things went according to his plan, when he was done there wouldn't be an operative in the organization, and certainly in the facility, who would think twice before obeying an order to kill one of *them*, seeing them not as equal to humans, but as strangers, outsiders, who must be destroyed.

And who knows what else he could get them to believe on the way. The organization's finest obeying his orders—his every order—that could go a long way toward achieving his own goals.

"Might take a while, but ultimately we'll have an army ready to move at our command against the Firsts." And against anyone else he told them to. Yes, the thought appealed to him.

"A while might be too long if they retaliate now."

"Some of this I can do immediately. The tiers in the facility I can already work with. I don't need to tell you what these guys can do. And I've read the assessments, Sir. The Firsts have had some weeks to retaliate and yet they've done nothing. Initial indications are they didn't expect what we . . . what Jennison did, so they might not be able to do anything at this time."

Richards's eyes were back on his wife's rose bushes, bent to a breaking point under the strengthening winds. This had better work, he thought. He didn't like this plan, certainly not after Jennison's plan had gone so wrong. But the fact was that there might be no choice but to have more people, operational people, know what was going on. Things with the Firsts were too uncertain and there was too much of a likelihood of more encounters with them.

"I've also stepped up recruitment to level training." Rozner continued, wanting to take his boss's mind away from any questions about this plan of his. He still needed to think about it, finalize it. Make it . . . board proof. "We'll need extra people if it turns out we need to get rid of any operatives currently on probation. If not, then we'll have more field operatives than we've had until now, which is fine with me. We'll need them."

Richards nodded. Rozner was thorough, no question about it. He'd been a field man himself, had advanced all the way up to tier two before choosing to head the training functions in the facility and then becoming the director of one of the secondary facilities, where he remained until he replaced Jennison. He was the right person to put the facility back on its feet as seamlessly and quickly as possible. And he was the best after Jennison, and unique in his drive, his capabilities.

In the danger he potentially posed. Damn Jennison, Richards thought.

But then he couldn't blame it all on Jennison, could he? It was under him that Jennison had done what he did. It was under him that a man like Rozner grew strong. And it was under him that the organization still hadn't put the resources it should have into studying the Firsts and preparing for the eventuality that was now here.

"What about the Italy office?" Rozner fished, interrupting his thoughts.

"Melake cleaned it and is heading it for now, we've got someone in mind for it." In fact, a director from another European office would step in. A damn good guy, a strong director who could perhaps one day be used to remove Rozner, but Richards was not about to let Rozner even suspect that. Nor was he about to tell him that they'd already gone through all offices and facilities of the organization, and have found too many who were Jennison's loyals. The idea itself that Rozner would know more than necessary made Richards uneasy, the man had a talent for latching onto weaknesses and filing them for later use. He didn't need to know how far the organization had been compromised by his predecessor. He didn't need to know just how badly the board had screwed up.

Rozner said nothing. He wasn't here to push. In fact, he wasn't sure why he was here. This talk, until now, could have been done by secure phone or in Richards's office. Why was he at his home?

"I want our intelligence capacity enhanced."

So that's it, Rozner thought. "Enhanced how, Sir?"

Richards met his eyes. "Enhanced so as to allow finding and monitoring all Firsts. Enhanced as in finding out their weaknesses. Enhanced as in unlimited resources." He paused, waiting to see the effect on Rozner. Nothing but a fleeting smile. Richards nodded. "And I want you to set up a covert operation for Kyle Rhys and the woman."

Rozner tilted his head slightly.

"Find them," Richards continued. "I don't care how. Watch them. Study them. I want to know what happened. I want to know why they're still alive, why Jennison failed." Richards's eyes bore into Rozner's. "And then prepare what we'll need to remove them. At my command." He lowered his eyes back to his glass. The ice cube had given up. "And this is on a need-to-know basis. That applies to everyone but the board and you."

"So, just identify and observe."

"For now." Richards confirmed.

Rozner turned away to hide his sneer. Weak, he thought. The man was weak. It was just a matter of time.

Rozner was more impatient than ever. He had finally landed and was just a car drive away from the facility. His facility. He itched to make the necessary calls, start getting the right people rounded up. But he didn't do any of it yet, not in the car. He was a careful man, who trusted only himself and didn't let anyone know more than they needed to. His experience had taught him that. He caught the driver's eyes in the rear-view mirror and reminded himself to look impassive. Rational.

That, what happened to Jennison had taught him.

He had spent his years in the organization planning carefully. As soon as he'd become a tier operative and had thus become privy to priority missions and gained access to high-ranking personnel, he began using them to learn. He was reliable, helped everybody, kept everyone's secrets. He became the man they depended on. And he never misused what he knew. The only things he wanted were to rise up in the organization—legitimately, with as little opposition as possible from within—and to learn everything he could about it, its goals, its secrets. When he knew enough and was positioned well, all he had to do was wait until his chance came.

Until Jennison made the wrong move. Or went off on a bender, more like it, as he did.

And now he had what he wanted. The facility. This facility. Its resources, its people, its power, to do with as he pleased. As long as he played his cards right, of course. Yes. He needed to be careful now. The organization would be watching closely, the Jennison fiasco had made them more distrustful than ever. He knew he had been given Jennison's job because they needed him, but doubted they trusted him. Richards certainly didn't.

Rozner would give them what they wanted, an intelligence force that would watch that other species, and a combatant force the likes of which had never been seen, bigger and better than ever. He knew what their plan was. Prepare and Deter. An all-out war would be bad for humanity. Wars tended to get messy and should, he agreed, be avoided, unless there was no other choice. The preferable way was to study *them*, find buttons that could be pushed, he agreed with that too. Only, he thought a way should be found to subdue their will. Make things, well, bad for them, then show them a better way to live, something they would latch on to out of despair—and enslave them. Kill those who dared rise up, use the rest. It wasn't like they were humans, after all.

Except, he thought, and this too he took care to leave out of his discussions with the board, told no one, why not do the same with humanity? Not now, of course.

Later. When there was no one to stand in his way.

The car finally arrived at the facility, and he got out and walked in briskly. He had work to do.

As inconceivable darkness surged, building up long sought-for power, confident that it could no longer be stopped on its path to its coveted dominion, and as reality tilted just that much farther away from all that was right and a critical mass was finally reached, a flicker appeared deep within the Light. Unseen, unfelt, unknown, it was beyond the grasp of even the ancient species who walked this world hidden, who had been so despaired when they had beckoned it, when it had answered their call.

Awake now, in its time that had almost come, it sent fine threads to its origins in ages long gone, rousing that which had been hidden beyond existence. In a crash of giants they danced, formed and reformed, then came together as in days past in one that swept on to times present when it would take its rightful place and restore the balance. As a destiny long decided was finally sealed, past and present met in a burst of power that resonated at a level underlying all, initiating that which would bring about what was meant to be, that which had long been foreseen. It spread, becoming one with the Light it had sent before it time and more ago, sending a whisper through forms past, ready to finally awaken within a never before seen form present.

Chapter Thirty-One

Neora stood at the entrance of the great house, Ahir beside her. Both were worried, Aelia knew, although they would not show it, not while all these people, Aeterna's staff and its residents, were looking on. It was all discussed and settled, but the fact remained that the First and the Protector were leaving, and would no longer have Aeterna's protection around them. And while Aelia could ensure that her people would have the confidence that she was always with them no matter where she lived, she could not relieve the worry of their two leaders who knew all the dangers and stakes involved, and who had come to care deeply about Adam and her. But there was no other choice. This had to be done.

Aelia smiled at them and got into the back seat of the car, the door closing behind her. Adam got into the front passenger seat. Rolly was at the wheel, wanting to see them off himself, and they were flanked by two SUVs, mirroring the way they had first arrived here, at Aeterna, except for the two stealth helicopters that followed them high above. As they drove away from the great house Aelia turned and looked at it as it grew smaller, until the vehicles rounded the hill and she could no longer see it. She leaned back and closed her eyes, feeling them, her people. Confident, she was pleased to find. Confident of her.

The jet, her jet, was a bit of a shock. Shining new, almost silvery in the light. Its markings were familiar, except for what she knew marked it as Serena's, instead of Aeterna's. And except for what marked it as carrying the First. Of course, only the Firsts would recognize either. That, and the way the jet would be tagged by their air traffic control systems wherever it would go. She took the time to walk around it, then climbed inside and looked around, curious. It was comfortable and had a designated place for her and Adam to sit together, and place for a security detail in the front. It even had a plush bathroom and a bed in a private area in the back. She'd never seen anything quite like it before.

Around her all was calm. This was Firsts territory, Aeterna's secure hangar, and she was safe here. The hangar was closed, and Adam was standing outside the jet, talking to Rolly. The security detail—a part of her security detail that Adam had brought along with him from Serena—was keeping an eye on the jet, and another detail from Aeterna was outside the hangar, always on the lookout, taking nothing for granted even on their turf.

A short time later she was sitting in her designated place, watching the sky outside. Despite its movement the jet seemed to be still, the hum of its engines unheard, so that it felt surreal, as if she were floating in the sky, unmoving, as if the clouds were the travelers, peeking curiously into the jet, then moving on. Movement close beside her shook her from her reverie, and Adam sat down in the seat opposite hers. She looked at the clouds for a moment longer, then turned to him, found him watching her.

He smiled. "A far cry from the flights we've been on so far."

She laughed. "Just the flights?"

The smile remained on both their faces as they watched each other. There was a new calmness in him, she could tell. This was it and he was ready. He still had that edge of constant alert, though. This alertness, it would be a part of him from now on. Those looking at him would see a strong man, an impenetrable wall, easily intimidating. He would not show weakness, and there would be no soft spots that could be mistaken as such by those who might wish to bring harm. But she would know what was in him, her he would, already did, let in.

She strained to look out as they landed, but caught only glimpses since the jet never stopped, instead rolling into its new hanger, the large doors closing behind it. A car was waiting inside, a black car, tinted windows. She didn't recognize the make, but she recognized the intention. It certainly looked as if it was here to make a statement.

The jet stopped, and she turned her attention to the door opening up front. Adam was already there. He descended the stairs, and she watched as he walked to the car without hesitation. As he neared it the car's head and taillights came on and it started. He got in and swiftly moved it near the jet. When he got out again he saw her standing at the aircraft's door, watching him with obvious curiosity. He smiled. It took her a moment to realize that they were alone in the hangar, except for the aircrew—the steward who stood at the door not far from her, the pilots still in the cockpit. The security detail that had arrived with them had filed out of the jet and left, and she didn't see any ground crew, it was nothing like Aeterna's hangar. Her eyes came back to Adam. He'd saved her the commotion, she realized, knowing what she needed, as he always seemed to. She descended the stairs and approached the car, and Adam surprised her by opening the passenger side door.

"It's just you and me," he said.

She got in and looked around her. Comfortable, and yes, luxurious. But she saw the additions, too. The security console, and a place for a gun, his gun, within his reach. Getting in behind the wheel, Adam saw her look. "It's reinforced, too," he said. "Ahir had it prepared for us and sent here."

She was about to ask more when they exited the hangar through a door that opened for the car, and two SUVs that looked exactly like Aeterna's security cars positioned themselves before and after them. She didn't realize Adam had seen her disappointment until he spoke quietly.

"Only until Serena," he said. "We're still new here."

She nodded and looked around at the small airfield.

There were people around, all of them Firsts, it was obvious to her. They stopped where they were, looking at the passing cars. Adam had the convoy go around the airfield, rather than cut through it, but it was still disruptive, for the obvious reasons. No one knew for sure yet who was in the escorted black car, but they *knew*. She felt them, their curiosity, their excitement—was it true? Was it Her? But the cars moved away from them, and from the village she only saw from afar, and toward more solitary terrain that was nothing short of breathtaking. They entered the woods, going up between hills and following the road until finally they came to a gate. As they approached it, the lead car moved aside. The gate opened and the car she and Adam were in drove through. Adam signaled the car they drove by, and as she looked back she saw the gate closing, both security cars on the other side, already turning and driving away. Something inside her relaxed as she realized.

This was the first time they were alone since they first fled to Aeterna.

Serena was wild and beautiful, a far cry from the city Aelia had lived in all her life, a pastoral calm after the attention she had received at Aeterna. After they passed the gate, Adam slowed the car down and opened its windows, letting her feel this place he had chosen for her, and that she had so far only seen in images that did not do it justice. He himself was less on edge now that they were here and that she had made the trip from Aeterna to Serena safely. He threw a look at the car console, which told him that Serena's sensors had been activated, had recognized the car, and were watching it, deactivating and reactivating certain security measures as they progressed toward the cottage.

The road curved to the right and downward. It continued underground for a distance, lights guiding the way in the translucent ceiling above, and then entered the underground complex, which was automatically opened before them by Serena's systems. Adam brought the car to a stop before the open elevator doors and Aelia got out and looked around her. Behind her was the exit back to the road, now closed. On one side stood a row of security SUVs, and beside them and closest to her stood what looked like a sturdy version of the car they had just arrived in. On her other side was a closed entryway, to the control center and the rest of the underground complex, she knew from the blueprints Adam had shown her.

Adam waited patiently, giving her time. She closed the passenger side door and walked beside him into the open elevator. Recognizing them, the security system closed the doors and took them up. The doors opened again, and she walked into a large space that led on both sides to stairs going up. A distance before her stood a partition wall that reached almost to the ceiling and was open on both sides. Skirting it from one side, she found herself in an open kitchen for which the partition was the back wall. Beyond it was a spacious living room. An opaque protective shield similar to the one she'd seen at Aeterna silently slid up, allowing the daylight in through a full glass wall with the lake and the mountains beyond it.

Behind her Adam spoke a quiet command, and the glass doors slid open, letting the fresh wind in. Aelia walked forward, drawn by the view outside, the picturesque landscape, its peace. Adam found that he was enjoying watching her. She was different here, just herself, in this lovely, quiet place. He watched her walk out, watched as she looked around her, her eyes lingering on the lake, then returned inside and walked around the room, her fingertips brushing the fireplace mantel, the back of a sofa. Then she turned back and walked to where he was leaning on the kitchen counter. She continued a little farther and peeked toward the stairs on both sides.

"Come see," Adam said and led her up the stairs on one side, to his niche—he stopped for a moment near the screens as they activated, letting him know the security system registered a vehicle entering the perimeter through the gate—and his bedroom. He showed her how to enter the corridor that connected their bedrooms and that opened automatically as either of them approached it, and they passed through it to her bedroom, and to the cozy niche just outside it.

She looked around her, then returned to her new bedroom and took in the organized closet, her bathroom, the way the cushions were placed on the bed. She smiled. "Sonea was here."

Adam nodded. "And then some."

Sounds from below let them know they were no longer alone. "Speaking of Sonea," Adam said and led

Aelia down the stairs on her side of the cottage.

"Welcome home!" Sonea, the only person who would dare do that, ran to Aelia and hugged her.

Aelia readily accepted the affection. She then greeted Nolan, who stood quiet and ever patient behind Sonea, and even he answered with a wide smile—anything that made Sonea happy, made him happy. As far as he was concerned, the First or not, she was family.

Good, Adam thought, watching them. If this were to work, Sonea and Nolan needed to be completely at ease around them, which would in turn ensure that Aelia and he would get used to having them around and relying on them for whatever they needed.

Sonea opened the bags Nolan now carried in from the elevator, Adam helping him. "They've got some great shops here, and the produce market, I simply can't say enough about it," she said as she stocked the refrigerators. She opened a cupboard, and Aelia saw that it was already full. "Nolan and I stocked this place the other day, the pantry too, but I had to leave most of the perishables until now. Mr. Kennard here said he'd be leaving the day after I arrived, but we weren't sure when you two would return. I cooked, too," she chattered on happily as she filled the refrigerators with enough food for a small country. "I'll do all the shopping around here, and I'll cook. You can cook, too, if you want, just tell me what you need and I'll get it for you, but you don't have to, I'll take care of everything, we will, Nolan and I. Don't you worry." She carried on, Nolan nodding vigorously now and then, obediently confirming everything she said.

A little over an hour later they were alone, Sonea having repeatedly promised to come back just a few days later. She wanted to return the very next day, but Adam wanted Aelia and him to have some time alone in Serena, to get used to their new home and to at least begin to get used to just the two of them being here, before fully introducing their two caretakers into their routine.

While Adam checked Serena's security and locked it down for the night for the first time with the First in it, Aelia forgot herself exploring the cottage. She then stepped outside to the balustrade that had been built around the roof and stood on it for a long time, looking at the falling dusk of the gently wintry day, not feeling its already cold edge. When the glimmer of the lake faded, she went back inside and down to the kitchen where Adam was busying himself with making dinner. She sat on the opposite side of the counter and watched him with interest as he began preparing a salad to go with Sonea's cooking which he was reheating. Her mind returned to that first night, after he'd shot her. He had carried her, unconscious, up to her apartment that day, and in that oddest turn of events had treated her wound, and had then prepared her dinner. He had looked comfortable in the kitchen then, just as he did now.

He slid a cutting board with cherry tomatoes on it and a knife across the counter to her, and she began cutting. "You cook," she said.

"You knew that already." He smiled a little, knowing where her mind had gone.

"Well, back then I saw you more as a shoot first and

cook later guy." She was amused, he saw. Good, she was comfortable in her surroundings, and with this situation they were in.

And with him. Which was mutual, but then he was all too aware of that already.

"I still shoot," he remarked, matching her amusement. "Except that now I shoot for you, not at you."

"I kind of like it better that way."

"Oddly enough, so do I," he said, then realized what he'd meant and changed the subject. "So?"

"I love the place," she said.

"Good. I think we'll be comfortable here."

"We will, Mr. Kennard." She used the formal address that Sonea had used, which everyone used now, when they were not referring to him as the Protector.

He raised his brows. "Yes, that takes some getting used to. Kennard."

"Hey, wait. I don't really exist anymore." She suddenly realized what she'd forgotten, the witness protection part of it, which made her former identity unusable.

He stared at her for a moment, then got it. "It's all right, we registered new identities, new names. Ahir and I set up backgrounds to fit us, and our people among the humans filled these in brilliantly with every possible detail. We also have bank accounts, and Aeterna deposited in them funds to reflect a certain elevated status so that no questions will be asked." He indicated the upper floor with his head. "We've got IDs, digital wallets, credit cards, cash in multiple currencies, everything a normal person needs anywhere in the world. It's all in my desk upstairs."

"Mmm. And you're back to being Adam Kennard."

"Yes. But I have credentials for another name, if I ever need it."

"Kyle Rhys."

"Yes."

She nodded. It made sense for him to keep the identity the organization knew, and after all the authorities had never connected that name to what happened at her apartment, or to her. And it wasn't as difficult for him as it might otherwise have been, using this name that reminded him of the past, since he now had his real name, his real family. She wondered if she would ever find hers. Pushing the thought away, she raised her head and looked at Adam resolutely. "So what's my name?"

"You're still Aelia," he said gently. "I thought you'd want to keep the name, and since we're constantly watching out to make sure you're not found, it's okay."

"Thank you." Her voice was equally soft. She tilted her head quizzically. "And the rest of it? My last name?"

He stopped mixing the vegetables and threw a look at her, and she was surprised to see him look somewhat self-conscious. She was about to ask again when she got it.

"You're kidding."

He shook his head, still finding the salad bowl so much easier to look at. He wasn't used to this. He'd never let himself get involved before. Before her.

"Kennard. You called me Aelia Kennard." She was in shock.

"Yes."

"Whose idea was that?"

"Mine." He continued quickly. "It was a given, really. Among the Firsts you don't even need a name. Yes, they know the name Aelia, but for them you're the Light, or, officially, the First. And that was enough in the past, when the Light lived protected among the Firsts, never venturing among the humans. But the decisions you've made will necessarily put you also around humans, in their world." He paused, contemplating how to say this. "When we're out there, you and I, I've got to have un-limited access to you, and it's crucial that no one will be able to question my being near you, or my right to be with you. Among our people, I am the Protector of the Light. Among humans, I need to have the one status no one can argue with. So, yes," he breathed in. "We're registered as husband and wife."

She lowered her eyes. He was right of course, it made sense. Still, it was . . . she didn't know what she was thinking, how to look at this, at him. Or at what, for just an instant there, she felt from him, before he managed to conceal it.

"Set the table?" he said, his voice a notch softer than it was before. "Dinner will be ready in a minute."

It was after midnight when Adam went up to his bed-room, after making a last round of the locked-down cottage and checking security through the system in his niche, the routine he would now fall to every night that they were here.

In her own bedroom, Aelia stood looking around her. Then she went to the windows that spanned two walls of the room and moved aside the light curtain—a mere decorative item, as no one would be able to see anything if they happened to be looking from outside. In the moon-lit night and with the gentle dimness of the room surrounding her, she could see clearly to the dark lake and to the far mountains of Serena beyond. She liked it here. She hoped that this time, this home she would not have to leave again so soon.

She prepared for bed, then walked into her closet— here too with the white robes she had never yet worn hanging in their own designated corner—chose a slip and a short robe and dressed unhurriedly. She climbed onto her bed and sat quietly in its middle. Her thoughts were calmer here, she realized. It was easier to distance herself, to find that place within her that would allow her some peace, here at this remote place where she was alone.

Not quite alone. She turned her head in the direction of Adam's rooms. But him being there felt right. He was in his bedroom right now, and he too liked it here, liked this place that he had chosen. Liked that she was finally there with him, that much she could tell.

Aelia didn't realize she was smiling.

Chapter Thirty-Two

Those first days they were just them, just Adam and Aelia, making a home for themselves in this place they had chosen for their refuge. They explored the woods around it, walked along the lake, and still there remained unexplored territory for them to see, whole mountains beyond. It was a serene solitude, a place to get away to, and it was all it was meant to be for them. Adam saw it on Aelia soon after they'd arrived, saw it in her eyes, in her smile. There was a new calmness to her. Serena was already shaping itself to be the sanctuary that she needed.

That they both needed. Under normal circumstances they would have been raised among the Firsts, allowed time to learn their destinies and their roles in the lives of their people, and for their abilities to develop gradually, with all the support they might have needed. As it was, they were thrown with unforgiving abruptness from lives they had grown into adults in, into an alien, unimaginable reality in which they were the most crucial players, responsible for the lives of so many. And these, their first days at Serena, were the first chance they had, since it all began, to smooth this transition over. They had each made a conscious decision to accept the role assigned to them, and that had allowed their transition to be completed. But that didn't mean they didn't need this time they now had, in this isolated place that was only theirs, to accept what had been done to them. And to accept what was now theirs.

While at Aeterna they were constantly surrounded by people, here they were alone much of the time. Sonea and Nolan came on most days to take care of the cottage, but otherwise Aelia and Adam were on their own. As for their loyal helpers, they loved their new life. Sonea chatted constantly about her new home, about the garden that Nolan—her Nolan, he already was—had prepared for her and the space he had set up for his carpentry in the shed at its edge, and about the market not far from the center of the village where people would stop and chat, everybody knowing everybody. She loved it here and she and Nolan loved being together, and Aelia was glad about it. She wanted Sonea to stay, felt comfortable having her around, but if she had not been happy here, Aelia would have sent her anywhere she would feel at home.

But their being alone here also meant no security and defense teams who could react if they needed them. The security detail Adam had brought from Aeterna lived in the village and was stationed in the structure beside the hangar. The village had people who could protect it if needed, but although they had regular training, the fact was that this had been a peaceful area for decades. They would not be able to stand up to the organization's killers. The Firsts did have a secure location where they trained their people and kept a defense force, one that the Protector had been aware of for a while now and that he had factored into Serena's security. It was equipped to launch teams anywhere globally, and would always know where the First and the Protector were. But still, these teams would take time to get to them.

This worried Adam despite the care he had taken to secure Serena. In the unlikely event that Aelia found herself here alone and in danger, he wanted her to be able to defend herself. He remembered what Ahir told him, that the Light could not be killed by anyone but her Protector. But the fact was that she had already been taken away from her people once, and he remembered all too well that she could be hurt. Worse, so far he'd only seen her protect others around her, and had seen no real indications that she was able to protect herself. Whatever her abilities were, he wanted her to also be able to defend herself as any person would.

Any person who had ruthless enemies.

And so he taught her how to access Serena's security, how to see their new home in images, holograms and data. He showed her all the security measures in and around the cottage and scattered around Serena's perimeter for miles around, and how to access the screens in his niche, the capabilities he had made sure were available from there. He made sure she knew how to access their underground control center, how to seal it with herself inside, how to watch and control Serena from it, and how to communicate from it. All communications involving Serena were routed, he told her, through systems that made sure they could not be traced, to prevent anyone tracking the First and the Protector to their sanctuary.

He showed her that when she accessed the screen in her own niche, she had a direct connection not only to Neora and Ahir, but also to Rolly and the control center at Aeterna. On her command or if Serena entered emergency mode, it would automatically establish connection with Aeterna's control center, which would in turn lock on to Serena, notify the defense center and alert the security detail on call at the airfield, even as it tracked her and Adam's movements and locked down safe sections around them to isolate them from potential pursuers. Serena's security was not designed to fail.

He also showed her where he kept his gun and his knife when they weren't on him, in his bedroom, and where the weapons arsenal was, in the cottage and under it. She refused to learn how to use a weapon. He insisted. There were some things he would not let even her argue with him about. And so she listened to it all, and tested her new knowledge. For him.

Later on that evening, the two sat together on the porch Adam had asked be built for Aelia, allowing themselves to enjoy this sensation of their new home settling down for the night in the dusk around them. Or at least, Aelia did. Sipping from his coffee mug, Adam still wasn't satisfied. His mind kept going again and again over everything he'd shown her, and everything that could happen to her, everything he feared and wanted to prevent. There must be something he missed, something he hadn't shown her. He thought—

The sense of danger, of Aelia needing his help, hit him so fast, so violently, that he dropped the mug he was holding, spilling coffee on his shirt. "What the—" He turned to the woman sitting right there by his side. "Hey!"

She stood up, and, walking by him inside, threw him an innocent look.

He followed her with his eyes for a moment and then laughed. Yeah, okay, she had a point. He got up and went upstairs to change his shirt, then joined her in making dinner, finally allowing himself to relax in their new home.

No less new was just this, their living together. Different rooms, different wings even, but still. A man and a woman who were used to being alone, to keeping apart from others, and who had been thrown into the necessity of spending their lives together. But this, despite both having wondered about it before they moved to Serena, proved to be so much easier than they thought.

And so right.

The village quickly got over its initial shock at the woman who was rumored to have arrived in the jet that now remained closed in its secure hangar at the edge of their small airfield. News traveled fast but the Protector was prepared, and he went to the village to remove all speculation. There was a purpose behind him doing this himself. It wasn't just that his experience had taught him the wisdom of having people trust him. These were his people, he was one of them, and he was born to protect them, them and their Light. Their history told them to trust him, but it was important to him to establish such trust himself, to let them know him.

He took the black car, to let them know who was coming, to bring it right to their midst. He chose a random spot to park, got out of the car, and walked down the street toward the village hall, in plain sight, intending for them to see him. He wanted them to accept his presence, as a stepping stone for their ultimate acceptance of Aelia's presence among them. But as he walked among them they stepped back. And they looked at him, not so much in fear, although fear of sorts was there, in these people who knew the power of the Protector. What he saw were mainly curiosity and awe—the awe that comes with a title and with stories told over centuries.

He let himself accept it. He would have to get used to it, he knew, to their reaction, to that powerful feeling that came with who he was. He would get used to it, and so would they, with time. When any fear would be gone, and only their confidence in their Protector would remain, as should be.

He entered the village hall, an ancient building with doors that sensed his approach and opened before he came near. As he walked in he saw the telltale signs he'd learned to recognize, which showed that this structure was equipped with the Firsts' security systems. He was pleased. He'd known the village was secure, but seeing indications of this himself made a difference.

Here, in the village hall, he met with the woman who was called in this place the village elder, since the village did not have its own council. She'd been briefed before by Ahir several times, while Serena was being prepared, and had provided her support throughout the duration. But now Adam came himself, as a sign of respect, to let her know that the First was at Serena, that this was now their home.

Later he walked through the village, getting to know it. He couldn't do this before, when he still wanted to avoid them knowing for certain through his presence who Serena was being prepared for. It was beautiful and quaint, and people here seemed at ease, friendly with one another. And at the same time, this place had everything. Every type of store, everything this village's residents might need. All understated, which did not surprise him.

He saw the local market peeking down a small street to his right and headed there. He chatted up people and they opened up to him, soon more at ease around this imposing man who talked to them at eye level. Ahir was right, these were good people. But then Adam had heard that from Sonea, too. The way this village had accepted her, and the security detail that now lived here, too, them, the aircrew, their families, said a lot about its residents. True, this wasn't their first time. After all, the Keeper had stayed in Serena. But still, this time they weren't just accepting the newcomers for a short visit. This small village, that had so far led a quiet, out of the way life, was welcoming their Light and Protector, and everyone they had brought with them here, for the long run, without reservation.

When he finally left, he was impressed. This was a small community that had chosen to lead a quiet existence in this remote haven. Its way of life, although here too outwardly disguised to avoid detection by humans, was the way of life of the Firsts, and its eyes were on a future with the Light in it, a future that was now here. They would, he left here knowing, stand strong beside her.

And then he brought Aelia there. A few days later, without first telling them. He didn't want preparations, didn't want this to be out of the ordinary. He just wanted the villagers to meet their new neighbor, and Aelia to be able to visit the place feeling normal. Like everyone. Yes, he knew this could not, would never truly be, for both them and her. She was the First, their Light. She could walk among them as if she was one of them, but she would always be recognized for who she was. Still, a Light who walked among them was different from a Light who was kept hidden away, safely protected, on a pedestal in an ancient mansion. This was who she wanted to be for them, thinking she could do more to help them this way, and this had to start now.

The day he chose was a cool, sunny market day. He

parked out in the open, in front of the village hall this time. He got out of the car, and so did Aelia, looking around her curiously.

"This way," Adam said, and led her down the street and to the market. He walked beside her, alert to everyone, every move, every sound. But there was no danger here, he knew. So did she, and he was sensing this from her. Still, he never let down his guard. Nor did he tell her that the security detail, scattered, had had eyes on them since they entered the village. Not because of the Firsts who were its residents. They weren't the ones he was concerned about.

She was liking this, he saw, pleased. She enjoyed walking in this picturesque village, in this lively market, almost like a normal person. Almost. She was surrounded by her people, by Firsts, and although she was calm and made every effort not to be noticeable, she, the Light, was *felt*. People stopped, gaped, took a respectful step back. No one spoke to her, no one knew what to say, how to behave. The First and the Protector beside her were awe-inspiring.

Adam began to wonder how he could change this, make them relax and accept her presence, when a small child broke her father's hold on her hand and ran forward, skidding to a halt before them. The father ran after her and stopped a few feet away, hesitant, when the girl asked with the daring innocence of a child, "Are you the Light?"

Aelia didn't think twice before she kneeled down on one knee in front of her. "Yes," she said softly, "I am."

And around them people began talking in low, awed voices at this admission that somehow made it all so much more real, and at the same time so much more possible to deal with. The father stepped forward and scooted the girl into his arms. "I apologize, Ma'am... First, she's young..." he said, his head bowed, the adult having learned to fear that which the child never would.

The girl began to cry, squirming in his hands. "No, I want the light, there is no light."

Aelia smiled and stood up, understanding what this small child, who was too young to understand, thought and needed. And right there, in the middle of the market, not heeding the adults but only this child who must grow with the confidence her parents had not known when they were her age, she reached into herself. And as the village looked on, the presence of the Light within them changed, taking on a subtly more powerful edge, and they could see a soft, bright halo around her, growing, expanding, there in its gentlest form. The child laughed happily, clapping her small hands with delight, while the adults stood awed, their reverence high, too high.

And then a squeal sounded, a delighted call, and Sonea pushed between them, an obedient Nolan immediately behind her, his arms full of shopping bags. Chattering excitedly, she took Aelia by the hand and pulled her through the crowd to show her the most delightful greenhouse berries she'd just found. Aelia, the Light receding, let herself be pulled, and it was this that

414

broke the spell on the people around her, sending them back to their stands and their shopping, chatting happily about the amazing Light that had chosen to live among them.

Adam followed, marveling. This might work after all. Perhaps, when it came to the First and her people, he should just let things be.

Gradually, as it realized it could watch them from afar, Aeterna relaxed and settled into a routine in which the Light and the Protector still lived among the Firsts, but away from the fortress prepared for them. It soon found it no longer had an immediate role in the Light's protection, as the Protector ran Serena's security with uncanny preciseness, constantly changing and improving it. What they did for Aeterna, he did alone for Serena, but no one in Aeterna's control center was surprised. The Protector of the Light had turned out to be everything the stories said he would be, and more.

As life at Serena settled down, both Aelia and Adam resumed learning what they would need to know, from those at Aeterna and others worldwide, from past records, and from that which was still revealing itself within her, for Aelia. But one other thing Adam never stopped doing was thinking about the organization. He never had the illusion that it would let go of its goals, the very reasons for its existence. He had no doubt it was regrouping, and knew what that would entail— getting rid of everything connected to Jennison, to him, to the failures, would not be easy. So he knew the Firsts were safe for a while. But he had no idea for how long, and when the hit would come. Or what it would be.

And that worried him. The simple reality was that he didn't know anything about what the organization's new plans might be, nothing but what his past with them taught him, and what little he heard from the bug in Rozner's office. Especially now, with the changes in the organization and, he feared, in its attitude toward the Firsts. And so he never stopped trying to anticipate what it would do.

Because that was the one thing he was sure of. That the organization would step up its preparations against the Firsts. And that when the time came, it would hit.

Chapter Thirty-Three

Soft light played over Serena, waking up the life that gentle winter days have been bringing to it for millennia, undisturbed but for the evolution of nature itself. In her bed, Aelia opened her eyes, her brow furrowed. She tried to understand, tried to grasp what it was that she was sensing, what it was that was within her, had been whispering to her in the deep of her sleep. She moved the soft blanket covering her aside and got out of bed, reached for the short robe that lay at its edge and put it on. She walked to the window that opened at her command and looked out at the silent water rippling with the gentle breeze, at the shadow of mountains clad with first snow beyond it. In the peace around her, the frown never left her face.

Something. Just beyond her reach.

Restless, she turned and left the room. She walked down the stairs and crossed the living room, opened the glass doors and walked out. This would register in Serena's security system, she knew, but would not alarm Adam. He would already know she was awake and about, would know it even before the system registered it. He too was awake, had been since before this wintry dawn. Rested, she could feel. He never slept more than a few hours, but he slept well. This place, and her being within his reach, her protection safely in his hands, seemed to be giving him some peace, and he had gradually relaxed these past weeks as they settled into their new sanctuary. Awake before her most days, he would go downstairs, turn the coffeemaker on, and go running along the lake, in the peaceful dimness that precedes the life that comes with full light, and, returning, would take his coffee upstairs to the niche beside his bedroom. To observe Serena, she knew, and connect to Aeterna's systems and to those of the Firsts' communities worldwide. Until she awakened, and then he would come downstairs and start the morning with her, as he did everyday.

She left the doors open behind her and walked to the lake, unheeding the cold, and stood on its shore near the edge of the pier, her eyes gazing around her.

Then closing slowly, as that which had roused her called to her from within. Turning inward she found herself standing alone, nothing around her but the Light, her form within it, head bowed, eyes closed. Not like then, no darkness now. She was the Light, and the darkness was no more.

Beyond her that which had called her appeared, surrounding her. It was endless, stretching back into the past, boundless on all sides in the present. It rose, unchecked, unhidden, and suddenly she understood, knew what it was, could perceive that which the Light had concealed within it and not even her people knew, not even her past forms. Knew that which was rising beyond the Light within her, had been, gradually, insistently, for days now, strengthening, preparing her for what was to come, in this place, this peace, his protection, that had given her what she needed to contain it.

Waiting.

She reached out to it, beckoned. Let it be, I'm not afraid.

And it came.

That which had come from ages long gone, from a timeless, boundless existence, now swept through her, taking over. Powerful, insistent, it erupted within the Light, that fraction of itself it had sent before it and that for a time and more had been enough, until now when it finally wasn't, overwhelming her with its force and reaching beyond her, sending Serena itself into a foggy haze. But she was not aware of this, was not there anymore, her awareness now beyond time, beyond bounds.

Around her all disappeared, replaced with an unfamiliar reality as it tried to tell her, warn her, as images chased one another, fast, faster until they crashed into her with staggering speed, hitting her with merciless vividness, as before her eyes the world itself came crashing down and reality escalated into pure chaos. She saw it all, saw destruction as it spanned the globe, her own life within it. She felt it all, as hope died with a feeble scream under a reign of hate and terror and oblivion, as the struggle for life grew desperate, as all the roads that must never be taken, were. She sensed it all, as hurt increased and swept the land, as the collapse became unstoppable. She stood helpless at the overpowering sights and sensations of it all, until the images came in which humanity fell, the Firsts alongside it, just before she herself crashed, falling into an endless abyss where the images, mercifully, stopped.

Inside the cottage, all screens went black as the most advanced system in existence could no longer register anything beyond the staggering potency of the energy that was interfering with it. But Adam wasn't seeing this. He was already running out to where he knew she was, toward the lake, through the soft haze that appeared all around him, that was growing thicker, brighter, with every step he took toward her. She was alone, he knew, no one had come anywhere near Serena, but whatever was happening was hurting her, overwhelming her, drawing from her inconceivable amounts of energy.

He sprinted toward her, his heart racing, afraid, terrified for her. From afar it looked like the Light was around her, the same Light he had seen emanate from her in the past, but it did not feel the same, and there was a new quality to it, a deeper essence, reverberating in it, dominating it, crushing powerfully against him, so that he had to put every effort into continuing, pressing on, not giving into that which was beyond even his abilities. It felt foreign, was just beyond his reach, as if he could not fully perceive it, as if his mind could not fully comprehend what he was sensing.

He couldn't see her inside this new Light but it didn't matter. He saw her as only he could. He pressed on, feeling its staggering strength, feeling it on his skin even as he could feel it inside him. As powerful as it was, as foreign as it was, he could feel the parts in it that were the Light he knew, could easily connect to that part of her that was always within him, just as that new essence of the Light that was so much more potent threatened to overwhelm him, as if for it the Protector was nothing to behold, as if it only regarded her, *was* only her. But all senses of it washed only fleetingly through the back of his mind, and were just as quickly crunched by his fear for her. Without hesitation, without even considering that anything would dare try to stop him from getting to her, he crushed through it and reached her.

And the Protector could see what she saw, see as if he was looking through her eyes, see without the force of it, without the sensations she was shielding him from, absorbing them all herself. At first he could not understand what he was seeing, felt like someone walking into a story too far into it, tried to grasp what—

And then it hit him. What her eyes were telling him, what her heart was telling him, what she was crying out to him in his name. And as the newly arisen Light within her finally ebbed, slowly withdrawing from Serena around him, disappearing back deep into her, now forever one with her, and as she collapsed, drained, and he caught her, cradled her in his arms, he understood.

The sun came up and the clouds made way for it to warm life in Serena below, help it recover from what had transpired under its skies only hours before. It was already high up and contemplating starting on its path to the end of the day when Aelia finally regained consciousness in her bed. She sat up and looked around her, as if trying to orient herself, to ensure that she was here, now. She remembered it all, up to the moment the last of her strength was drained and then it all disappeared. She knew what happened, knew what it meant, what she was, the Light as was never before that was now within her.

The Light was stable now, although she was still weak. She breathed in deeply. It would take a while for her to regain her strength, and even more time until she could safely use that which she now was, but it would be so. She got out of bed slowly, and walked to the window. Stood looking outside, her eyes on the spot she had stood in earlier that day.

"You saw," she said softly.

On the edge of her bed, Adam continued to gaze at her for a long moment. Finally he got up and came to stand close beside her, his silence a confirmation.

She felt no fear, and not a shadow of a doubt or

question. It was as it should be, and it would be as foretold. She now knew why. Why her, why now. Why *this* Light. Knew the purpose, the part only she could play in it.

And in the future of life in this world, in this era that the Light, so much more than anyone had known, had chosen to return in.

"What now?" the Protector asked.

The First stood tall, looking at an unseen horizon. "Now we save them."

End of Book One

Join our mailing list on www.authorandsister.net
for updates about Book Two and additional
books by A. Claire Everward

CPSIA information can be obtained
at www.ICGtesting.com
Printed in the USA
LVHW082049140821
695338LV00008B/344